# The Irish Midwife

Seána Tinley is an Irish author of saga historical romance. She also writes regency romance as Catherine Tinley.

After a career encompassing speech and language therapy, Sure Start, being president of a charity, and managing a maternity service, she now works as NI Country Director for a leading UK charity.

Seána was appointed as chair of the Romantic Novelists' Association in August 2024.

# The Irish Midwife

## Seána Tinley

HODDER &
STOUGHTON

First published in Great Britain in 2025 by Hodder & Stoughton Limited
An Hachette UK company

The authorised representative in the EEA is Hachette Ireland, 8 Castlecourt Centre, Dublin 15, D15 XTP3, Ireland (email: info@hbgi.ie)

1

Copyright © Seána Talbot 2025

The right of Seána Tinley to be identified as the Author of the Work has been asserted by her in accordance with the Copyright, Designs and Patents Act 1988.

All rights reserved. No part of this publication may be reproduced, stored in a retrieval system, or transmitted, in any form or by any means without the prior written permission of the publisher, nor be otherwise circulated in any form of binding or cover other than that in which it is published and without a similar condition being imposed on the subsequent purchaser.

All characters in this publication are fictitious and any resemblance to real persons, living or dead, is purely coincidental.

A CIP catalogue record for this title is available from the British Library

Paperback ISBN 978 1 399 74768 4
ebook ISBN 978 1 399 74769 1
ebook ISBN (US-only) 978 1 399 74809 4

Typeset in Plantin Light by Manipal Technologies Limited

Printed and bound in Great Britain by Clays Ltd, Elcograf S.p.A.

Hodder & Stoughton policy is to use papers that are natural, renewable and recyclable products and made from wood grown in sustainable forests. The logging and manufacturing processes are expected to conform to the environmental regulations of the country of origin.

Hodder & Stoughton Limited
Carmelite House
50 Victoria Embankment
London EC4Y 0DZ

www.hodder.co.uk

*For my family, and for all the handywomen and midwives down the generations*

# PART I

# 1

*Belfast, Thursday, 31 January 1935*

The day Peggy Cassidy's life changed forever began with the birth of a baby. At the ripe old age of sixteen – nearly seventeen – she had seen almost a hundred babies born, and every single birth had been unique.

'The baby's coming!'

There was fear in Mrs Murray's voice – fear that could be a problem. Thankfully, Peggy could see the baby's head descending in a perfectly normal way.

'Yes, it is,' she said soothingly. 'It's all right, Mrs Murray. You're doing a great job, so you are.'

Thankfully, this seemed to settle Mrs Murray. Occasionally, first-time mothers would get themselves in a panic, which could make the birth slow down. Behind her, she could hear Aunty Bridget getting ready for the baby. Mrs Murray had provided clean, soft towels, a wee vest, and some terry nappies, and it was clear they would be needed very, very soon. The most important thing she and Aunty Bridget could do now was to help Mrs Murray stay calm and focused.

Taking a thin piece of wool from her pocket, Peggy tied back her long, dark hair in readiness for the birth. The last thing she wanted was for her own unruly curls to get in the way.

*Seána Tinley*

'Now, another pain is coming in a minute, and you'll feel yourself pushing again, Mrs Murray. Are you comfortable the way you are, or do you want to get onto your knees?'

'Can I?' Mrs Murray looked red-faced and tired, but the labour had only been going on since late yesterday, so Peggy knew she would still have good reserves of strength. First babies could be slow to come. A quick glance towards the window told her it was now almost morning, weak light penetrating the thin curtain. The January nights had seemed endless, reluctantly giving way to allow a few minutes of extra daylight each day.

With Aunty Bridget's help, she supported Mrs Murray to flip onto her knees and grip the wooden headboard of her sturdy bed. And not a moment too soon, for she was pushing again – loud, guttural groans coming from her throat. Peggy and Aunty Bridget's eyes met – the same eyes, for Peggy had inherited the Doyle blue eyes from her ma. A sense of connection, of shared purpose, flowed through her. This was important work, and she and Aunty Bridget were doing it together. Soon all the hours of patient waiting would be done.

Together Peggy and her aunt arranged towels on the bed between the woman's knees, ready to receive the baby. Sensibly, Mrs Murray had covered her mattress with a rubber sheet before making it up with cool cotton bed linen. The bed was normally pushed up against the wall of the small bedroom, but with Mrs Murray's agreement Peggy and Aunty Bridget had pulled it out when they arrived yesterday, to allow them to get around both sides of it.

There was a discreet knocking on the door, which Peggy ignored. Once Mrs Murray's contraction had eased though,

## The Irish Midwife

she left Aunty Bridget murmuring soothing words to Mrs Murray and went over to open it a crack.

As expected, it was Mr Murray, his face pale and his brow furrowed. 'How is she? I can hear her from downstairs.'

'She's fine. It won't be long now. Can we have some more hot water?'

'Yes, of course.' He disappeared speedily, and Peggy suppressed a smile. Some of the men would go to the pub during the evening, but once they were back in the house they often needed to be given jobs to do. Besides, she and Aunty Bridget were sticklers for hygiene, and washed their hands with soap and a nail brush on a regular basis while attending a birth, so the hot water was genuinely needed. Mr Murray had been taken for pints by the menfolk yesterday evening, but had spent the night downstairs with his wife's mother and sisters, as well as his own ma. Peggy had heard the reassuring hum of conversation from downstairs through the night, and knew Mrs Murray would have been comforted by it, too. Sometimes a woman would want her own mammy in the room, which was fine, but more often than not she was content just to have the handywomen.

Having a baby, Aunty Bridget always said, was the most natural thing in the world, but that didn't mean it should be ignored or taken for granted. A new member of the Murray family was about to come into the world, and the significance for the whole family could not be overstated.

*And I am to be part of it!* Peggy thought. It never grew old – the feeling of privilege that, in her role as trainee handywoman, she got to be part of special moments for so many women. The numbers she had supported were nothing, of course, not in comparison to Aunty Bridget's experience. For more than forty years Bridget Devine had served the women of West Belfast and as a result, she was held in high esteem throughout the community. All the handywomen were.

Not that there were that many of them. Peggy knew of only four in the west – Aunty Bridget and her great friend Mrs Clarke, as well as Mrs Kennedy and Mrs Quinn. That was why Aunty Bridget was training Peggy, for they knew there would always be a need for five or six handywomen for their sprawling community based around Belfast's Falls Road. Apparently there had been more handywomen needed at one time, but more recently wealthier women were choosing to pay doctors' fees and have their babies in hospitals and maternity homes. Not so the working women of West. While emergency care was free, they wouldn't have the money to pay for a doctor every time they had a baby.

Not that doctors were needed, anyway. Not for straightforward births, which most births were. That was women's business. The business of the women and the handywomen.

Mrs Murray began groaning again, and Peggy nodded in satisfaction. The pains were coming one after another, which would hopefully prevent the baby's head from slipping back up the birth canal.

About ten minutes later the head was out. Peggy watched as it moved – a full quarter turn to align with its shoulders. It was fascinating how that happened, every time. Gently, Aunty Bridget checked the cord, and Peggy saw her frown.

'Try not to push for a minute, Mrs Murray,' she said, and Peggy saw that the cord was wrapped tightly around the baby's neck. She held her breath as Aunty Bridget worked at it, trying to resist the instinct to be worried. *Babies don't breathe the way we do*, she reminded herself. Before birth they got their oxygen directly from the blood in the cord, so the only problem would be if the cord was nipped so much it wasn't able to pulse into the baby. Peering closely, she saw that the cord was a healthy colour, plump and purple.

Aunty Bridget's clever hands, spotted with age and wisdom, were working deftly to release the cord, and a moment later Peggy saw her slip it over the baby's head. Peggy watched closely, as she'd only seen it done a couple of times, but as before, there was no issue. The cord was still a good colour, its natural springiness ensuring the blood had kept flowing to the baby.

It struck her then that she *knew* things – that she was genuinely learning from Aunty Bridget. Well, and why wouldn't she? She'd been helping with births – and with laying out the dead – since leaving school at fourteen.

Nearly three years of it, being sent for after working her shifts in the mill, on her days off, or on Sundays when the mill was closed. She hated being a milly – as the Belfast mill-girls were called – and couldn't wait to work as a handywoman full-time. She even got paid a bit already, if there was enough money. Sometimes the women paid Aunty Bridget in favours or food, because they couldn't afford her modest fee. It didn't matter, for Bridget Devine would help anyway, and everyone in West Belfast knew it.

'Now then, Mrs Murray, it's time. With the next push, your baby might be here.'

Mrs Murray nodded, then the urge to push took her over again. A moment later the baby was out, landing squarely on the towels. Its colour was good, the cord was beating healthily, and within seconds it began to cry.

'Move this leg . . . now turn . . . that's it.' Aunty Bridget directed Mrs Murray to turn around safely, then helped her pick up her baby. 'A wee boy. *Maith thú*. Well done!' Aunty Bridget still spoke Irish occasionally, particularly when emotional.

'Oh, oh, my baby! I can't believe it!' Mrs Murray was holding him close, rubbing his wee head and back. 'Look at that head of hair! Look at his wee hands!'

'And a good size too, Mrs Murray. I'd guess he's a seven-pounder.' Aunty Bridget was covering his wee back with towels – it wasn't good for newborn babies to get cold. Peggy congratulated the new mother then added coal to the fire. Mrs Murray's house was identical to her own, and the fireplace in the upstairs front bedroom of these houses rarely got used. Now that the baby was born, the room needed to be a lot warmer.

Knowing that Mr Murray was probably on the landing, she opened the door again, a little. There he was, along with his mother, Mrs Murray's mother, and three of her sisters. 'All well,' she said. 'A boy. We just need a wee while longer. And bring us that bucket, please.' She sent a meaningful look to the women crowding the narrow landing.

'Ah, that's great. Right, everybody! Downstairs. Time to put the kettle on.' Mrs Murray senior was taking everybody in hand. Still smiling, Peggy closed the door and went back to the new mother, who was already undoing the buttons at the top of her nightdress.

'My ma told me to feed the baby straight away, so she did.'

'And she was right!' Aunty Bridget agreed. 'But let him do it himself. Here, let me fix these pillows.' She arranged the pillows so that Mrs Murray was still sitting, but slightly laid back. 'There. Now you can be comfortable, love.'

Peggy was keeping an eye on Mrs Murray's bleeding. A steady trickle, nothing major. And only the tiniest tear, thankfully. Leaving Mrs Murray to coo at her baby, she and her aunt tidied the room. One of the women brought the bucket – and in the nick of time, for Mrs Murray was groaning again, as the afterbirth announced its imminent arrival.

Peggy took the baby, checking that the cord had finished its work. Sure enough, it was now white and limp – a strong contrast to the purple pulsating of twenty minutes ago. Tying it off in two places with strong wool, she cut between them with scissors cleaned in the freshly boiled water, then took the baby to the foot of the bed to dress him in nappy, wool pants, and vest. The afterbirth was now out, so the baby went directly back to his mammy, wrapped in a wee knitted blanket, while Aunty Bridget inspected the afterbirth before carefully placing it in the bucket.

'That's us now,' she declared with an air of satisfaction, the familiar words delivered in an accent that was pure Belfast. *At's us nai.*

And it was. Another baby safely born. Another contented mother holding her wee one close.

Another good day.

# 2

'Are you ready to show him off?'

The baby had had his first feed and all was well. Mrs Murray, beaming, agreed and Peggy left the room, closing the door behind her. This was such a lovely part of her role, inviting the new father and the grannies in to see the wee one.

A minute later Mr Murray was bounding up the stairs, followed in a much more dignified manner by both grannies, who were even now sharing an indulgent look and rolling their eyes. Peggy grinned, relief and exhilaration coursing through her. Tragedies did still happen during childbirth – no one knew why sometimes – though they were rare. Still, it was always comforting to get to this point, with baby safely out and mammy and baby doing well.

As the women passed her on the landing, Mrs Murray's mother told Peggy to go to the kitchen, where some fresh toast and a cuppa tae were awaiting her. She needed no second bidding, and a few moments later Aunty Bridget joined her. They had eaten nothing since yesterday teatime, and the toast was all the nicer for it. Mrs Murray's ma had taken tea and toast upstairs for the new mother, who would be even more ravenous.

They sat chatting idly, warmth coursing through Peggy at the knowledge that all was well. How many times had they done this – sitting in a kitchen after a birth? Night or day, the routine was the same – tea, toast, and a sense of satisfaction.

'You done well, Peggy,' said Aunty Bridget, popping the last morsel of toast into her mouth. 'You'll make a fine handywoman, so you will.'

The warmth flooding through Peggy at her aunt's compliment made her smile.

'Ach sure, I'm only learning.'

'Another six months or so and you'll be ready to go to births on your own.'

Peggy's eyes widened. 'Really?'

'Aye. You're a good girl, Peggy. And a great learner.'

Peggy blushed and stammered. Around here, people didn't usually say nice things so openly.

'Don't you be getting all mortified now, Peggy.' Aunty Bridget's tone was firm. 'You're like a daughter to me, and that's a fact.'

It was true, but Aunty Bridget had never said it out loud before. Her husband had died before Peggy was born – a hero of the Easter Rising – and Aunty Bridget had never remarried. Her nieces and nephews all adored her, but Peggy had often wondered if Aunty Bridget had a soft spot for her. After all, she had been the one selected to train as a handywoman alongside her aunt. The deal had been done between Ma and Aunty Bridget, and Peggy had been delighted when they had told her of it.

'I know,' she said softly. 'I'm lucky enough to have two mammies – although that does mean double the telling-off sometimes!'

Bridget laughed, throwing her head back and guffawing the way she did sometimes. Affection coursed through Peggy at the sight. Aunty Bridget's hair was grey now, her face increasingly wrinkled. But she was one of the most *alive* people Peggy knew. It was probably because she had managed to avoid a lifetime in the mills. Mill-hands died young – mostly of accidents or lung diseases. The handywoman's other job was sitting with the dying, and Peggy could recall nights trying to comfort frightened people struggling to get a breath. It was not a good way to die.

Thank God Bridget was unlikely ever to suffer that way, but Peggy worried about the rest of them – Da, who worked long hours in the mill, and Peggy's brothers and sisters along with him. Ma had escaped because she needed to be a mother instead, and Granda was too old to work now, but Gerard, Antoinette and Sheila all worked full-time as mill-hands. The wee ones – Joe and Aiveen – were too young yet, but their time would come, too. Every penny of wages was needed to cover food and rent. Peggy was lucky the family had taken the hit of her staying a half-timer so she could train as a handywoman.

'Aye, well sometimes you need a good telling-off, my girl – though to be fair it's only a now-and-again thing. I recall my own ma – your Granny Doyle – was a fierce woman. I used to dread her shouting at me!'

'Aye, I remember she was a strong woman.'

'We all are, Peggy – all us Doyle women.' Aunty Bridget leaned forward, her blue eyes pinning Peggy's. 'You might be called Cassidy but you're a true Doyle, and never you forget it!'

'I—'

Abruptly, there was a pounding at the front door. Peggy and Aunty Bridget looked at each other, both rising and making for the living room. Peggy's inner sense of satisfaction was giving way to fear. Who would make that racket in a house where everyone knew there was a woman having a baby? God, was somebody not well? She bit her lip.

'Open up! Police!' The voice was loud, demanding, and utterly terrifying.

What in God's name did the police want?

# 3

The pounding on the door was continuing, louder than before.

'Jesus, Mary and Joseph!' Aunty Bridget made the sign of the cross then stepped forward – just as Mr Murray's ma reached the bottom of the stairs and opened the front door.

Immediately the house was invaded. Two burly men, both wearing the insignia of the dreaded Royal Ulster Constabulary. One headed straight upstairs, while the other came into the living room. Peggy's heart was thumping like a hammer in her chest, and her palms were suddenly sweaty with fear. *What do they want?*

The RUC constable was tall and broad, with a red face and a cross expression. He looked at them all, his eyes narrowed. 'Mrs Bridget Devine?'

Cold fear pooled in Peggy's stomach. She clutched her aunt's arm, feeling the tension in her.

Aunty Bridget straightened. 'I am Mrs Devine. Why?'

'We have reason to believe that you are practising midwifery without a licence. There have been complaints.'

Peggy gasped. Aunty Bridget was highly respected in the community. Who on earth would complain about her? She moved forward, leaning against Aunty Bridget from behind. *I am here.*

Bridget straightened. 'Complaints from whom?'

'Not one but two doctors.' He consulted his notebook. 'Dr Fenton and Dr Sheridan. They say you're putting lives at risk.'

At this, Peggy felt her sag slightly. Aunty Bridget *saved* lives! Never would she do anything risky with the women who trusted her.

'Dr Fenton,' Aunty Bridget mused, shaking her head. 'But I'm surprised about Dr Sheridan. I thought he was better than this.' She turned to Peggy, her face pale but her voice remarkably steady.

'Peggy,' she murmured, 'tell your ma not to fight this.' She looked her in the eye. 'Will you do that for me?'

'But—' Peggy could barely contain her outrage, her terror on Aunty Bridget's behalf. The community could have a crowd outside the police station in no time if needed. There would certainly be anger enough.

How dared the police challenge Bridget Devine née Doyle – a woman who was well known and well respected, and who had never broken a law in her life! Or at least, had never broken a *sensible* law.

'Will you *do* that for me?' Aunty Bridget's look was intent, and Peggy nodded.

'And who is this?' The policeman was now looking at her, his expression disdainful. 'Another so-called handywoman?'

'She's nobody. My sister's girl.'

'You wouldn't be training her up, now would you?'

Peggy could feel the blood draining from her face, but Aunty Bridget was well fit for them. She laughed – actually *laughed*, saying, 'Sure she's only a chile.'

Just then, his colleague reappeared. 'New baby and mother upstairs. Our information from the pub was correct. She swears she had it alone, but' – he jerked his head towards Bridget – 'you got her?'

'I have indeed. Right, come with us, please.' He stepped back, indicating that Aunty Bridget should pass him. Helplessly Peggy watched, noticing in that moment that Aunty Bridget was walking confidently, head held high. The sight of her grey hair secured in its usual neat bun seemed incongruous, somehow. Were the RUC really lifting her aunt? A woman who had recently turned sixty? And for what? For helping other women? Rage blazed through her. *How feckin' dare they!*

Outside a crowd was gathering, as it always did when the RUC came into their tight-knit community.

'On yiz go, yiz bastards!' shouted one elderly man, and a chorus of jeers echoed out.

'Leave the Murrays alone!' shouted a woman. 'They're good people!'

Peggy could almost feel the moment when the crowd realised what was going on. A wave of gasps and shocked exclamations rippled through the crowd, with people exclaiming:

'It's Mrs Devine!'

'No!'

'Oh my God!'

'Leave her alone!'

'What the hell are you doing with Mrs Devine?'

Stony-faced, the police ignored them, putting Aunty Bridget into the back of the police car, then climbing in the front.

*Oh, poor Aunty Bridget!*

As the motor car moved off some of the young lads ran after it, hurling insults until it turned the corner and was gone. Peggy, tears rolling down her cheeks, could only stand there, entirely helpless.

# 4

'So where did they take you?'

Peggy watched silently as her ma questioned Aunty Bridget about her ordeal. It was midnight and Aunty Bridget had finally reappeared in her tiny house, one street down from Peggy's home. It was the house Bridget and Peggy's mammy had grown up in. After the Rising, when the news had come of her husband's death, Aunty Bridget – widowed and childless – had moved back into her home house with her ageing mother. With never a complaint about the hand that fate had dealt her, she had looked after her elderly mother until Granny Doyle's death. And now this. It was so unfair!

Following hugs, and the kettle going back on, Aunty Bridget was now sitting in her own armchair by her own fire, answering Ma's questions.

'The main police station – the one where the Andersonstown Road meets the Glen Road, you know?'

'And you walked home? In the dark? At midnight?'

'And sure why wouldn't I? I know all these streets and everybody that lives in them!' Aunty Bridget chuckled. 'It takes more than intimidation from a few eejits to properly scare me – though I have to admit it was a shock when they landed into Mrs Murray's house. Is she all right?' Her gaze swung to Peggy, who nodded. 'And the baby? Good.

Absolutely disgraceful carry-on, invading the home of a woman giving birth.'

Ma shrugged. 'It's the RUC. What else do you expect from a pig but a grunt?'

'Ah, now,' said Aunty Bridget. 'Don't you be giving pigs a bad name, Mary!' They laughed then – laughter that held a great deal of relief. Despite her light-hearted words, Peggy could see strain in the lines of Aunty Bridget's face. It was as if she had aged twenty years since this morning.

'Did they formally arrest you, Bridget?'

'Aye, but it's nothing to worry about, Mary.'

'Nothing to worry about? You could be put in prison!'

Bridget shrugged. 'It's not as simple as that.'

Ma's brow was furrowed. 'I don't follow you.'

'They brought in a law to say only midwives and doctors can attend births. They've made it a crime all right, but the punishment for handywomen who get caught is a fine, not prison. The whole "you're under arrest" play-acting was only to intimidate me.'

'How much of a fine?'

Aunty Bridget grimaced. 'Ten pounds.'

Ma blessed herself. 'How are you supposed to find that sort of money? It's a fortune!'

Aunty Bridget's eyes danced with mischief. 'I have a good wee bit put by, but damn sures they're not getting it!'

Mammy looked puzzled. 'Then what—'

'They can put me in prison as a debtor, I suppose . . . but they're still not getting my savings.'

'Now, Bridget—'

'Don't you *now, Bridget* me, Mary! I would remind you that I am the eldest, and you the youngest. And you might be Mrs Cassidy now, but in this house you'll always be Mary Doyle, the baby of the family!' She pursed her lips. 'I haven't been working for forty-five years just so the RUC and a couple of big doctors with notions about themselves can steal it from me!'

'Yeah, who were the doctors who reported you? Do you know them?'

'I do.' Aunty Bridget nodded briskly – as though they weren't discussing the fact she had been detained in a police cell all day. 'Fenton is a big-shot in the Royal. Thinks he is somebody. Doesn't surprise me in the least that he did this.' She paused. 'Dr Sheridan though . . .' Her face twisted and Peggy suddenly realised that Aunty Bridget looked *hurt*. 'He's a general practitioner in South Belfast. I never had much to do with him, for he has very few patients here in West. But he always struck me as a good man. Fair, you know?' Her eyes became unfocused. 'Just shows you, you never really know anybody, do you?'

'Ah, this is a disaster.' Ma's hand was on her forehead. 'We'll talk about it in the morning. Peggy, you'll stay here tonight.'

Peggy nodded, even as Aunty Bridget protested that she didn't need a babysitter and Ma overruled her with all the authority of a mother of six.

'She's staying, and that's final.' She turned to Peggy. 'You'll miss work tomorrow – our Antoinette can tell them you're sick. She can pick up your wages too.'

'But that'll mean less money this week. Will we manage?'

Ma looked after all the money in the family, everybody including Daddy dutifully handing over their wages every Friday.

Ma shrugged. 'We manage when you're at a birth or a wake. We'll manage this week.' Her tone was firm. 'Now, go and fill a hot-water bottle for your aunty Bridget, for it's freezin' tonight.'

Peggy complied, and she was upstairs putting the rubber bottle into Aunty Bridget's bed when she heard a shriek from below. 'Peggy! Come quick!'

Hurrying down the stairs, her heart pounding at the fear in Ma's voice, she dashed into the wee living room. Aunty Bridget was slumped in her chair, one side of her face sagging, and Ma kneeling beside her.

'It's all right, Bridget,' she was saying softly. She turned to Peggy. 'Go and get Dr Gaffney, quick!'

Peggy didn't need to be told twice. Grabbing her coat, she ran out the door, heading down to the bottom of Rockdale Street and turning right, passing her own street, Rockville, then Rockmore Road and Rockmount Street. The 'Rock streets' as they were known, for obvious reasons. Those who lived here had a tight-knit sense of community.

Peggy knew exactly which house to go to – the big house on the Falls Road beside the chapel. In her three years helping Aunty Bridget, she had been sent for the doctor a few times – for a woman who had a fever, a woman who bled, a woman whose baby wouldn't come. Dr Gaffney had come, and each time he had arranged for an ambulance, and praised Aunty Bridget for doing the right thing. Emergency care was free, unlike hiring a doctor or midwife. The women and babies had been fine afterwards, thank God. Dr Gaffney, she knew, would never have dreamed of complaining about a handywoman.

## The Irish Midwife

As she ran, under her breath she was muttering a decade of the rosary. First, an Our Father, then ten Hail Marys . . . And all the while she was wishing, praying, *begging* for a miracle.

Aunty Bridget's house in Rockdale Street was identical to the Cassidy family home one street over. Living room to the front, kitchen to the back, with an outhouse in the backyard. There was running water for the kitchen sink as well as electric lights and even two power sockets. Upstairs were two bedrooms, usually stuffed full of people. At home Granda Joe (who was Da's da) and Peggy's brothers Gerard and wee Joe shared the back bedroom, while Peggy shared the front bedroom with her sisters Antoinette, Sheila, and wee Aiveen. Ma and Da slept downstairs on a big mattress that got hauled upstairs every morning. Still, Antoinette and Gerard were both courting and saving to get married, so in a few years the house would be a bit emptier, with two of the six children up and away.

Because Aunty Bridget lived by herself in Granny and Granda Doyle's old house, that meant there was usually at least one of the Cassidys or their cousins staying over in her back bedroom. Her two-up two-down seemed enormous for just one person. Tonight it would be Peggy's turn to stay over – especially with poor Aunty Bridget not being well.

Dr Gaffney had come, confirmed it was a stroke, had shaken his head sadly, and left again. Da had been sent for, to carry his sister-in-law up to her bed, where Ma and Peggy had made her comfortable. By morning she was opening her eyes, and even talking – her speech slurred and hard to make out at times. She kept having nosebleeds and was complaining of a bad headache. Dr Gaffney had said Aunty Bridget's blood pressure was very high and had warned she might have a second stroke. Peggy had only a vague idea what blood pressure was, but Dr Gaffney's demeanour told her everything she needed to know. He was deeply concerned.

Peggy, used to sitting through the night with women in labour, had made Ma go to the back bedroom to sleep a few hours ago, and had then taken a turn at sleeping herself, but when it got to half-five in the morning Ma came back, letting Peggy go to help Antoinette with Ma's jobs at home.

Da was already up when she got home, the mattress leaning against the wall ready to go upstairs. It would be stored in the boys' bedroom for the day as usual. Da had had his strip wash in the kitchen and was currently buttoning up his shirt. With Ma away there was no porridge made, but she saw that he had made himself tea, as well as taking some bread-and-dripping.

'How is she?'

Peggy grimaced. 'Talking, but slurred. No power on her left side. It's not good.'

He nodded, sadness in his eyes, then straightened. 'Right,' he declared briskly. 'I'm away to work. Come and get me if you need me.'

*If she dies.* 'We will, aye.'

# 5

Walking through to the kitchen, Peggy started preparing breakfast, her mind elsewhere. Tea. Porridge in the big pot. Checking the bread bin, she saw there was very little left, so she made fresh farls, mixing flour with baking soda, salt, and buttermilk, then kneading it out. After forming the dough into a circle she cut it into four, cooking the farls on the iron griddle on top of the stove.

The smell of the fresh soda farls attracted the attention of Granda Joe along with Peggy's brothers and sisters, and soon downstairs was bustling. Wee Joe started clearing out the fire, and Gerard, Antoinette, and Sheila went to the table with Granda, eating their porridge as quickly as they could. Once they were done, Peggy gave them half a farl each and sent them on their way – Gerard and Antoinette to get ready for work, Sheila to tidy the bedrooms before school. Everybody did their bit – except Granda of course. At nearly ninety, he had more than earned the right to be looked after. Wee Aiveen, the youngest at only two, had to be changed so Antoinette did that, coming back to the kitchen afterwards to wash her hands and talk again about poor Aunty Bridget.

'I'll say one thing,' she declared, fire in her eyes, 'it's no coincidence she took a stroke after being held in a bloody RUC station all day!'

Peggy nodded, but said only, 'Don't let Ma hear you saying bad words like that.'

'What bad words? RUC?'

Peggy smiled, Antoinette's wit lifting the clouds from about her for the briefest of moments.

'Here, take the chile,' Antoinette added, passing Aiveen across. Peggy settled her wee sister on her hip, stacking used plates and cutlery with the other hand, and talking to her in a baby voice. Wee Joe, who was nine, had finished doing the fire – brushing the hearth and setting a new fire with paper twists, sticks, and coal, ready for later. After washing he took his turn at the table, and Peggy put Aiveen into the corner chair, well propped up so she wouldn't fall. While they were eating their porridge – Aiveen getting it everywhere but her mouth, of course – Peggy washed the first set of dishes, then filled a bowl of porridge for Ma, placing it in one of the wee compartments under the stove to keep warm. There was enough left for half a bowl for herself, and she ate it standing by the stove, unable to settle.

After that she cleared out the big pot and washed it, washed Aiveen in the sink, then started peeling the spuds. A notion took her. Today was the first day of February, St Brigid's Day – the saint that Aunty Bridget had been named after. St Brigid, the patron saint of women, of midwives, of healing, and of art. Maybe it was a sign that Aunty Bridget would recover. On the other hand, if she did die today, on the feast day of her name, it would be somehow fitting.

Peggy closed her eyes briefly. Hopefully Aunty Bridget would be all right. Besides, she had too much to do to be wasting time thinking right now. By the time she had filled

## The Irish Midwife

the big pot with peeled potatoes covered in water, cleaned Aiveen up, and made sure Joe had washed properly, they were running late.

'Let's go, Joe!' Even though some of the local boys ran to school by themselves every day, Ma usually went along with Joe, calling at the chapel afterwards to light a candle and say a prayer, while making sure her youngest son actually went inside the school. Today of all days, Peggy would do the same.

After cleaning the house from top to bottom while Granda Joe kept an eye on Aiveen, Peggy hoisted the toddler onto her hip and made her way back round to Rockdale Street. A few of Aunty Bridget's neighbours were out at their front doors, and Peggy made slow progress up the street. Word had gone out that the doctor had called to the house during the night, and again an hour ago, and now it seemed the priest had been sent for. Peggy's heart sank at the news.

'What we all want to know, Peggy,' said Mrs Elliott, her arms folded over her faded cotton apron, 'is did the RUC harm her? For if they done anything to that wee lady, I swear—'

'No, no, nothing like that,' Peggy hastened to answer, seeing Mrs Elliott's fierce expression. 'Definitely a stroke. She can't talk right, and she's lost the power of movement all down one side.'

'Ah, God love her.' Mrs Elliott blessed herself. 'What time did the polis let her out?'

'Just before midnight. She was there a good few hours.'

'Aye, then had a stroke a coupla hours later.' Mrs Elliott looked ragin'. 'Them bastards mightn't have put a hand on her, Peggy, but they killed her all the same.'

'As did the doctors who reported her,' Peggy replied, her throat tight. 'They're glad of the handywomen when it suits them. But to do what they done to my lovely Aunty Bridget – it's not feckin' right.'

'You're spot on, Peggy. I'm so sorry.'

Peggy thanked her, moving on before she started to cry. Aunty Bridget was not dead, but the signs weren't good.

Sure enough when she got to Aunty Bridget's, Father Fullerton, the parish priest, was coming down the stairs, a green stole around his neck and his box of holy oils in his hand. He had clearly just given Bridget the Last Rites.

'Ah, hello there, Peggy,' he said, his kind eyes soft with sadness. 'Mrs Devine has made her confession and had communion. The doctor thinks she won't do, so I offered' – he indicated the box of oils – 'and she accepted. She knows she doesn't have long.' He pressed a hand to her arm briefly before greeting Aiveen, who hid her face in Peggy's shoulder. 'She's asking for you,' he added.

Peggy nodded, thanked him, then began the long climb upstairs. Surely thirteen steps had never been so difficult before? Taking a breath, she stepped into the front bedroom.

'Ach, here's our Peggy, Bridget.' Ma's eyes were red, Peggy noticed.

Aunty Bridget was lying motionless in the bed, arms outside the covers. Ma and Sister Mark from the parish were sitting on hard chairs beside the bed. Aiveen reached for Ma, her wee face troubled. *Even wee Aiveen knows something is wrong.*

'Peggy.' The word was almost a whisper, the sounds shaped rather than fully formed.

## The Irish Midwife

'I'm here, Aunty Bridget.' Sitting on the edge of the bed, Peggy took her right hand – the good hand, for her aunt squeezed it.

'Good girl.' She stopped, took a few breaths, then, with visible effort, spoke again. '*Éist liom.*' That was 'listen to me' in Irish. 'Now, second drawer, at the back.'

Peggy's mind was sluggish. Seeing Aunty Bridget like this – a woman who, until just a few hours ago, was hale and hearty and fiercely independent . . . it made no sense to Peggy's brain.

'Peggy.' Aunty Bridget's tone was urgent, bringing Peggy's attention back to the present. Her mouth was turned down on one side, Peggy saw, the lines in that side of her face smoothed in unwanted idleness. 'Second drawer. Now!'

Peggy went, crossing the small room and opening the second drawer in what had originally been Granny Doyle's chest of drawers. At the back, Aunty Bridget had said. Feeling her way amid cardigans and blouses – all clean, pressed, and neatly folded – Peggy suddenly came upon something else. She drew it out, bringing it to Aunty Bridget. A cloth bag, hand-stitched from an old pillowcase, that emitted a metallic clink as she moved it.

'Open. Go on!'

Peggy opened it, her jaw dropping at the number of coins and notes inside. Turning her head, she looked at her aunt.

'Saved for years, so I did. Thought I'd need for retirement. God has other plans. Go you to Dublin, Peggy.' She took a breath. 'Midwife school. Too many know you as a handywoman around here. It'll go against you.' Given her condition, this was a long speech and she stopped, breathing laboriously.

## Seána Tinley

'No, Aunty Bridget, no.' Peggy could barely speak. Her throat was painfully tight, her cheeks wet with hot tears. 'I can't.'

'Can.' Aunty Bridget patted her hand. 'Great handywoman. Great midwife. *Is féidir leat.*' You can.

'Don't you be arguing with your aunt now, Peggy.' Sister Mark spoke firmly. 'She's telling you what she wants done with her money, and it's her right to do so. Now just you say "thank you" and be grateful.'

'Thank you,' Peggy managed in a small voice. Her mind was reeling. Aunty Bridget was dying – they all knew it. Giving away her life savings was proof. And Peggy couldn't possibly take the money.

'Mary. Peggy.' Aunty Bridget wanted them both this time.

'We're here, Bridget.' Ma took her sister's other hand. *How many times had the two of them held hands as children?* Peggy wondered. Bridget would have helped rear her youngest sister, there was no doubt. Fifteen years between them. *Same as me and Aiveen.*

'I want a good wake now, chile. D'ya hear me?' Whether this was directed to Ma or Peggy was unclear. It was likely that Bridget thought of them both as children right now.

'The best,' Ma said, tears streaming down her cheeks. 'I might even get Granny Doyle's china out when they all come.'

Half of Aunty Bridget's face smiled at this. 'Music. And craic. No yappin'.'

'Oh, there'll definitely be music,' Peggy said, hearing the thickness of her own voice. 'And we'll have the best of craic. But we'll cry too, Aunty Bridget. We'll all miss you. I'll miss you.'

## The Irish Midwife

There was no response. Checking anxiously, Peggy saw that Aunty Bridget was still breathing, but had sunk into sleep.

'Tanty Biddit sick?' asked wee Aiveen, who had been watching and listening carefully.

'Yes, love. Aunty Bridget is sick. But she's sleeping now.' Burying her face in Aiveen's dark curls, Ma kissed her wee head repeatedly, then rose, letting go of Bridget's hand. 'I better get the dinner on. Won't be long till dinner break at the mills, and they'll all be landing in demanding their champ!'

'I peeled the spuds this morning,' Peggy offered.

'Ah, you're a good girl, Peggy.' Ma squeezed her shoulder. 'If you get the chance, see if you can gather up all your granny's china and put it on the kitchen worktop.' She turned to Sister Mark. 'Thanks, Sister. I really appreciate you being here.'

'I'm glad to be of help, Mrs Cassidy,' Sister Mark replied. 'And me and Bridget go way back. Best friends we were, along with Róisín – Mrs Clarke. Now go you on and feed your family. I'll sort out something for Peggy and me here.'

Sister Mark was as good as her word, boiling a few potatoes and mashing them with butter and milk. 'Your champ's ready, Peggy,' she said, entering the bedroom. Peggy glanced at Aunty Bridget, who hadn't woken since. Her breathing was slowing, with brief pauses between breaths. Having sat with the dying many's a time, she knew what that meant. 'Go on,' Sister Mark urged. 'I've had mine. You need to eat.'

So Peggy went, eating her champ at Aunty Bridget's table, her only company the ticking of the clock. The silence was eerie, wrong. Mealtimes were normally bustling and noisy. Everything about today was wrong.

After washing up she checked in all the cupboards, assembling a collection of delph – both Aunty Bridget's plain crockery, and Granny Doyle's precious china. Mrs Clarke arrived then – another handywoman Peggy knew well.

'Ach, I'm so sorry, Peggy.' Mrs Clarke hugged her. 'I can't believe we're going to lose our Bridget. One of the best women I've ever known.'

'You were best friends, Sister Mark said?' *Why do I not know more about Aunty Bridget's past?* And now it was too late. Too late to ask. Too late to hear the stories of how Bridget had become a handywoman or how she had met her husband. *Too late.*

'We were, aye. Still are, I suppose. Me and Bridget and Mary McKeever – always together, and hardly a bit of wit between the three of us. We had quare craic!' She chuckled, then sighed at whatever memories were going through her mind. 'Me and Bridget became handywomen and Mary went into the convent. Then Bridget married Ned Devine and I married my Brendan, and we all got sensible and grown-up.'

'She told me yesterday that I was like a daughter to her.' Peggy heard the tightness in her own voice. *Don't cry. Not yet.*

'Well, and that can't have surprised you, surely?'

Peggy frowned. 'I suppose. But she wants me to use her life savings to train as a midwife. In Dublin.' Dublin was a hundred miles away. A hundred miles!

'Does she now?' Mrs Clarke considered this. 'I suppose it would do no harm, having one of our own in among them. And it would protect you from the likes of what happened yesterday.' Her brow furrowed. 'I knew that bloody law would make trouble for us one day. But I don't think any of us thought a handywoman would actually get lifted over it.' She sent a sharp glance at Peggy. 'You do what your aunty tells you, Peggy. You hear me?'

Peggy shrugged, knowing an outright refusal would only cause more trouble. Mrs Clarke went upstairs then, and Peggy returned to her dishes. Carefully, she washed each piece, stacking them on the worktop ready for the wake. *Aunty Bridget isn't even dead yet, and I'm washing dishes for the wake.*

That done, she returned upstairs with cups of tea for Sister Mark and Mrs Clarke. 'No, don't get up!' She put a hand out to prevent the nun from rising. Perching on the edge of the bed, she looked properly at Aunty Bridget. Death was coming. She'd seen it many times before. Her aunt's breathing had slowed even more – she counted to ten in her head while awaiting her aunt's next in-breath.

It was going to be a long day.

Sitting with the dying was a privilege. Peggy had done it as a handywoman, many times. Birth and death held many similarities – beginnings and endings, a family on edge, the need to soothe and to hold and to make things as calm as possible. A good death, she knew, was just as important as a good birth – and both were better at home.

Today, Peggy was struck by a kind of double vision. She herself was that grieving relative awaiting the death of a loved one. And at the same time she was supporting everyone around her, using the skills and wisdom of a handywoman. Skills and wisdom passed on to her by Aunty Bridget herself.

Once the mills closed for the day there was a steady stream of relatives through the house, all wanting to speak to Aunty

Bridget, to hold her hand and have a wee cry, or to tell her things. Ma swore that her sister squeezed her hand at one point, but she never woke up properly.

Peggy and Sister Mark had based themselves downstairs, making continuous pots of tea and soothing people's distress. Mrs Clarke had been called to a birth, reminding Peggy again of the eternal cycle. Births and deaths in their community every day, every night.

But why did Aunty Bridget have to be taken, and her only sixty?

Thankfully it was just close family in the house for now – Peggy's brothers and sisters, cousins, aunties and uncles. Once the wake began there would be hundreds of people calling to say a prayer and pass on their condolences. Ma had come downstairs to bake two dozen scones this afternoon, and the women of the family were discussing what they would each bake or bring for the wake.

By late evening the house had settled into silence again – Sister Mark resting, Ma away home to sleep, and Peggy holding Aunty Bridget's hand. As it should be. Together they had held the hands of countless women in labour, and many more grieving the loss of a loved one. The doctor came around eleven, checked her pulse, and listened to the long, long gaps between breaths.

'I think I'll stay a while, Peggy.'

She nodded, knowing he thought it would be soon.

Sure enough, just before midnight, in the dying minutes of St Brigid's day, Aunty Bridget went to her eternal rest.

# 6

'Dr Sheridan!'

Dan turned, as someone was hailing his father.

'Dr Fenton,' Father hissed, and Dan straightened. Dr Fenton was one of the leading obstetricians in the Royal Maternity Hospital, and Dan's best hope for a junior house officer post after he qualified. At nineteen he had already decided to follow in his father's footsteps with a medical career, and knew that making a good impression on the senior doctors in the Royal was equally as important as doing well in his pre-med university studies. Which was why his father had brought him along to this drinks reception at Queen's University, to which all the leading doctors in Belfast had been invited.

Dr Fenton made his way through the crowd in the university medical school meeting room, drink in hand. They greeted one another cordially, Dan noticing that his father seemed a little tense. The two men chatted for a few moments, then Dr Fenton glanced his way.

'This your boy, Dr Sheridan?'

'Aye, this is Daniel.'

Dan squirmed inwardly. His parents always insisted on calling him Daniel, even though he preferred the shortened version. And he wasn't a boy.

'He's in pre-med and is going to be doing the medical post-grad in Queen's. He's interested in obstetrics.'

'Ah, good lad, good lad.' Dr Fenton patted his shoulder. 'We'll look after you.' He turned back to Dan's father, and Dan felt as though he had been dismissed. 'After our conversation last week I put in a complaint about one of those awful handywomen a few days ago. West Belfast, name of Devine. I put your name on it along with my own.'

'You did? Why?'

Dr Fenton looked taken aback. 'Well, after our chat about them—'

'Having a chat doesn't mean a formal complaint though. Many of the handywomen do a good job. Bridget Devine included.'

'Ah, come on! We both know how dirty they are, and clueless. What would women know about medicine?' He thought for a moment. 'And besides, they charge a pathetic amount, undercutting us.' Outrage was clearly apparent in his tone and expression.

Uncharitably, Dan wondered if the man was more outraged by the financial loss than by any risk to health, but stifled the thought. He needed Dr Fenton.

'Some of them are all right, as I said when we talked last week,' said Dan's father. 'But I wouldn't have put in a complaint. And certainly not about Mrs Devine.'

'See, there's where we disagree. None of them are all right,' said Dr Fenton firmly.

'Well, you shouldn't have added my name,' said Da firmly. 'I didn't give you permission, and I don't agree with it. In fact, I might need to formally withdraw my name.'

## The Irish Midwife

Dr Fenton now looked decidedly uncomfortable. 'Ah, no need to do that, Sheridan. I'm not sure they even took it seriously anyway. I wouldn't expect anything to come of it.'

'Well, I'm relieved to hear that.'

They talked on for a few minutes more – of mutual acquaintances and upcoming events – until any hint of awkwardness was smoothed over, then Dr Fenton made his escape, saying, 'Ah, I see Professor Wendell is looking for me. See you later, Sheridan.' And he was gone, without even a nod to Dan.

'My God,' said Dan. 'So arrogant!'

'Wheesht! And don't you be taking the Lord's name in vain.'

'But he is. Arrogant, I mean.'

Father sighed. 'Most of them are. I don't know whether the role attracts arrogant men, or whether they become arrogant once they're in the role. They think that general practice work like mine isn't real medicine, you know.'

'So why are you encouraging me to go for a hospital role?'

He shrugged. 'The money is better, and the respect. You make sure you stick it out and develop a hospital speciality. But until the day I die I'll defend general practice.'

Dan nodded, his mind now returning to Dr Fenton's complaint. 'What will happen to the handywoman?'

'Not being a lawyer, I don't know much about it. There would be a fine, I think – if they do act on it, which – as Fenton said – is unlikely.' He frowned. 'Fenton shouldn't have put my name on it without my permission, though.'

'Arrogant, like I said.'

'Aye. But keep in with him. He has great pull at the Royal.'

Dan set his jaw. He wasn't so green as to think he could fix the world, or bypass the power networks that riddled Belfast. There were many who wouldn't even consider opening doors to a medical student who attended Mass rather than Sunday Service. Dan would be tolerated by some of them simply because his own father was a doctor.

A notion struck him. West Belfast, name of Devine. The west of the city was dominated by Catholic areas – apart from the Shankill, which was mainly Protestant and aligned with King and Crown. Devine was an Irish name. Why had Dr Fenton not reported a handywoman from East Belfast called Smith or Simpson or some other English name?

He sighed. Obstetrics was one of the specialities that attracted him – getting things right for mothers and babies at the start of life would make a huge difference to the babies' life chances. But that meant dealing with pompous eejits like Dr Fenton. Eejits who might well be sectarian as well as arrogant.

'Good morning, dear. Did you sleep well?'

Dan bent to kiss his mother's presented cheek. 'Good morning, Ma.'

She frowned. 'I have told you a hundred times not to call me that. I am your mother, and I would appreciate you respecting me.'

He stifled a sigh. 'Good morning, Mother.'

'Thank you.'

She gave a nod of approval as he seated himself opposite her at the breakfast table. As usual, it was set formally with silver-plated cutlery and fine china, courtesy of Mrs

## The Irish Midwife

Kinahan, a middle-aged woman who worked for the family. His father's chair was empty – Father preferring to breakfast alone before heading to his surgery in leafy South Belfast. Today was Saturday, so Father would likely only work a half day.

'Now, Daniel, tell me again what Dr Fenton said to you yesterday.'

'Well, it was nothing really. He just said "We'll keep you right" or "We'll look after you" or something.'

'Well, which was it?'

He shrugged. Somehow, when Mother was questioning him, he had the overwhelming urge to resist her. For all that he was nineteen years of age, she still had the knack of making him feel a decade younger. He ran a hand through his thick, dark hair. 'I can't really remember.'

'Honestly, Daniel, you will need to pull your socks up. You're going to be a medical student soon! It won't be easy, qualifying as a doctor. And the worst thing would be if you had to give it up, now you've told everyone that's what you're doing.' She shuddered. 'I cannot even *imagine* what I would say to people.'

*Would that really be the worst thing?*

'I've no intention of giving it up, Ma— Mother. I *want* to be a doctor.' *At least, I think I do.* The doubts that plagued him occasionally threatened to rise up again and, ruthlessly, he suppressed them. It would never do for Ma to realise he was unsure of his path.

She sniffed. 'Well, you'd better concentrate on taking in important details then. No, don't pour from that jug, dear. Use this one first.'

Biting back the retort that had sprung to his mouth, he complied. Some of his school friends had chosen to be accountants or lawyers, and every one of them would be qualified and free to marry and move out of the family home in just two or three more years. Not he. The four more years of medical school ahead seemed endless. He wouldn't be qualified until the summer of 1939, which seemed a lifetime away. If he didn't want it so much he'd have been sorely tempted to base his career choices on whichever option would allow him to escape as soon as possible.

# 7

The black ribbon was on the door, all the curtains closed, and the undertaker had been spoken to. Peggy and Sister Mark had washed and dressed poor Aunty Bridget in her Sunday best – a service that handywoman Bridget Devine had performed for many a poor soul over four and a half decades. Now the wake was properly underway – even though most of the callers would come later, after the mills closed. Peggy herself was of course still a 'milly' – one of the hundreds of girls from the area who worked in the cotton and linen mills dotted around the city. Peggy was special though, for she was still only a half-timer, despite having finished school. Three days in the mill, three days working with Aunty Bridget. Sundays a day of rest. Until now.

What would happen to the women, now that Aunty Bridget was gone? She supposed Mrs Clarke and the other handywomen would pick up the extra responsibilities. While she had been making progress, Peggy wasn't yet ready to work independently at births, though she could still sit with the dying and help lay out the dead.

The notion of training as a midwife in faraway Dublin was so ridiculous she barely passed any remarks on it. Her life was here, and she would dearly love to be a handywoman, not a milly. But with Bridget gone she couldn't continue to work as a handywoman, for local women wouldn't want somebody half-trained. She bit back a sigh. And it had been going so well.

Dr Fenton and Dr Sheridan were to blame. Standing with her hands in the sink washing yet more teacups, Peggy felt a wave of anger ripple through her. She had never hated anyone, but right now she hated the two faceless doctors who had reported Aunty Bridget, leading to her death. There was no doubt at all in Peggy's mind about the cause of Aunty Bridget's stroke, for she had seen for herself how aged and strained her aunt had looked on returning from the police station.

Da and Gerard had gone to work as usual – the family couldn't afford for everybody to miss a day – but Peggy, Antoinette, and Sheila were all off, getting ready for the evening when hundreds would come to pay their respects. Once the undertaker had returned with the coffin, Aunty Bridget was placed within, rosary beads laced around her fingers. She looked like herself, which was nice, for not all the deceased did. Chairs and candles were placed around the front bedroom where she lay, and a picture of the Sacred Heart moved up from downstairs to hang on the bedroom wall.

Taking turns to sit with Bridget – who was never to be left alone – Ma and the girls moved furniture, adding a line of borrowed hard chairs along the wall of the living room, and setting out rows of sandwiches and scones on the living-room table, all covered with clean tea towels. Father Fullerton's housekeeper had loaned them three large teapots, and there were kettles and pots for boiling the water.

'Joe, Joe, leave the chile alone!' Joe was annoying wee Aiveen, and Peggy picked her up to comfort her. 'Now go and fill the coal bucket out the back, like you were told. And check there's plenty of newspaper in the outhouse!'

He went – grumbling, but he went. To distract her, Peggy sang a wee song to Aiveen, who stopped crying to listen, thumb going to her mouth. '*Beidh aonach amárach,*' she sang, '*i gContae an Chláir,*' *There'll be a fair tomorrow in County Clare*. As she sang, Granny Doyle's precious clock struck nine. Aunty Bridget had been gone a little over nine hours.

Oh, why could the clock not be turned back? If Aunty Bridget hadn't been lifted. If the doctors hadn't reported her. If, if, if . . .

\* \* \*

'I was talking to Mr and Mrs Moore yesterday.'

Mother's words seemed innocuous enough, but there was something in her tone that had Dan's senses on sudden alert.

'Oh?' he offered, helping himself to another slice of nicely cooked bacon, half-noticing that the clock was striking nine. Mother had spent the last fifteen minutes talking about the new king, and the old one. She heartily disapproved of Mrs Simpson, whom she referred to as 'the American'. According to Ma's second cousin in Baltimore, the twice-married lady had led King Edward astray – as though the man had had no choice in the matter. But at least when Mother was rabbiting on about the royal family her attention wasn't directed particularly at Dan. Not like this. Right now she was entirely fixed on him, her gaze hawk-like.

'Yes. Their daughter Melissa is home from school for a short break. Lovely girl.'

He nodded neutrally, hoping his expression had remained blank. *Here we go.* For the past year or so, Mother had become increasingly obvious in highlighting 'suitable' girls for his consideration – as if he wanted or needed his mother's assistance in finding a girlfriend.

He knew plenty of girls, had even kissed a few – including some who were students at the university – but of course Mother would never approve of such young women. No, in her view women only needed education in household management, social graces, and fashion. He shuddered. The notion of marrying someone who would likely turn into a clone of Mother and her friends was horrifying.

Catching the direction of his thoughts, he told himself off internally. Mother was a good person. She had raised him well, with a good mix of love and firmness. He had been neither over-indulged nor treated with coldness. But since he had started university her ambition – always there, he knew – had become more overt. He was to succeed. He was to become a hospital doctor. He was to marry well.

'You remember Melissa, don't you?'

'Vaguely,' he said, knowing full well it would frustrate her. But he couldn't risk her thinking he might actually be interested in Melissa Moore, or in any other girl for that matter.

'Well, she's home, and her mother is going to bring her along to some of our committees. I'm sure she'll fit in beautifully. Even though she'll be at finishing school for another couple of years, it's never too early to be getting her used to things.'

'How nice for her.' She sent him a sharp look, but his mild tone meant she could not accuse him of irony. 'She won't go to university, then?' he continued, before she had time to question his meaning.

'Lord, no!' Mother gave a trilling laugh. 'She's been raised to be a lady, not a . . . not a . . .'

Dan was thinking of some of his female university friends. Smart, determined, and just as capable as the boys when it came to examinations.

'Not a . . . ?' he prompted, one eyebrow raised questioningly.

'Ladies should be feminine, dear,' Mother said firmly. 'Not mannish.' Her tone dripped with contempt.

'Is it mannish for a woman to use her brains, then? Surely all of us must use our God-given talents, or is that rule only for men?'

She sniffed. 'I will not let you bait me, Daniel. Now, finish your eggs and bacon. You're going to be late.'

Since he had intended to reach the university library by half past nine, and the distance from their home in Derryvolgie Avenue to the university was less than a five-minute cycle ride, he realised this comment was not actually about the time, but was intended to shut down his attempt at discourse that she found entirely too radical. He shrugged inwardly. A win, of sorts. Now maybe he could enjoy what was left of his breakfast in peace.

* * *

Mrs Clarke had returned, with confirmation that the West Belfast community had recently welcomed its newest member – a baby girl, born in Beechmount in the small hours. She hugged Peggy fiercely and got stuck into the work as though she was one of the family. Which she was in a way, given her close friendship with Aunty Bridget.

Sister Mark arrived a little later, and the two women shared a long hug and a few tears. As they worked they shared some memories and Peggy listened, fascinated. They'd be laughing one minute and crying the next – all part of the wake, Peggy knew. That was the point – to celebrate Bridget's life, share stories about her, and let the tears flow.

Wee Joe was listening too, Peggy saw, while Aiveen was curiously exploring one of Granny Doyle's cupboards. It was good for children to be at wakes. Peggy remembered many of them, going right back to her earliest days. It was part of the rhythm of life here. Of life, and loss.

\* \* \*

Following a long day of study, Dan made for the university quad, trying to clear his head with a walk outdoors. Exams were never far away, and there were always essays to be completed. Queen's University used *Cunningham's Anatomy* rather than Gray's – probably because Professor Cunningham had taught in Dublin, where Dan would eventually go for his accredited practice, if he stuck with his plan to specialise in pregnancy and childbirth.

Queen's was not yet fully accredited for obstetrics, and so placement in the Rotunda Maternity Hospital in the capital was a must. Ironic, really, that the Unionists all crowed about the partition of Ireland and how wonderful it was still to be part of the British Empire, yet most things were organised on an all-Ireland basis.

'Dan!' He turned, smiling as he saw three of his friends approaching.

'Well,' he said. 'What about ye?'

Grinning at his deliberate informality, they surrounded him, informing him they were on their way to Lavery's pub and he definitely needed to go with them. Sorely tempted, he managed to resist, promising that he would join them after dinner.

'You'd better!' they laughed as they walked away, and Dan was struck by how carefree they seemed. Once they'd graduated, all three – two girls and a lad – planned to go straight into work. They'd be earning money and would be independent. Was he mad to be persisting with medicine? With his education, accent, and demeanour he could walk straight into a good job in a bank or the civil service after graduation – despite his Catholic surname.

Shaking his head, he continued on his way to the quad. He would have to go home for dinner shortly, and he needed to appear calm and serene in front of his parents – even if his insides were twisting with uncertainty.

# 8

It was five in the morning, and Peggy Cassidy was exhausted. She had slept for a few hours yesterday evening, having volunteered to be one of the women who would stay awake through the night for Aunty Bridget, but this was now her second night without proper sleep, and she was feeling it.

Mrs Clarke was with her, and they had just finished reciting a decade of the rosary. The rhythm of it was soothing, and Peggy's mind – despite a fogginess from lack of sleep – was blissfully numb.

'I was thinkin', Peggy . . .'

'Yes?'

'How far on were you with your handywoman training?'

'Aunty Bridget said I could go to births by myself in about six months.' The memory of that conversation brought fresh tears to Peggy's eyes. How recent it had been, and yet how much had changed in the meantime.

'We'll definitely need you, especially with Bridget gone. There's only three handywomen now for the whole of West – though some of the others will help us out if we're stuck. I was thinking of taking on an apprentice anyway, but I'll finish your training first.'

'Would you do that for me? Oh, thank you!'

Mrs Clarke's brow was furrowed. 'You surely didn't think I was gonna leave you hanging? No, I'll train you – for Bridget's sake, and yours, and my own. We'll be desperately short until you're ready, and again when you go to Dublin.'

'I'll not be going to Dublin!' The very thought made her feel sick. Leaving everyone she knew behind, to go so far away? Not a chance.

'Oh, I think you might be – though not yet. So you might as well keep going as a handywoman. That is, if you want to?'

*If I want to?* Without even a flicker of hesitation Peggy replied, leaving Mrs Clarke in no doubt about her enthusiasm.

'Good. Bridget would be pleased, I think.' She addressed the corpse. 'D'ye hear that, Bridget? I'm taking your Peggy under my wing, so I am. I'll finish training her, and if she's half the handywoman you were, she'll be excellent!'

Peggy glanced at her aunt. Bridget looked serene, despite the pallor of death. Many people believed the newly-dead often stayed around for their own wake and funeral. If so, Bridget would surely be enjoying every minute. Or at least Peggy hoped so.

'You were an amazing handywoman, Aunty Bridget,' she declared. 'And so long as I live I will never, ever forgive Dr Sheridan and Dr Fenton for what they done to you!'

\* \* \*

It was five in the morning, and Dan Sheridan was having trouble sleeping. Having spent a few hours in the library drafting an essay and diligently learning the names for the different parts of the liver, he had enjoyed a quiet dinner with his parents before heading to Lavery's. Unfortunately, his friends were much further on with their Saturday evening of alcohol-fuelled congeniality than he, and so he had felt strangely detached from it all.

He was unsettled, and he knew exactly why. Two paths lay before him. One, the easy road of a handy job after graduation. The chance to marry sooner, to be financially independent, to buy his own home, to become a father. And bloody hell, how much he wanted those things! He was ready for all of it – more than ready.

The other option was to delay all those things for at least three more years, in order to become a doctor. What should he do?

Tired of tossing and turning, he got up, washed in the bathroom, and got dressed. Noise from downstairs told him Mrs Kinahan was already up, and so he made for the kitchen – as he had been doing since he was about five years old.

'Ach, it's Dan. Sit down there, son.' She indicated the sturdy, well-scrubbed table. 'Tae?'

He accepted, and they chatted idly while she started on Father's breakfast. Mrs Kinahan's kitchen was – apart from the sanctuary of his own bedroom – his favourite place in the house. Here, there was no scrutiny, no expectations. Just tea, and acceptance.

His da always breakfasted early so as to arrive at the surgery and get a head start before the place officially opened at half past eight. Or at least, that was always the reason he gave for not breakfasting with his wife and son. Even on Sundays Da would often go in to catch up on his paperwork before Mass, then do any urgent call-outs afterwards. Being in general practice was more a way of life than a job.

Without a word, Mrs Kinahan made enough bacon, eggs, and toast for both father and son, and he helped her carry it to the dining room, despite her protestations. His father's face lit up when he saw him.

'Daniel! Early start for a Sunday.'

Dan slid into his usual seat. 'I wondered if I could come to work with you today.' Perhaps spending the day with an actual doctor at work would lift his mood, remind him why it was worth delaying his independence for years.

His father looked at him sharply, but said only, 'Aye, course you can. No problem. But what about your studies?'

Dan shrugged. 'No lectures on a Sunday. And I'm well on top of it all. Next essay is due next week, but I already have it drafted.'

'Good, good.' They chatted then, the sort of idle conversation where very little is said, but where a sense of companionship is built. Dan could feel his muddled head begin to ease. Whatever was right, would happen. Somehow, he would know which path to take.

★ ★ ★

Ma arrived at eight having made the breakfast at home, and sent Peggy off to nine Mass, then home to sleep. Peggy dreamed of being alone at a birth; in her dream, when the police came, they introduced themselves as Fenton and Sheridan. The two of them loomed over her with accusations, and all the while Peggy muttered, 'I'm only a chile. Only a chile.'

Awakening with terror coursing through her and her cheeks and neck damp with tears, she tried to settle herself with reassuring logic.

## The Irish Midwife

*It's all right*, she told herself, *I won't be on my own before I'm ready. Mrs Clarke will see me right.* But the fear would not leave her. Looking after women and babies during birth was no small thing, and only now was she beginning to realise how much she had taken for granted Aunty Bridget's calm wisdom and clever hands.

Sighing, she sat up. She was wide awake, and might as well go back to the wake house to help. Besides, Aunty Bridget was there, and tomorrow after the funeral she would be gone for good.

★ ★ ★

'My son is with me today, Mrs McGeough. He's going to be a doctor. Do you mind if he sits in?'

'Not at all. Sure that's great!' Mrs McGeough declared enthusiastically. 'Come in, and welcome. Holy God, he's a fine fella, Doctor! Big and strong and good-lookin'.'

Dan stepped inside the narrow doorway. They were somewhere in West Belfast – alien territory for him – and his father was doing his Sunday call-outs.

'He is that!' Was that pride in Da's tone?

'I betcha all the girls be after him!' Mrs McGeough chuckled, then finally addressed Dan directly. 'So you're gonna be a big doctor like your da?'

'That's the plan, Mrs McGeough.' *Probably*, he added inwardly, conscious that he was being treated as though he were a child. *Though some day that may change.*

Mrs McGeough's husband had had a mild heart attack almost a week ago, and Father had wanted to check on him. As Mrs McGeough confirmed that her man hadn't so much as put a foot to the floor since Sunday, as per the doctor's instructions, Dan looked about him. The living room was tiny, with a small settee and four hard chairs, along with a sturdy cupboard along the back wall. The only art was a picture of Our Lady above the fireplace. Everything was plain, spotlessly clean, and entirely depressing. From the kitchen five pairs of curious eyes watched him – Mr and Mrs McGeough's children, aged between about four and twelve, he guessed. It was Sunday, so no school today.

'Will you take a cup of tea, Doctor?'

'Ah, no thanks, Mrs McGeough. Lots of calls to get through, as I'm sure you'll understand.'

'Aye, you'll be flat out. Come on ahead upstairs. I have to warn you though – he's like an imp!'

Having lived with salt-of-the-earth Mrs Kinahan all his life, Dan knew this to mean that Mr McGeough was cross, out of sorts, or in bad form. Hardly surprising, he thought, if the man had been confined to bed for six days.

*Like an imp* . . . It was a good phrase, evoking images of grumpy goblins and demented demons. Fleetingly, it occurred to him that going to West Belfast from the south of the city was like travelling into a different world. The people here were Catholic, and Irish, but the class differences were very real.

Following his father and their hostess upstairs, he realised there was no bathroom, making his eyes widen briefly. Of course he knew – had always known – that he and his parents were privileged to have a plumbed-in bathroom, but it struck him forcefully that for the McGeoughs that meant going outside to an outhouse every time you needed to relieve yourself. Even in the middle of the night. Even in winter.

'How are your children, Mrs McGeough?'

## The Irish Midwife

'Ach, all doing well, Doctor. The big three all have jobs at the cotton mill, thank God, so we've plenty to eat. They're at Mass at the minute, for I always let them have a wee lie-in on a Sunday, so I do. I took the wee ones to eight Mass.'

Shock briefly rippled through Dan. Eight children, then. And three of them out working. Judging by the fact the younger ones were like steps-and-stairs, he'd hazard a guess that the older ones were aged between thirteen and sixteen. He swallowed. And here was he, complaining because he had opportunities that these children could only dream of.

While his father examined Mr McGeough, Dan could see the care he was taking, the way he focused on the man, how intently he was listening. Had Dan himself got that ability? Day after day, for forty-odd years. To give of oneself, unceasingly.

Dan saw in himself the potential for laziness. Were his doubts about the profession, or about himself? He could not say. Anyone could earn money. As a millworker, a mechanic, or a medic.

But young men of his class did not have to work in the mills or the shipyard. Was it bad to feel relieved about that? Oh, why was it all so damned *complicated*?

★ ★ ★

Ma was washing more dishes. 'Have you thought about what Aunty Bridget said to you, Peggy?'

'What do you mean?' Peggy knew full well what she meant, but had no answers for Ma.

'About going to midwife school.'

'Sure, I couldn't do that. It's impossible.'

Ma stopped and turned to face her, wet hands on hips. 'And why could you not?'

'Well for one, we could never afford it. And if you think I'm going to waste Aunty Bridget's life savings on a fancy course, you're mad.'

'That's exactly what you'll do, my girl, for that's what she said the money is for. Anything else would be nearly theft, and we don't hold with thievery!'

'But—'

'But nothin'. Me and your da wouldn't have the first notion about these things, but I bet Sister Mark could find out how to go about it. I'm going to talk to her later. You can't go yet, for I need you in the house. But maybe when you're twenty or twenty-one. Now brush that floor, and give me no more of your nonsense.'

Silenced, Peggy did as she was told. Her heart was thumping at the very notion of it. The whole idea was ridiculous. *It'll never happen,* she told herself. *It couldn't.*

Fear and anxiety raced through her at the notion of leaving her home and family behind, and going to a place where she knew nobody, and nobody knew her. And that was even before she considered the preposterous notion that she could train as a midwife in some sort of fancy hospital with stuck-up girls whose parents didn't work in mills. She was a milly, and that was that.

Peggy had been on a train once, to Bangor. It had been exciting, but Ma and Da and the whole family had been there. Without them, she couldn't imagine it being enjoyable in any way.

'Mrs Cassidy! Come quick!'

*The Irish Midwife*

'Lord save us, what's wrong now?' Ma bustled from the kitchen, Peggy and Sheila right behind her. One of the neighbours was at the front door, her face flushed. As they passed through the living room Peggy scooped up Aiveen without even thinking about it.

'You'll never believe it. Thon Dr Sheridan is in the McGeoughs' house!'

'What? I knew they had a different doctor to the rest of us. I didn't realise it was Sheridan though. The nerve of him!'

'Exactly.' She glanced up towards the McGeoughs' house. 'Wheesht! He's coming out!'

They stepped outside, and Peggy followed. If the evil Dr Sheridan was there, she wanted to look into his face.

\* \* \*

'Only for an hour or so to start with, all right?'

Mr McGeough was beaming at the prospect of being allowed out of bed. 'Aye, Doctor, and thank you.'

Downstairs, Mrs McGeough paid Dan's father, taking the money from a drawer in her living-room cupboard. 'Here you go, Doctor. Thanks again.'

Father took the money, then handed something back to her. 'That's plenty, Mrs McGeough.'

'Thank you, Doctor. I appreciate it. I'll light a candle for you, so I will.'

Following the farewells they left, walking slowly down the street outside. Father had parked the car down on the main road, as there had been an enthusiastic game of Kick the Can going on when they had arrived, eight or nine local urchins milling about.

'Did you give her some money back?' Dan asked curiously.

'Don't tell your mother!' The two exchanged a glance filled with humour, then Father shrugged. 'Let's just say my prices are on something of a sliding scale.' He frowned. 'What's this?'

They had seen on the way up that there was a wake underway in one of the houses, but now something curious was happening. While there were often people standing outside wake houses chatting, this was different. No one was talking, and every one of them – men and women alike – were staring.

'Are they looking at us?'

'Mm-hmm. Keep walking.'

As they got nearer, Dan couldn't help looking – trying to figure out what was going on. The crowd was mostly middle-aged women, it seemed, with a smattering of older men and younger people. One young mother caught his eye.

She must have been about seventeen or eighteen, of medium build, but with a fine figure. Standing motionless with a toddler on her hip, he saw that she was looking directly at him and his father. She was beautiful, with clear skin and dark, lustrous hair twisted around a black ribbon which was fighting a losing battle in containing her curls. Her little girl was very like her, with the same dark curly hair and the same deep blue eyes. But while the child's expression showed curiosity, the mother's—

He caught his breath. Was that *contempt* he saw in her expression? Surely not?

'Good morning,' Father declared cheerfully as they approached.

## The Irish Midwife

Not one responded. Instead they continued to stare balefully at them. Dan could feel the space between his shoulder blades twitching as they walked past and down the street.

They were at the car. Exhaling, Dan climbed inside. 'What on earth was that about?'

'No idea,' said Father. 'But this area is associated with the McKelvey GAA club. Their hut is just up there, in Rockmount Street.'

'McKelvey's? Is that the GAA club where you have to be an IRA member to play?'

'The very same.'

'So what's that to do with us? We don't like partition either! And I play Gaelic football and hurling.'

'And your granda was a Sinn Féin man. Never forget that.'

'Course.' Sinn Féin had won a landslide in the 1918 elections. It still hadn't prevented the British government from partitioning Ireland a few years later. 'But why be hostile towards us?'

Father shrugged. 'They don't know us – I have very few patients in this area. It's usually Dr Gaffney around here. But Mrs McGeough's own family are mostly in service in South Belfast, and are all on my books. That's even though her children are mill-hands – a pity. Working in a house isn't as dangerous as working in those awful mills.' He frowned, returning to the strange behaviour of the mourners. 'They could be fearful. Who knows? Maybe the deceased was in the IRA and they're wary of the wake or funeral being disrupted.' He pursed his lips. 'Joe McKelvey was anti-treaty even though many of the IRA leaders in the North went along with Dev. Might be something kicking off around the divide.'

'Fair enough.'

'I'm only speculating, like. No idea what's actually going on. Best to put it out of your head.'

Dan did. Or at least, he tried to. While his mind was quite ready to forget the hostility and not labour overmuch on the cause, there was one thing he could not seem to forget. The beautiful young mother and the stab of regret he had felt at the notion they were from different worlds, and could never be friends. He would likely never see her again.

\* \* \*

Peggy watched them continue down the street. So that was Dr Sheridan? How dare he appear on Aunty Bridget's street, bold as brass, and her lying in her coffin upstairs? And who was the younger man with him – the one who looked like a young film star? Thankfully her neighbours were equally curious.

'Who was the young fella, Mrs McGeough?'

Mrs McGeough had joined them. 'That's Dr Sheridan's son. He's gonna be a doctor too. Why, what's goin' on?'

As the Rock women explained Dr Sheridan's contribution to Aunty Bridget's death, Peggy kept her eyes fixed on the young man as he walked away. *Oh, he has it all, doesn't he! Wealth, good looks, a fine future taking money off people that can't afford it . . .* The jolt that had gone through her just now when their eyes met must have been disgust.

'Away on back to the Malone Road or wherever you're from,' she muttered to his retreating back, 'and leave me and my aunty Bridget alone.'

# 9

Two days after the funeral a small boy came to the Cassidy door looking for Peggy. 'My granny says can Peggy come to Mrs O'Connor's house in St James's Gardens,' he recited, clearly having rehearsed his message all the way to the Rock streets.

Peggy, who was home from the mill for her dinner break, felt her pulse quickening. Was this to be a birth? Or was someone dying? It mattered little. She was needed, and she would go. Antoinette would let them know at the mill she wouldn't be in for the afternoon shift, and they would dock her pay accordingly. They were used to her coming and going, and assigned her to wherever they needed her that day when she did come in.

After a quick wash she made her way across the Falls Road towards the network of streets on the other side collectively known as St James's. Mr and Mrs O'Connor, Ma had said, lived in the first house on the left – the one with the blue door – and were fairly young. A birth, then. Or so she hoped.

It was awful even when elderly people died after a full life. She couldn't imagine how she might support a family where a young person or a child was dying. Bridget hadn't been elderly, and her death had been unexpected. Tragic. Because she had been taken too soon.

A young man answered the blue door, his brow creased with the now-familiar concern of a childbirth father.

'Hello, Mr O'Connor. I'm Peggy. I'm here to work with Mrs Clarke. Is she here?'

His brow cleared. 'She said there'd be a second handy-woman coming. Come in, come in!'

'I'm an apprentice,' she said, keen to be clear.

'Ah right. They're upstairs. Let me know if you need anything.'

'Hot water, always. Towels? Nail brush?'

He nodded. 'All upstairs. I'll boil more water.'

Mrs O'Connor was a tall, brown-eyed woman with a cloud of dark hair and a ready smile. Peggy recognised her from who-knew-where. She had seen most people who lived around here hundreds of times over the years – at Mass, and at funerals, wakes and weddings. After the usual introductory conversation where they each shared their clan details ('My mammy was Doyle to her own name') they realised they had a mutual cousin by marriage on the Cassidy side. Mrs O'Connor paused then, to lean over the back of a chair in her bedroom and breathe slowly and carefully.

Mrs Clarke quietly explained that this would be Mrs O'Connor's fourth child and Peggy nodded. *Might be fairly quick then.* The other children were with one of the grannies – Aunty Bridget had often said labour seemed to get going properly once a woman knew she had only herself to think about. Herself, and her next wee one.

After the contraction had passed, Mrs O'Connor was all talk again. She had picked out her names already – Sheila for a girl and George for a boy. The nappies and vests were in the second drawer, all washed and ready, and her mother had knitted a wee matinee coat in yellow for this baby.

'It's nice for a baby to have something new, only for them,' she declared firmly. 'Hand-me-downs are great an' all, but this baby is *itself*, you know? God, I'm not explaining it very well!'

'No, you are,' Peggy said. 'Every baby is unique and special.'

'That's it exactly! I— Hang on.'

Peggy waited, resting her hand gently on Mrs O'Connor's arm.

'That was stronger!' the woman declared after the pain had passed. 'I think it might be time to get my nightdress on me.'

'Right so.' Peggy lifted a brushed cotton nightdress which was sitting pressed and folded on top of the tallboy. 'Is this it?'

Mrs O'Connor confirmed it, and soon was changed and ready. 'Would you mind if Peggy has a feel of your tummy, Mrs O'Connor?' Mrs Clarke asked. She had said very little since Peggy arrived, and abruptly Peggy was worried she'd been talking too much. Aunty Bridget's first rule was about keeping the room cosy, comfortable, and *quiet* – but only after you had built some sort of connection with the woman first.

'I don't mind at all,' Mrs O'Connor declared cheerfully, so Peggy washed and scrubbed her hands carefully in preparation. Once the next pain had passed she carefully laid her hands on the sides of the woman's distended abdomen. This was a skill she was still learning, and she had a flash of anxiety at the thought she might disgrace herself in front of Mrs Clarke.

Putting it out of her mind, she concentrated on what she was feeling. There was space at both sides, the baby clearly lying up and down, not across. That was good, for babies lying crossways literally couldn't get out.

Next, she felt along the middle from top to bottom, clearly feeling a solid, continuous shape. That was the baby's backbone, so the baby was facing its mother's back – a good position for birth. Leaving one hand on the baby's back, she then pressed gently at the top of Mrs O'Connor's abdomen, keen to work out if the baby might be breech. Breech births were fine, but it was a little easier if the head came out first. There was something round and hard there, under Mrs O'Connor's ribs, but was it the baby's head or its backside? Gently, she moved that part of the baby sideways – and the whole of the baby's back moved too.

'Well?' Mrs Clarke had been watching intently.

'I think the baby is head down, facing Mrs O'Connor's back,' Peggy declared confidently. 'I think this up here is its bottom.' If it had been the head she'd have been able to move it slightly without the entire torso moving too. No, the head was tucked nicely into Mrs O'Connor's hips, she reckoned.

Mrs Clarke smiled. 'Agreed. I checked earlier. Well done!'

'How long have you been training?' Mrs O'Connor asked curiously as Peggy helped her up.

'Nearly three years,' Peggy confirmed, 'but only part-time. I'm in the mill as a half-timer.'

'God help you! I was never so glad as when I was having my first and had to quit!'

Peggy smiled wryly. 'Aye. I'd love to get out of there. It'll be a while before I can be a full-time handywoman though.'

Mrs Clarke raised an eyebrow and Peggy suddenly remembered the midwife plan. *Not happening.* No matter that Ma and Sister Mark and Mrs Clarke and even poor deceased Aunty Bridget were all ganging up on her. *No way am I going away to Dublin!*

Mr O'Connor knocked on the bedroom door then, the latest pot of water having boiled. He took away the used basin, too, informing them that he was going to the pub shortly with his brothers-in-law.

'Aye, don't let my ones give you a skinful!' Mrs O'Connor admonished, but her eyes had softened on looking at him. For a fleeting moment Peggy wondered what it might be like to love like that. To be loved. To have a husband. Shaking herself out of it she reminded herself she was not even seventeen yet, and had more important things to worry about. Like completing her apprenticeship without Aunty Bridget.

Once he had gone, things began to progress more rapidly. Before long Mrs O'Connor had stopped talking altogether, all her attention going inside herself.

*Now we wait.*

★ ★ ★

It was hard to believe that things could change so quickly. From having major doubts only a few days ago, Dan was now certain of his path once more. Seeing his father work – how he listened, how he cared, how he made a difference . . . Never in a hundred years could Dan find that sort of meaning in his work if he went for the civil service or the bank. Yes, it meant putting off freedom for another few years, but getting married and becoming a father was a theoretical goal at present anyway. Much as he liked his female friends at university – and disliked the privately schooled society girls Ma kept trying to hint to him about – he had no girlfriend, so was unlikely to be getting married any time soon anyway. Briefly, his mind flitted again to the beautiful young mother he had seen in West Belfast. Whoever her husband was, he was a lucky man.

Still, Dan's path was now clear. He would train to be a doctor, like his father. And he would do his best to emulate him once he qualified.

\* \* \*

'You're doing great, Mrs O'Connor.' Mrs Clarke's tone was soothing. 'The head is right there.'

It was nearly four in the afternoon, and she and Peggy were either side of the bed. Mrs O'Connor had Peggy by the hand, and was squeezing tight every time a pain came. She groaned again, eyes tightly shut, and this time the head finally emerged. But—

Peggy's eyes flew to Mrs Clarke's. The head looked *wrong*, somehow. As it turned to align with the shoulders, Peggy saw that, while the baby's face looked normal, and the skin was perfectly intact everywhere, the head was flat at the back – as though half of it had not developed.

She and Mrs Clarke exchanged concerned looks, Mrs Clarke shaking her head slightly. But there was no time for more, for Mrs O'Connor was pushing again, and now the baby slithered all the way out.

Quick as a flash, Mrs Clarke gathered it with a towel, presenting the baby to its mother with the back of the head covered. It was yet to breathe.

## *The Irish Midwife*

'Another boy!' Mrs O'Connor looked delighted. 'George!'

'Mrs O'Connor.' Mrs Clarke looked grim.

'What?' Mrs O'Connor gasped, realising something was amiss. 'What is it? What's wrong?'

'I'm sorry, love. Your baby is not well.' Deftly she folded the towel around the baby, leaving the cord dangling and hiding the misshapen head.

'What do you mean, "not well"?' Mrs O'Connor's gaze roamed over her baby, confusion marring her face. 'He looks all right to me.'

The baby moved, then began to breathe shallowly. He did not cry. 'Oh, thank God!' Mrs O'Connor cried. 'He's breathing, see?'

'I know. But it won't do, I'm afraid. He's not gonna do, Mrs O'Connor.' Mrs Clarke turned slightly. 'Peggy!'

Peggy was holding Mrs O'Connor's hand with both of hers. 'Yes?' Her voice trembled.

'I need you to go and get Father Fullerton. Now! We don't have much time.'

'Right.' The baby was breathing, but Mrs Clarke clearly expected it to die very soon. 'I'll run all the way.'

Leaning forward, she hugged Mrs O'Connor, who seemed frozen with bewilderment. 'I'm so sorry.'

As she left, she could hear Mrs Clarke begin to explain, and shuddered. *Maybe the mills aren't so bad after all.*

She ran non-stop all the way to Father Fullerton's house, rapped the door, then bent over, gasping. The priest's housekeeper opened the door fairly quickly, and confirmed that he was in. 'Why? What's wrong, Peggy?'

'A wee baby in St James's. Just born, but it's not gonna do. St James's Gardens. Mrs O'Connor.'

'Ach, Lord save us! Here, sit down a minute, catch your breath.' She indicated an upholstered chair in the hallway. 'I'll get him.'

A couple of minutes later the priest appeared – the same box of holy oils in his hand that she had seen only a few nights ago. She had run to Dr Gaffney's house that time, hoping for a miracle. It was not to be for Aunty Bridget, and there could be no miracle for Baby George either.

'Well, Peggy.' His brow was furrowed as they stepped out, and it occurred to Peggy that Father Fullerton's life included involvement in every death in the parish. *God love him!*

'So why is Mrs Clarke so certain this baby won't live?' he asked as they hurried along.

Peggy explained, and he shook his head sadly. 'And is Mr O'Connor in the house?'

Peggy gasped. 'No! She has nobody with her – only Mrs Clarke. Mrs O'Connor's brothers were taking him to the pub.'

'He needs to know.'

'Aye.' Peggy stopped. 'You go on, Father. I'll get a message in to him then follow you to the house.'

He agreed, and hurried on, while Peggy crossed the Falls Road to where the Rock Bar stood on the corner. It was perfectly located at the heart of their community – on the Falls, beside the Rock streets, across from St James's. She stood dithering for a moment, for women and girls didn't go into pubs under any circumstances. Luckily a cart laden with barrels was unloading at the side, so she made her way to the cellar opening, where the delivery man was rolling barrels down to someone from the bar.

'Mr O'Neill?' she called, half-recognising the owner.

'Aye? Who's looking for me?' He peered up at her.

'I'm Peggy Cassidy. I'm a handywoman.' Now was not the time for unnecessary details about apprenticeships. 'I need one of your customers to come home.'

'Good news, I hope?' When she shook her head he tutted. 'Ah, no.' Hauling himself up, he stood on the road beside her while the delivery man, seemingly oblivious, lit a cigarette. 'Right. Who do you need, Peggy?'

She told him, and he frowned. 'He's in one of the snugs with his wife's brothers. Poor lad. Wait here.'

She waited, feeling dreadful, until Mr O'Neill brought Mr O'Connor out. 'What's goin' on? Oh, Peggy the handywoman! What are you doing here?' He read her expression, and visibly paled. 'What's wrong? Is my wife all right?'

'Mrs O'Connor is fine.' She placed a hand on his arm, hoping there would be a tiny bit of comfort for him in doing so. 'But the baby isn't well. Father Fullerton is away to your house.'

'To baptise it before it dies?'

She nodded. 'I'm so, so sorry.'

'Boy or girl?' His tone was clipped, his expression one of utter bewilderment.

'A wee boy.'

'George,' he murmured. 'After my da, Lord rest him.'

As they began to walk, Peggy asked, 'Is there anybody else you'd like me to tell?'

'Does her ma know?' Peggy confirmed that nobody had been told but himself and the priest, so he gave her Mrs O'Connor's ma's name and address. 'And my ma,' he added, giving her details. They all lived close by.

'I'll go to them next,' she promised.

'I hope the priest got there in time.'

'Aye.' If the baby was baptised it would go to heaven and its wee body would be buried in holy ground. That was so important.

They soon reached the house and went inside. Thankfully the baby was still breathing, and the baptism was done. They went upstairs to find Mrs O'Connor was holding the baby, the towel still carefully arranged so as to hide the back of his head. Baby George's mother did not look well. She was pale and trembling and clearly shocked, but Mrs Clarke was there by her side.

'Tea for Mrs O'Connor, please, Peggy. Three sugars.'

As she left the bedroom after Father Fullerton, Peggy saw Mr O'Connor embrace his wife. Mrs Clarke stepped away, and the young couple clung to one another over their baby, united in shock and grief.

As she waited for the kettle to boil, Peggy took a deep breath. *This is so hard.* Aunty Bridget was only buried, and now a wee baby was about to die.

'How do you do it, Father?'

The priest had accompanied her to the kitchen, and had sat himself at the wee table.

'Do what?'

'Keep going? Amid death and sadness and grief? How?'

He spoke to her then of faith, and of not being alone, and how he deemed it a privilege to be able to support his parishioners at most of the important moments in their lives – baptisms and marriages, sickness and funerals. Afterwards she felt a little better, and after serving tea to everyone – adding extra sugar to both Mrs O'Connor's and her husband's cups – she made her way to the homes of both grannies, breaking the news as gently and compassionately

## The Irish Midwife

as she could. The woman next door agreed to mind the children, and the grannies made for the O'Connor house.

By this time Mrs O'Connor's neighbours had worked out that something was wrong, and as Peggy approached the house accompanied by Mr O'Connor's ma, she was able to share basic information with them. The community would rally around, she knew. It was one of the best things about West Belfast.

Baby George O'Connor died just after six o'clock in the evening, taking his last breath to the sound of the Angelus bells. Mrs O'Connor took great comfort from this, saying it was a sign that Our Lady would look after him.

Once satisfied that she was physically well, with no sign of bleeding or infection, Mrs Clarke and Peggy left, Mrs Clarke promising to call in the morning. Dr Gaffney had also called, recommending bandaging the chest to stop Mrs O'Connor's milk coming in.

Silently the two handywomen walked up St James's Avenue, their steps in unison, neither speaking. Peggy felt exhausted – as though she had gone two nights without sleep.

'You did well, Peggy,' Mrs Clarke said quietly as they reached her house on the corner. 'I was glad to have you with me.'

Peggy shrugged. 'I did very little.'

'Now don't put yourself down, my girl! You made a bad day for the O'Connors a wee bit less bad, and that's more than most people get to do in a year. Bridget would be proud of you and the way you handled yourself today. You were calm, and warm, and most of all you were kind. That's one of the most important qualities a handywoman can have. And you have it, Peggy. You're a quick learner, you've a good brain and good hands, and you have the compassion. You have it all.'

*You have it all.* Mrs Clarke's words kept coming back to her. Not just that day, but in many of the days that followed. By June she'd started handling births by herself, and her confidence was boosted. She sat with the sick and the dying, and laid out the dead, and held women's hands as they laboured and birthed. She helped first-time mothers to learn to feed their babies, and it thrilled her to run into one of the women she had supported, seeing those babies sitting up and laughing.

By March 1937 when she turned nineteen, she considered herself a competent handywoman, and was even able to help support Mrs Clarke's new apprentice, a girl from Beechmount called Kathleen Gallagher, who had been two years below her in school. She and Kathleen soon developed a strong friendship, forged in long nights sitting with women or comforting the dying. Kathleen was smart, and warm, and very pretty, with fair hair, blue eyes, and a warm smile. Like Peggy, Kathleen was keen to escape the mills, but unlike Peggy, there was no vague threat in the background of her life to waste a fortune by sending her to Dublin to train as a midwife.

Thankfully, the idea had only occasionally been mentioned since Aunty Bridget's death, and Peggy was increasingly confident it would come to nothing. And a good thing too! The last thing she needed was to leave her family and her community behind. No, Peggy was entirely content with her lot, and planned on being a West Belfast handywoman until the day she died.

# Part II

# 10

*Rotunda Hospital, Dublin, September 1938*

'Welcome, girls, to the best midwifery training hospital in the world. My name is Davidson, and I am the master of the hospital. You may be seated.'

Peggy sat with the others, her hands trembling and her insides twisted and sick. For the past six months – since her twentieth birthday – Ma and Mrs Clarke and Sister Mark had been at her about coming here, until finally they had sent in her application themselves, paying the twenty-two pounds for her place with the bulk of Aunty Bridget's savings.

*Twenty-two pounds!* The amount was shocking, and represented a near-fortune. As a milly half-timer Peggy had earned only a few shillings a week, topped up by her modest income as a handywoman. The rest of Aunty Bridget's legacy – a fairly small amount – would be Peggy's pocket money for the next year while she completed her training, as the fee included accommodation and food.

Yesterday she had travelled by train all the way to Dublin. After Mass, Da had taken her to the station in a pony and trap borrowed from his cousin up the Springfield Road, and had hugged her fiercely before saying goodbye. Peggy, still devastated by all the other goodbyes at home, had managed not to cry in front of him, saving her tears for when she was in her second-class seat and the train was underway.

Thoughts of Ma and Da, of Granda Joe and Gerard and wee Joe, of Antoinette and Sheila and wee Aiveen almost broke her. How would she survive without them all?

But change had already come to the Cassidy home. Both Gerard and Antoinette were married now – a joint wedding in August had meant double the celebrations for the same price. Both sets of newlyweds had managed to rent houses within walking distance of home – Antoinette had got Granny Doyle's old house, where lovely Aunty Bridget had died.

No doubt babies would be coming along shortly. Peggy had promised to be there for any births – a promise she did not honestly know if she could keep. She was to stay in Dublin until next summer, with a short break home at Christmas, so if either Antoinette or Gerard's wife Colette were having honeymoon babies, they'd be born before Peggy's return. Aiveen would be six by the time she moved back to Belfast. *I hope she still remembers me*, Peggy thought now . . .

Refocusing on the present, she tried to listen. Master Davidson was talking about the history of the Rotunda Hospital – how it had opened way back in 1745 thanks to a man with the unlikely sounding name of Bartholomew Mosse, and how it had been a training hospital for both surgeons and midwives from the start. The current building had followed, opening in 1757, and partly funded by charging an entrance fee to the Rotunda Gardens, and by Handel concerts.

Under other circumstances this might have been interesting, but Peggy was overwhelmed simply by being here. How was it right that a wee girl from West Belfast was sitting in such a prestigious building, hearing talk of Handel? To her

## The Irish Midwife

knowledge, she had never even heard any music by Handel. They had no wireless at home, although Ma and Da were saving for one. *See, Aunty Bridget's money could have gone on that!*

'. . .and I wish you all the best.'

Master Davidson had done, it seemed, and as he strode out, Matron urged them to rise briefly. This they did in total silence, and she then took over, going through what seemed like hundreds of rules. They were to be in the nurses' home each weeknight by nine o'clock, unless on duty. They were not to smoke or to drink alcohol while resident there. They were to ensure their uniforms were always correct, clean, and pressed, and that their caps were securely fastened. They were to obey any order from a doctor or qualified midwife instructor instantly, correctly, and precisely.

'Those of you who are already qualified nurses may expect to earn your midwifery badge in around six months, so long as you pass the examination set by the Central Midwives Board. The rest of you will require a further six months. And remember, the Midwives Act of 1918 means that only those who have successfully completed a training programme such as ours may be described as midwives, and may refer to themselves as midwives. The Midwives Act which followed in 1931 states that others, including so-called *handywomen*' – her tone dripped with contempt – 'shall be fined the princely sum of ten pounds if they dare to pose as midwives without proper training.'

Peggy was clenching her hands so tight that, were her fingernails not cut short they surely would have been digging into her skin. Ten pounds. The same ten pounds that meant she was here might have been taken from poor Aunty Bridget. The ten pounds that had been a substantial part of Aunty Bridget's life savings. She was going to have to be very, very careful not to reveal her work as a handywoman, it was clear.

'As well as understanding birth, you will learn basic anatomy, physiology, and pathology. You will undertake studies in antenatal and postnatal care, as well as care of the newborn.'

It all sounded very daunting. There were to be written and oral examinations as well as tests of their practical skills, which was terrifying. Peggy had been an apt pupil in school – the nuns had said when she left that they were sad to see her go without even a junior certificate. Being able to fly through reading, writing, and arithmetic did *not* mean, however, that she would be fit to cope with passing midwifery examinations. Some of the words Matron had said sounded like the Latin used at Mass, and she had no idea what they even meant.

As they filed out after Matron's speech, Peggy said as much to the girl beside her. Thankfully she agreed.

'I know! Thank God I only finished school in June, so I hope my head is still in the way of it.'

'You did? How old are you, if you don't mind me asking? My name's Peggy, by the way.'

'Nice to meet you, Peggy.' The girl smiled brightly. 'I'm Anne. From Galway. I'm eighteen. How old are you?'

'I turned twenty in March.'

Anne was pure Irish-looking, with riotous red curls and a pretty face peppered with freckles. 'Ah, so it's been a while since you left school then.'

Peggy squirmed a bit. Anne was clearly assuming she'd stayed at school until eighteen – something that was unheard of where she lived. Only girls from wealthy families stayed at school that long.

'A good while, aye.' *Six years ago.* 'Hopefully there won't be too much book learning.' *God, am I even fit for this? Maybe I'm not smart enough.*

'I love your accent. You're from the north?'

'Aye, Belfast.'

'Is there no midwifery training hospital there? I thought there was.'

Peggy was ready for this. 'There is, but I preferred to come to the Rotunda. It's the oldest, and apparently it's special.'

'You are so right! My auntie is a nurse, and she is so proud of her Rotunda badge.'

Peggy exhaled. 'I've the full year to do, so no point in thinking about badges yet. You?'

'Same.' Her eyes danced with mischief. 'Still, that gives us more of a chance with the medical students – if we have a full year.'

'What do you mean?'

Anne rolled her eyes. 'If I go back home without getting engaged I'll end up with a clerk or a farmer, and I'd much rather have a doctor. Would you not?'

Instantly – and frustratingly – the image that popped into Peggy's head was that of the good-looking young man she'd seen three years ago in Rockdale Street. The son of the man for whom she retained an anger bordering on hatred.

In a mistaken attempt to be reassuring, Sister Mark had told her that any doctors training at Queen's University had to do their childbirth training in either Edinburgh or the Rotunda, and that the Catholic ones tended to come to Dublin.

'That means there'll be young ones from the North down there in Dublin, so there will,' she had said, causing Peggy's heart to sink. Young Mr Sheridan's handsome face and confused expression had stayed with her, despite her best attempts to shake it, so Peggy had not welcomed this news. *Chances are he's a Unionist anyway.* Many wealthy people supported the union with Britain, which served them very well. So hopefully he would be safely away to Edinburgh, and she wouldn't have to meet him.

'I suppose,' she said as Anne was clearly awaiting a response. She had never thought about marrying someone from outside her own area, her own class. Since turning sixteen she had occasionally walked out with a lad, but nothing had ever come of it. She had never liked any of them well enough even to allow him to kiss her – apart from once, and that had been a disaster. No, she was here to get that precious badge, and then she'd return home – hopefully to get a midwife's job at the new Royal Maternity Hospital, and keep looking after the women of West.

'There's a list,' Anne said. 'Me and some of the others found it yesterday morning. We explored the place a bit. When did you get here?'

'Not until yesterday evening.' She had taken a wrong turn on leaving Amiens Street station, and had been weary when she had finally arrived at the brand-new nurses' home beside the hospital. 'What list?'

'Come with me. No, really, we have time. Matron said we've to be back in the lecture hall by half-nine, and it's only twenty past.'

Leaving the others, she led Peggy down a small corridor to their left. 'See? These are the main notice boards.'

Peggy's jaw dropped. Even the feckin' notice boards were ornate and beautiful. The meticulously carved wooden boards had the legends *Obstetrics* and *Midwifery* painted at the top in gilt cursive script. Going directly to the medical board, Anne pointed out a list of names. *August 1938 intake* was the title, and the names were arranged alphabetically by surname, with their university named in the next column. *August*, Peggy thought, *so the medical students have been here a month already*. Naturally, Peggy's eye immediately went to near the bottom. *Scanlon . . . Sheehan . . . Sheridan!* Daniel Sheridan. Queen's University, Belfast. *Feck.*

Daniel. It was a good name. Solid, and clear, and popular with those who saw themselves as Irish. Such a pity his da was a hateful, small-minded person. And he was likely the same. Like father, like son. She sighed. *Why did Daniel Sheridan have to come here?*

'One of them boys is for me!' Anne declared, perusing the list. 'The problem is, I don't know yet which one!'

Peggy considered the matter dispassionately. Anne was pretty, and seemed kind. There was no reason why she couldn't find a husband in the next year if she wanted one. That was, after all, generally how it worked. For Peggy though, here under what felt like false pretences, it was nowhere near possible. She would have her work cut out simply to survive without anybody discovering she was a fully qualified, experienced handywoman.

'And look at this!' Anne was saying, pointing to a notice on the midwifery board. Peggy's blood ran cold. It was a newspaper cutting about a group of handywomen being prosecuted in Mayo a few years ago. There was also a more recent prosecution in Wicklow. Thankfully Aunty Bridget's case had never progressed, and so her name had been kept out of the papers.

'God help them,' Anne said. 'I mean, it's not their fault the law changed. There's always been handywomen in Ireland.'

'Aye,' Peggy agreed, her heart racing. 'Probably going back thousands of years.'

'Look at this though.' Anne pointed to another pinned page, marked *Report from the Carnegie Trust*. One sentence had been circled.

*We are disappointed*, it said, *that the handy woman is still allowed to practise her nefarious trade unchecked, and to carry the germs of childbirth fever from one victim to the next.*

Reading it, Peggy felt a rush of anger. Yes, there may have been some handywomen who did not take care with hygiene, but the West Belfast handywomen like herself and Aunty Bridget and Mrs Clarke and Kathleen Gallagher *always*—

She took a breath, glancing to the right, where the last of their classmates were filing past the opening. 'We better go.' Thankfully her tone sounded reasonably normal. God, this was going to be so hard!

\* \* \*

Life in the Rotunda suited Dan perfectly. Here he could live in the medical students' hall, and even though he was sharing a room with a fella from Cork called Paudie (whose accent was so thick he could barely understand him at times) and his days were dominated by his studies, he had more freedom than he had ever enjoyed in his life. More than boarding school. Way more than home.

## The Irish Midwife

He had been in Dublin for a month, and he could already feel the burden of scrutiny lifting from about him. Oh, he was still under close observation. The master and the qualified doctors were demanding, the complications some of the patients were presenting with challenging, and there was of course his own desire to get things right – both for the women and for himself.

The difference was that here, he was no longer simply Dr Sheridan's son, nor was he Daniel, his mother's showpiece. He was simply Dan Sheridan, medical student, and he had never felt better.

'The new midwifery students are here.' Paudie nudged him hard in the ribs. 'The boys can't wait to get a look at them. Plenty of lashers among them, no doubt!'

Dan grinned. Much as he had been raised to be totally respectful towards women of all ages, he knew exactly what Paudie meant. Most of the midwifery students would be young women, some were bound to be good-looking, and they'd be working closely alongside the medical students for months. Much more interesting than the qualified midwives, most of whom were older than Dan and Paudie.

'Yous are all terrible, you know that?'

'Ah sure,'tis only a natural thing. You'll be looking at them just as much as we will. Assessing their structure and function, if you know what I mean.' He jiggled his eyebrows, making Dan laugh aloud. Paudie's irreverence was exactly what he needed in his life. Having almost completed his medical training, this was Dan's last clinical placement, and he was already feeling energised and inspired by working to ensure babies made it into the world alive and healthy, and that their mothers were alive and well, and ready to nurture them.

And now there were forty-five young women arriving, some of whom had never been in Dublin before. They would maybe benefit from a guiding hand, and he and his new friends would oblige. Oh, yes. Things were definitely looking up.

# 11

Peggy was feeling a sense of bewilderment. For three days, they had learned nothing. Well, that was not exactly true. Some of the other girls had struggled to make the beds in the way that Matron and the qualified midwives required, and had expressed surprise at the hygiene regime that was being impressed upon them. But for Peggy, there had been no new learning, beyond memorising how to tuck a corner folded sheet the way they wanted it, ensuring the bedclothes were entirely smooth. One or two had really struggled, making Peggy wonder if they weren't used to making beds at home. Surely to God you'd make your own bed, even if your family employed a servant!

Today there had been a timed test, the girls working in pairs to make up a bed in less than a minute. Afterwards they had stood by their beds while Matron inspected their work – and their uniforms.

Peggy had to admit to a secret liking for the uniform. A dark linen frock with no fraying or bare patches, trimmed with white cuffs and collar. She had honestly never owned anything so fine. Over the dress they wore spotless white aprons that had to be changed the moment they became soiled. And of course, the cap. Made of stiff white cotton, the midwifery students helped one another pin it in place each morning. Eventually they would doubtless be skilled at pinning it themselves.

A couple of the girls owned tiny fob watches, which they pinned to their dress. Fobs were worn upside-down, which meant they could see the time without having to lift it.

Da had a watch, but Peggy had never owned one. Thankfully most of the pupil midwives didn't own a fob watch, so Peggy wouldn't stand out as the poor girl. Which was a good thing, for she really, really didn't want to be seen that way.

The main difference in appearance between the students and the qualified midwives was the midwifery badge. Shaped rather like the circular part of the Celtic cross, it was made of brass and featured the motif of a woman and two small children along with a crown, the Irish harp, and the year of the hospital's foundation, 1745. It was a beautiful thing in its own right, and for the first time yesterday, Peggy had felt a surge of emotion when imagining that one day she might earn the right to it.

But three days of hand-washing and bed-making? It made no sense. Twenty-two pounds for *this*? Peggy could feel her frustration rising, but held it back, for today they were to have an actual lecture from an actual professional.

They had been issued with brand-new notebooks and pens, and even that small thing had pierced her. The other girls – who no doubt had houses full of books and pens at home – had not even blinked, but Peggy had clutched the book to her chest in something like a hug. Her family were certainly not illiterate – they had a bible, as well as quite a few children's books and a well-thumbed copy of a W.B. Yeats collection. Peggy knew some of the Yeats poems by heart, so often had she read them.

Da also bought the paper every Friday. In recent weeks the *Irish News* had been dominated by the Spanish Civil War and the Sudeten crisis. With the Great War and the Irish War of independence still fresh in the minds of those who'd lived through them, Peggy hoped that something could be done to resolve the issues between the Sudetens and Czechs, although Da had said the Nazis didn't really care about that and just wanted to make Germany bigger. Peggy sighed, thinking about it. In Ireland they well knew the consequences of imperialism.

Finding a seat in the lecture room, she exchanged a nervous glance with the girl beside her before focusing her attention on the man at the front of the room. He wore a crisp white coat as all the doctors did, and his bald head gleamed in the daylight streaming in from the tall windows either side of the blackboard. There was a human skeleton hanging on a stand beside him, and more bones on the table in front of the blackboard. The hum of chatter died as soon as he opened his mouth to speak. *My first ever lecture.* A shiver went through her at the enormity of it.

'Good day, ladies. My name is Professor Folan. Today I will cover the anatomy of the human pelvis. This is a male pelvis, and this a female. This is the anterior side, this posterior, and these lateral. You will note the difference in size. The android pelvis is also narrower than the gynaecological version, its inlet heart-shaped due to the sacral promontory projection, and the sacrum itself is longer, narrower, and straighter than the female sacrum.'

*Wow!* The man had barely taken a breath, and most of the words he had used were incomprehensible. However Peggy could clearly see the difference between the two sets of bones, and had immediately equated 'posterior' with 'backside'. From all her days and nights of tending women, her hands knew and recognised the hip bones, the tailbone, and the front bone – which often ached in late pregnancy. And now her eyes could see what was normally hidden beneath the skin.

It was obvious, really, that women's hips were wider to facilitate childbirth. Over the next hour, the professor raced through his description, providing Latin names for every lump, bump, hole and promontory on the bones. Like the girls around her, Peggy tried to make notes, but since she had never heard most of the words he used, she had no idea how to spell them. The girl beside her scribbled something in her book, then nudged Peggy to look at it. *What's a foramina and how do you spell it?* she had written.

They exchanged a glance – humour mixed with helplessness – then went back to writing down what they could. As the large clock finally reached half past ten, thankfully the lecture came to an end.

'You will now go into the next room for your practical session. This will last until twelve noon, at which time you may take your dinner break. Please then return to this room at twelve thirty for a lecture on the circulation of the blood.'

Peggy's shoulders sagged. It was over! As they made their way through to the adjoining classroom at the front, Peggy saw that the medical students were entering the lecture hall from the rear door. Well she assumed they were the students. There must have been nearly fifty of them, all young, all in white coats. Quickly averting her eyes, she put her head down and hid as best she could in the crowd. Not that *he* would know who she was, anyway. Why would he?

For the anatomy practical session they were placed in pairs and given a wooden box and a large book. Peggy had been paired with a girl called Mary from a place called Donnybrook. From the way she talked, it seemed to be somewhere in Dublin. Despite being close to home, Mary too was living in the nurses' home, regardless of the extra cost – an

## The Irish Midwife

extravagance that made it clear to Peggy that Mary's family was wealthy. There were a couple of day girls, but Matron strongly recommended living in.

One of the midwifery teachers then told them they had to learn the names of the parts of the pelvis, and that there would be a test later this afternoon. That was enough for Peggy. With a mix of nerves and determination she exchanged a glance with Mary. They opened the box to find two human pelvises, one wider than the other.

'Are they not called pelves?' Mary asked with a wry smile, but Peggy had no idea what she meant.

The book was filled with diagrams, arrows showing clearly which Latin names applied to which parts. *I can do this!* While there were undoubtedly going to be many challenges ahead, at least this one looked achievable with concentration and brain effort.

By lunchtime, she and Mary had figured out the key differences between the two sets of bones, and had learned a good deal of the names. Sitting in the dining hall with Anne and a girl from Longford called Joan, they tested each other on as much as they could remember while eating bacon with potatoes and peas.

*Meat again!* Peggy thought, with surprise. *And it's not even Sunday!* Was this really how the professional classes lived?

By the end of the day, she had learned about bones, and blood, had done her best in the test, and had, she hoped, made some new friends.

'Let's swap rooms so we can be together!' suggested Anne, and the others enthusiastically agreed.

'Are we allowed to do that?'

'Oh yes,' Joan said blithely. 'My cousin trained here last year. They don't really care.'

And so, once they were done for the day, Peggy packed up her meagre possessions and took them from the room she'd shared last night with an uncommunicative girl with long dark hair, moving down the corridor to Anne's room, while Anne's former roommate cheerfully reciprocated. Joan's room was next door to Anne's and so Mary moved in there. There was a bathroom two doors down, and Peggy was astonished by the flushing toilet and the large bath with running water. While there were toilets in the mill, she had only ever bathed in the Cassidy tin bath in front of the fire, in water already used by Ma and Antoinette. They bathed in order, oldest to youngest, with Aiveen still being washed in the sink if she got grubby while out playing. The boys had their baths on a different day, and the women would leave the house and let them at it. Peggy could not wait to fill the bath with warm, clean water that was just for her, and to enjoy privacy and comfort.

Placing her things in the small wardrobe – towel, facecloth, clean underwear, Sunday dress and coat, and plain but shabby linen day-dress – Peggy was struck by how little she owned compared to the others. Her toothbrush, nailbrush, and hairbrush she placed carefully on her nightstand, and her nightgown under the pillow. That was it. No spare outfits. No photographs of loved ones. No novels. Her beloved shawl had been left in Belfast, as only millies and farmers' wives wore shawls. Well-off women wore coats, not shawls – even on workdays.

Yesterday, she hadn't minded. But today, seeing the fine possessions that her new friends owned, she hoped they wouldn't ask any awkward questions. Anne had noticed, for Peggy saw her looking, but thankfully she said nothing, for which Peggy was grateful. They all sat for a while in Anne and Peggy's room, chatting. To Peggy's relief, both Joan and Mary reported being present when women in their family had given birth, and so knew a little about how things happened. Indeed, for both girls, it had been why they wanted to be midwives and not nurses. *Hopefully it won't be too obvious that I know too much about labour and birth!* Peggy thought anxiously. She could hide behind the life experiences of the many young women who had been drafted in to support their sisters or cousins. It was vital that nobody find out she had been working as a handywoman as recently as three days ago, and had attended hundreds of births.

'Let's go out for a walk before supper!' Joan's suggestion was well received, and so they changed out of their uniforms, hanging them carefully away, then stepped out into Parnell Square. By mutual agreement they turned away from the pretty gardens behind the hospital, making instead for the bustle of O'Connell Street – Dublin's main thoroughfare.

'Have any of you been to Dublin before?' asked Mary.

Joan, it emerged, had been once – on a trip round the shops with her mother last December – but neither Anne nor Peggy had ever visited the capital.

'Excellent!' Mary was delighted. 'I'll soon show you about!'

And so they went down the hill together, from Parnell Square to O'Connell Street. The place was packed, trams and motor-cars mixing with horse-drawn carriages and carts on the roads, the pavements thick with people. They passed the Pillar with the statue of Admiral Nelson on the top, and the GPO, where, Mary reminded them, the 1916 Rising had begun. That was where Bridget's husband had died, during the Easter Rising. Peggy shuddered. So many lives lost!

'Thank God we've got our independence,' Mary said sunnily, then put a hand over her mouth. 'Oops! Sorry, Peggy, I forgot!'

Very politely, Peggy told her it was fine, but inwardly she was beginning to suspect that Da was right, and the Free Staters had no intention of ensuring the north was included any time soon. The six northern counties still suffering under British rule seemed to be an afterthought.

Thankfully, Anne and Joan were happy to exclaim at the sights, and so Peggy felt able to join in with enthusiasm. Daringly, they went into Clerys department store, and Peggy tried not to be too much of a milly, gaping at all the beautiful and expensive items, and hoping she wouldn't crash into anything and break it. *God, it's so different here!*

Despite being technically a city girl, this was all new to her. She had been in Belfast city centre only a few times, for West was like a town in itself. They had everything they needed there – mills, shops, schools, churches, sports clubs . . . Peggy's brothers played both hurling and Gaelic football, and tentatively she raised the topic, hoping the others might also have some family involvement in Gaelic games. Luckily, this proved to be correct, and the next half-hour – even as they continued to explore, crossing the River Liffey to the south side – was spent rehearsing past victories for their local clubs and their counties. County Kerry was dominant in football, while Dublin had recently beaten Waterford to become the new All-Ireland hurling champions.

'Oh, wow! Look at that!'

'College Green,' said Mary primly. Clearly, she was enjoying her new friends' reactions. 'That's the old parliament building. And that' – she pointed to her left – 'is Trinity College!'

Peggy had heard of Trinity. It was a university, but mostly for Protestant men. While they had finally dumped the oaths that had effectively barred Catholics, they had not allowed

## The Irish Midwife

women to study there until early this century. Even though the rules had changed, Peggy knew that someone like her could never be welcomed there. *Religion, sex, class.* These things defined one's life – subtly, immutably. As a working-class Catholic woman from Belfast, Peggy's life was set for her, with limitations on all sides. Aunty Bridget's legacy was challenging that for Peggy, but her sisters were destined for the mills, or, if they were lucky, shopwork or a life in service.

The university was certainly impressive, Peggy had to admit. Stepping inside through a dark archway, they emerged into another world, or so it seemed to her. It was *quiet*, and the contrast with the bustle of the city was striking. The cobbled square led to large greens with venerable trees dotted about. The whole thing was framed by beautiful buildings – some with fancy pillars to the front – and in the centre of the space, dead ahead, was a tower which looked like it might contain a bell. People were everywhere – gawpers like themselves contrasting with the determined pace of students in academic gowns crossing from one side to the other with an air of purpose.

'That's the chapel,' said Mary, pointing to the building on their left. The door was open, so they peeped inside. The lower half was bedecked in rich wooden panelling, giving way to plaster-decorated walls and beautiful stained-glass windows.

'It's Church of Ireland,' Mary offered, and Peggy bit back a sarcastic comment. *Of course it is.* This did lead to a riveting discussion though. Joan, it turned out, was Protestant – Church of Ireland specifically – while Mary and Anne were both Catholic.

Peggy wasn't sure she'd ever met an actual Protestant before – apart from RUC officers, who hadn't exactly given her a positive impression of their faith. It was an interesting experience, for Joan seemed to her to be no different to Anne and Mary. *Maybe class is more important than religion in the Free State.* In the north the two were aligned, with most wealthy people being Protestant, seeing themselves as British not Irish, and politically supportive of British rule. Religion, class, nationality, and politics – divide reinforcing divide. Most Catholics on the other hand were poor, Irish, and entirely opposed to British rule. Families like the Sheridans – *wealthy* Catholics – were small in number, and their politics varied.

That made her think again about Daniel Sheridan's handsome face and blithe lack of awareness – or lack of compassion – about what his own father had done to Aunty Bridget. Logically, she knew he was not to blame for his father's actions, yet something in her remained angry with him. It now occurred to her to wonder what his politics were. *Probably an I'm-all-right-Jack imperialist.*

'How much will we work with the medical students, do you know, Joan?'

Anne laughed. 'Are you thinking about what I said yesterday, Peggy?'

There was a knowing humour in her tone, which had the other two girls immediately clamouring to hear more. 'Why, what's this? What did you say yesterday?' By the time Anne had outlined her plans to find a husband, and the others had teased her about it, Joan would have been forgiven for forgetting Peggy's question, but she came back to it.

'We'll work with the medical students all the time, apparently. They're nearly qualified as doctors, so they'll be taking full responsibility for patients by Christmas. And our job – at least according to my cousin – is as much about helping them as helping the women.'

# The Irish Midwife

'Handmaids to the doctors then, rather than being proper midwives.' Peggy had said it without thinking, but was relieved to find the others agreed with her.

'Only in hospitals though – remember what Matron said. We are expected to be autonomous professionals when we're out in women's homes.'

A shiver went through Peggy at the reminder. *Autonomous professionals*. It sounded so fancy. And daunting. And yet she had done it. She knew – none better – the value of being her own boss, alongside Aunty Bridget or Mrs Clarke as a handywoman. It was so much better than the spinning room or weaving shed in the mills, with supervisors watching you every minute of every day.

'Once we're qualified we'll be based in a hospital, but we'll be doing all the home births for uncomplicated women,' Anne said. 'That's proper midwifery.'

'Where will ye all be working?' asked Joan, and they replied with the names of their local hospitals.

'For me it'll be the Royal Maternity Hospital in West Belfast, if I can get in,' said Peggy.

'And sure why wouldn't you get in? You'll have a Rotunda badge!'

'They train their own midwives though. They mightn't want me.' *Especially if they find out about my past.*

'Course they will. But, if you don't mind me asking, why come to Dublin? Why not train up there?'

Peggy managed a shrug. 'The chance to live in Dublin. And, you know, the Rotunda badge.'

They seemed to accept this at face value, but Peggy was feeling decidedly guilty at not being honest with them. They were nice girls. They didn't deserve lies and half-truths. But she couldn't risk it. If she got kicked out of the Rotunda for being a handywoman then she'd have wasted Aunty Bridget's money, and achieved nothing. No, biting her tongue was the only sensible option.

Part of her hated the fact she had to hide who she was. Being a handywoman had been the greatest achievement of her life, and being with women giving birth was a privilege – even when the outcome was tragic. Her mind flicked back to the O'Connors, and wee George who had not been destined to live. Mrs O'Connor had made a point of inviting Mrs Clarke and herself to her home, a year after George had died. Mrs Clarke had refused to take any payment from her, given the tragic outcome, and so Mrs O'Connor had given them gifts of her own hands – socks and hankies that she had made, along with a pair of fine cotton pillowcases for each of them which she had embroidered with bluebells – the flowers that festooned Sliabh Dubh, the Black Mountain – every May. Peggy had carefully packed away her pillowcases, thinking that she would use them if she ever married. The gift was special, and precious, and she would treasure it for life.

And that's what it meant, to be a handywoman. It meant being part of women's families for a special time – a happy time, or sad. Midwifery so far seemed more about rules and control than about truly connecting with women. Making a bed neatly and having a fancy uniform and a fancy badge – these things were all very well, but Peggy had yet to be convinced that midwives could ever be as good as a knowledgeable handywoman. Still, here she was, and she would make the best of it.

# 12

September came and went, and Peggy began to feel a bit more settled. Her friendship with the other girls was deepening and so far, she was doing all right in the training. The classroom learning and tests still scared her, but she had managed to pass everything up till now. Thankfully, they now spent a good half of their week working directly with the women, where Peggy knew *exactly* what she was doing.

Oh, she still had to be careful – to pretend to be learning things she already knew in her bones. But she was starting to realise that the midwife teachers knew their craft, and they knew women. That in itself gave Peggy confidence.

Having absorbed Aunty Bridget and Mrs Clarke's way of working as her own, Peggy dreaded the day they would make her do something different. But childbirth was childbirth, and being the woman in the room whose job it was to support the woman in labour differed little whether that woman was called 'handywoman' or 'midwife'.

In Irish, she knew that both midwives and handywomen were referred to by old, old words: *cnáimhseach, bean cabhartha, Cailleach, bean ghlúine*. Bone-person, helper woman, wise-woman/witch, woman of the knee. Kneeling was certainly a big part of supporting women, and Peggy had spent many hours of her life kneeling beside a woman who was on all fours or sitting as her labour progressed.

The different meanings of *cailleach* were significant, too. Was a handywoman-midwife a witch or a wise-woman? It would probably depend who you asked. And were midwives only acceptable because they worked under the direction and supervision of obstetricians – in other words, men? Peggy had been fascinated to learn that the English term 'midwife' came from the old version of that language, and meant simply 'with-woman'. So long as they were allowed to work like that, Peggy knew all would be well.

Peggy had supported four different women in the past week, alongside various medical students. The senior midwife (confusingly called *Sister*, although none of them were nuns) allocated the pupil midwives as the women arrived or progressed, while the medical students were assigned by their own tutors. Crucially, even though the doctors' role was to act when things went wrong, the Rotunda's approach was to ensure the medics had a good grounding in normal, straightforward birth, and so the medics were placed with new midwifery students, under the supervision of qualified staff.

It was odd not knowing the women, and only meeting them for the first time when they were in labour. Once she and Mrs Clarke had begun working together regularly, Peggy generally made sure to meet women a couple of times in late pregnancy – and of course they would usually have shared connections in the area. She was however good at connecting with women quickly, and so had been able to manage.

This morning, following uniform and hands inspection, Peggy had been assigned to a cheery Dublin girl called

## The Irish Midwife

Philomena Carney. Mrs Carney was alone, her mother looking after her other children at home and her husband at work, and she had decided to come to the Rotunda rather than have this baby in her bedroom. The room she had been given was bright and airy, with a bed, an armchair, two hard chairs, and a small table where Peggy laid out the items she would need for the birth, while getting to know Mrs Carney a little. In the corner beside the door stood a small wooden crib, awaiting the arrival of the baby.

'I'll be honest with you, Nurse,' the woman confided, walking behind the armchair and leaning on the back of it. 'I'm hoping to get a bit of a rest. With three children and a husband to feed and clean for, I'm worn out!'

Her Dublin accent was strong, and Peggy couldn't help echoing the last word in her head. 'Out' had sounded more like 'eyo' when she had said it. *Worn eyo. Worn eyo.* Having been surrounded by broad West Belfast accents her whole life, Peggy was loving the diversity, and spotting the differences in both pronunciation and in words used between her friends from Dublin, Cork, and Longford. Within Dublin city and county there were multiple accents, too – Mrs Carney's working-class brogue sounded nothing like the polished tones of Mary from Donnybrook.

'Well, you deserve it, Mrs Carney! What were your other births like?'

'Call me Philomena, love. Sure there can't be more than a year or two between us!'

As Philomena began telling her birth stories, the door opened. Turning her head slightly to see which medical student she'd been paired with today, Peggy saw familiar blue eyes, dark hair, and a face that was far, far too handsome.

On Rockdale Street, conservatively dressed, he had been good-looking. Over three years later and wearing his white medical coat, he was drop-dead gorgeous. Her heart stilled, then raced.

Having recognised him fairly easily weeks ago, she had managed to avoid talking to him before now. Still it was inevitable that their paths would cross eventually.

'Good morning!' he announced. 'I'm Dan Sheridan, final year medical student. Is it all right if I stay for your birth, Mrs Carney?'

Philomena frowned. 'Am I sick? Do I need a doctor?'

*Great question, Philomena!*

'No, no,' he reassured her. Not at all. But they like us to really understand normal birth so that . . . well . . .'

She brightened. 'I get it. Aye, why not? But birth is women's work, so would you mind if Peggy here is the main one looking after me?'

Peggy stifled a smile. This was why she loved working-class women. The rich ones did what they were told and deferred to any man in the room. The confident working woman knew how to stand up for herself. And which battles to fight.

'Of course, of course,' he said. 'Hello, Peggy.'

Their eyes met. 'Hello.' She could feel a slight flush building, so turned straight back to Philomena. 'So, keep going. What about the second birth?'

'Houl' on.' Philomena closed her eyes, breathing slowly and carefully, while rocking from side to side.

'That's good,' Peggy said soothingly. 'Just go with it.'

'You're from the north?' It hadn't taken Dan Sheridan long to spot her accent. *He clearly hasn't remembered me.*

She nodded, not taking her eyes from Philomena.

'I'm from Belfast,' he offered.

*I know.* This time she did glance at him, nodding again before tearing her eyes away. 'Me too.'

*Damn!* What in the name of all that was holy was happening to her? Her insides were all twisted up, her heart was pounding, and even her breathing was doing something weird.

*It's because I dislike him. Because of what he and his da did.* Thankfully, the anger was still there, and she used it to regain her equilibrium, ignoring him and focusing entirely on the woman.

Once the labour pain had passed, Philomena asked if it was true that a midwife could hear the baby's heart beating, if she pressed her ear to the mother's stomach.

'Not quite.' Peggy smiled, crossing the room to take the Pinard stethoscope from the table. It was a wooden implement, the wide end horn-shaped to gather the sound, and the narrow end flat so it could be pressed to the ear of the midwife or doctor. Or handywoman. 'We use this. Would you like me to listen?'

Trying to ignore the man in the room, Peggy assisted Philomena to lie on the bed and adjust her clothing. Covering her lower half with a sheet to protect her dignity, she waited while Philomena lifted her simple cotton dress, then felt the woman's abdomen with knowing hands.

'Right,' she said, 'baby is head down. Its bottom is . . . *here* and it's facing your back. So I'm going to look for the heartbeat' – she placed the Pinard on Philomena's skin – 'here.'

And there it was. The near-miraculous proof of the other human being in the room with them, as yet unseen.

'Bop-bop-bop,' she said aloud, giving Philomena a sense of the heart rate. 'All sounds well.'

Helping Philomena up, she supported her to sit on the side of the bed as the next pain had arrived. 'That's it,' she said in her soothing voice. 'Just breathe. You're doing great.'

Out of the corner of her eye she noticed that Dan Sheridan was watching her intently. *What?* Instinctively she patted her hair, checking in case any of her curls had escaped their pins. No, all was well. *What, then?* God, hopefully he wouldn't figure out where he'd seen her before – outside Bridget Devine's wake house, sending him daggers with her eyes. She threw him a look and hastily, he shifted his attention to the labouring woman. Thankfully, this time he did not speak.

Peggy had often felt that being in a woman's labour room was a bit like being at Mass. Quiet, reverent, with a clear focus, one only spoke when needed. Would men understand that? Would someone like Mr Sheridan there, accustomed no doubt to giving orders, be able to sit on his hands and bite his tongue? Most of the other medical students had struggled with the need to just . . . *wait*.

In a way she could understand it. Men and boys were raised to *do*. To make, or fix, or destroy. Oh, women were active, too. The hard physical labour of working in the mill, or in the home, was a key part of women's lives. But women also learned patience. The ability to feed a baby who wanted to suckle for hours, or the calmness to sit with a sick child or an elderly relative, perhaps someone whose life was ending, or a woman in labour. She and Aunty Bridget had often knitted while awaiting progress – the clicking of their needles echoing the rhythm of the woman's breaths and groans as the pains came and went. Sadly, knitting was not permitted in the Rotunda Hospital.

The hours passed, and with them a kind of harmony came to the room. Despite the un-home-like odours of carbolic and antiseptic, together Peggy and Dan Sheridan crafted a sense of safety for Philomena, built of silence and support. Gone was the woman's need for conversation, for the pains were lasting longer now, and with very little time between them. Her eyes were closed, her expression serene. She was an absolute trouper, as the saying went.

All was proceeding perfectly well, and Peggy was confident that baby would be here before long. Catching Dan Sheridan's eye, she could not help but return his smile – then turned away quickly, as if to pretend to him and to herself that it had never happened. She needed to be careful. So, so careful.

★ ★ ★

*She smiled back!* Quite why this felt like such a victory, Dan was uncertain. Despite having noticed her a few times over the past month – for she was remarkably pretty – Dan had never managed even to speak with her before today. Perhaps she was shy. *Peggy*. A good name. Down to earth. Her northern accent had made him catch his breath in surprise, even as his heart had been thumping in recognition that finally, he was going to spend time with her.

Along with Paudie, he had managed to speak to quite a few of the pupil midwives, and they had even gone to the cinema with a group of them last Sunday. This week though, the medical lectures and antenatal clinic work had finally given way to being allocated to women giving birth, and Dan was delighted. This was the centre of it all. This the privilege. Doctors were the only men in Ireland permitted to step inside a birth room, and the responsibility of it was enormous. And this morning, to enter Mrs Carney's room and see the prettiest trainee of them all was the cherry on the cake.

Not that he had made much progress in getting to know her, for they had not spoken since the initial greetings. To be fair they had been told in lectures that labour would progress better in a quiet environment, but the other trainee midwives had interpreted that information much more liberally than Peggy-from-Belfast.

And he could see why. In letting go of the conventional need for chatter, he had been quietly watching her and Mrs Carney for hours. Drinking in Peggy's beauty. Blue eyes, framed by thick dark lashes. A fine figure. Clear, pale skin. Dark curly hair constrained by pins . . . For a moment the shadow of a vague memory came to him, but was lost before he could catch it.

In watching, he also found himself carefully observing, and learning. As a midwife, Peggy was astounding. The way she had so quickly built a relationship with Mrs Carney. The way she seemed to know *exactly* what to say, and when. They were all learning abdominal palpation – Dan had felt the bumps of probably a hundred pregnant women in the clinic this past month. But Peggy had so skilfully confirmed the position and presentation of the baby, so deftly placed her Pinard and found the heartbeat . . . She seemed so serene and relaxed as well, unlike the other midwife trainees. It was hard to avoid the conclusion that she was very, very special.

He shook his head slightly in wonder. Beautiful, skilled, with the sort of inner confidence he was only beginning to develop . . . she was even from Belfast. In that moment, Dan knew that he had to try to befriend her. Court her. The half-flirtations he had been enjoying with a few of the other girls suddenly paled into nothingness. Peggy was the one he wanted. Or at least, wanted to get to know better.

And for all he knew, she might already be spoken for. Some of the other lads had wasted no time in pursuing their preferred girl. When he and Paudie had gone to the cinema with that group of girls, they had seen three Rotunda couples on what was clearly their first excursion. Paudie had seemed a little worried over this, nudging Dan to say they'd need to make a move sharpish, or all the best ones would be gone.

At the time, Dan had laughed, having assumed this was a joke. Now, looking at the side of Peggy's perfect face, he wasn't so sure. Had one of his classmates already befriended her? Or had she a sweetheart back home in Belfast? He needed information, and soon. *Damn it!* Why could she not have been one of those friendly, chatty midwives? Why did he have to pick the one who seemed more interested in the woman in labour than in him?

Hearing the arrogant ridiculousness of his own thoughts, internally he advised himself to give his head a wobble. He had no right to her attention, and Mrs Carney did. And part of the reason he was admiring her so much today was the fact that she *was* ignoring him in favour of Mrs Carney.

'Well, and how are we doing?' It was Dr Small, one of the medical tutors, and he was clearly here to check on Dan and his patient. Fleetingly, Dan noted that Dr Small had entered the room like a showman, whereas the midwifery sister had come in quietly, taking Peggy aside each time for an update on Mrs Carney's progress. *Perhaps that is why women are more suited to supporting other women through normal labour.*

Leaping to his feet, he greeted the man who, along with his colleagues, held Dan's future in his hands. After a keen look at Peggy and Mrs Carney, Dr Small nodded, then hit Dan with a series of questions about Mrs Carney's situation, health, and obstetric history. Thankfully, Dan was able to answer with a fair degree of fluency, having perused Mrs Carney's file in some detail during the past hours.

'Carry on, Mr Sheridan.' And with that, he was gone.

Exhaling, Dan turned back into the room. Mrs Carney was in the armchair, leaning forward and quietly rocking. Hopefully she had not allowed the intrusion to disturb her. Peggy met his gaze, her expression a mix of mischief and – was that approval? Turning away, she focused on Mrs Carney again, but once again, Dan felt an inner thrill at connecting with her, however briefly.

Outside, the sun was setting, the light dimming. Peggy turned on the light and closed the curtains, tutting that it was too bright.

'Hang on,' said Dan, leaving the room. The nurses' desk at the end of the corridor had a plug-in table lamp, he was sure of it.

'Can I borrow this?' Giving the midwife there a bright smile, he explained that he wanted it for a labour room.

She frowned. 'So long as you turn on the big light if anything goes wrong.'

'Of course!' With a word of thanks he took the light back to Peggy and Mrs Carney, reflecting that as well as wanting dim light for the woman, he wanted Peggy's approval. *I'm like one of those male birds, trying to attract their chosen female with gifts of pebbles.* The notion made him laugh at himself.

## *The Irish Midwife*

As he entered the room, he sensed that things were progressing with Mrs Carney's labour. She was moaning now, and muttering about it being too hard. 'You can do this, Philomena. You're a strong woman. And I'm here for you.'

Mrs Carney clutched her hand. 'You won't leave me?'

'I promise.'

'All right. Oh, here's another one!' Mrs Carney seemed to be struggling to regain her calmness.

Quietly, Dan plugged in the lamp, setting it on the floor beside the socket as there was nowhere else to put it. He then flicked the wall switch up to turn off the big light. Instantly the room changed, the atmosphere less clinical.

'That's better,' said Peggy. 'Now, do you want to change position, Philomena?'

For answer, Philomena dropped to her knees, turning to lean on the seat of the armchair. Taking the pillow from the bed, Peggy placed it beneath her.

'Now, let me know if this helps at all,' she said, pressing the heel of her hand to Mrs Carney's tailbone.

'Oh, that's good,' said Mrs Carney, while the hairs were beginning to stand up on Dan's arms. How in God's name did Peggy know so much? Something was not right. A notion struck him, and his jaw loosened. *Might she be . . . ?* He dared not finish the thought. Every one of his lecturers and tutors were scathing about the now-illegal handywomen. *No. She couldn't be. Could she?*

# 13

*Damn it!*

Seeing the look in Dan Sheridan's eye, Peggy knew he was on to her. *And this is how I will get found out.* But how could she avoid using all her skills and knowledge, when the woman beside her was struggling with labour pains? It would be just wrong.

'The way you were moving made me wonder if your back was sore,' she offered, hoping it would obscure her recent demonstration of expertise. She just needed him not to be certain. *And from now on I need to be more careful.* She could almost hear Aunty Bridget's voice in her ear. *Do what you can, but keep yourself right.*

Philomena was no longer listening, for Peggy heard with satisfaction that she was beginning to bear down. The sounds the other woman was making were unmistakable – even, she hoped, for a pupil midwife.

'You're pushing, Philomena. Great work.' Despite herself, she met Dan Sheridan's eye. The suspicion she had seen there a moment ago was gone, replaced by clear interest in the progression of Philomena's labour. Hopefully she had got away with it.

They stayed like that for a little while, Peggy gently encouraging Philomena, who was pushing now with each pain. As this was Philomena's third, Peggy knew this part was likely to be fairly quick.

Suddenly the door opened.

'What on earth is going on here?' It was Sister Guinan. Turning on the big light, she tutted. 'Get that woman up on the bed immediately!'

Blinking in the harsh light, Peggy saw the anger on Sister's face and knew she was beaten.

It killed her to do it, but she muttered, 'Yes, Sister.' Leaning close to Philomena, she said, 'I need you to stand, Philomena. Can you do that?'

The woman nodded, and Peggy helped her up and walked her the few short steps to the bedside. As she did so, there was a whoosh and splash.

'Her waters have gone,' said Sister Guinan – as though it hadn't been obvious. Thankfully the puddle was by the side of the bed, and the pillow had escaped unscathed. Wordlessly, Dan picked it up and put it on the bed as Peggy helped Philomena onto it.

'On her back, please, Peggy,' Sister Guinan said, her tone snappish. 'Underwear off. I need to assess her.'

By the time Peggy had helped Philomena remove her underwear, another pain was coming. It was absolutely clear. Despite this, Sister Guinan separated Philomena's legs, pushing two fingers inside the birth canal.

'Ow! Ow! Get off!' Philomena tried to push her hand away, while Peggy stood, aghast. *This is horrific!*

'Now, now,' Sister Guinan said, her tone that of an adult to a small child. 'We'll have none of that carry-on, thank you very much! The head is right there, so you have work to do, Mrs Carney!'

*Well of course the head is right there*, thought Peggy. It was obvious from Philomena's progress. Bending, she had a look. The head was indeed right there. No need whatsoever for what Sister Guinan had done. *And they talk about sepsis, and the need to reduce childbirth infections?* Yes, and they blamed handywomen for poor hygiene, while they – or at least, some of them – were sticking fingers into women's private parts unnecessarily! Anger raged within her, but what could she do? It was almost as though Sister Guinan wanted to punish Mrs Carney for daring to labour on the floor.

'Me back, me back!' Philomena moaned. Tears were running down her face.

Peggy's heart was breaking for her. *She needs to be on her knees*. Aunty Bridget had been a great believer in letting women find their own most comfortable positions. Most women, she had always said, wanted to be kneeling or sitting while pushing. Even when a woman was exhausted from a long labour she tended to lie on her side, not her back. Sure it made no sense, asking poor Philomena to push her baby out uphill.

*At least some of them are kind*. The sisters who had been in charge earlier in the week had been much more supportive of women finding their own positions. This one, though . . . She did not dare look at Dan. What was he making of all this?

'I'll be back in a minute,' said Sister Guinan. 'And you and I' – she sent Peggy a challenging look – 'need a little talk after this.'

'Yes, Sister.' Chastened, Peggy dropped her gaze. *What a cow! What an absolute cow!* No, that was an insult to cows, who were gorgeous creatures who looked after their young very well. Sister Guinan had been more like a bull – dominant, uncaring, and frightening.

She left the room, and Peggy had an idea. *By God, she'll not do this to Philomena!* Bending, she whispered in Philomena's ear. 'Do you want to get back onto your knees?'

'Oh yes, please. I'm beggin' you, Peggy. The pain in me back just doubled!'

'Right then!' Helping her rise, she rearranged Philomena's clothing as the woman turned to kneel on the bed, leaning over the headboard. 'Don't let her bully you into lying down again!' she whispered, and Philomena nodded.

'No,' she said to Dan Sheridan, who had come to help. 'Don't be part of this.' No point both of them getting into trouble.

'Fuck that!' He hung the pillow over the bedhead, making a more comfortable rest for Philomena's arms.

Her eyes widened at his strong words, then she grinned. Maybe he wasn't as bad as she had assumed. His da though . . .

By the time Sister Guinan came back with one of the cleaners, Philomena was back in her flow and pushing well. Ignoring the clank of the cleaner's mop and bucket as she cleaned up the puddle on the floor, the woman simply kept her eyes closed and kept pushing. *Why would Sister Guinan bring a cleaner into Philomena's room right now?* Could it not have waited? Or why could Peggy not have been allowed to clean it up at a suitable time, instead of bringing another stranger into Philomena's room?

'Mrs Carney!' Sister Guinan was outraged. As she turned to face Peggy and Dan, Peggy could see fury in her eyes. 'Why is this woman not lying down? We are not animals, you know!' She tutted. 'On the floor. Kneeling on a bed. Disgusting.'

## The Irish Midwife

'I'm sorry, Sister.' Peggy opened her eyes wide. 'I didn't know.' The lie was absolutely worth it, so long as Sister Guinan didn't interfere with Philomena again.

'Now, Mrs Carney,' Sister Guinan said sweetly, 'I need you to lie on your back.'

Shaking her head, Philomena said nothing.

'It's to keep your baby safe,' she cooed, and Peggy held back a gasp at the blatant lie. It was nothing to do with safety, and everything to do with Sister Guinan's need to win.

Her own direct lie a minute ago had been to protect Philomena. Sister Guinan was now telling a vulnerable woman a straight lie – and she was doing it out of her own selfish need to domineer.

If Peggy hadn't known better – if she'd been the woman in labour putting her trust in the world famous Rotunda Hospital – she might have believed her. Instead, she muttered *Bullshit* inside her head – with an apology to her absent mother, who would be horrified at her use of such a word.

Thankfully, Philomena continued to ignore her, and before long the head was crowning. Naturally, Sister Guinan took over at that stage, giving Philomena curt instructions. Her hands were good, Peggy conceded, and her commands appropriate. It was just her manner . . .

An hour later the afterbirth was out, and Philomena's baby girl was suckling contentedly. Philomena herself was in great form – Peggy had often noticed that women were usually on top of the world in the first few hours – and full of praise for Peggy.

'She's an angel, that girl,' she was telling Sister Guinan. 'I can't thank you enough, Peggy.'

'All our girls are great,' Sister Guinan replied, and Peggy only just prevented herself from rolling her eyes.

'It was lovely to be here with you, Mrs Carney,' she said, uncomfortable with Philomena's praise. 'Any names for baby?'

'I was debating, but my husband's granny was Margaret. Peggy, you know? So she can be christened Margaret, but I think I'll call her Peggy.'

Peggy put a hand on her chest. 'Ah, that's so lovely!'

'That's perfect,' said Dan, and Philomena beamed at him.

'You're a good lad too! I hope you learned plenty!' She sent him a cheeky wink and he laughed.

*Jesus!* Peggy blinked. As if he wasn't good-looking enough with a sober face.

'I certainly did!' he replied then, more softly, 'I certainly did.'

Peggy swallowed. *What does he mean?* Her mind returned to the look he had sent her earlier – something like shock mingled with realisation or . . . *knowingness*. Had he guessed her secret?

There could be nobody worse, for he undoubtedly shared his da's disdain for handywomen. Hopefully her explanation had been reasonable – or at least plausible enough to prevent him reporting her, the way Dr Sheridan senior had reported Aunty Bridget.

'Come with me, Miss Cassidy!' Sister Guinan's tone was sharp.

Peggy's heart sank. *Time to be told off.*

'Yes, Sister,' she said meekly, following her to the door. Unable to resist, she glanced back. Philomena was busy repositioning her baby, but Dan lifted his right hand towards her, his fingers crossed to wish her good luck.

Inexplicably, this boosted her courage. Squaring her shoulders, she followed Sister Guinan out of the room.

★ ★ ★

'Well?' Dan spoke quietly. Peggy had just returned, having been gone for a full fifteen minutes. They stood in the corner of Philomena's room, speaking in low tones so she couldn't overhear.

Peggy shrugged. 'Last time I experienced something like that, I was being told off by the head teacher for pulling our Antoinette's hair in the playground. Could have been worse.'

'How so?' He was searching her face, seeking to work out how upset she was. *Bloody hell, she's pretty!*

'Well, I could have been kicked out. That didn't happen, so I'm grateful.'

'Kicked out? For supporting a woman to be comfortable?'

'Well, that's what I thought I was doing, but apparently I was contributing to the demise of civilisation by allowing a woman to behave like an animal.'

He snorted. 'I've been at five births this week, and some of the other Sisters did exactly as you did.'

'Well, that's what I thought! I even told her that.'

'And what did she say?'

'She sniffed and told me that others could do what they wanted but that she herself would adhere to the highest standards, and she expected *her* students to do the same.'

'So basically you have to practise differently depending on who's in charge that day?'

'Looks like it.'

He sighed. 'It's the same for us, you know.' He went on to describe conflicting advice he'd had from two of the medical tutors, at the same time noticing how she seemed to have thawed towards him over the course of the day. Daringly, he decided to push the conversation in a more personal direction. 'So where in Belfast are you from?'

Her expression became closed. 'Near St James's.'

St James's. The name was familiar, but he couldn't quite place it. At his puzzled look, she added, 'West Belfast.'

'Ah.' Now he knew exactly where she meant. West Belfast was not as genteel as the south of the city. No doubt Mother would disapprove. But Mother was far away. 'I'm from Derryvolgie. Near Queen's.'

'Aye, I thought you might be.' She turned away, heading to Mrs Carney's bedside. 'Are you getting afterpains?' she asked. 'They often come on during a feed, especially for mothers who've had more than one baby.'

'Aye,' Mrs Carney replied, her face creased in pain. 'As bad as early labour pains, they are.'

'Ach, God love you,' said Peggy, her expression filled with compassion. Something about the exchange brought a lump to Dan's throat, and he shook himself. Sentimentality had no place in medicine. Medicine was about science, always, and emotion could cloud the judgement.

And yet, had he and Peggy not been acting on emotion, on sympathy, on *instinct* when they had defied Sister Guinan? He thought about this. Perhaps it was about moral values, not sentiment. Emotion as a pathway to one's inner compass. He recalled Father not taking his full fee from Mrs McGeough, that day when he had decided to stick with his plans to enter medical training. Some might scorn Da for that, as they did for doctors who went for general practice rather than hospital medicine. It was all about choices, in the end.

Tiredness washed over him, and he checked his watch. It was heading for midnight – no wonder he was exhausted. Mrs Carney's labour and aftercare had lasted the full day. Still, at least he would get to bed at a reasonable hour tonight. The birth he'd observed two nights ago hadn't happened until three in the morning, which meant that he had been seeking his bed just as Paudie was rising.

Within the hour the night sister had returned from her rounds, and told them both they were now off duty. Sister Dolan was one of the nice ones. 'We'll see you at eight in the morning,' she said. 'And well done.'

'That was kind of her,' he said to Peggy as they headed down the dimly-lit corridor after bidding Mrs Carney goodnight. The place was eerily quiet – almost as though only the two of them existed. The hairs stood up on his arms as a sense of . . . of *magic*, almost, tingled around them. The night, the silence, the company . . .

'Who? The night sister?'

'Aye. They're not all like Sister Whinface.'

This earned a giggle, quickly stifled, and a surge of happiness within him. He was definitely making headway, despite those moments when she withdrew from him.

'It was a long day,' she sighed.

'Aye. We'll sleep well the night.'

Her lips twitched at his use of 'the night' – the northern way of saying 'tonight' – but she didn't comment on it. Calculating that he had maybe two or three minutes more before their paths would diverge, he decided to jump right in.

'Do you fancy going out for a walk sometime?'

Instantly her expression changed, and he knew a *No* was coming. Hastily, he backtracked. 'Nothin' funny, like. I'd just like to pick your brains about midwifery.' He grimaced. 'Sometimes it seems like they think people from the north are another species entirely.'

'I know what you mean. I think they're all wary of us reviving the civil war.'

'Which, to be fair, could easily happen. It does seem as though they've abandoned us entirely. The Free State, I mean. It might take another war for us to get out of the British Empire.'

She sent him a sideways look. 'I have to admit I took you for a Unionist.'

He recoiled theatrically. 'How very dare you! No, I'm an Irishman through and through. You?'

'I'm from West. We're all Irish there — apart from the Shankill, that is.'

They had reached the end of the main corridor. Here their ways would part — she to the nurses' home, he to the accommodation reserved for medical students. 'We should talk more about this.'

'Maybe.'

'Ah go on, sure what harm would it do to go for a wee walk? I don't actually bite, you know!'

Was that a hint of a smile? 'I'll think about it.'

'That'll do.' *For now.* 'Nice to meet you, Peggy . . .' he faltered. 'What's your surname?'

'Cassidy.' She almost seemed reluctant to tell him.

'Ah, yes. Sister Guinan called you Miss Cassidy.' He took a breath, looking her directly in the eye. 'Nice to meet you, Peggy Cassidy.'

Turning, he headed for his room, feeling as though his world had just got brighter.

# 14

Peggy couldn't sleep.

It was often this way after a birth. The same euphoria that frequently overcame the women could hit the handywoman just as much. For Peggy it was typically a mix of 'All went well' and 'That was amazing'. *But I'm not a handywoman any more. Or am I?*

The truth was, she had no idea. Being a handywoman had been her main idea of herself for years, and now it was leaving her. She was not yet a midwife – not until she had earned their precious badge – but she was changing. She loved the science they were teaching her – understanding how the body worked, being able to picture the various organs and bones beneath the skin and comprehend fully how everything fitted together. Combining it with her experience and instincts as a handywoman had been easy so far, and she often experienced moments of insight during the classes.

There were challenges too. Keeping her knowledge hidden. Managing her anger when they spoke so disparagingly of Aunty Bridget – for Aunty Bridget, to her, was the Handywoman personified. Feeling on edge when they assumed everyone in the room was middle class. To be fair, that was not particularly outrageous, since it was highly unlikely that any working-class family could afford twenty-two pounds to train a daughter. It was a miracle she was here. Or a tragedy. A miraculous tragedy? No. A tragic miracle. That was better.

Caterpillar, chrysalis, butterfly. Maybe the chrysalis stage was the most painful. The incident with Sister Guinan earlier had really unsettled her. Never would Aunty Bridget or Mrs Clarke have chastised her like that. And never in a thousand lifetimes would Aunty Bridget or Mrs Clarke have treated a woman like that.

It was almost as though the sister had enjoyed the power of barking out orders and belittling her *and* Philomena. Peggy had taken her dressing down like a good girl, while inwardly seething.

Anger rose again now. How dared Sister Guinan, who had put her fingers inside Philomena without permission, how *dared* she tell Peggy off for genuinely being focused on the needs and the safety of the woman and her baby? It was almost as if there was a gap between what they *said* – the lovely talk about what a privilege it was to be 'with-woman' during the most important day in the woman's life – and what they *did*. Or at least, what some of them did. And in that gap between words and actions, there was room for cynicism to grow in Peggy's heart.

It was early days though. She knew better than anyone that it would be wrong to judge an entire group on the basis of the worst among them. What had that report said about handywomen? That a handywoman should not be allowed to practise what they called 'her nefarious trade' and to 'carry the germs of childbirth fever from one victim to the next'. So who was it who might have introduced germs into Philomena's body today? Certainly not Peggy.

## The Irish Midwife

She turned over, trying not to disturb Anne's sleep. The other thing keeping her awake was of course Dan Sheridan. A 'fine thing' the other girls would call him, no doubt. A good-looking young man. But she distrusted him.

For a moment earlier, when he'd asked her to go for a walk with him some time, she'd actually thought he fancied her, which had set her heart a-pounding like there was no tomorrow. But he'd quickly clarified that it was for his own learning about midwifery. Probably a dose of nordie solidarity in there too. No, he didn't fancy her.

Which was a good thing, for that would really have complicated matters. Here she was, handywoman masquerading as trainee midwife, her dead aunty needing loyalty from beyond the grave.

A notion struck her. Thank God she and Aunty Bridget had different surnames. Aunty Bridget had been married, and had been Peggy's ma's sister, not her da's. If she and Peggy had both been called Doyle, he might have put two and two together. As it was, the name 'Cassidy' would have meant nothing to him – even though anyone from St James's, the Rock streets, Beechmount, Whiterock, or the Falls Road would have known the connection. But then, he wasn't from West.

Dr Sheridan had been defiant that day, walking past Bridget's wake house as if it was nothing to do with him, his son by his side. The fact was that Dan Sheridan's da had reported Aunty Bridget – an action which Peggy believed had contributed to her beloved aunt's early death. And Dr Sheridan's son would therefore likely report her too, if he realised who and what she was. She felt sick to her stomach as she recalled the shocked look he'd given her earlier. Almost as if he had *known*.

No, she needed to stay far, far away from the boul' Dan. Even though, she admitted to herself in the secret silence of the night, under normal circumstances she probably would fancy him.

On Sundays, most of the pupil midwives had the day off, apart from five who were rostered to cover. After Mass in the nearby Dominican, they enjoyed a Sunday roast dinner in the canteen with the medical students, following which they were free. Some of the girls were already stepping out with particular young men, and Peggy watched them go with something of a wistful air. But it would be too risky to get close to a medic here. Who knew what they might think of her? Or what secrets she might be tempted to reveal?

It was hard enough trying to keep up with her friends. Their world, their life experiences were in many ways very different to hers. From offhand things they said they all had parlours, and inside bathrooms, and a scullery as well as a kitchen. She suspected a lot of them had at least one servant, too. Their fathers were lawyers, or well-off farmers, and when they asked Peggy what jobs her father and brothers had, she replied blithely:

'Oh, nearly everyone in Belfast works in the shipyard or the mills. The northern economy is really strong.'

They had looked impressed by this, clearly assuming that her family was in some way benefiting from Belfast's industrial boom. Well, it was logical, given that she had a paid place on the midwifery programme.

Thankfully, both Anne and Mary were also from large families, and she was able to join in with funny stories about her siblings without standing out. But it didn't sit well with her to deceive them. *I'll have to tell them.* Would they judge her? Would she be dropped from their friendship group? She was not, after all from the sort of background their parents would approve of. The uncertainty worried at her, so she continued to bite her tongue for now.

'Let's go to the cinema!' Joan suggested. She, of course, had attended Sunday Service in the beautiful chapel in the Rotunda itself. Not that it mattered. One of the good things about being here and mixing freely with Protestants like Joan and some of the other girls, was realising it didn't seem to matter at all down here.

'Or the theatre, maybe! We're in Dublin after all! Every town in Ireland has a cinema, but the theatre is special.' Mary's alternative suggestion was instantly backed by both Anne and Joan, who immediately began perusing a copy of the newspaper at the back of the canteen for details of that day's shows.

'The Abbey is showing something called *The Silver Jubilee*. Never heard of it.'

'Ooh! *Julius Caesar* is on at The Gate. Tickets one shilling. Should we?'

*A whole shilling!* A shilling could buy a stone's weight of potatoes, Peggy knew. Or a pound weight of prime ribs. The notion of spending it on something as frivolous as a theatre or cinema ticket seemed impossibly extravagant. But the girls were excited, and how could Peggy possibly tell them that a shilling was a significant amount of money for her? Maybe she could pretend to be unwell.

Yet despite her misgivings, something in her suspected that if Aunty Bridget was standing beside her right now, she'd be urging her to 'away on and enjoy yourself'.

*Ah, sure why not?* Throwing caution to the wind, Peggy decided to go. After all, she had spent not a ha'penny since arriving over a month ago. Her uniform, food, and accommodation were all included in her fee. As it bloody should be, given how outrageously dear it was.

One of the medical students was approaching. 'Hey, girls. Can we get a look at the paper after you've done with it?'

'Certainly you can!' Anne sent him a glance filled with mischief. 'Is that a Cork accent?'

'It is. And where are you from yerself?'

'Guess!' She gestured to all of them. 'And guess my friends' counties, too!'

'Challenge accepted.' He turned. 'Sheridan! Get over here!'

Peggy's insides clenched at the name. Nerves? Excitement? She couldn't tell. But her heart was racing and her mouth was dry. And there he was. No white coat, but a shirt and tie. God, he looked well.

'I'm Paudie,' said the other medical student, and they all gave their names, Joan reminding Paudie that they'd worked together the week before.

'Dan. Dan Sheridan.'

'Ooh, well that accent's easy! You're definitely a nordie!' Anne declared.

'Ah, but which county?' he asked, a smile in his eyes.

*Are they flirting? Is he flirting with Anne?* Suddenly her stomach felt sick.

'Peggy! Your call!' Anne turned to her.

Peggy spread her hands wide. 'Dan and I were allocated to the same woman a couple of days ago, so I know he's from Belfast.'

'So that's Antrim, right?' Mary offered, and now he turned his smiling eyes on her. 'Is that your final answer?'

Mary nodded.

'Yes and no.'

## The Irish Midwife

They clamoured at him to clarify, Peggy joining in. Suddenly the eyes were on her, with the same teasing smile. 'As Peggy knows, I live on the Antrim side of the river, but my family's from Down, so I was reared as a Down man.'

'Ardsman or Mourne man?'

He pursed his lips, his beautiful lips. 'Me da's originally from a place where the Mountains of Mourne . . .'

'Sweep down to the sea!' In unison, they finished the line from the song.

'Me da', Peggy noted. Not 'my father'. As Dan and Paudie started flinging wrong guesses at Joan, she mused on this. From what little she knew of the Belfast middle class, they didn't usually say ma and da. *Interesting*.

Mary's Dublin accent was little challenge to them, so now they were focusing on Anne again.

'I'm gonna say . . . Mayo!' declared Paudie, and Anne flinched theatrically.

'Ooh, you've done it now!' laughed Mary. The rivalry between Mayo and Galway was renowned.

'Ah no. Galway?' He bowed theatrically. 'My sincere apologies, Anne.'

'That's like me saying you're from Kerry!' she declared, feigning a pout.

'I'm a gom, a gowl, and maybe even a langer!' he declared, all contrite. 'Can you ever forgive me?'

'I'll think about it!' she said primly, but her eyes were dancing.

'So what are ye going to see?' he asked, and Anne told him.

*Uh-oh. I know where this is going!*

Sure enough, within minutes the lads had been invited along, and they said they'd bring a couple of others they'd half-agreed to tag about with. Peggy stood silently while

Paudie and Anne made the arrangements, unsure what she was feeling. Of course there was nothing wrong with a group of them going to the theatre together. And Anne was on the prowl for a husband. It was just...

Was it Dan? *Well yes*, but in a surge of honesty she realised it was all of them. It was everything. She was a milly, a shawlie – a millworker from one of the poorest areas of Belfast, known for always wearing the poor woman's shawl. She was only here because Aunty Bridget's life had been cut short.

She didn't know if she even *wanted* to be part of them. They were all nice people as individuals. Even Dan seemed nice. But they were alien. They thought differently. They dressed differently. They had different expectations to her.

*Stop it!* She was thinking too much about it – a habit of hers, she knew. *Just enjoy the experience. You don't have to be changed by it.*

The matinee was at two, and so the boys offered to go straight round to the box office to secure the tickets.

'That's very kind of you,' said Anne. 'Thank you.'

'Sure it's no bother!' declared Paudie, and off they went. The girls exchanged glances that varied from the mischievous (Anne) to wry (Joan and Mary) and bewildered (Peggy).

'Nice,' said Anne. 'Two handsome lads, don't you think? I enjoyed the banter with Paudie. Definitely a possibility.'

At this, the others responded with exaggerated outrage, making her laugh. 'Sure it's all only a bit of craic, girls.' She set Peggy a sly glance. 'Big Dan seemed mighty interested in you, Peggy.'

Peggy flushed. 'No, no, it's only because we're both from the north. And we were together looking after a woman the other day.'

'Together, were ye?' Anne winked.

'No! Not *together*, just . . .'

'Aw yeah, we get it, don't we, girls? Right! Let's go and get ready.'

Off they went, Peggy's discomfort gradually easing as the conversation moved on, to her great relief. After taking turns to visit the bathroom – Peggy now almost accustomed to the luxury of it – they donned their coats and made their way downstairs to meet the lads.

# 15

'I assume you're after the nordie girl, are you?' There was a knowing look in Paudie's eye.

'A hundred per cent,' said Dan, grinning. 'What about you? The one from Galway? Or one of the others?'

He pretended to consider this. 'For today anyway, yer one from Galway. I might change my mind if she's not as sound as she seems.'

'Or if she doesn't like you!'

He laughed. 'That too.' He turned to Eugene and Desy, who had the bedroom next to theirs, and with whom they'd formed something of a friendship over card games after-hours. 'That means you two can focus on the Dublin and Longford ones.'

'Ah here!' said Desy. 'Now you wouldn't be giving us the ugly ones, would you?'

'Definitely not,' said Paudie. 'Four total lashers, I swear.' He dug Dan in the ribs. 'Wouldn't you say, Dan?'

'I can confirm,' said Dan loftily, 'that all four young ladies are definitely pretty.' He grinned again. 'But if any of yous try to chat up Peggy from Belfast, you'll have me to contend with!'

It was all said in a light-hearted way, and Dan knew they had no idea how much he meant it. Thankfully Paudie's intervention had allowed him to warn his friends off Peggy. *In the end she may not like me, but at least I'll not have to deal with the lads trying to make a play for her.*

They had each paid for two tickets, and as the girls arrived Paudie marched straight up to Anne, apologising again and offering her his arm. After pretending to consider it she grinned and took his arm, at the same time declaring that it would take more than a ticket worth a shilling to earn her forgiveness. *She likes him, though.* Dan could see it. They'd be doing a line in no time, if he wasn't mistaken.

The boys were busy introducing themselves to Joan and Mary, which meant . . .

'Shall we?' Mimicking Paudie, he offered his arm, and Peggy – with a noticeable hesitation – took it. No play-acting; she seemed genuinely uncertain. He stifled a sigh. She looked beautiful with her hair down, dark curls spilling over her shoulders and framing her pretty face. Hope mingled with pride as he walked by her side into the theatre.

The Gate Theatre was part of the Rotunda complex, the entrance round to the side of the hospital, and the interior was in the same style as the hospital itself. High, plastered ceilings, ornate plasterwork, and portraits hung about the walls. Making their way to the auditorium, Dan looked about with curiosity. It was a neat little theatre, with probably around four hundred seats. There was no upper circle or boxes, all the seats being in the stalls.

Their tickets were for row M, in the raised area towards the back. 'Ten and eleven,' he said, realising they were by the aisle. He indicated she should precede him, then took his own seat. Paudie and Mary were already there, in the next two seats down, and a moment later Desy, Eugene, and the other two girls sat in the row in front. This arrangement pleased them all, for it was much easier to speak to them than if they'd all been strung out in a single long row. Peggy, like the others, shrugged out of her coat and straightened it behind her.

'It's so beautiful.' She was looking around her, her gaze drawn to the ceiling, which was adorned with plasterwork flowers within lozenges of white, and picked out with dark blue paint, creating a striking effect. The rest of the ceiling was painted in warm cream, the walls a deep green. It was indeed beautiful, and he said so.

'I've never actually seen *Julius Caesar* before,' he offered, 'though I've read it, of course. I went through a Shakespeare phase a few years back.'

'Oh.' She didn't seem to have anything to say to this, so he tried again.

'Have you seen this one performed before?'

'No, I haven't.' She looked decidedly uncomfortable, making Dan wonder if he'd done the right thing in singling her out. *Does she dislike me?* He dismissed the notion instantly. *She knows nothing about me. And besides, what have I done that could make her dislike me?*

So with determination he chatted away, hoping to see something of the spark she had showed while they were together with Mrs Carney. It was hard work. She answered all his questions with polite reticence, asking none of her own. To their right, he could hear Paudie and Anne chattering away, and the contrast was marked. It was almost a relief when the chandeliers were dimmed and the play began.

After a few minutes he glanced towards her. Oh, *now* she was animated, seemingly enthralled by the spectacle. Suddenly he lost all interest in fully watching the play himself, instead turning constantly to see how she was reacting to this or that. Then Act I was done, and the lights came up.

Exhaling loudly, she looked at him, momentarily speechless.

'I know!' he offered. 'Strong stuff, isn't it?'

She found her voice. 'It's fascinating. The way they make the meanings clear even though the words are so old-fashioned. I got the gist of all of it, which I'm really surprised about. I was sure I'd be sitting here lost.'

So maybe she'd never seen *any* Shakespeare performed before? He tucked this nugget of information away into the back of his brain somewhere. 'I know what you mean. Some of it is really obscure, but they make it clear using their tone of voice.'

'And facial expression.'

'Even their body movements, too. Confident, cringing, sly . . .'

She nodded, then frowned. 'I don't like that boy Cassius. Yes, Julius Caesar might be a bit cocky, but there's no need to turn his friends against him, is there?'

'Totally.' Thinking hard, he managed to remember a quote from a few minutes ago. '"The fault, dear Brutus, is not in our stars, but in ourselves, that we are underlings".'

'Well that's pure nonsense, for a start!'

'You don't think we are masters of our fates?'

'I don't, sadly. Oh, we can change small things, of course. We all have choices to make. But the big things, the overall journey of our lives – most people have no control over it.'

'In what sense?' He was reviewing his own path, the choices he had made so far. Never had he felt constrained by fate. Why, he had even debated dropping the idea of studying medicine a few years ago, then decided to carry on. His own choice, freely made.

She shrugged. 'Class. Sex. Religion. These things define us, set limits on our choices. You must know it.'

He frowned. 'The religion thing is bad in the north, granted. I suspect some of my tutors in Belfast might be a wee bit . . .' His voice tailed away. Suddenly, he was reluctant to say it out loud.

'Sectarian?' She grimaced. 'Of course they are. Not all of them, but enough. And they are already in all the key positions of power throughout the north. Politics. Universities. The law. Medicine. If you do become a hospital obstetrician, I bet you'll be one of the first Catholics to make it that far in the north.'

'My father is a GP.'

'I know. And somebody was telling me the hospital doctors sometimes see GPs as less important.'

'How?'

'What?'

'How do you know my da's a GP?'

She blinked as if surprised, then shrugged. 'Dr Sheridan. I've heard of him.'

'Oh.'

There was a pause. 'So you get the religious thing. Now think about sex. How many girls are there in your course?'

'Five,' he said promptly, 'and all interested in obstetrics and gynaecology. They're all away to Edinburgh together to do their maternity training.'

'All Protestants then?'

'No, I . . .' He thought for a moment, then frowned. 'Actually, yes.'

She shrugged. 'Five women, out of what? Eighty medical students? And they all *happen* to be Protestant?'

He grimaced. 'I see where you're going with this. I haven't really thought about it before.'

'No. You wouldn't have.'

Ignoring the implied criticism, he thought finally about class. 'Not too many shipyard workers training to be doctors either.'

'Exactly. Now imagine a working-class Catholic girl. Class, religion, sex. Her ma and da both working in the shipyard or the mills. What sort of choices might she have?'

He swallowed hard, nodding. 'She'll work in the mills herself.'

Her gaze became unfocused. 'Once we've done twenty births and been signed off, apparently we're allowed to go out "On the district". I'm hoping to get there by January.'

'On the district? Oh, does that mean you go out to the Dublin home births? That's optional for us. Once we finish this part we'll be starting in theatre. Actually operating.'

'It's good that they encourage you to see normal birth. But I suspect that if the medics had to do a lot of home births it would give you a better understanding of people's real lives. Are you going to take up the option?'

'I wasn't going to, but maybe I should consider it.' He thought for a moment. 'Back to your earlier point. My father swears that being a GP is more important than being a surgeon. He's in people's houses six days a week, sometimes seven, and often talks about some of the poverty and

## The Irish Midwife

malnutrition he sees. Overcrowded houses, poor diets. He swears a lot of ill health is poverty by another name.'

'Does he now?' There was an edge to her voice that he couldn't place. 'Tell me this, do you call him "Da" or "Father"? I've heard you say both.'

Now he was on safer ground. 'I'd like to call him Da, and I know he doesn't mind, but I've been trained to say "Father".'

'*Trained?* Who trained you?'

'My ma.' He rolled his eyes, half-laughing. 'Jaysus, she'd be ragin' if she knew I'd called her that. She insists on "Mother" and "Father".'

'What was her own background?'

*Killer question.* 'See, that's the interesting thing. Her own da – my granda – was a coalman. Delivered all around North and West Belfast with his horse and trap. But he was a good businessman, and made enough money for her to go to a fancy school.'

'Fair play to him. He's still alive?'

'Aye, though we don't visit him very often.'

'Let me guess. Your ma came out of the fancy school with notions about herself.'

'Exactly.' He frowned. 'Don't get me wrong, now. She's a good person. She was warm and loving towards me as a boy, and she does loads of charity work.'

'As a boy? Is she still warm and loving?'

'I suppose so. But I'm an adult now. It would be odd if she was still hugging and kissing me, don't you think?'

'I dunno. My own ma still hugs us, even though our Gerard and Antoinette are both married now.'

'Does your ma work? What does your da do?'

'Wheesht now, it's starting again.' She was right. The lights were dimming, and a moment later the curtains opened for Act II.

# 16

*Jesus, Mary and Joseph!* That had been a close one! It was becoming harder and harder to avoid revealing the truth – at least, the truth about her family background. While it was highly unlikely that anyone would ask her if she had worked as a handywoman (unless she gave it away herself), finding out about each other's families was a perfectly reasonable thing to do while building friendships.

She couldn't expect to live on her wits forever. But once again she had managed to avert disaster.

Meanwhile on stage, Caesar's wife was trying to persuade him to stay home, having dreamed that bad things might happen to him that day – the Ides of March. *He should listen to her.* Women knew things that men's rationality could never touch. But no, Caesar, confident in his invincibility, could only suggest she was encouraging him to be a coward. 'Cowards die many times before their deaths,' he said, 'the valiant never taste of death but once.'

There was definitely something in that. How many times with her friends had she imagined being uncovered as the impostor in their midst? Today they were all out with a group of nice young men, and all she could think about, as usual, was getting caught. God, it was tiring. And she really wanted these people to like her. The girls were lovely, and Paudie seemed lovely, and Dan . . .

Dan was special. When she was with him something strange happened to her insides. And when he looked at her . . . She had honestly never felt anything like it before. At the grand old age of twenty, she finally knew what it was to have a soft spot for a particular lad.

And even more oddly, she liked him despite everything. Despite what his da had done, which could never be forgiven. Despite the privileged life he had had. Dan had, she sensed, an open mind, and possibly an open heart. Naïveté? Perhaps. Even though he was three or four years older than her, she had the measure of him in life experience. What did he know of the value of a penny? What did any of them know?

On stage the play continued, and she watched as the wives of Caesar and Brutus pleaded for understanding, to be informed, to be listened to. *Are they really going to do this thing?* Well, she knew they would, for she knew the history.

The curtains closed again, and rather than converse with Dan she muttered a word of excuse then made for the ladies' room. There she lingered, pretending to fix her hair in front of an ornate gilded mirror, until she judged the interval must be nearly done. *Oops!* The lights were dimming and she hurried, brushing past Dan and into her seat just as the curtains opened.

Transfixed, she watched as Caesar was struck down. The sadness of 'Et tu, Brute' pierced her heart. That trust should be betrayed so cruelly! Poor Caesar! And the self-righteousness of his murderers, congratulating themselves on their good deed! Had Dr Sheridan felt like that, after reporting Aunty Bridget? She sensed Dan moving beside her, then he pressed a soft cotton handkerchief into her hand. It was only then that she realised her face was wet with tears.

Embarrassed, she patted dry her cheeks, then found her own handkerchief in her coat pocket and blew her nose into that. The play had moved on, and Mark Antony was reading out Caesar's will, vindicating him. Peggy was entirely gripped by the whole thing . . . the acting, the poetic way they spoke, the drama of the events unfolding before her. She had been to a play once before – a pantomime in the Grand Opera House in Belfast. Granda Joe had taken her, having bought two tickets as a Christmas present for her when she was eight. Shakespeare was very different to pantomime though.

She refocused her attention on the actors. A rebellion was now underway in Rome, and it stirred her blood as Da's blood must have been stirred when he went to fight in the War of Independence. Two years he'd fought, coming home once the treaty had been signed. Uncle Ned – Aunty Bridget's husband – had not been so lucky. He had died in the GPO on the third day of the Rising, leaving Bridget all alone.

Da had refused to get involved in the civil war that followed the signing of the treaty, even though he had been devastated at the betrayal by his fellow Irishmen, who had taken their own freedom, abandoning the north to continued British rule.

'Irishman against Irishman,' he always said, with an air of sadness. 'I cannot believe Collins did this to us.' *Et tu, Brute.*

Still, Da was proud to have played his part in the fight for Irish freedom from the British Empire. And what reward had he been given? Recognition from the Free State government.

A medal, a small amount of money, and continued British rule in the north. *Bah!* She was getting all wound up about things she wasn't in control of.

Another interval, and this time she sat where she was.

'Are you enjoying it?' Dan asked.

'Enjoying . . . ?' She thought about it. 'No. This is not enjoyment. My insides are twisted up at the injustice of it. And now the mob is taking over. It's . . . powerful stuff.'

'It is. Shakespeare, right?'

'I must admit I haven't read his works. W.B. Yeats is my favourite. "A terrible beauty is born" and all that.'

'Yeats is wonderful. Romantic. Isn't there one where he says he has spread his dreams under her feet? "Tread softly, for you tread on my dreams".'

'Yes.' Her voice sounded strange, so she cleared her throat. 'Yes, that one is "Aedh Wishes for the Cloths of Heaven". It's a beautiful poem.'

'Shakespeare can be romantic too, you know.'

'Really?'

'Absolutely.' He gave a short laugh. 'Now if I was a proper renaissance man I'd be quoting from one of his sonnets. Sadly, I'm a medic.' He shrugged.

'And I'm a midwife. Or at least I'm going to be. I think.'

'You think?'

'There's a lot of hurdles to get over first.'

'Like the exams? You'll be fine. You're smart, and dedicated, and . . . you are an amazing midwife.'

She could feel her colour rising. And he was giving her *that look* again – the one that melted her bones and made her all confused inside.

Her eyes dropped. 'Thank you.'

They moved then to let Paudie out, and when they sat down again the moment had passed. Thank God, for Peggy didn't know what to make of it. If anybody else had said it she'd have been just as scundered, but was she imagining it, or was there a *particular* warmth in his eyes when he looked at her?

More importantly, would it be a betrayal of Aunty Bridget to want that? *Of course it would.*

The rest of the play was less gripping to Peggy. Just men fighting one another, posturing like dogs, or so it seemed to her. By the time it was done she was well in control of herself, smiling and making cheerful comments to the others as they all filed out.

Surprisingly, it was dark outside. The sun had set while they were in the theatre, the short winter day making way for night. *The dark cloths of night and light and the half-light*, Yeats had said, but no way was Peggy going to start quoting poetry again. She needed to keep her feet on the ground.

Less surprisingly, it was cold, and the wind had picked up since earlier. They had barely taken ten steps when a gust of wind blew straight through her coat (which was, admittedly, fairly thin), making her wrap her arms around herself and suck in her breath.

'It would founder you!' Dan half-shouted to be heard among the gusts.

'Certainly would!'

'We're heading to Bewley's!' Paudie and Anne were huddled together. 'You coming?'

Bewley's. The name was vaguely familiar from the day Mary had taken them around the city centre, but Peggy couldn't recall exactly what or where it was. Desperately hoping it wouldn't involve spending money, she went along with the plan, and they all headed southwards towards, apparently, Westmoreland Street. As they passed Clerys she nearly stumbled as a particularly strong gust hit them, and Dan put an arm around her to steady her.

'You all right?'

She nodded and matched her steps to his, giving him a clear signal that she was happy for his arm to remain. The others had all paired up in the same way, so it might have seemed rude to throw him off. Or so she told herself.

God, it was good to feel his arm around her. She felt safe, protected, cared for. She also felt something else. Something dark, and mysterious, and new. Something was stirring in her body. She wanted him. *Desire.*

The absurdity of it struck her. Her first brush with physical desire, in the middle of Dublin, on a windy November evening. With the son of her family's greatest enemy. It was straight out of *Romeo and Juliet*, and while she hadn't had the chance to read any Shakespeare, she had heard how *that* story had ended. As they crossed the bridge the wind picked up, the wide banks of the Liffey allowing it to swirl and gust freely. Dan's arm tightened around her, and she leaned into him. Had his lips just brushed her hair? No, she must have imagined it.

Bewley's Oriental Café, the sign said. Inside was cosy, warm, and very noisy. The place was jammed, the hum of lively conversation accompanied by the staccato rattle of crockery. There were mosaic tiles under her feet, beautiful stained-glass windows around the edges, and the open space in front of her was filled with little square tables and fancy wooden chairs with curved backs.

## The Irish Midwife

The lads were already moving, bringing a couple of empty tables together to create a larger one. Belatedly she went to assist, moving the chairs along with the others until they had arranged things to their satisfaction. They sat then, hanging coats on the backs of chairs. Peggy stole a glance at what the other customers were eating and drinking. Tea or coffee, buns and scones. *I wonder how dear it is?* She had put two shillings into her coat pocket earlier, and hadn't spent anything yet, for Dan had bought her theatre ticket. Surreptitiously she checked. Yes, the shillings were still there, alongside Dan's handkerchief. Unable to help herself, she stroked it briefly before withdrawing her hand.

A waitress had arrived to take their order, and Paudie was consulting Anne about her preferences. Peggy had, to be fair, been in Mooney's Café in the Belfast Cornmarket a few times, her and Antoinette treating themselves to tea and an iced fancy for an extravagant five pence.

'I'll get this,' said Dan. 'What would you like?'

'Tea, please.' She sent him a grateful smile. Even though she had to watch the pennies, he most definitely didn't, and she was relieved that the lads' chivalry would spare her the regret she would feel if she had to break into one of her precious shillings.

'Two teas,' he told the waitress. 'And' – he turned to Peggy–'scone, or layer cake?'

'Oh, layer cake, please!'

'Two, please.' The waitress moved on to the others, and Dan rubbed his hands together. 'Thank God it's warm in here!'

Peggy was looking around. 'Is it always this busy?'

'Not sure. I've only been in here a couple of times – though I've never seen it quiet, to be fair. And with that wind, I'm sure a lot of people had the same idea as us – get in from the cold.'

'Too right!'

The conversation widened out then, and Peggy took a particular interest in Eugene and Desy, trying to work out what if anything was going on between them and her other friends. She was being watched in the same way, she knew, and so she kept everything very neutral when interacting with Dan. The hot tea was welcome, the layer cake delicious, and Peggy's bones were now warming up. Just for a moment she tried to imagine describing today to her past self of a couple of months ago. Shakespeare. Layer cake. Stepping out with a doctor's son. An inward giggle threatened to bubble up, and she suppressed it.

Whether she would eventually be found out didn't matter right now, for right now she *belonged*.

# 17

*November 1938*

Working on the district was tough. It was hard seeing the sheer scale of the poverty in the tenements of inner-city Dublin. At least in West Belfast most families – even poor families – had their own front door and back yard. They had running water in the kitchen and a fireplace that worked.

In this part of Dublin there was none of that. Some of the families lived in one room, with a table in one corner and a couple of mattresses in the other. The Free State government were funding the councils to build new houses, and the contrast in standards was stark. Yesterday, Peggy and Mary had attended a woman in labour in a tenement slum – a faded building at least a hundred years old, with high ceilings and peeling plasterwork. She had given birth with no complications in the darkness of the evening, her husband and other children having been banished to his sister's flat for the duration. They'd all come back last night just as Peggy and Mary were leaving, to exclaim over the baby. Some things were universal.

This morning the girls were completing a series of antenatal and postnatal visits around Stoneybatter, the neat brick houses very similar to Peggy's own home house up in Belfast. Two rooms upstairs, two down, and the outhouse. These homes were nearly forty years old apparently, but Peggy had heard that some of the newer council houses had plumbed-in bathrooms.

Oxmantown Road was long and fairly broad, the street a hive of activity. A vegetable man was selling his wares, his horse-drawn cart placed strategically in the middle of the road. Children too young for school ran about, while many of the women were out, the morning being dry. Some were cleaning windows, or kneeling to scrub their front step. All wore the same aprons that Peggy knew well from home. She sighed in satisfaction. These were her people.

'Let's stop here,' she called to Mary and they dismounted, leaning their bicycles against a gable end wall where Oxmantown Road met Cowper Street. Only fifteen of the trainee midwives had been approved to go on the district, Peggy among them. The others had been adjudged as needing more births under the eye of the sisters before being trusted to care for women at home. Thankfully, Sister Guinan had not blamed Peggy for what she described as Philomena's 'disobedience'. On hearing this word used to describe the woman, Peggy had clenched her fists and managed to say nothing, but *feck!* it had been hard.

And now this – working on the district – was her reward. It almost felt like being a handywoman again, except that now she was wearing a heavy nurse's cloak and riding a black bicycle marked *Rotunda Hospital*. Taking her leather midwife's bag from the basket, she conferred with Mary about which houses they would each visit, checking their list and the crudely drawn map they had copied from the one on the wall in the midwives' common room in the hospital.

'Meet you back here afterwards!'

Waving a farewell, Peggy started her list. She had three women to see, all at different stages. After visiting two postnatal women – checking that their wombs were shrinking down appropriately, that they were showing no signs of fever, and that their babies were attaching and feeding well – she circled back at last to 63 Oxmantown Road, checking her list once more. Mrs Halliday was due soon, and so today's visit was for Peggy to see her home, chat with her, and hopefully, to listen to her wishes.

The door was ajar, so she knocked. 'Midwife calling!'

'Ah, howya, Nurse!' Mrs Halliday hobbled towards her with that distinctive gait of late pregnancy. 'Come in, come in. Will ya take a cuppa tae?'

'I will, and thanks.' Peggy knew well how important it was to accept a woman's offer of hospitality if she could. 'I'm Peggy,' she added, 'Peggy Cassidy.'

'You're from the north?'

Setting her bag down on the settee, she followed Mrs Halliday through to her back kitchen, watching as the other woman filled the kettle and placed it on the stove. The house was spotless, the kitchen neat and tidy.

'I am. Belfast.'

'My husband is from up there. County Antrim. A place called Cushendall.'

They chatted while the tea brewed, then chatted again while drinking it. Mr Halliday worked on the railways, and this would hopefully be their first living child. 'I've had two miscarriages and a stillbirth before this,' the woman said, her tone matter-of-fact, but Peggy wasn't fooled for a moment.

'I'm so sorry, Mrs Halliday. That must have been terrible.'

'Aye. It was.' She rubbed her abdomen. 'But this is farther than I've ever got, so hopefully this time it'll be all right.'

'And how are you feeling in yourself?'

She managed a smile. 'Some days I do be fine. Others,' she shrugged, 'it feels like it'll all go wrong again. You know?'

'I do, aye. You'll only be properly all right when you have your wee baby in your arms.'

'Exactly!'

'How far on are you?'

'I'll be nine months next Tuesday. So close!' She grimaced. 'I just keep worrying, feeling like something's not quite right, you know?'

Peggy did know. The problem was there were two possibilities here. Mrs Halliday might simply be anxious because of losing the other babies – a perfectly reasonable reaction. But Peggy had supported enough women to know that sometimes a mother's instinct that something was wrong would turn out to be correct.

'So tell me about how you're feeling physically.'

'Ach, I'm all right.'

'No, honestly. I know we're told not to make a fuss, but I genuinely want to know.'

Mrs Halliday sent her a long look, then nodded. 'Well, it's hard to get air into me lungs, and I've an awful headache these two days. Me head is bustin', so it is. Plus I'm running to the outhouse all the bliddy time, and producing only a few drops. And me back is killing me.'

Peggy nodded sympathetically. 'Any nosebleeds or convulsions?'

'No, thank God.'

That was reassuring. The breathing thing was common in late pregnancy, as was the constant weeing, and even the back pain. Both the lungs and the bladder were now physically constricted as the baby was so big, and the back and

## The Irish Midwife

pelvis were under tremendous strain. In her mind's eye she could see the bones and how they articulated. Anatomy lessons were definitely useful.

The headache *might* be just a coincidence, but something deep inside her was alert and paying attention. Not wanting to contribute to Mrs Halliday's anxiety, she offered sympathy and suggested she rest in a darkened room.

'Can I? I'd love to lie down, but I don't want somebody landing in and thinking I'm lazy!'

'You're not lazy,' said Peggy firmly, realising Mrs Halliday needed someone to give her permission to rest. 'Now, go you on up and I'll bring you a nice cool cloth for your head.' Going through to the kitchen she turned on the tap, then opened drawers and cupboard until she found a pile of neatly folded tea towels. *Perfect*. Soaking one in freezing cold water, she wrung out the excess then folded the cloth and carried it upstairs, along with her midwife's bag.

Mrs Halliday was in the front bedroom, struggling to get her shoes off. 'Here, let me help you.' The woman's feet were swollen, Peggy noted. Her hands too. 'You have a wee bit of swelling there,' she noted.

'Aye. I'm told it can happen but I thought I was getting away with it. I was grand until last night. Had to take me wedding ring off – and a good job I did. Look!' She spread her fingers, which were tight and very swollen. Peggy's concerns were deepening by the minute, but she managed to appear calm – one of the key skills of a handywoman. And a midwife.

'Ah, they're definitely swelled. Good job you noticed and got the wedding ring off in time. I've seen women having to have it cut off them!'

Mrs Halliday sucked the air in between her teeth. 'Shockin'!'

'Do you mind if I feel your tummy and listen to the baby?'

'I don't mind at all,' said Mrs Halliday, swinging her legs round and lying on the bed.

'Sorry, my hands might be a bit cold,' Peggy murmured as she began palpating Mrs Halliday's abdomen. *Palpation.* Another new word she'd learned these past months, but the meaning was the same. Feeling for the baby's lie and position.

'Ah, never worry, Nurse.'

'Right, baby is head down, facing the right way, and slightly to the right.' She reached for her Pinard, taking a minute to find the best spot. And there it was – baby's heartbeat, sounding reassuringly regular.

'Lovely!' she declared. 'Baby's happy as Larry in there.' She paused. Mrs Halliday's womb was tightening – she could feel it under her hand. 'Are you getting any pains?'

'I am. On and off all morning. Do you think it might be labour starting?'

'It's hard to tell. Either way, you need to rest. Now, lie you round on your side and I'll put this cloth on your forehead.'

'Oh that's lovely, Nurse. Such a relief!'

'Good.' Peggy pulled the curtains, encasing the woman in cosy darkness. 'Now, I'm going to go, but I'll call back later if that's all right with you?'

'Aye, no bother, Nurse. I might have a bit of a sleep here.'

'Exactly what you need,' said Peggy firmly, gathering her things and tiptoeing out.

Mary was waiting for her by the bicycles.

'Well, how did you get on?'

Mounting, they started pedalling briskly down Oxmantown Road. Thankfully, it would only take ten minutes to cycle to the hospital.

## The Irish Midwife

'The two postnatal women were both well,' Peggy said, as Mary cycled alongside her, 'but I'm worried about Mrs Halliday.' Briefly, she outlined the woman's symptoms.

Mary gasped. 'Sounds a bit like what we learned in that lecture last week. Early stages of toxaemia. Eclampsia, right?'

'That's what I thought. Course, I could be wrong.' As a handywoman, one of the most important moments was knowing when to send for the doctor. The health and the life of the mother and baby were paramount, and even though most of the women she and Aunty Bridget had supported couldn't really afford the services of a doctor, Aunty Bridget and Mrs Clarke had both had an excellent working relationship with Dr Gaffney, and always called him when needed. A few times each year someone from the house, Peggy herself, or even a neighbour would be sent to fetch him – and with time to spare for him to get the woman to the hospital if needed.

Mrs Halliday was all right at present, but if she developed full eclampsia, as Peggy now knew the condition was called, her life and the life of her child would both be at risk. Women had been known to die from fits – or, heartbreakingly, from not breathing during fits, or choking on their own saliva and mucous. The pupil midwives and medical students had been treated to a special joint lecture highlighting the importance of ensuring the woman continued to breathe during a convulsion. Apparently a former master of the Rotunda, Mr Tweedy (now retired) was an expert on the condition, and the so-called 'Dublin treatment' was influencing practice throughout the British Isles. Mortality rates for women with eclampsia were as high as eight per cent, so everyone took the signs seriously.

## Seána Tinley

One thing was for certain. Mrs Clarke would have been sending Dr Gaffney for Mrs Halliday. Peggy would do no less.

'They'll probably tell you to go back and stay with her,' Mary said as they pulled in to the Rotunda yard. 'Here, take this.' She unpinned her fob watch. 'It'll come in handy.'

'Ah, you're a star!' said Peggy, grateful for the loan. Fob watches were very expensive, and she promised to take good care of it.

They dismounted properly. 'I'll see to your bike,' Mary said. 'Just go!'

Thanking her, Peggy grabbed her bag from the basket and dashed inside, forcing herself to walk, not run along the corridor. In her head she was rehearsing what to say. She mustn't leave anything out!

'Sister.' Her heart sank. It was Sister Guinan. *Of course it bloody would be.*

'Yes, Miss Cassidy?' Sister Guinan lifted her head from her ledger, her demeanour that of someone barely tolerating an interruption to a vital task.

'I have a concern about an antenatal woman.' Peggy took a breath. 'Mrs Halliday of Oxmantown Road in Stoneybatter. Age 30, previous stillbirth and two miscarriages. No living children. Due next Tuesday.'

'Go on.'

Out of the corner of her eye Peggy saw the twitch of a white coat, hovering as if its wearer was listening.

'She has a severe headache lasting two days, as well as sudden swelling of the hands and feet.'

'Convulsions?'

## *The Irish Midwife*

Peggy shook her head. 'No. I did ask.'

'Have you written up your notes on the official Central Midwives Board form?'

'Not yet, Sister. I thought it was important to tell you straight away.'

'Right,' said Sister briskly. 'Ask the tutors to assign you a medical student, and write up your notes now. I will need to check them before you go back to the house. Keep her in a dark, quiet environment, follow the Tweedy diet, and allow her labour to progress naturally. If she fits once, you and the medical student will manage the situation appropriately. If she has multiple fits, St John Ambulance will bring her here. I will speak to them about the possibility, so they are aware.'

Peggy waited.

'That is all, Miss Cassidy. You may go.'

'Yes, Sister.'

Turning, she saw Dan at a nearby desk, white coat and all.

'Miss Cassidy!'

Eyes dancing at his formality, she walked towards him. It had been a few weeks since their theatre outing, and their group were now firm friends. Each time Peggy saw Dan though, her heart skipped – much as it was doing now. And then she would feel guilty – much as she was feeling now. He was the son of the man who had basically killed Aunty Bridget. She should not be fraternising with him in any way.

'I've thought a lot about our chat about poverty at the theatre that night,' he said, keeping his voice low. 'You said that if medical students did a lot of home births it would give them a better understanding of people's real lives. So I decided to ask for some experience on the district.'

Her jaw dropped. 'You did?' It was strange to hear that she had influenced him. Strange, but nice. *Oh, God.* This whole thing was a mess. Why the hell did the son of the hated Dr Sheridan have to be so . . . so . . . ? She swallowed.

He nodded. 'The assistant master told me earlier today I can do it. I'd really like to take on the case you just mentioned.'

*Interesting case. Good learning. Perfectly logical.* She mustn't read anything else into it. Not that she should be even hoping he liked her in a particular way. He was entirely out of bounds.

'Oh, good!' she said brightly, hoping her inner turmoil wasn't showing. 'Do you want to come with me and we can ask the tutor together?'

'Absolutely.' He turned to walk alongside her, and she took a step to the right, walking with him but clearly apart. Wouldn't do for Sister Guinan to think there was anything going on. Peggy could almost *feel* the woman looking at them. And of course there was nothing going on between them. Nothing at all.

# 18

The assistant master was in charge, as it happened, and once he had heard the details he commended Peggy for her observation and reporting. 'We cannot be too careful,' he said, 'and we need the midwives to remember the possibility of eclampsia. Well done, Nurse Cassidy.'

'Thank you, sir.' Peggy could feel herself blushing. 'I'm going to write up the notes now.'

'Sheridan.' He turned to Dan. 'I suggest you both get something to eat before returning to this woman's home. You'll need to stay with her through the night. I'll send someone to relieve you in the morning.'

'Will do.'

'Oh, and I'll get one of the others to prepare a medical bag for you. They can bring it to the dining hall. Magnesium sulphate and morphine, and keep an eye on the hypertension. No examinations – stimulation is to be avoided.'

'Yes, sir.'

They were too early for tea, but once they understood what was happening the kitchen staff made them sandwiches and a cuppa. Having finished her note-writing, Peggy sat across the table from Dan, hugging her cup with both hands and trying not to stare at him too much. He quizzed her again on Mrs Halliday's obstetric history and current symptoms, and she offered to borrow an extra bike from the nurses' shed to save him the walk.

'Only ten minutes if we cycle, but a good half-hour to walk!'

Although only half past five, it was already dark when they ventured out. Down Parnell Street they went, turning into Capel Street. They chatted as they rode – mostly about the dreadful events in Germany, where businesses and homes belonging to Jews had been attacked the night before last. *The world can be such a bad place*, Peggy thought, half-wondering if her mind was mixing up her shock and horror about the stories on the news with concern for Mrs Halliday and memories of what Dan's da had done to lovely Aunty Bridget. The night was cold and clear. She could see her breath, and the air was cold enough to hurt her throat.

Peggy had learned the route earlier, so she led the way as they headed to Brunswick Street, then down Manor Street and finally into Stoneybatter proper. It was like a village within the city, she mused – a tight-knit community where the people seemed to look after each other. Rather like the Rock streets in West. A pang went through her as she wondered what Ma and Da and the rest of her ones were doing right now. Despite her worries beforehand the homesickness had been manageable up to now, but occasionally it pierced her. She could hardly wait to go home and see them all for Christmas. *Only a few weeks more.*

The truth was there was no time for homesickness. She fell into bed every night exhausted, slept deeply, then was immediately back into the busyness of life as a pupil midwife as soon as she rose.

Leaving their bikes at the gable end, they made their way in silence to the Hallidays' door. It was closed, but there was

## The Irish Midwife

a hint of warm light at the edges of the living-room curtains. Peggy knocked, and a moment later a young man with rolled-up shirtsleeves opened the door.

'Midwife calling!' said Peggy with a smile.

He opened the door fully, beckoning them in. 'Are you Nurse Cassidy who came earlier? From Belfast?'

'I am indeed. And this is Dan Sheridan, a medical student.' She smiled. 'He's from Belfast too.'

'Well, isn't that class? Nice to meet some northerners! Come in!' In they went, and within minutes the men were talking about the state of hurling in Antrim and in the Ards. Mr Halliday had lit the fire, and the living room was cosy and warm.

'Is Mrs Halliday still lying down?'

'She is. I brought her tea a wee while ago. I hope that's all right.'

Peggy nodded noncommittally. 'I'm just going to go up and check on her.'

She knocked gently at the bedroom door, hearing Mrs Halliday's voice inviting her in. 'How are you doin', Mrs Halliday?'

'I think it's happening, Nurse.' She was sitting on the bed, rocking from side to side. The big light was still off, but Peggy could see her clearly via the landing light. The room was cold, though. Mrs Halliday closed her eyes and continued to rock.

'Oh, that's great to hear.'

Toxaemia (also known as eclampsia) seemed to resolve itself after the birth, Peggy knew. Sometimes it happened straight away, but in the lecture they'd heard about a small number of women who'd continued to have convulsions for a few days afterwards. The cure for eclampsia, the doctor had pronounced, is to have the baby. They were reluctant to perform caesareans on these women, as apparently the mortality rate was even higher with a surgical birth. She swallowed, praying that Mrs Halliday and her baby would come through the night safely, and would survive the next few days.

Once the pain had passed, Mrs Halliday opened her eyes. 'I haven't told Will I've started – my husband, I mean. I don't want him getting all worried.' She rolled her eyes. 'He'll only make my nerves worse.'

'We can tell him later, once things really start to progress.' Peggy was already getting her Pinard out. 'Can I have a listen? No, just sit there, as you are.'

Women with suspected eclampsia were to avoid any form of stimulation – no food, no vaginal examinations, not even palpation of the abdomen. Gently, Peggy held her Pinard against the same spot where she had found baby's heart earlier. Thankfully, the heartbeat remained strong and steady, and Mrs Halliday seemed in good form. 'How's the headache?'

'It's eased a bit, thank God. Lying down in the dark really helped.'

Peggy placed a thermometer under her tongue. 'Good. We need to keep the lights low.' Once the thermometer had been in for a good minute she checked it. No fever. *Good.* If anything, Mrs Halliday was a little cold, which was hardly surprising. It must be close to freezing outside, and there seemed to be no heat at all coming up from the living room below..

She glanced around. 'Do you mind if I light the fire? We'll be up here for a while.'

## The Irish Midwife

'Get Will to do it.' She bit her lip. 'So, do you really think this could be it?'

'Maybe. You never know for sure at this stage. Labour can start and stop for a few days, or sometimes it just goes ahead steadily from the beginning. Have you had a show in your underwear?'

'Yes! Yesterday. Sort of mucousy. With blood.'

'Fresh blood?' Peggy's heart skipped in concern, but Mrs Halliday shook her head.

'No. Old and brownish.'

*Whew.* 'Good. All normal.'

Mrs Halliday tilted her head. 'I hear voices downstairs. Who's down there?'

'A medical student called Dan Sheridan. They're allowed to do some work on the district at times. Is it all right with you if he's here?'

'Yes, no bother.' She sent Peggy a keen look. 'Is something wrong with me?'

'I'm going to be honest with you, Mrs Halliday. The fact that your swelling came on so quickly worries me. Plus the headache. It might be nothing, but I'd like Dan to check your blood pressure if that's all right?'

'Yes, aye. Bring him up.'

'Thank you.'

Another pain came then, and Peggy sat with her, encouraging her as she breathed carefully through it. It was always amazing that women seemed to know what to do – unless they were panicked. The rocking, the breathing . . . instinct was a wonderful thing.

A little later, with the fire lit and a small table lamp plugged in by the bedside cabinet, Dan came up. Mrs Halliday had been complaining that her headache was getting more intense again, and worse, the room was spinning, she said, and there was a strange tingling all over her. *Not good.*

Dan's manner was excellent, Peggy noted. He came across as reassuring and competent, without talking down to Mrs Halliday. Taking the sphygmomanometer from his medical bag, he attached the cuff to Mrs Halliday's arm, inflating it using the attached bulb. He then pressed the end of his stethoscope to her inner elbow, listening carefully and watching the pressure gauge.

'Right.' He released the cuff. 'Your blood pressure is fairly high, Mrs Halliday.'

'What does that mean?'

'It means the force of the blood pushing through your arteries is too strong. It can happen in late pregnancy.' He went on to discuss the sudden swelling in her feet, ankles, and hands, as well as the headache and the tingling. She confirmed she had had no visual symptoms like flashing lights or blurred eyesight. All the while Mr Halliday stood beside them, his shoulders tight and his brow furrowed.

'So what do we . . . Oh, I don't feel a bit well.' Mrs Halliday put a hand to her head. A moment later convulsions overtook her and she fell onto the bed, her body stiffening and jerking.

# 19

Dan and Peggy sprang into action. Peggy's heart was thumping, but she knew what to do. Glancing at the tiny fob watch pinned to her uniform, she noted the time: six forty-five. Dan turned on the big light, then together they placed Mrs Halliday on her side so she wouldn't be harmed by bumping into the headboard or bedside table. Peggy was keeping a careful eye on her breathing, making sure she hadn't swallowed her tongue. Carefully, she loosened Mrs Halliday's clothing, undoing the zip of her dress and unhooking her undergarment. At the same time Dan was preparing the magnesium sulphate injection, which he then administered deftly into Mrs Halliday's thigh.

'What's happening? What's going on?' Mr Halliday's voice was panicked.

'Your wife is having convulsions, Mr Halliday. Can you boil some water for us, please? We will need a large bowl of hot water, as well as some clean cloths.'

At Dan's words – spoken with calm authority – Peggy could see reason return to Mr Halliday's eyes.

'Hot water. Cloths. Yes.' He made for the stairs, his energy entirely focused on the important tasks he had been given.

'Tonic-clonic seizure,' Dan said. 'Grand mal.'

'Yes. Likely eclampsia.' Peggy angled Mrs Halliday's face towards the ground, and thankfully the foaming saliva and mucous began to drain. Grabbing the cloth she had placed on the woman's forehead earlier, she caught the thick fluid with it, using a corner to mop the side of Mrs Halliday's mouth.

'Hopefully the mag sulph will do the trick.'

'How high was her blood pressure?'

'High, but not severe. 140 and 90.'

Peggy exhaled. 'So hopefully we can manage this. Hopefully she won't keep fitting.' Their eyes met briefly. *I'm glad he's with me.* She knew she shouldn't feel that, but she did.

'I'm glad you're with me.' His voice was low, but she caught her breath. It was as though he had read her mind.

'I was thinking the same.'

Mrs Halliday's body was stilling. 'It's stopping.' She glanced at her fob. 'Nearly ten to seven. Four minutes.'

'It seemed longer.' He exhaled in relief.

'Mary lent me her fob – it's so handy to have it!'

He agreed, then turned back to their patient. 'Let's keep an eye on her breathing and check her pulse.'

Mrs Halliday's breathing was laboured, her throat filled with phlegm. Peggy ensured she was securely on her side, gently lifting her chin in the hope it might help her breathe better. Dan was checking her pulse, and Peggy noted there was no sign of blueness around Mrs Halliday's lips or in the space below her nose. *Cyanosis.* That's what the tutor had called it. It was a sign of low oxygen. She checked the woman's fingernails too, just to be certain. Healthy and pink. *Good.*

By the time her husband returned with a bowl of steaming hot water, Mrs Halliday was conscious again, and sitting on the edge of the bed. She seemed a little

## The Irish Midwife

confused, fairly drowsy, and appeared to have no memory of her fit.

Mr Halliday set the bowl down on the chest of drawers beside Peggy and Dan's equipment then, wordlessly, he dropped to his knees before his wife, enveloping her in a hug. Peggy's eyes met Dan's and they both turned away – Dan to tidy away his syringe and mag sulph bottle, Peggy to retrieve her Pinard. She would listen in to the baby's heartbeat again in a moment. The bowl of water was too near the edge of the chest of drawers, and spontaneously they both reached out to push it to the back. Their hands touched, and Peggy held her breath, looking at Dan. They both stood frozen, hands touching and eyes locked on one another, while behind them a man cried from love and relief, and a bewildered woman soothed him.

Peggy swallowed, a surge of emotion flowing through her. *Dan. Dan Sheridan. Dan.*

Behind them, it sounded as though Mr Halliday was getting to his feet. 'I'll get those cloths,' he muttered, his voice thick.

'Thanks, Mr Halliday.' Peggy turned, but he was already halfway out the door. 'Now, how are you feeling?' she asked Mrs Halliday.

'A bit dizzy, to be honest.' She was gripping the mattress beneath her with both hands.

Peggy sat beside her. 'It's only to be expected. Take big deep breaths and stay where you are.'

Mr Halliday was more composed by the time he reappeared. He had questions though – lots of questions. Sensibly, Dan took him downstairs – the very fact that Dan was leaving the room would be reassuring to both Mr and

## Seána Tinley

Mrs Halliday. Peggy then explained as best she could to Mrs Halliday what had happened, and that Dan had administered medicine via an injection. She rubbed her thigh in wonder.

'I don't remember it at all!' She shuffled, then frowned. 'Is my zip down?'

'Aye. I needed to loosen your clothes – but I made sure you were respectably covered.'

'Thank you. You're an angel.' She bit her lip. 'Is the baby all right?'

'Let's see.'

Mrs Halliday lay down and Peggy helped her lift her dress. Once again she carefully placed the Pinard horn where she had found the foetal heart earlier, pressing her ear to it. Reassuringly, there was a steady little heartbeat within. 'All good,' she confirmed. 'Now, can I help you into your nightdress?'

'Ah, that'd be lovely. Thanks, Nurse. Second drawer.'

'Here you go. And I see you've got your nappies and baby clothes here too. These are beautiful.'

Mrs Halliday smiled shyly, placing a hand on her bump. 'We're married over five years, with no children.' She began rocking gently – something that Peggy noticed, but did not comment on. 'I can afford to spend a bit more.'

'Quite right too!' Peggy turned off the big light, enveloping them both in the cosy glow from the fire and the lamp. 'Now, let's wait a while and see if this baby still wants to come tonight.'

\* \* \*

Dan was shook. His insides were in absolute turmoil. While giving (he hoped) the appearance of calm reassurance to

Mr Halliday, inwardly his mind was beginning to look analytically at what had just happened. He had managed emergencies before. He was nearly qualified, after all. But never before had he been so far away from all medical colleagues – from equipment, and surgery, and expertise. *This is what my da does.*

Being the only doctor in the building felt very different to being part of a team of doctors and being told what to do, or knowing someone more experienced was there to correct him if he drifted from the right path. All his life, he had been obedient. A good boy. A good son. A good student. Does what he's told. *Yes, sir. No, sir. Three bags full, sir.*

Tonight, it had all been down to him. Peggy beside him as a reliable, competent midwife and he, doing things without direct instruction. Once more, he reviewed his own actions in caring for Mrs Halliday. *Yes. All correct.* He exhaled, conscious that gradually, inexorably, he was changing. And in that change he was discovering who he was and what he could do.

'Looks like it's boiled,' he said lightly, pointing to the kettle. Mr Halliday had already spooned some tea into the china teapot, and he watched as the man added boiling water, his hand shaking ever so slightly.

*He's shook too.* Shook, he mused, was a very useful word. They didn't use it in the north, but he was glad he'd come across it, for it perfectly described the shaken up feeling within him. Mrs Halliday was safe with Peggy, and he'd left the door between the living room and the hallway open in case she should call – even though it represented the cardinal sin of Letting the Heat Out.

*Peggy.* Understanding flooded through him. The other reason for his inner bewilderment was Peggy, and the moment they had shared upstairs. Never had he felt so close to another human being. It was actually . . . *scary*.

Yes. He was frightened of this. Of the enormity of his own feelings. Of the power she had to hurt him. For, despite moments like this, she was not pursuing him the way he was pursuing her. *Be careful*, he warned himself.

He didn't *want* to be careful. He wanted to ask her to be his girl. To be his everything. But instinctively he knew that if he pushed too hard, he would lose her entirely. Something was holding her back, he knew not what. But until he could find out what it was, he was powerless to address it. And since she still mostly kept him at a friendly arm's length – well out of kissing distance – he hadn't even been able to deepen their friendship. *Until tonight.*

That moment upstairs had changed things between them, he was sure of it. But instinct told him Peggy was more likely to run from it than embrace it. But why?

'There y'are.' Mr Halliday passed him a cup of tea, then sat opposite him at the kitchen table.

'Thanks. So, you work on the railways, Peggy said?'

'I do, aye.' As the conversation went on, Dan gave Mr Halliday his full attention, pushing all other thoughts aside for now. This was as big a part of his job as checking blood pressure or administering medicines, and he was beginning to understand why.

★ ★ ★

## The Irish Midwife

Mrs Halliday's baby was born safe and well at five thirty in the morning. Peggy couldn't help but shed a wee tear as she witnessed the joy with which Mrs Halliday welcomed her son. She was crying and smiling all at once, her garbled words a mix of wonder, delight and absolute amazement. Dan had returned to the bedroom an hour before, explaining that Mr Halliday was asleep in an armchair by the fire. When the baby was out and safely in his mother's arms, he and Peggy shared a grin, giving Peggy a hint of that tremendous feeling she'd felt earlier. This though, was fine. Shared joy, connection, but it was . . . *contained*, somehow. Nothing too big for her to handle.

'Can I bring him up?' he murmured to her.

She nodded. Normally the fathers weren't invited in until after the placenta was delivered, but this situation wasn't normal. 'Aye, but only for a few minutes. Make sure he knows.'

Dan nodded, and a few minutes later he returned with a groggy-looking Mr Halliday – who cried again, then apologised for crying. They told him to wise up, that lots of fathers cry, and not to be worrying about it.

'Father,' he said in wonder. 'I'm a father!'

By the time Desy and a qualified midwife called Dolores arrived at eight thirty, the afterbirth was out, the baby had had two feeds, and Mr Halliday had cooked bacon and eggs for himself, Dan, and Peggy. Mrs Halliday was ravenous – as well she might be – and was tucking into her own breakfast of tea and toast in bed, having been told she needed to wait the recommended twelve hours from her convulsions before having anything too heavy – as recommended by Master Tweedy. Her baby – a gorgeous wee thing who had been looking about him with great curiosity before being overcome by sleep – was swaddled and tucked in beside his mother. Peggy was standing by the chest of drawers enjoying the food, the delicious tea, and the relief of knowing that all had gone well. By nine o'clock she and Dan were on their bikes, having been given hugs and handshakes by the grateful parents.

'Wow,' said Dan as they began cycling. 'That was some night.'

'We did good.' Both knew there was still the possibility that Mrs Halliday would have another fit in the coming days, but with the baby out the risk would now begin to reduce.

'Aye, and Dolores and Desy get the easy part!'

'I assume we'll be off duty today,' he said. 'How does that actually work on the District?'

She shrugged. 'I plan to sleep, then call back to see Mrs Halliday later.'

'Let me know when you're going, and I'll come too.'

'All right.' She could hear the reluctance in her own voice, and almost over-corrected it by saying something more. Something warm. *But no.* Better if she didn't get too involved with him. Last night's incident had to serve as a warning. He was Dan Sheridan from Derryvolgie, son of a doctor. Son of the man who had reported Aunty Bridget. And Aunty Bridget had died that night. Her family would never forgive his, and she could do no less. Aunty Bridget had *died*, for God's sake!

As well as that she was Peggy Cassidy, former handywoman, from the Rock streets, daughter of two millworkers. He was a rich doctor's son from South Belfast, and he'd be a doctor himself next year.

And doctors didn't pair with millies. It simply wasn't done.

# 20

*Tuesday, 20 December 1938*

Christmas break had finally come, and Dan and Peggy had decided to take the same train home to Belfast. Fearful of the power she had to hurt him, Dan had done his best to maintain a cool air with her – which was difficult since Paudie and Anne were now doing a steady line, and the group of four lads and four girls all sat together at every meal and spent all their off-duty time together. While this had given Dan plenty of opportunities to build a *friendship* with Peggy, he couldn't honestly work out if he'd made any progress in *wooing* her. Of course it didn't help that he was too nervous to woo her openly. Did she even know how much he fancied her?

They had all got to know each other much better – their opinions, moods, sense of humour . . . Peggy had a dry wit that wasn't always obvious, but which Dan had learned to spot and appreciate. She chewed her lip when she was worried, became a little curt when cross or anxious, and would go out of her way to support someone who was feeling sad or frightened. She was an absolute diamond.

She remained friendly to everyone, interested in everyone, and seemed just as happy to be conversing with Paudie or Eugene or one of the girls as she did with Dan.

Yet something within Dan *knew* she liked him more than the others.

He now believed that she liked him against her better judgement, which was why she gave him little hints to back away at times. Like a wary horse or nervous dog, she'd send out signals that said 'Keep away', and he was getting sick, sore, and tired of it. Eventually, for his own good, he knew he'd either have to bring things to a head, or give up on her.

Booking the same train had been the obvious thing to do. The medics were returning to Dublin the day after Boxing Day – or St Stephen's Day as they called it in the Free State – while the pupil midwives didn't have to return until a few days later on the thirtieth of December. Mr Halliday had spotted them at Amiens Street station while on duty and promptly issued them with first-class tickets, which Peggy seemed particularly delighted about. Baby Halliday was apparently thriving, his wife had had no further health issues, and he was on top of the world.

Sitting opposite Peggy on the train as they passed through various towns on their way north, Dan eyed her surreptitiously and wondered if maybe the whole damn thing was in his imagination. He was going to miss her terribly. Oh, he would miss his whole life in Dublin – the freedom and independence he'd enjoyed these past few months had been amazing. But he would miss her most of all.

They passed through Malahide and Balbriggan, the winter sun sparkling on the sea. Then Drogheda, a busy junction. They had spent the journey so far chatting idly about their work, their friends, the Rotunda . . . even the news.

## The Irish Midwife

Many Irishmen were fighting in the Spanish Civil War – on both sides – while the papers reported that the British were building up their supplies of arms. At the same time the Nazi government continued to introduce anti-Jewish rules and laws. They were even planning a law that prevented Jewish women from acting as midwives. None of it boded well for continued peace in the world.

Dan was looking forward to discussing it all with his da. Mother would probably not be very interested – unlike Peggy, with whom he had had many conversations about politics and world affairs. Had she someone at home that she could talk to about such things?

It occurred to Dan now that he knew very little about her family. And since he could, in his head, name most of their other friends' brothers and sisters, surely that was a bit odd? Thinking about it, he realised that when those conversations came round in their group Peggy almost always gave general answers, then turned the question on someone else. With a sense of experimentation, he decided to try something.

'You're from a fairly big family, aren't you? Will they all be at home for Christmas?'

Was he imagining it, or were her shoulders suddenly a little tense?

'There's only six of us, plus Ma and Da and my granda. That's not a particularly big family.' She sent him a challenging glance. 'Aren't you an only child? I'd say that's small.'

He had to laugh at this. 'Yeah, fair point. One-child families are very definitely not the norm in Ireland. My ma once said she'd had "women's problems" when someone dropped a hint to her about having another child. I remember it, because even though I was young, I recall how angry she was afterwards. Kept going on to my da about how rude the woman was.' He eyed her keenly. 'But enough about me. Six children. Are you somewhere in the middle?'

'Gerard, Antoinette, Peggy, Sheila, Joe, Aiveen,' she listed in a singsong voice. 'Our Gerard and our Antoinette both got married in August, so the house felt half empty. Then I went away in September.'

He had names. *Definite progress.* 'So you'll be back, but are Gerard and Antoinette living elsewhere now?'

She bristled. 'Of course they are. They both found houses to rent fairly near home.' Her expression became thoughtful. 'I'd guess our Antoinette and her husband will come to Ma's for Christmas dinner. Gerard might go to his wife's family. That'll be really odd.'

*Rent, not buy.* Peggy always wore the same clothes on a Sunday, so he'd already realised her family weren't particularly well off. Enough money to cover her training fee, but not enough to buy houses for their children. Perfectly reasonable. His own parents wouldn't be able to buy six houses! 'How old are the younger ones?'

'Our Sheila's fifteen now. Joe is eleven. He hates school – and loves the hurling.' She frowned. 'Or at least he did, when I last saw him at the end of the summer.'

'You miss them.' It was a statement, not a question.

'I – I do.' There was a hint of thickness in her voice. 'Wee Aiveen most of all.'

Dan couldn't quite believe she was telling him all this. 'How old is Aiveen?'

'She's six now. She was five when I left.' Her chin trembled a little, and her hands were twisting in her lap. 'She'll probably have forgotten me.'

## The Irish Midwife

Without even thinking about it, he reached across and pressed his hand over hers. She froze – there was no other word for it – and he withdrew. *Damn! And I was finally getting somewhere.*

'So,' she said brightly, 'tell me about your Christmas. What will yous be up to?' Her gaze held a hint of challenge. Oh, he knew *exactly* what she was doing. And there wasn't a damn thing he could do about it.

'Ach, it'll be quiet. We'll eat too much, Da will fall asleep in his armchair, and we'll have loads of visiting to do.'

'Visiting? Friends of your parents?'

'Mostly, yeah. We'll go see my granda too – my ma's daddy. He lives with my ma's sister on the Antrim Road. My aunt Mary never married.'

'I'm glad you're going to see them,' she said softly. 'Family is important.'

He nodded, but inwardly he was feeling uncomfortable. Apart from his parents, Mary and Granda were all he had, and he rarely saw them. *I should try harder.*

'My ma is Mary too.' Her lips clamped together, as if she regretted offering him more information, unsolicited.

'Most common girl's name in Ireland.'

'In Catholic Ireland, anyway. Although,' she pursed her lips as she mused, and he had to glance away, so powerful was the urge to kiss her, 'did you know that Joan, who is Church of Ireland, has a sister called Mary?'

'I did know that. I think we probably know most names in our friends' families.'

Now it was her turn to look uncomfortable. Yes, he had realised that she'd been reticent. Should he say it out loud, ask why perhaps?

173

'And then you've to go back on the twenty-seventh?' she asked, clearly changing the subject. 'This day week?'

'Aye.' *Best not to push her.* 'It'll be a pain, but sure they need us, so they do.'

She frowned, saying slowly. 'Strange to think that by next Christmas I'll be qualified and hopefully working in the Royal. I might not get any time off over Christmas as apparently they roster a lot of the newest girls for Christmas and New Year.'

'You're not tempted to go for a job in the Rotunda?'

'Definitely not. I couldn't be that far away from our ones. You?'

*I'd be happy enough being far away from my—* He refused to finish the thought. 'I honestly don't know what I'll do. The plan was always to come home and work in the Royal, but I do love Dublin.'

'Ah, Dublin's a great city, that's for sure.' *But not for me*, her tone clearly said.

*Right.* He needed to wise up. He was actually letting her influence his future plans, even though there was no understanding between them. No words, no kisses, nothing. He'd put an arm around her once, that first night on their way to Bewley's. She'd even seemed to like it.

But since then he'd had nothing concrete. The occasional touch of a hand. Their eyes meeting. *I am cracked on her though.* His gaze roved over her, trying to commit every detail to memory. Ten days without seeing her wee face. Without hearing her voice. Without that buzz within him when they spoke, or when she looked at him. How was he going to manage?

Turning his head, he looked out of the window. They were stopped at Newry, and soon would cross the Egyptian

## The Irish Midwife

Arch and the viaduct – a feat of engineering that had always impressed him. Eighteen arches, sweeping across the landscape in a graceful curve. As they left the town behind and gained speed he looked down as the ground dropped away, giving a sense that they could almost be flying. Below, he saw a small whitewashed cottage near the foot of the arches. A woman was standing outside, a little one on her hip, pointing up at the train. Birth, growth, parenthood, old age, death. That baby would grow, would most likely become a parent some day, would show their own child the trains . . .

He wanted that. Wanted to share his life with the right woman and make babies together. Sons or daughters, he'd show them the steam trains and the Eighteen Arches and the Lanyon building at Queen's. He'd take them to Bangor to paddle in the sea and up the Cave Hill to see the views over Belfast. He'd bring them to Dublin, to the zoological gardens and the Botanic Gardens, and he'd point out the beautiful residence in the Phoenix Park now occupied by Ireland's first president, Douglas Hyde.

In each of his fantasies, the woman by his side was Peggy. And he hadn't even kissed her.

They'd been silent for a while, and he was craving her attention again. *Jesus, I'm like a child!* 'Have you brought any books home to study over Christmas?'

She went a little pink. 'I have actually. I know the others think I'm mad. But I'm not mad, am I?'

'Not even slightly. I've brought two or three textbooks home, plus my lecture notes.'

'Aye, but you'll have written exams in February.'

He shrugged, pointing out that she had practical tests all the time, where she had to demonstrate understanding of anatomy, physiology, and pathology.

She smiled. 'I remember hearing those words on my first day, and not having a clue what they meant!' She went on to describe her first anatomy lecture, and how the professor had launched into detailed labelling without even explaining the basic anatomical terms. 'We survived it though, and I'm proud to say I can now distinguish the obdurator foramen from the sciatic foramen.'

'Ah,' he replied wryly, 'but can you locate the greater sciatic notch?'

The next while was spent on safe ground, discussing their studies. While tempted to refer to specific women and the complications they'd seen, they knew not to – the Rotunda valued respect, and confidentiality was part of that.

All too soon the countryside gave way to the streets and mills of Belfast. *Linenopolis*, it was known as. Apparently there were more linen and cotton mills in Belfast than anywhere in Europe, and Belfast was still the linen capital of the world. It was reassuring to spot familiar landmarks again, but at the same time Dan was dreading the parting of the ways that now loomed over them.

'You live near St James's, right?'

'I do.' She raised an eyebrow. 'I'm impressed you remembered.' She didn't look impressed though.

He tapped the side of his forehead. 'Over three years of medical lectures, plus my degree studies before that. I can hone in on details when I need to.' *Gerard, Antoinette, Peggy, Sheila, Joe, Aiveen,* he recited inwardly, hoping he'd still remember the list later. 'Whereabouts near St James's?'

'Oh,' she waved a hand vaguely, 'between St James's and the Whiterock.'

## The Irish Midwife

He knew the Whiterock Road. 'Near Corrigan Park? The GAA pitch opposite the cemetery?'

'You've played there?'

'Aye. Hurling and football. St John's have bate us many's a time.'

Now she looked impressed. 'Our Gerard plays for St John's. Wee Joe too. What's your club?' She seemed genuinely curious.

'St Malachy's. It's fairly new. I never really played for a club growing up. Got plenty of Gaelic games at school though. My school was called St Malachy's, too.'

She frowned. 'St Malachy's College? But that's up near the Antrim Road – North Belfast. It's practically in the countryside! Would you not have gone to school somewhere nearer home?' She raised an eyebrow. 'Like Inst maybe?'

Inst – the Royal Belfast Academical Institution – was renowned across the north as the cradle of leaders. Industry, medicine, law, politics . . . Many of the top people in the north had gone to Inst, or to Methody – the Methodist college.

'Inst is Presbyterian,' he replied flatly, not liking the edge to her voice.

'I thought they were open to all denominations.'

'In theory, maybe. In reality, they only ever have a handful of Catholics. Some of my parents' friends sent their sons to Inst.' He shrugged. 'Besides, my ma is from North Belfast originally. And my da went to St Malachy's.'

'So how did you get there every day? That's some hike across the city.'

'I was a boarder.'

'Course you were.' Her tone was mild, but somehow he'd known she would disapprove. 'Your da was, too, because I recall you saying he was from Mourne.' He nodded. 'You didn't fancy becoming a priest then? Isn't the seminary attached to the school?'

'It is, but I had no notion of being a priest. I used to pray *not* to get a calling when they did the vocations thing!'

She laughed. 'Same! The nuns used to do the rounds every year trying to recruit. Not that there's anything wrong with being a nun. It's not for me though.'

Their eyes met, then slid away again. The silence that followed held a hint of awkwardness.

'What about you? What school did you go to?'

'St Dominic's,' she said, naming the main convent girls' school in West Belfast. 'Ironically,' she continued, 'it's more or less straight across the road from the new Royal Maternity Hospital. It's like my life is lived in a triangle. Home, school, work . . . all of it within a square mile.'

'A square? I thought you said it was a triangle.'

She rolled her eyes at this, so he added, 'You also had a massive detour to Dublin!'

'True.' She seemed to reflect on this for a moment. 'I'm glad to have seen somewhere else, lived somewhere else. Most of the people I know have never left Belfast.'

'It changes you, doesn't it? Being in the medical student rooms is a bit like boarding school. Same craic.' He thought for a moment. 'But the independence of being in Dublin is something else.'

As he spoke, the train began slowing, having reached its final destination. Once it stopped he stood, handing down Peggy's bag before grabbing his own. The ache in his chest at the upcoming goodbye was a real, physical pain.

'Who's picking you up?'

## The Irish Midwife

'I'm not sure. I wrote to them last week once we knew which train we were taking.' She sent him a look that he couldn't quite read. 'Let's say goodbye here.'

'Of course.' He took her hand as if to shake it, then lingered. 'I hope you have the best Christmas with all your ones. I look forward to seeing you again in time for New Year.'

She left her hand where it was, making his heart thump so loudly that surely she must hear it. 'And the same to you, Dan.' Standing on her tiptoes, she pressed a fleeting kiss to his cheek, then went to turn away.

'Peggy!' She turned back to look at him, and in her eyes he saw all the longing he could have hoped for. Then she was in his arms, and his lips were on hers, and everything in the entire world was perfect.

# 21

Hurrying down the platform, Peggy did not look back. Already she was regretting her impulsive action. The kiss had been . . . she had no words for it, but inwardly she sensed wonder, and desire, and something beautiful, and enormous. Too enormous. It would not do.

She bit her lip. The last thing she wanted to do was to lead Dan on. Oh, she had felt for a long time that he liked her. Or at least, she had been fairly certain. But while he had been enjoying all the benefits of being a boarding school boy at St Malachy's, she had been working as a half-timer in the mills – three days at school, three days in the noise and humidity of the spinning room – until leaving school at fourteen. *And* she had been a handywoman – a job generally despised by doctors. *And* his father had reported Aunty Bridget. It was impossible. Completely and utterly impossible.

No matter what her heart said.

'Peggy!' Ma and Da were both there, looking real and solid and *oh*, so familiar. And beside them, holding Ma's hand, was wee Aiveen. They were all in their Sunday best, for going into town to the train station was an important event. Da would have taken time out of work, too – not something that happened very often.

The next few moments were a blur of hugs, and tears, and garbled half-sentences.

'Here, let me take your bag,' said Da. 'Bloody hell, it's heavy! What have you got in here? Spuds?'

'Even better – books,' said she with a grin, still making use of her handkerchief. The last time she recalled crying was during the play, and Dan had given her his. She had returned it a few days later – washed, cleaned and pressed, and it had cost her a pang to part with it. Aye, even back then she had liked him too much.

They began moving off towards the exit. The station was busy, but Peggy couldn't help but look for Dan in the crowd. *He's probably gone.* The notion pierced her, as she briefly anticipated the long days ahead without him.

'See you, Peggy!' Suddenly there he was, striding past with an older couple who must be his parents. She didn't recognise Dr Sheridan at all from that day outside Aunty Bridget's wake. But then, her attention had been focused elsewhere. Dumbstruck, she managed to half-lift a hand in acknowledgment.

'One of your new friends from Dublin?' Ma's tone signalled mild curiosity, but her eyes were darting all over the Sheridans. *Please don't let her recognise him!*

'Aye. He's the only medical student from Belfast and I'm the only trainee midwife from here, so we got the same train. We actually' – she used an exaggerated tone, hoping to distract Ma – 'were upgraded to first class!'

'What?' She and Da looked suitably impressed. 'So you were waited upon like a queen the whole way from Dublin?'

'I was. Free tea and everything!'

'Will you take me on a train some day, Peggy?' Aiveen had her by the hand, and Peggy felt like never letting her go.

## The Irish Midwife

'I will of course. It goes so, so fast. And there's steam, and sometimes the driver pulls the whistle. You will love it.'

Outside the horse and trap was waiting. Da threw Peggy's bag up and lifted Aiveen while Peggy and Ma climbed aboard. It was a two-wheeled trap, still common even in the city, and a tight squeeze, so Peggy put Aiveen on her knee as they set off. The chile was clearly delighted to see her, and chatted excitedly all the way home.

★ ★ ★

'Who was that?' Dan stifled a sigh at his mother's sharp tone.

'One of the pupil midwives. She's from here.'

'What's her name? Whereabouts is she from?' Ma was wasting no time.

'She's called Peggy Cassidy and she's from somewhere near St James's. I don't know exactly where.'

She sniffed. 'St James's is a mixed area, so that tells me nothing.'

Dan frowned in puzzlement. 'Mixed? I thought it was almost all Catholic?'

'I mean in terms of the *sorts* of Catholics who live there. St James's has some fine detached houses, but also rows and rows of two-up two-down rentals.'

'And what's wrong with that?' Dan's hackles were rising, but Da sent him a quelling look, so he subsided. He had promised himself not to let Mother wind him up. They weren't even in the car yet and already he felt like turning around and getting back on the train to Dublin.

'Well, nothing. Not really. They're probably good people,' Ma said, her tone decidedly patronising. 'But you should be making friends with people who are from better areas.'

*Better areas.* His eyes were rolling so hard already. *How does Da stick it?* It was going to be a long, long week.

\* \* \*

The days leading up to Christmas were always hectic in the Cassidy home. All the shillings and pennies Ma had been putting by all year were now being spent in a wave of extravagance. Extra meat – including the turkey – and vegetables. Bottles of beer, and a single bottle of whiskey. Dried fruit, spices, sugar, and any other ingredients needed to make the fruit cakes, pudding, scones, buns, and apple pies that would be baked and consumed during the Twelve Days of Christmas – all the way from Christmas Day to the feast of the Epiphany, which was known as 'Little Christmas'.

Ma had the clever knack of spending some of her Christmas savings from about mid-November. All of them were well used to the corner of the larder that contained treats including jellies, tinned fruit, and even occasionally, chocolate. These were assigned for Christmas, and well dare anyone touch them!

Wee Joe and his friends had been up the lower slopes of Sliabh Dubh gathering greenery, and the holly, ivy, and mistletoe had to be hung around the house. The Christmas crib was brought down from its box in the roof-space and reverently assembled on top of the living-room cupboard. Ma kept the wooden baby Jesus figure behind the crib, to be added to the tableau at midnight on Christmas Eve.

## The Irish Midwife

All the mills closed at noon on Christmas Eve, and that was the moment when Peggy always felt Christmas had begun. The twenty-fourth was a busy day for the whole family, especially the women and girls. Peggy, Ma, and Sheila spent the afternoon cleaning, baking, and preparing the meat and vegetables for tomorrow's feast, but once darkness fell, they paused, the whole family coming together to light the Christmas candle.

This privilege always fell to the youngest, and Aiveen was suitably solemn as she took the taper from Da and held it to the tall candle, which had been set in the traditional hollowed-out turnip. They all clapped, and Ma put the candle in the window, as she had done every year of Peggy's life. The women then returned to the kitchen to serve the Big Supper of red (smoked) fish with potatoes and butter. It felt like having two dinners in the one day, and was always a delight after the fasting and abstinence of Advent. There was even 'afters' – delicious rice pudding cooked in Ma's best baking dish.

Afterwards the boys and men would sit, while the women put younger children to bed, cleared away the supper, and completed their preparations for the next day – including preparing another rice pudding. Once wee Aiveen was settled – going up to bed after hanging one of Da's socks on the fireplace, and demanding stories of Santa alongside her prayers – Peggy headed back downstairs to help.

Passing through the living room, Peggy realised that Granda Joe was talking to Joe about the famine, and so she hovered in the kitchen doorway to listen, broom in hand. Granda Joe was over ninety, and had been alive during the famine – the *Great Hunger* as it was called in Irish.

## Seána Tinley

'And was there no food at all, Granda?' Joe's eyes were wide and round.

'Oh, there was plenty of food, son. That's why it was never a true famine. Boats filled to the neck with corn, and wheat, and barley left these shores every day for England. But they gave none of it to the Irish people. My mother and sisters starved to death. I had one uncle made it to Amerikay, but me and me da were the only ones left here by the end. Another one of me da's brothers tried to steal some food for his family, and was transported to Australia on a prison ship.'

'And what happened to his family?'

'They all died too. Died of the hunger.'

Joe looked shocked. 'How come you didn't die?'

'Me and me da walked all the way to Belfast for a place in the union workhouse. Their rations kept us alive. After the famine there was plenty of work, and very few to work it.' He put a hand on Joe's shoulder. 'So enjoying a grand feast like we're after eating is something special, son. Now don't you forget it!'

\* \* \*

The days leading up to Christmas were always hectic for the Sheridans. While Mrs Kinahan had the food shopping and the cooking under control, Ma always planned a series of visits around all of her friends' houses, and usually insisted on dragging Dan along.

Father would get out of it by working right up to the twenty-third – yes, and sometimes on Christmas Eve too, if needed. Dan could escape some of it by claiming he needed

## The Irish Midwife

to study, but his mother insisted he accompany her to at least two visits each day.

He also managed to get into town on the Thursday to buy his gifts. Ma, Da, Granda, his aunt Mary, and something for Mrs Kinahan. Not many people to buy for – only five in total. He stopped in the street as a sudden notion took him, then made for Sinclair's department store, emerging not long after with a sixth package, neatly wrapped in Christmas paper by the sales assistant. He mightn't be able to give it this side of Christmas, but simply buying it made him feel better.

On Christmas Eve they had been invited to a drinks party at the home of the Harbinsons on the Malone Road. Mr Harbinson was a lawyer, and his son Richard was about Dan's age. Years ago Dan had enjoyed playing with Richard – or perhaps, more accurately, with Richard's *toys* – when they visited. Nowadays of course it was all polite conversations while clutching a glass and trying not to yawn. As they parked the car on the drive and walked towards the large, brightly lit house, Dan braced himself for the evening ahead.

Briefly, he wondered what Peggy was doing. Whatever it was, it had to be better than this.

★ ★ ★

Peggy was exhausted. She had been working flat out all day, with only a break for the Big Supper, and there was still more to be done. Throwing another peeled potato into the pot of cold water, she reckoned four or five more would do it. The turnips were the hardest, being tough and hard to cut. She and Sheila had done them earlier – partly because one was needed for the candle – and so they were all chopped up and in a separate pot, ready to be cooked for tomorrow's dinner. Antoinette had come to help, too, and it had been lovely working alongside her. But it had been a long, long day. Peggy's back ached from having to bend over the table all afternoon and evening, and her feet were sore from standing.

But inwardly, she was contented. She was home, and home was wrapping her in the cosiest, warmest blanket of love and familiarity and safety. Her life in Dublin already seemed far away, almost as though it had all been a dream. Yet it was all too real – the books on the windowsill upstairs were a reminder of that. She hadn't so much as opened one since arriving home on Tuesday – there just hadn't been time. She shrugged inwardly as she peeled the next spud. Hopefully she wouldn't have forgotten everything by the time she went back to Dublin. Yes, she reckoned she could still locate the greater sciatic notch. The thought made her smile, and fleetingly she wondered what Dan was up to. Would he even think of her at all?

# 22

'Well, and what are you up to these days, Daniel?'

Dan gritted his teeth, exhaled deliberately, then took a sup of fine whiskey. Once it had hit the spot, he managed, 'I'm still in medical training, Richard. I've been down at the Rotunda in Dublin since August.'

They were standing by the supper table, which contained enough food to feed about five times the number of people present at the party. Still, no one would accuse the Harbinsons of stinginess, which was probably the point.

'Still training? You're at that years, man. When will you be done?'

'Next summer.'

'And what will you be at then? Will you stay in Dublin or will you work up here?'

Suddenly Dan had an inkling of how Peggy must feel under questioning about things she didn't want to reveal. 'Haven't decided yet. What are you up to yourself?'

'I'm a solicitor now. Working with Father in his firm.' He lowered his voice. 'Making a tidy sum already. More than the average doctor, I'd bet.' He glanced towards Dan's father. 'Still, we all need doctors now and again, so I'm glad some of you do it.'

'Whereas thankfully most people rarely need lawyers.'

Dan's jibe failed to pierce Richard's confidence. 'Ah, but they'll pay a good bit when they do need us.' Laughing at his own witticism, he then added, with a confidential air, 'Have you seen that Melissa Moore is finished boarding school? She's quite the looker!'

Ignoring the final statement, Dan contented himself by saying that yes, he was aware that Melissa had finished school. Well, how could he not be, since his ma brought her into the conversation at least three times a day? Melissa was here tonight, and he dreaded to think how much scrutiny he would be under if he so much as said hello to her. But *not* speaking to her would be rude, so he took the opportunity to tell Richard that he hadn't chatted to Melissa yet, and would do so straight away.

'Aye, you go for it, lad,' said Richard, his expression mournful. 'See if you have any more luck with her than I had.'

Exhaling, Dan walked away, seeking out Melissa. There she was by the window, with her mother and – *damn!* His own mother was with them. Bracing himself, he prepared to be nice under scrutiny.

'Ah, there you are, Dan! I was just telling Mrs Moore and her daughter how well you're doing with your medical studies.'

'Oh, I don't know about that, Ma – Mother.' He gave a twisted smile. 'They haven't kicked me out yet, for which I am very grateful.' *Jesus, I fell at the first hurdle.* So much for his determination to be nice.

Mother looked displeased, but Mrs Moore laughed lightly. 'You were always so clever at school, Dan. I've no doubt you'll make a fine doctor.'

He shrugged slightly. 'How are you doing, Melissa?' *No point in avoiding it.*

'I'm good, thanks. I finished school a few months go.'

'Aye, so Mother was saying. Good for you!'

'She's really thrown herself into charity work though.' Mrs Moore was the picture of pride. 'Haven't you, dear?'

Melissa shrugged. 'I might as well. It gives me something to do.'

'She's on the Royal Maternity fundraising committee,' Mother offered. 'Isn't that exciting?'

'Very worthwhile,' he said, then frowned in puzzlement. 'I thought they'd already raised all the money they needed for the building project.'

'For the hospital itself, yes.' She looked up at him, holding his gaze for a little too long. 'We're currently fundraising for another nurses' home.' She gave a tight smile. 'Can't have all those working girls living in squalid flats now, can we?'

'I suppose not.' The way she'd said 'working girls' had an insulting edge to it.

She slipped a hand into his arm. 'Let's go look at the tree. I spent *ages* today decorating it. I was quite *exhausted* afterwards, I can tell you!'

'Yes, go and enjoy yourselves!' Ma and Mrs Moore had the same indulgent expressions. Trying not to shudder, he walked with Melissa towards the huge Christmas tree.

★ ★ ★

The women were always last to bed on Christmas Eve, and the first to rise on Christmas morning. Peggy didn't mind one bit. This was important work, making a Christmas they would all enjoy. Antoinette had headed home about nine, Sheila was sent to bed at ten, and Peggy and Ma had kept going. By half past eleven they were done, so they made themselves a last cup of tea and sat quietly chatting, awaiting the midnight chimes. Ma then solemnly placed the baby Jesus figure into the crib, making a sudden lump form in Peggy's throat.

Had Our Lady been attended by other women when she gave birth in a stable nearly two thousand years before? It was entirely likely. And it mattered little whether those women were called midwives or handywomen. The job was the same – to be with the woman as she went through the day and night that would make her a mother. Or make her a mother again.

Being away from the Rotunda was making it easier to *see*. Peggy was still using all the skills she'd learned at Aunty Bridget's side, and honed during her apprenticeship with Mrs Clarke. But now she had a better understanding of how the body worked, and what complications to watch out for, and even the location of the greater sciatic notch. Midwifery training was basically making her a better handywoman. As she climbed into the big bed beside Sheila and Aiveen, she reflected that she had finally, it seemed, accepted Aunty Bridget's gift.

'Thank you, Aunty Bridget,' she murmured softly. 'Merry Christmas.' In her mind she started a wee decade of the rosary for Aunty Bridget, but was only on her third Hail Mary when sleep overcame her.

\* \* \*

## The Irish Midwife

Having dutifully admired the Christmas tree, Dan had managed to escape Melissa Moore by excusing himself to go to the bathroom, then taking up with Richard again when he came out. *It's a bad do when Richard is my best option.* Da had then rescued him from Richard, and they had shared a few moments companionship in a corner of the Harbinsons' enormous parlour.

He remembered getting on quite well with Melissa Moore when they were younger, although he'd never fancied her. Melissa hadn't changed. But he had – and it was partly because of Peggy. The filter of her worldview meant he had another lens through which he could view the world when he chose. And because of Peggy, he had been on the district this past month, seeing for himself the conditions that the working families of Dublin had to endure. The Hallidays with their neat two-up two-down in Stoneybatter were well off compared with the tenement families. He had no doubt that Melissa Moore would be horrified if she ever found herself entering such a building.

The Moores and Harbinsons and, yes, the Sheridans enjoyed luxuries that people like the Hallidays could only dream of. Da understood, thank God. But the others . . . Despite the fact he knew these were all nice people, he felt as though he no longer fully belonged in this world.

'I meant to say to you, Dan. Do you fancy a game of football over Christmas?'

*Anything to escape this.* 'Yeah, sounds good. When and where?'

'It's just a challenge match. A fundraiser for St John's. Corrigan Park on Boxing Day.'

Dan managed to remain outwardly calm. 'Will be good to get out of the house,' he said neutrally.

'Great! We can let the Malachy's boys know at Mass in the morning.'

Inwardly, Dan was delighted. Corrigan Park to play St John's! The two clubs had played each other quite a few times, but on previous occasions Dan hadn't known Peggy. Nor had he known that her brother, Gerard Cassidy, played for the club. Christmas was suddenly looking a lot better than it had been.

The remainder of the evening was reasonable. Dan circulated, told stories, listened, and generally set out to be agreeable, his mood lifted by the news he'd be in Peggy's neck of the woods on Monday. He could, it seemed, still act as though he belonged here.

Finally it was over. 'Goodnight, goodnight!' Mother was kissing Mrs Harbinson on the cheek, Da standing by with barely concealed impatience. Ma had had a few too many sherries, as many of them had. In fact the amount of alcohol consumed at the party was astounding. Dan himself had enjoyed a few Jamesons, preferring quality over quantity. Like Da, he preferred keeping his wits about him.

Midnight had been their signal to leave, but given the protracted farewells it was around half past when Dan finally got into bed. Sleep came to him quickly, buoyed by the whiskey, the lateness of the hour, and the knowledge that he would see Peggy the day after tomorrow. Life wasn't so bad, after all.

## 23

Christmas Day was still strange without Aunty Bridget. This would be the fourth Christmas without her. But they had Antoinette and her new husband Jim, and later hopefully Gerard and Colette would call.

Wee Aiveen woke early and was delighted with her gifts from Santa Claus – a new bow for her hair, a picture book and an orange. Everyone else exchanged the usual sorts of presents – knitted socks, a new tie for Da, neatly-sewn handkerchiefs made from old pillowcases, and ribbons for the ladies along with Mackintosh's toffees, new gloves, and even stockings.

Ma and Da then astonished them all by bringing out their gift to the family – a brand-new Murphy A34 wireless that they had been saving for since the weddings in the summer. It was beautiful – made of polished wood, with a gold-coloured grille to the front. They couldn't get it working at first, and had to wait until after Mass to have a proper go at it. So while the women worked on the dinner, the men set up the wireless.

'Jesus, Mary and Joseph!' The sound of a choir singing 'O Come All Ye Faithful' had just come through, clear as day. Cooking was momentarily forgotten as they all paused to listen. Ma blessed herself. 'It's like a miracle!' she declared.

Naturally they had listened to the wireless before – a few of the neighbours had sets – but having one in their own house was special. In Belfast, you could pick up both the BBC and Radio Éireann, which basically meant that the people of the north had access to double the channels available to those in Britain or the Free State. *One of the few benefits*, Peggy mused, *of being in this contested place.*

For the grand sum of sixpence Da had also bought a copy of the Christmas edition of the *Radio Times*, and they all perused it eagerly. As well as the programme listings it had puzzles, articles, and even photographs of the inside of Broadcasting House, including the control room. They soon spotted that a programme called *Irish Rhythms* would be broadcast at twenty past five, featuring jigs, reels, and hornpipes, and decided to tune in then. On the Irish radio news there was more information about the men who'd been lifted by the Belfast police under the Special Powers Act on Thursday morning. Apparently it was related to some sort of device that had been found in a diplomat's bag.

'Well!' declared Ma. 'We're gonna know everything there is to be known, that's for sure!'

There was plenty of eating too, with the roast turkey the centrepiece. While waiting for seats at the crowded table, Peggy and Sheila brought plated-up dinners to a couple of their elderly neighbours who lived alone but had decided to spend Christmas Day together. By the time they got back a few of the others had finished, so they were able to sit and enjoy the delicious food at their leisure.

## The Irish Midwife

After dinner everyone declared they were so stuffed they'd never eat again, yet when Ma and Peggy served the rice pudding after the Irish music, somehow they all found they had room for it. A few hours later at supper time, there was tea and cake, and once again, they all ate their fill.

They had turned the wireless off after the Nativity play, taking turns to perform songs and recitations by the fire. After Sheila, Gerard, and Granda had had their moments, Peggy took her turn with a creditable version of 'The Minstrel Boy', before getting them all going with a rousing chorus of 'A Nation Once Again'. Wee Aiveen sang 'Silent Night' all by herself, to great acclaim, Ma recited 'Ach I Dunno', and Da then brought them back to rebel songs with 'God Save Ireland'.

Gerard had called in time for supper but didn't linger. His last words to them all were not to forget there was a challenge match tomorrow. 'Corrigan Park at noon!' he said, waving a hand.

'So we'll have to make the dinner for a bit later then,' Ma decided, 'for we'll all want to go and see the game. Yous may all take a good breakfast, for it's all yous'll get till later on.'

Sheila groaned. 'I can't even think about eating tomorrow when I'm this full of fruit cake!'

'Aye, you'll soon learn, love. Bellies empty quicker than women can fill them.' Ma rose. 'Right. Let's get this lot cleared off, then it's bedtime!'

\* \* \*

Over the years Dan had played in many, many games of Gaelic football and hurling – including a schools final, once. He was a decent club player without ever having been in danger of being selected for the county, but he did enjoy both sports. Having dug out his old boots from the back of his wardrobe he stuck them into his canvas bag along with clean trousers and socks wrapped in a towel. At the last minute, he retrieved the package from Sinclair's department store and slipped it into the bag. *You never know what opportunities might arise.* He then made his way downstairs, no doubt a comical sight in football socks and shorts teamed with an old jumper and a pair of battered loafers. He'd be issued with a team jersey just before the game.

The journey by car to Corrigan Park was relatively short, and Dan's neck was near twisted off him as they drove through St James's and then up the Whiterock Road, wondering where Peggy lived, if she'd be at the game, if one of the houses they were passing was hers. While there were quite a few people walking towards the football field, he couldn't tell which one was Peggy, if any.

'Ah, good lad, Dan,' said Eddie, the *bainisteoir* – team manager, as Dan entered the St Malachy's team changing room. Taking a pencil from behind his ear, he wrote Dan's name on the sheet in front of him. 'You're starting at wing-back. How's your fitness?'

'Shouldn't be too bad,' said Dan, thinking about the hours spent on his feet every day as a medical student.

'Here, copy that out, son, would ya?' Eddie handed his team list to a young boy, who diligently began making a copy of the names and positions.

## The Irish Midwife

Dan was busy greeting the other players, glad to see them after so many months away. They were from all sorts of backgrounds, with many of them from the working-class Markets district. *Now*, he thought, *this is a hundred times better than making polite conversation with Richard Harbinson!*

'Jerseys on, lads!' Eddie threw the bag of jerseys to the ground and they all fished inside to find the right one. The jerseys were numbered 1–15, each number representing a specific position and role – 1 for the goalkeeper all the way through to 13–15 for the full-forwards, who would hopefully get a good few scores today. Dan quickly found the number 7 jersey and put it on, throwing his jumper on top of his bag. He had already put on his boots, sitting on the slatted bench to tie the laces. They ran out soon afterwards, immediately followed by their rivals, and the crowd in the small stand mustered up a decent cheer. Oh, it was a good feeling, to be running out onto a playing field again in an amber-and-black jersey!

The referee approached the manager, taking both copies of the team list – one for himself and one for the other team. He handed Eddie the St John's names, and Dan had a look over Eddie's shoulder. *Bingo!* Gerard Cassidy, top of the left. Peggy's brother.

'Have a bit of a run there to get warmed up. It would founder you, so it would.'

The stand was reasonably full for a club game, but there was no sign of Peggy. She might be there somewhere, but he hadn't spotted her. Interestingly, all the women on the St John's side were wearing the shawls he associated with mill-workers. Well, it made sense. Most of West Belfast worked in the mills.

'Let's go!' The referee was calling both teams to line out. Dan jogged into position, shaking the hand of the opposition number 10, whom he would be marking for the next hour. A moment later the referee threw the ball up, and the game was on.

★ ★ ★

Peggy pulled her shawl more tightly around her. The wind could be fierce in Corrigan Park.

'C'mon the Johnnies!' Da shouted as the ball was thrown in, and Peggy's heart skipped. Ah, there was nothin' like the exhilaration of football or hurling – standing with your family and all your neighbours to watch local young men don the blue-and-white and play for the pride of their parish. Her heart warmed, and suddenly the wind seemed not as fierce, the day less cold.

'G'wan, Gerard!' she called as her brother won a long ball from midfield. He managed to lay it off to the advancing centre half-forward but the resulting kick went wide. As the opposition keeper prepared to take his kickout, she looked at the team properly for the first time. Amber and black. Her heart skipped. 'Is that St Malachy's we're playing?'

'It is.' Kathleen, her handywoman friend, was by her side. It had been so good to see her again – and Mrs Clarke too. She had missed them both almost as much as she had missed her own family. *Well, they are family really.* Kathleen – as much a St John's supporter as anyone – didn't take her eyes off the game for a minute. 'We should beat them all right.'

## The Irish Midwife

But Peggy wasn't worrying about whether the Johnnies would win. Instantly she scanned the Malachy's players. *There!* Her heart skipped. *Bloody hell, it's him!* Dan Sheridan was playing at wing-back.

The rest of the game went by in a blur. Peggy was torn between supporting the Johnnies, cheering on Gerard, and watching Dan. *He's not a bad player.* And, *feck!* He looked good stripped out for the GAA. Unaccountably, she felt a sort of pride every time he did something skilful, almost as if he was in some way *hers*. That bloody kiss had made her heart worse, not better.

At half-time Father McCudden, the new parish priest, went down both lines to invite them all – both teams and their supporters – to the parish hall for a cup of tea after the game. Peggy's heart sank. How was she supposed to get out of going?

'You're very quiet, Peggy.' Ma's look was intent. 'Anything the matter?'

'No, no, not at all,' she lied, turning her gaze back to the game. 'That was off the ground, referee!' She could feel Ma looking at her, but maybe if she kept her focus on the game Ma would let it go.

Somehow she made it through the second half without, she hoped, awakening further suspicions in her mammy. The game ended in a comfortable win for the Johnnies – who were, after all, the current Antrim junior champions, and the crowds started making their way to the Whiterock Road end.

'Don't forget!' It was Father McCudden. 'Tea in the parish hall!'

'Actually, I think I'll go straight home and get the spuds on,' said Peggy.

'Indeed and you will not!' Ma's tone was firm. 'Father McCudden has invited us to the parish hall and that's where we're going! All of us.'

'But the chile's freezin!'

'D'ye think the priest has no heat in the hall?' She nodded firmly. 'We're going, and that's that.'

That was indeed that. Despite being twenty years of age, Peggy could not and would not openly defy her mother. So with the rest she trooped down the hill and along to St John's, Aiveen's little hand in hers and her chattering all the way.

Inside, Father McCudden's housekeeper was putting the final touches to the tea party she'd laid out. As well as dozens of cups and saucers there were plates of sliced fruit cake and buttered soda bread – the woman had clearly been working for hours to prepare everything. So they all exclaimed, and thanked her, and were grateful. Kathleen and a couple of other women went behind the big table and started pouring tea, and before long the hall was full of warmth, conversation, and laughter.

Peggy had made sure to stand in a corner, facing the door. Chatting with Ma and Gerard, she saw Dan the minute he came in. He seemed to be looking about, and she ducked behind Gerard – who was tall enough to hide her, or so she hoped. *Dan's looking for me!*

Ma was frowning, and looking from Peggy to the door and back again. 'Peggy?'

'I think I'll go and help in the kitchen,' she said, diving to the left.

'Wait!' They only heard that tone from Ma very, very occasionally. But when she used it, you obeyed. 'Stay here, Peggy.'

## The Irish Midwife

'But—'

'But nothin'. You're stayin' here, Margaret Cassidy.'

*God!* When your Ma used your full name you knew it was serious. Besides, it was too late to argue further. She had been spotted, and Dan was on his way. Heart pounding, she turned to face him. 'Hello, Peggy.'

He looked gorgeous, his hair wet from the bath and his skin glowing from all the healthy exercise. He was wearing a battered old jumper and some old loafers with plain trousers, and he blended right in with the St John's lads. She had never seen him look better. Or maybe she had, she realised, recalling the bemused expression on his face as they had surfaced from their astonishing kiss last Tuesday.

But they were in her parish hall, and Ma and Gerard were right there, and *feck!* This was so awkward.

She gave a strained smile. 'Oh, hello, Dan. Er . . . happy Christmas.'

'And the same to you.'

There was a pause. 'Is this your Gerard then?'

'Aye. Gerard, this is . . . This is Dan. He's training in the Rotunda too.'

'Ah, the wing-back. You done all right today.'

Dan laughed. 'Not well enough. Yous beat us fair and square.' He glanced towards Ma.

Peggy gave in, accepting the inevitable. 'This is my ma.'

He offered a hand. 'Nice to meet you, Mrs Cassidy.'

Ma eyed him assessingly. *Oh, feck.* 'Dan, is it?'

'That's right.'

'Tony!' She called Da, who was chatting nearby, and he came straight over. 'This is our Peggy's friend Dan. We saw him at the train station.'

His eyes widened briefly, then he shook Dan's hand. 'Good to meet you, Dan.'

Peggy had never felt as uncomfortable in her life. Strangely, everyone else seemed totally relaxed. The whole time they were chatting – about the game, the weather, the Christmas – she was praying for it all to end.

Then the personal details started to be exchanged. 'So are you from the Markets, Dan?' A logical assumption on Da's part, given that Dan was playing for St Malachy's.

'Eh, no. From Derryvolgie. Near St Brigid's church.'

'Oh, is that right?'

'You're Dr Sheridan's son, are you?'

*Bloody hell. Nothing gets past Ma.* She must have recognised Dan's da at the station that day. Peggy's insides were twisting with anxiety.

'I am.'

'Dr Sheridan?' Da looked at Ma. 'The one who—'

'—And you're following in your father's footsteps by studying medicine? Good for you!' Ma clearly and decidedly diverted the conversation away from Sheridan senior.

'Just like I followed you into the mills, Da!' said Gerard easily. He seemed unaware of the undercurrents.

'And you're doing great, son.' He turned to Dan. 'He's already a supervisor, and I reckon he'll be a manager before long.'

Dan looked suitably impressed, and murmured something appropriate. There was a pause. 'So do you go back to Dublin on the thirtieth, like Peggy?'

'No, I'm back tomorrow. No rest for the wicked medical students!' His laugh was self-deprecating. 'Right! I'd better go. See you in Dublin, Peggy.'

'Aye. See you then.'

As he walked away, Da and Gerard got stuck in analysing the game, and Gerard's performance. Avoiding catching Ma's eye, Peggy made for the kitchen, and stayed there washing dishes until the St Malachy's men were all gone.

★ ★ ★

Dan was gutted. While it had been lovely to meet Peggy's ma and da, and 'our Gerard', Peggy's demeanour had been anything but welcoming. She'd looked awkward and uncomfortable, and while technically reasonably polite had avoided even looking at him except when forced to. *She regrets kissing me.* She couldn't have made it more obvious. All his hopes were now crashing about him.

She had been so tense just now. *Because of me. Because I was there.* It struck him forcibly that her discomfort might be similar to his own experience of being forced into reviewing a Christmas tree recently, and he cringed in mortification at the parallel. Melissa Moore. *Is that how I make her feel?*

In the car on the way home he said very little, while Da drove and whistled a tune. Inwardly, his mind was racing and his stomach sick. *She didn't want me to meet her family.* But why? They were perfectly nice people, and he, hopefully, was not the sort of lad to embarrass her. By rights he should be more worried about her meeting his family, for his own ma could be a bit stuck-up to say the least.

One thing was clear. She didn't want to get to know him better, or for him to get to know her better. And she clearly regretted kissing him. As the realisation began to sink in, there was a roaring in his ears, everything else fading into meaningless oblivion. It was the sound, he realised dimly, of his own heart breaking.

# 24

*Dublin, Saturday, 31 December 1938*

'How's it going in here?' It was Sister Dolan, who often seemed to do night duty. Her voice was quiet, respectful of the labouring woman.

'All good,' Peggy replied softly. 'Mrs Dempsey is making good progress, and managing really well.'

'Labour pains increasing?'

'Yes. Every two minutes now, and lasting longer than the gap between.' Sister Dolan nodded. They both knew Mrs Dempsey was likely to be pushing before long.

'It's only twenty minutes to midnight. This might be our first new year baby!'

'Or even our last one of this year. She does have three children at home.' Parous women – those who'd had babies before – often progressed quickly.

'Grand so. I'll send you in another midwife or a medical student for the birth.' Many of the pupil midwives were now trusted to fully manage the births themselves – particularly those who'd gained crucial experience and confidence by working on the district. Including one who had years of experience as a handywoman behind her, though no one here knew that. There were always two people for the birth itself though – one to focus on the mother, one on the baby.

Nodding, Peggy turned back to Mrs Dempsey, who was in the full birth trance – eyes closed, rocking gently, breathing slowly and carefully.

Murmuring soothing words, Peggy rose and walked to the side table, checking that she had everything she needed for the birth. It was good to be back with labouring women again. She had reported for duty mid-afternoon today, and been immediately assigned to Mrs Dempsey. The hospital was busy, the babies of Dublin seemingly in a race to see who would be the firstborn of the New Year.

When it came to her work, Peggy hoped that her new serenity would persist. All last term she felt as though she had been fighting with herself in her head – almost as if becoming a midwife would be a betrayal of Aunty Bridget and all the other handywomen down the centuries. She knew better now. Midwives *were* handywomen, and she was both.

Tonight she had been consciously integrating all of her previous knowledge – the knowledge of the eye, the hands, the heart, the gut – with her new knowledge – the intellectual knowledge of the brain. And it felt right.

In being fully with the woman tonight, she had also had to manage her thoughts of Dan. How amazing it had been to see him play Gaelic, to have him meet some of her ones, to see how charming and natural he had been.

If only he hadn't been Dr Sheridan's son! If only he hadn't been wealthy!

Yet he had chatted easily with her family, seemingly unaware or uncaring that they were of a lower class to his own parents. And despite the fact he was son of the hated Dr Sheridan, the conversation had gone reasonably well. Not that Ma could ever approve of any particular friendship between a Cassidy and a Sheridan. Politeness was fine. Friendship, not so much.

There was another problem, and one that she didn't want to think about too much. That kiss had spoiled things, even though it had been one of the most wonderful things that had ever happened to her. She couldn't forget it, and she also needed him to understand that they couldn't do it again.

Her own fear and awkwardness had left her stilted and remote that day at the parish hall, she knew. Hopefully he hadn't particularly noticed or been hurt by it. While she knew they were worlds apart, and that there could never be anything between them, she also didn't want to lose his friendship. It meant the world to her.

Ever since that encounter on the day of the Gaelic football game, she'd been agonising over it all. Thankfully, nobody had mentioned Dan afterwards, and the dreaded interrogation from Ma hadn't happened. Briefly, she wondered why. It wasn't like Ma to be subtle about anything.

*Maybe*, she thought as she selected a couple of soft towels in which to receive and wrap Mrs Dempsey's baby, *maybe she doesn't care enough to even mention it*. Because the Sheridans from Derryvolgie Avenue were so far removed from the Cassidys from the Rock that she didn't have to. Maybe she trusted Peggy to have a bit of common sense and keep away from lads that were completely unsuitable. Including a lad who just happened to be the son of their enemy.

A groan from behind her brought her attention back to Mrs Dempsey. *That sounds promising.* The woman was sitting on the bed, leaning slightly against the headboard – her choice. She looked comfortable, so Peggy prepared to receive the baby there. Sister Guinan wasn't on tonight, thank God.

'That's good, *good*, Mrs Dempsey.' Waiting until the contraction eased, she quickly brushed Mrs Dempsey's hair back from her face in case it was annoying her.

'Pin it,' the woman muttered, and Peggy jumped to find a couple of hairpins. There were usually some in the middle drawer . . . *yes*!

As she straightened, the door opened. *Dan!* Seeing her, his eyes widened briefly, then his expression seemed to . . . *close*, somehow. Peggy, already returning to Mrs Dempsey's side, sent him a bright smile.

'Well! Mrs Dempsey, Dan Sheridan has joined us. He's a medical student and he'll be here to help with the birth. Is that all right with you?'

Mrs Dempsey nodded, then began the groaning-pushing sound again, bearing down with every part of her. Bending, Peggy lifted her nightgown a little to check. *Wow!* The head was already visible. 'Well done, Mrs Dempsey. The head is right there. Now breathe it out slowly, slowly . . .'

The contraction eased. Seeing her chance, Peggy deftly pinned back the strands of hair that were irritating Mrs Dempsey, at the same time explaining that she should try her best to let the head come out as slowly as she could. The last thing Peggy wanted was for the woman to have a bad tear, which seemed to happen more often when the head came out too quickly.

## The Irish Midwife

The woman nodded, unable to speak as her body was gripped once again by the overwhelming urge to push. Peggy could see her trying to slow it down, but Mrs Dempsey's body had other ideas, and the head emerged all at once, accompanied by fresh blood indicating a torn perineum – the skin between the woman's birth canal and her backside.

Keeping her voice calm, Peggy said, 'Well done! The head is out. Now breathe for a wee minute. Just breathe.' Watching as the baby's head rotated, she checked gently for the cord, then leaned back to await the next contraction. When it came, she gently eased her fingers around the anterior shoulder, gently helping it out from under the pubic bone. The second shoulder emerged smoothly and the baby slithered out onto the towel.

'Congratulations, Mrs Dempsey. A baby boy at' – she glanced at the clock on the wall – 'nearly one minute past midnight! Happy New Year!' She passed the baby up to his ma.

'Oh, oh!' Mrs Dempsey clutched her wee one, joy and relief written on her face. Peggy rubbed the baby's back gently with a second clean soft towel, then used it to cover both baby and mother. Important to keep them both warm.

The bleeding was continuing. Exchanging a professional look of concern with Dan, she bent to assess the tear.

'You're gonna need a couple of wee stitches there, Mrs Dempsey. Dan here will do that once the afterbirth is out. Is that all right with you?'

Mrs Dempsey didn't care, it was clear. She waved a vague consent, completely focused on her baby and the relief that her labour was over. Going through her usual post-birth routine, Peggy tidied up while awaiting the birth of the placenta. When it came she transferred it into a metal bowl, then gave way to Dan, who had been sitting quietly in his usual respectful way.

While she was tense to have seen him so soon after her return to Dublin, Peggy realised now it was a good thing. Get any awkwardness out of the way, and go back to their previous easy friendship.

She watched with a fair degree of admiration as he deftly stitched Mrs Dempsey's perineum while she held the light. Her other hand was resting on Mrs Dempsey's arm and she spoke softly to her throughout the procedure, the baby safely tucked in beside his ma.

'All done!' said Dan, stepping back to wash his hands again in the sink in the corner of the room. *That's his third time washing his hands since he came in.* Like the midwives, the medical students were very conscious of trying to prevent infection, which was good. Apart from the unnecessary vaginal examinations, which happened much more frequently than Peggy liked.

Once done, he dried his hands, bade them both a cheery goodnight, and left, leaving Peggy feeling decidedly deflated.

Sister returned then, with tea and toast for Mrs Dempsey, and soon afterwards baby had his first feed. Sister Dolan also confirmed that Baby Dempsey was the Rotunda's first baby of 1939.

'Congratulations!' said Peggy, enjoying Mrs Dempsey's delight. 'The last year of the 1930s. Hopefully it will be a good one!'

An hour later Peggy was allocated to support another birthing woman in another room. Two births in one night. That was new. But she took it in her stride, knowing it was a privilege to be with any woman during such a sacred time.

## The Irish Midwife

It occurred to her to notice how confident she was feeling in the role of midwife. By summertime, please God, she'd be fully qualified and seeking a job, having earned a Rotunda badge. Apparently she needed to write to the matron of the Royal Maternity Hospital in Belfast sometime in late June. They held interviews in late July – a prospect that seemed much more daunting than the regular tests she and her friends faced here. What did one do or say during an interview? She had no idea.

The medical students, too, would qualify this year – though their last exams were in August. Would Dan return to Belfast, or stay here? When they had spoken on the train, just before . . . When he had talked about it she had had the distinct impression he was considering staying in the south.

The second woman gave birth before six in the morning, and Sister Dolan – who was so kind – told Peggy to finish her shift a little early and get some rest. Gratefully, Peggy thanked her and headed back to the nurses' home.

Anne was just leaving as Peggy arrived back in their room. They spoke briefly about the New Year baby, then Anne rushed off, anxious not to be late. Once alone, Peggy finally allowed herself to think about Dan again.

He had been professional, polite, even friendly while they had both been caring for Mrs Dempsey. And yet she felt unsettled – sad, somehow. Something wasn't quite right. Something other than her own awkwardness about the kiss-that-shouldn't-have-happened. She couldn't put her finger on it, but there had been *something* different. Something missing.

Methodically she prepared for bed. Having access to the indoor bathroom again was bliss after ten days of an outhouse toilet and washing at the sink, and so she savoured each luxury as if experiencing them for the first time.

It was hardly surprising, she supposed, that Dan also might be a bit awkward with her. Their last two encounters had both been fairly dramatic. First, the kiss. And then, him meeting her family – or some of them, anyway. Still, at least now he knew something of her background.

While she was proud of her family, and loved them dearly, she was certain that Dan's parents would not want him to be in any way involved with a girl from the Rock streets whose whole family worked in the mills. Da's talk of Gerard's promotion to supervisor might have muddied the waters though – maybe suggesting they were all earning decent money. And he wouldn't necessarily have worked out that the Cassidy women – including fifteen-year-old Sheila – were also millies. She tutted at herself in exasperation. She couldn't honestly work out what he knew, and what he didn't.

Having reviewed Dan's behaviour that day a hundred times since, she couldn't fault him in that regard. He had been warm and charming, and had seemed genuinely interested in them all. The fact she herself had been lost in mortification throughout the conversation meant that she hadn't said much at the time. Afterwards, her hands plunged in hot water washing teacups in the parish hall kitchen, she had berated herself for behaving so awkwardly. She certainly wouldn't like him to think she was odd!

And now? As she climbed into bed, insight finally came to her. Dan hadn't done anything differently last night. What she had noticed somewhere at the back of her mind was not a *something*, but a *nothing*. It was an absence. Gone was the

*The Irish Midwife*

special way he'd always looked at her. Gone was the warmth in his eyes.

She was no longer special to him.

The pain that lanced through her was as powerful as it was illogical. Was this not what she had wanted? Friendship? An acknowledgement there could never be anything more between them? *Yes. Yes it was.* But now that she had it, she was overcome by emotion. Sadness. Loss. Devastation. It could never be. But oh, how she wished it could! Pulling the covers over her head she turned on to her side, crying bitterly.

# 25

*Wednesday, 1 March 1939*

Spring came, and with it – thank God – a hint of milder weather. The medical students had all passed their February exams, and were now focusing on their final few months in the Rotunda. The pupil midwives were also progressing well through their programme. Peggy was less and less afraid of revealing her shocking past as a handywoman, as all the midwifery trainees were rapidly gaining skills, knowledge, and confidence, and she was less at risk of standing out.

There were now quite a few pairings among the students. Anne and Paudie seemed cracked on one another, and at least three other couples were doing a steady line. Peggy had gone to the cinema with a medical student from Wicklow called John – mostly to divert her friends away from questioning her as to what had happened between her and Dan. She had stuck to her story that there had never been anything between them, and that they had always simply been friends. Anne in particular had looked sceptical, but had let it go.

John was a nice fella, but he didn't make her heart skip or race. Not even slightly. She thanked him at the end of their outing, but gave a clear *No* when he asked if she'd like to go with him again sometime.

Two weeks later, Dan started walking out with Fiona Ruane. Peggy knew Fiona fairly well. She was also a pupil midwife – from County Mayo – and sickeningly, she was a lovely girl, both good-looking and kind. On hearing the news from Anne, Peggy had managed to shrug and wish them well, saving her tears for the bathroom. Locking the door, she allowed her distress out, collapsing to the floor in a fit of sobbing.

'I've lost him,' she kept repeating – even though she knew she had never had him in the first place. 'I've lost him.'

She ran a bath, which served to both drown out any noise she might be making and hopefully explain why she was in the bathroom for so long. Anyone who needed the toilet in the meantime would go to the next bathroom at the end of the corridor. By the time she came out – the bath water almost cold and her freshly washed hair half-dry – she felt empty inside. There was nothing. No emotion. No distress. No regrets.

Dressing to go down to supper with the others, she prepared to act normally – just as though her heart had not been ripped from her chest, leaving a gaping, aching hole of nothingness. Thankfully, Anne chatted in a lively way the whole way down to the dining room, requiring only monosyllables from Peggy. Dan and Paudie were already there at their usual table, Eugene and Desy joining them as Peggy arrived. Joan was there too, but Mary was on night duty. Peggy and Anne took their usual seats – Anne beside Paudie and Peggy directly opposite Dan. *I can do this.*

Supper in the Rotunda was the same whether you were a woman in the ward or a staff member in the dining hall. Tea, toast, soda bread, and butter. Peggy made a show of adding milk to her tea before taking a slice of soda bread and buttering it slowly and carefully. The conversation ranged as widely as it usually did – from the cases they'd been involved in that day to the conclave electing a new pope, and the ongoing tensions in Europe.

Even in the midst of her own heartbreak, Peggy was worried, as they all were. What did it mean for them all? For Peggy's family? If war came, as some were predicting, would there be conscription in the north? The last thing she wanted was Da and Gerard going off to fight in some meaningless war between competing empires. Although, she acknowledged, that boy Hitler was a bad, bad boy – stirring up hatred among his own voters and ushering them blindly into going along with his incursions and ambitions. And now the Italians were at it as well, with their Fascist party banning Jews from being members. And Spain was already a lost cause. *Arrogance*, thought Peggy, recalling Julius Caesar's friends. *Manly arrogance*.

The so-called Great War was still a recent memory – their parents had all lived through it. Since the outbreak of war in 1914, Ireland had also experienced the Easter Rising of 1916, the War of Independence, and then the civil war. They were all bone-tired of war, and had hoped their generation would know peace. But with Germany and soon perhaps Italy seemingly determined to defy everyone in order to expand their empires, it seemed war was a possibility at the very least.

'Anyway, enough about that,' said Anne brightly. 'It might never happen.' She eyed Dan directly, and her next words sent horror through Peggy. 'What's this I hear about you and Fiona Ruane, Dan, eh? Come on! Spill the beans.'

Mortifyingly, Dan glanced fleetingly towards Peggy before dropping his gaze to his plate. 'Nothing to tell. We've been out for a walk a couple of times.' He looked up. 'Jesus, you can't do anything around here. Yous are like the British Army intelligence corps!'

'Nah,' Anne retorted evenly. 'British Army intelligence were useless. Do you not know they had no idea what Michael Collins even looked like, and that he used to deliberately cycle past Dublin Castle every day?'

'A great Cork man,' said Paudie sadly. 'The rebel county!'

Peggy couldn't help snorting, the anger rising within her finding an appropriate target. 'Collins was the only rebel yous had, and yous killed him!' Her words emerged with rather more vehemence than she had intended, and they all looked at her briefly, before Anne returned to the topic at hand.

'We're more like Collins's own intelligence branch,' she declared, 'for we actually have the information. Now, stop trying to get out of it and tell us the craic!'

Dan's shoulders were tense. 'I told yous, I've nothing to tell.'

'So you're saying there's nothing going on between you and Fiona then? Well, that's not what her roommate is saying!'

Despite looking deeply uncomfortable, he managed a respectable shrug. 'Her roommate can say what she wants. Doesn't mean it's true.'

'Really?' Anne was merciless.

*What the hell is she doing?* Peggy was powerless to intervene, as to stand up for Dan would only make things worse.

'For I was told,' Anne continued, '*specifically* that you and Fiona have been out alone together, and that you'll likely be doin' a line soon.' She leaned back, an air of I-rest-my-case about her.

'And what?' Dan now looked fairly agitated but, crucially, did not deny it. Ignoring the pain lancing through her, Peggy concentrated on the awkwardness of the moment. *Anne needs to back down. Jesus!*

'Everybody goes out walking all the time,' Dan continued, his voice unusually harsh and his brow furrowed. 'In fact you and I walked down the street last Saturday to buy the paper, but I don't see Paudie thinkin' there's something between us.'

'A fair point, Anne, you have to admit.' Paudie's eyes were dancing. He was clearly enjoying Dan's embarrassment. 'Now leave the lad alone.'

It was too late for Dan, who now looked really annoyed. 'Can people not go for a walk without bloody rumours starting?' He was glaring at her, his expression tight and a hardness in his eyes. *Jesus, he is seriously ragin'!*

'Ooh,' said Joan in a sing-song tone, trying to inject some humour into the situation, 'Somebody's getting thick.'

'Yes, I feckin' am!' said Dan angrily, rising to his feet. 'I mean, it's not as if I took the girl on a date to the cinema, is it?'

And with that he stomped off. As if by some sort of unspoken agreement, all eyes turned to Peggy. Cringing inside, she met their gaze without even blinking. *Don't say anything. Don't even breathe!*

'Interesting . . .' said Mary.

'Very interesting indeed,' Joan concurred.

Paudie spread his hands wide. 'I'm keeping well out of this one, and I advise every one of ye to do the same!'

'Not a chance!' said Anne, sending Peggy a look that clearly signalled they'd be talking more on the matter later.

'I'm sick of certain people dancing around each other. Something had to be done!'

Peggy suppressed a sigh. Could this day get any worse? Not only was Dan clearly in the early stages of going out with Fiona, but her friends were determined to bring her into it. She needed to survive their company, then make for the bathroom again, where she could look into her own eyes in the mirror and cry in peace.

★ ★ ★

Dan had reached College Green before he began coming to his senses. Oh, he was still angry. In fact he was furious. With himself. With Peggy. With their friends. With Fiona Ruane's roommate.

The Rotunda was like a wee world in itself, and any gossip was seized upon and exaggerated beyond recognition. When he'd been told about Peggy going on a cinema date with John, it had reopened the wounds he'd been trying to heal since Christmas. Trying, and failing.

He knew what he *should* do. He should put Peggy out of his head. He wasn't going to chase after a girl who clearly didn't want him. His decision to take Fiona out was an attempt to forget about Peggy.

But it hadn't worked.

On he walked, up Grafton Street and on towards St Stephen's Green. The park was, naturally, closed for the night so he headed for Kildare Street, turning left before the Shelbourne Hotel then down past the Dáil to Nassau Street before heading back up past Trinity and back over the bridge to the north side.

## The Irish Midwife

Walking helped. It definitely helped. It used up some of the furious energy within him. But ultimately, it hadn't solved the fundamental problem – that he couldn't get past his feelings for Peggy Cassidy. Nine weeks since New Year. Nine weeks of hiding his heartbreak. Nine weeks of agony – seeing her every day, and knowing she didn't want him. Nine weeks of trying to pretend to himself that it was all fine – that he had just fancied a girl who didn't fancy him back.

He had no right to her affection, no right to her time, no right to any attention from her. So he had tried to turn heartbreak into anger, and anger into a stubborn resolution to be *fine*. But he was not fine. He was not one bit fine.

What was it about her that called to him so clearly? She was beautiful, yes. And smart. But frankly, quite a few of the other pupil midwives were fairly gorgeous – including Fiona Ruane. And they were all pretty smart.

But Peggy was special. Even as a midwife. She was capable, skilled, unflappable. Honestly, having worked with most of the trainee midwives at this point, he was convinced she was the best of them. She had a – an *instinct* that set her apart. Midwifery, like medicine, was a science. But it was also an art, and Peggy just had it.

*She's a strong woman. And I always knew I wanted a strong woman.* His thoughts flitted to Melissa Moore. If he was lazy enough not to fight his mother, he'd end up married to her. Married to Melissa, and miserable. He'd probably make her miserable too . . .

He reflected on this. *Maybe not.* Melissa seemed to want nothing more than the sort of life his mother enjoyed – flower arranging and charity committees. He shuddered. While there was nothing wrong with either activity, the world was changing, and many women wanted more than that.

He had to face facts. Peggy didn't want him. And he was an eejit. He couldn't even *see* a perfectly nice girl like Fiona, simply because she wasn't Peggy. Twice, he'd tried. He'd gone for fairly long walks with her. They'd had good conversations. Fiona had a good mind, a kind heart, and a pretty face. Her only flaw was that she wasn't Peggy.

So what could he do? He'd been trying to keep a distance, treat Peggy as simply a friend. It wasn't working. He was now halfway up O'Connell Street and running out of thinking time. Always his mind kept returning to the fact that he had firmly believed – right up until Christmas – that Peggy liked him in the same way he then liked her.

Was it all in his head? Or did she like him, but had some reason for not taking things further, despite their kiss at Christmas?

A mad notion occurred to him. Maybe he should just ask her. The idea was worth considering. After all, he couldn't be any more humiliated than he'd felt at the supper table. It would take courage, he knew. He might well bottle it. And he might not even get an opportunity to be alone with her. But at least he might have clarity from her, once and for all, which would surely help him get over her.

Yes, it was maybe worth a try.

He certainly didn't want to waste the rest of his time in Dublin chasing after a girl who was never going to go out with him. Anger surged through him. He deserved better. She was dangling him on a string – playing with him. Not deliberately, to be fair, but that was the effect. While he reminded himself again that he had no right to any attention from her, he knew he needed to draw a line under it all. So maybe he would ask her, and then he would let her go.

# 26

'Peggy Cassidy. Sit down.' Anne's tone was stern. She was sitting on her bed and indicated that Peggy should sit opposite, on her own bed. Peggy had just returned from the bathroom, and both girls were in their nightgowns, hair plaited for the night.

'What? Why?' Feigning a lack of understanding would only gain her a few seconds' grace, but it allowed Peggy's racing mind time to try to prepare for what was coming.

'I heard you in the bathroom.'

'What do you mean?'

'Earlier. After I told you about Dan and Fiona. I saw in your eyes that you were devastated. You pretended to just be mildly interested, then went straight to the bathroom. I followed you.'

'You followed me?'

'Yes. Because I care.' She leaned forward. 'I know you, Peggy Cassidy. You're my best friend. We've been living in the same room for seven bloody months! I *know* you.'

Peggy looked at her blankly. It was true. She and Anne were as close as sisters. *She knows. She feckin' knows.*

'So yes, I followed you to the bathroom and listened at the door. You were bawling in there.'

Peggy dropped her gaze. 'Please, Anne. I can't talk about this.'

'But *why*? Why can't you? It's obvious to everyone that you and Dan are cracked on each other. So why won't you go out with him?'

Peggy glanced at her, her heart soaring that 'everyone' thought Dan liked her. *I didn't imagine it.* She couldn't help the joy inside her. The notion that he might like her as she liked him was like a candle in the darkness of her misery. Even though it could never be. Even though he had gone cold on her since Christmas.

'He *used* to like me, maybe. But he's changed his mind. And as to why I could never go out with him . . .' She took a breath. 'Because it would never work. Not in the real world.' Her tone was flat.

Anne's brow was furrowed. 'But this *is* the real world, and it'll certainly work!' She paused, considering. 'Wait – by the real world, do you mean Belfast?'

Peggy thought about this. The Rotunda was like a place apart – a place where she could get away with pretending to be something she wasn't. In Belfast, it would all fall apart. Her family. His. Aunty Bridget. *The one who*—

How could she put Ma through that sort of pain? So long as she lived, Ma would mourn the early demise of her lovely sister. Aunty Bridget had had years left in her before the police had lifted her that day. Lifted her on the say-so of doctors Sheridan and Fenton.

A familiar rage rose within Peggy, as fresh as the day Bridget had died. The unfairness of it all was an open wound that never closed, never healed. There could never be any sort of resolution or justice for her family, for no one could bring Bridget back. The least Peggy could do would be to stand by them. Family loyalty. Community loyalty. That meant something.

To bring home a boyfriend who was the son of Dr Sheridan would be the worst betrayal imaginable – a slap in the teeth for her own mother, for every member of her family. She could only guess at the hurt it would cause Ma – would cause all the Cassidys, all the Doyles.

Not only could there never be true friendship between a Cassidy and a Sheridan, there was another problem. Being his girl in Belfast would inevitably lead to Dan discovering Peggy was a handywoman. She had done well these past months in Dublin, being careful not to reveal her skills and knowledge, desperately watching the other pupil midwives to work out what she was 'allowed' to know at each stage . . . The strain had been terrible and was only now beginning to ease as her fellow students gained knowledge, skills, and confidence by the day, and Peggy felt more secure hiding in their midst.

So why, having worked so hard to keep her illegal activities a secret, would she risk everything now? If she and Dan were together when they returned to Belfast, he would have to meet her family on a regular basis, as well as Kathleen Gallagher and Mrs Clarke – two handywomen who were precious to her. Inevitably the truth would come out – how she knew them, what her work had been. And what would he do then? Keep her former profession a secret from his own father? Or report her, as his da had reported Bridget Devine? No, it was impossible.

She nodded slowly. 'We're from different worlds, him and me.'

Anne was like a dog with a bone. 'Different how?'

Peggy just shrugged.

Anne's eyes widened. 'Is it civil war politics? I know you're anti-treaty – even though you like Collins. Is Dan on the pro-treaty side?' She inhaled sharply. 'Or is he one of them Unionists?'

'He's no Unionist. I've managed to work that one out. And I suspect that, like most northern Catholics, he's not too enamoured of the treaty or the way the Free State has abandoned us. My da says Collins must have had a plan to get the north back – if he hadn't been killed by eejits.'

'Never mind that. So what is it then, if it's not politics?' Anne's tone turned pleading. 'Tell me, Peggy. I'm trying to understand.'

Peggy took a breath. *Maybe I could tell her some of it.* 'Will you promise not to tell him?'

Anne blessed herself. 'On my mother's grave, I won't tell him.'

Peggy's hands were trembling. 'The twenty-two pounds for this training. How did your family pay for it?'

Anne's frown deepened. 'Well, you know we have a little shop in our village? My ma and da aren't rich, but they've put money by for our education. Why?'

'My ma and da are poor,' Peggy said flatly. 'Oh, we always have enough to eat, but we only have meat on a Sunday, and we've no inside toilet or bath.'

'Oh!' Anne thought for a moment. 'Oh.'

'We all work in the mills for shillings. Our Gerard has been made a supervisor, but the rest of us do the basic labouring.' Peggy's heart was thumping, her stomach sick, as she finally revealed her impoverished background. 'My family are brilliant, and we are all very close, but you couldn't call us anything but poor. Our house is a wee two-up two-down which

## The Irish Midwife

Da and Ma rent. We have very few clothes or books, and I had never been to the cinema until John took me that time.'

Anne was nodding slowly, her expression thoughtful. 'So how come you're here then? Where did your parents get the money for your fees?'

'They didn't. My aunty Bridget died and left me her life savings, with instructions it was to be used to send me to midwifery training.' She reached for a handkerchief from her bedside table and blew her nose. While she had been forced by circumstances to give details of her working-class background, there was no way she was going to share her other secret – details of Aunty Bridget's work.

Anne sat back. 'I'm confused. Why would you have hidden this all this time? It's not like I didn't suspect, like. I'm not stupid. You've only the one Sunday dress and coat and you never spend a ha'penny unless you have to.' She shrugged. 'I also don't understand why you think this is such a big issue. Nobody will think any less of you, you know.'

'What?' This was not the reaction Peggy had expected.

Anne gave a cynical half-laugh. 'We're all Irish, after all. None of us had a ha'penny until recently. My own grandparents all lived in thatched cottages with no running water.' She took both Peggy's hands. 'We are the lucky ones, Peggy. We all had a grandparent or a great-grandparent who survived the famine and had a child. As a nation we are only starting to understand what we're capable of. Seven hundred years of British occupation and oppression, remember?' She jiggled her eyebrows, sending Peggy a knowing look.

Peggy blinked. 'You're actually right.' She managed a shaky laugh. 'And I had never thought about it that way before.'

'Do you know,' Anne continued, fire in her eyes, 'I actually think it's wonderful that somebody with your background has done this. You've a great way with the ordinary women – because you're feckin' one of them! And the world is changing. Nobody should be hemmed in by what their parents do or earn. This is 1939, and all those old rules about class are starting to shift in Ireland. Most of the Big Houses have been burnt down and the upper-class landlords have fecked off back to England. This is our place now. Well, at least in the Free State it is!' She pointed a finger at her own chest. 'We survived the famine.' She enunciated every word. 'We can do anything.'

'My granda Joe literally survived the famine.'

'And he's still alive?'

'He is. He was talking to our Joe – my wee brother – about it over Christmas.' Briefly she told Anne Granda Joe's story, glad the attention was off the topic of Dan Sheridan – for now at least.

Anne looked fierce. 'I'm telling ya. The feckin' empire has a lot to answer for. Did you ever hear the story about when Michael Collins went to Dublin Castle after the signing of the treaty?' Peggy gave her a puzzled look. 'He was to ceremonially accept the keys from the British boyo – the viceroy or governor or whatever he was called. Anyway, the boul' Michael strolls in. "You're seven minutes late!" says the British lad. "Well, you're about seven hundred years late handing back our country," says the Big Fella!'

Peggy smiled. Inwardly, her heart was beginning to settle down. Anne, it seemed, was genuinely not that bothered by Peggy's modest background. And by the sounds of it, her family mightn't actually be that rich themselves.

## The Irish Midwife

'So you don't mind that I'm not like everyone else, Anne?'

She shook her head. 'That's not what I'm saying at all. I'm saying you *are* like everyone else. You're an Irish girl who's training to be a midwife, the same as the rest of us. And from what I've seen, you're gonna be a damn good midwife!'

'Aw, you didn't have to say that.'

'I bloody did. You're a bloody marvel, Peggy Cassidy.'

*Only because I'm a cheat.* The word 'handywoman' was swimming around her mind, daring her to admit to it. She clamped her lips firmly together.

Anne wasn't done. 'So. I'm gonna ask you again. Why will you not go out with Dan Sheridan?'

Peggy sighed. 'He really is different. He's the son of a doctor – not a farmer or a shop owner or anything more down to earth. They live in South Belfast and he's an only child. He went to feckin' boarding school, for God's sake!'

'And? He likes you, Peggy. I think he *really* likes you. Why don't you give him a chance, at least? What you're doing isn't fair, and that doesn't seem like you.'

Peggy eyed her uncertainly. Fairness was important. She wouldn't want to be unfair to him. *Am I being unfair?* God, it was all so confusing!

'What you're doing,' Anne continued, clearly sensing her advantage, 'is snobbery. Only the other way round. Are you a snob, Peggy Cassidy?'

'No! Of course not!'

'Well then, go out with him!'

Peggy searched around in her mind for an answer. *Why? Why not?* The truth erupted from her then. 'But it'll never last!'

Her own words surprised her, but they were true. If – and it was a massive if – *if* he still liked her, then she might be able to be Dan's girl here in Dublin, but reality would hit them like the north wind once they returned to Belfast. No way would his parents want a girl like her for their Daniel! And no way could she hurt her family by being with a Sheridan.

'And what?' Anne looked unconcerned. 'You think you can only go out with a fella if you're gonna marry him? It's 1939, Peggy! We can kiss a few frogs before we find our prince!'

Peggy tried to laugh. 'Are you saying Dan's a frog? More importantly, are you saying *Paudie* is a frog?'

Anne shrugged. 'I don't know yet what Paudie is. But sure, isn't that part of the craic?'

Peggy laughed helplessly. 'You're some girl, Anne!'

Anne shrugged. 'It's the twentieth century. As young women we have choices now that our mothers and grandmothers never had.' She sent Peggy a keen glance. 'So what about Dan? Will you go out with him?'

'I don't even know for sure that he still wants to go out with me. He seemed pretty annoyed this evening. And since Christmas he hasn't . . . I think he's changed his mind about me.'

'Never worry about him. You need to think about what *you* can do, what *you* want. Now, if he asked you, would you go out with him?'

Peggy's insides were swirlin' something terrible. This was, she knew, the thing she wanted most in the world. To be Dan's girl. To kiss him. To hold his hand. To be known as his girl. For him to be known as her fella.

But then she thought about her parents, and his, and the Rock streets, and Aunty Bridget . . .'I honestly don't know.'

'Well, will you at least *think* about it? Sure what harm?'

## The Irish Midwife

Peggy held her gaze for a long moment, then exhaled in exasperation. 'Fecksake, Anne!'

'Ah, I knew I had ya.' Anne winked. 'Now you're not mad at me, are ya?'

'Course not! Come here, you!' They hugged, and went to bed – Peggy feeling as though she had just gone ten rounds with a welterweight. Anne was a good friend, and a feckin' pain in the backside. How was Peggy supposed to get any sleep tonight, with her head wrecked and her heart veering between blissful hope and dark doubt?

# 27

Peggy did eventually sleep, but her dreams were troubled. *Da and Dan are arguing. Now our Gerard is fighting with Dan during a game of football. And Ma is looking at me, shaking her head sadly.*

When she awoke, she was no nearer to knowing the right thing to do. *Am I really a snob?* Would Dan really be all right with her being a milly, from a whole family of millworkers? He knew Gerard was in the mill – but Gerard was a supervisor, and hoped to get a manager's job some day.

And then there was Aunty Bridget. Had she known that by pushing Peggy to train as a proper midwife, her niece would be thrown into a new world? And would she have wanted that for Peggy? Only an instant's reflection told her that, yes, Aunty Bridget would have wanted Peggy to 'better herself'. She might even have been happy to see Peggy walking out with a medical student – someone like Paudie, or Eugene, or John.

What she would never have wanted – and could never have foreseen – was Peggy going out with Dr Sheridan's son. The same Dr Sheridan who had reported her. Dan was not his da, but it was hard to get past what his da had done. And Peggy couldn't expect her family – especially Ma – to have to face that.

As Peggy went through her day – breakfast, lectures with the midwifery tutors all morning, a late dinner with the girls as their session overran – in the back of her mind she was thinking constantly about Anne's challenges to her. Snobbery. Inverted snobbery. Post-famine Irish solidarity across class and geography. And the radical yet delicious notion that you could go out with a fella even if you saw no future in it. Living for now, they called it. It had been a big thing in England and America before the Wall Street Crash. The roaring twenties. Did those people regret having such a good time? Some of them, maybe. But certainly not all of them.

And what would she be risking? This afternoon she was working at an antenatal clinic and thankfully Dan wasn't around, so she was using every spare minute to think. If she did go with him, they'd have to break up at the point at which she left Dublin. If he decided to stay here, then so much the better.

Might it work?

Would she end up with a broken heart?

She shrugged inwardly. Her heart was broke, regardless. At least this way she'd have good memories to look back on . . . *Feck!* How was she supposed to know what to do for the best?

And were all these imaginings completely impossible? Was it too late?

*I've lost him.* Or had she? Recalling her despair when she'd heard about Fiona, she closed her eyes briefly. He'd been adamant at supper last night that he and Fiona were not a couple. Not yet, anyway. *Maybe I haven't completely lost him, then. Not yet.*

★ ★ ★

Dan was still scundered. He remained annoyed with Anne and Joan, and the whole bloody lot of them, and he wasn't

## The Irish Midwife

a bit pleased with Paudie either. His friend might not have taken an active role in the ambush at the supper table last night, but Anne was Paudie's girl, so Dan had no doubt they'd been talking about him.

It sickened him to imagine it. Were they gleeful at having some gossip to discuss, or were they pitying him now for still being cracked on Peggy? By the time he'd got in last night Paudie had been asleep, thank God, and this morning he lay on feigning sleep until Paudie was gone.

Timing everything to perfection, he swung into the dining room just as the staff were clearing away the remains of breakfast, grabbed two pieces of toast and took them outside to eat in the gardens. It was a beautiful morning, full of dew and birdsong and false hope. No doubt the blue sky would turn to rain by afternoon.

Thankfully though, the day flew by – helped by the fact he got to perform his first caesarean operation. The woman's baby had been stubbornly lying transverse – straight across. Strange to think that in days gone by, both mother and baby would most likely have died. Thankfully the surgery went well, the assistant master even praising Dan for a job well done. After that he helped review some postnatal women in the ward, and then suddenly it was eight o'clock and the night team were arriving.

Eugene was on, and he gave Dan a strange look when he arrived. Rather sheepishly, Dan recalled that the last time he'd seen him, he'd lost his temper and stormed off.

'All right, Eugene? What about ye?'

'Dan, what's the craic?' There was wariness in his eye. 'Busy today?'

Briefly, Dan gave details of the women he'd looked after that day. By the time Eugene had asked a couple of questions and Dan had responded, things were a little less tense. *Bloody hell. Will I have to do this with all of them?*

It was fair enough, he supposed, as he made his way to his room. He'd seen Paudie, Mary and Joan at different points today, but hadn't had time to properly talk to them. Peggy he'd seen only once, from a distance, sending the usual pain arrowing through him. Glancing out of the corridor window, he saw that it was now raining. Of course it was.

Paudie was already in their room, lying on his bed reading the paper.

Taking a breath, Dan said, 'Paudie?'

His friend moved the paper slightly, and Dan could now see wariness in his eyes – the same wariness he'd glimpsed in Eugene's expression.

'I was out of order last night. I apologise.'

Paudie grinned. 'Apology accepted. And I apologise, too. We shouldn't have wound you up like that.' Sitting up, he folded the newspaper, placing it on his bedside table. 'Right. So I have something to tell you, Dan.'

'Sounds ominous.' Dan sat on his own bed, facing Paudie, and slipping his shoes off at the same time. God, it was good to be sitting down. He'd been on his feet all day.

Paudie was frowning. 'I'm actually not sure I *should* tell you. Peggy made Anne promise she wouldn't tell you, so she told me instead.'

Dan's heart sank. *Peggy.* 'Is it bad?'

*She hates me. She thinks I'm a creep who won't take no for an answer. She and John are going steady.* His mind was racing, his stomach sick. 'Just tell me, Paudie. Put me out of my misery.'

## The Irish Midwife

'All right.' Paudie took a breath. 'Last night after supper she admitted to Anne that she really likes you. But she thinks it will never work because her family is poor and yours is well off.'

Dan couldn't believe it. Like, literally could not comprehend that what Paudie was saying was true. Shock arced through him. *This* was the reason? *This feckin' nonsense?*

'What?' he managed. 'That's it? That's why she won't go out with me?'

'Yup.' Paudie nodded slowly. 'Took Anne ages to get her to admit it, too.'

'But that's – that's pure horse-shite! I'm not going to think any less of her just because of what sort of house she grew up in!'

'And if you did, you're not the man I took you for.'

'Bloody right.' His mind was flying all over the place, his heart thumping. Images flashed before him. The rows of tiny red-brick houses in West Belfast. Peggy's father talking about Gerard's job in the mill – and his own. Peggy's disapproval of Dan's past as a boarding-school boy. What assumptions had she made about him?

One thing was for sure. The sooner he spoke to her, the better.

'I wonder when her off-duty day this week is?'

'Friday. Tomorrow, like. Anne already told me.' Paudie winked. 'Anne's all over this, I tell ya. She's some girl!'

'She is.' *He really likes her.* His heart lifted. They might even be a foursome, going on trips and nights out together. *Paudie and Anne. Dan and Peggy.* 'Right.' His decision was made. 'I'll get somebody to swap with me so I'm off too.'

'Desy's off tomorrow.'

Dan sent him a wry glance. 'You have this all worked out, don't you?'

'Oh, aye.' He sniffed. 'Couldn't have you two lovesick eejits moping around the place any more.'

Dan threw a pillow at him, his heart lighter than it had been in a long, long time.

★ ★ ★

'It's your day off, isn't it?'

It was Friday morning, and Peggy and Anne were heading down to breakfast. 'Aye. Such a good feeling!'

'Any plans?' There was something in Anne's voice. Peggy sent her a sharp look but Anne's expression was neutral.

'The weather's good, so I thought I'd spend some time in the Rotunda Gardens with Sir Comyns Berkeley.'

'Ah, the lovely *Handbook of Midwifery*.'

'Yeah, have to study for that test next week.' She sighed. 'Why is the weather always good on days when we have to study?'

'It's a rule of nature, don't ya know?'

'I suppose. Still, studying outside in the sunshine is better than being stuck inside.'

'Too right.'

Dan was at breakfast, acting totally normal. He seemed to have got over his anger of a few days ago, for these past couple of days he'd been polite and friendly, with no sign whatsoever of any deeper feelings. Peggy was still torn by the daring notions that Anne had put into her head. Fair enough, they could never be together long term, but wouldn't it be amazing to get even one more kiss from him?

*The Irish Midwife*

She sent him a covert glance. *Feck!* He was so gorgeous! Thick dark hair, blue eyes that were way too beautiful, a strong jaw, and a fine figure.

Her mind wandered back to the game in Corrigan Park. She had memories stored from that day – images of him fielding a high ball, giving his opponent a good shoulder, punting the ball beautifully up the field to his team-mate . . .

She had other favourites, too, from their time together caring for women. They mostly involved his hands. A gentle hand on the shoulder of a woman. Deftly drawing up a syringe. Even watching him writing up notes was a joy. He had great handwriting – sharp and fluid.

'. . . do you think, Peggy?'

'Sorry, what?'

'We're planning to go to Stephen's Green on Sunday, if the good weather holds.'

'Sounds good!' On Sundays, because most of the students were off, they had more time together. After breakfast, Mass, and then dinner, they'd then be free until suppertime. As a group they had got into the habit of going for walks if the weather was dry, or playing cards in the common room if it was too wet to venture out.

A thought struck her. If Dan did start going out with Fiona, no doubt he'd want her to join their friendship group, and Peggy's Sundays would be forever changed. But no. She wasn't going to let her mind linger on the worst possibilities. She was going to hold onto hope for as long as she could.

The others left – Dan walking out alongside Anne and Paudie – but Peggy lingered, enjoying an indulgent second cup of tea, not in a rush to get anywhere on her day off. A few minutes later the kitchen team started clearing up, so she rose, picked up her books from her room, and made her way outside.

The Rotunda Gardens were beautiful. Apparently people had paid a shilling entry fee back in the day, the money helping to fund the hospital. More recently, the leaders of the 1916 Easter Rising had been held here before being moved to Kilmainham Gaol, where most of them had been executed. Poor Uncle Ned hadn't even made it that far.

Those executions had sparked widespread outrage and ultimately had led to the War of Independence, when Ireland – or at least, twenty-six of its thirty-two counties – had finally won independence from Britain. A British politician called Winston Churchill had apparently said at the time, 'The grass soon grows over a battlefield, but never over a scaffold.'

A surprisingly insightful statement, Peggy thought, for someone from his background. The same man had also described Chamberlain's Munich Agreement last year as 'a total and unmitigated defeat', and events once again were proving him right. Poor Czechoslovakia was basically gone, swallowed up by Hitler's aggression.

Peggy shivered, even though the sunshine was beautifully warm. People were dying in Europe right now, and she was debating with herself whether or not to go out with Dan Sheridan, if he asked her? *Yeah, feck that.* Life was short, and precious. *Live while you can.* Anne had given her a solution – if Dan was prepared to agree to it. They could be together in Dublin, then break up before going home to Belfast. Now, how was she supposed to woo him, to work on him, to try to revive whatever liking he had had for her before?

Settling herself on the long grass she opened her book, but her mind was elsewhere. She couldn't shake the notion that maybe he, too, had regretted their kiss. Maybe beneath his politeness to Gerard and her parents, he had been horrified by the fact they were so different to him. It would certainly explain his coolness towards her since Christmas. The difficulty was that the kiss and him meeting the Cassidys had happened one after the other, making it nearly impossible for her to figure out which event had made him go cold on her.

A figure on her right caught her eye and she turned her head, her jaw dropping as she saw who was approaching. It was as though she had conjured him up with her thoughts. What was Dan doing in the gardens? He was supposed to be on duty! Her heart pounding, she prepared to say hello.

# 28

*There she is!* As they were leaving the dining room, Anne had mentioned – quite deliberately, he had no doubt – that Peggy planned to study in the gardens this morning. And so Dan had continued up to his room, grabbed a couple of his own books, waited a few minutes, then headed back down again.

'Well!' Deliberately he used the northern greeting, rather than the Dublin 'Howya' that they were all adopting these days.

'Well, Dan. What brings you to the gardens?'

He indicated his books. 'I've studying to do, and studying is always nicer outside in the sunshine.' He pointed to her textbook. 'I see you had the same idea.'

She rolled her eyes. 'What a coincidence. Studying outside is definitely nicer. Not sure it's particularly effective though.' There was a look of puzzlement on her face. 'So how come you're off?'

'Swapped with Desy. Do you mind if I join you?'

'Go ahead.'

He settled himself on the ground beside her, abandoning the books. There was a brief silence where their eyes met, then both looked away.

*Say something.*

'Peggy.'

'Yes?'

Damn, she was so pretty! The sun was on her face, spotlighting her perfect skin, clear blue eyes, and guarded expression. He swallowed. 'I want to apologise for my wee tantrum the other night.' He sighed. 'I was out of order, storming off like that. I know Anne was only slagging me, that she didn't mean anything bad.'

'Oh, don't apologise for that! Anne went too far. I was mortified for you. But I couldn't stick up for you, because then . . .'

'Then everyone would have slagged us both even more.'

'Yup.' She shrugged. 'We're tortured, like. They just won't let it go.'

'You do know what the obvious solution is, don't you?'

'What?' She seemed to be holding her breath.

'Go out with me. Be my girl.'

She bit her lip, but he could see something in her eyes. Something that made his heart pound even more loudly than it already was.

'Well?'

'M-maybe.'

'Right?' *This is progress.* 'What would put you off?' He had to get her to put her worries into words.

'A few things.'

'Go on.'

She exhaled slowly. 'Firstly, Fiona Ruane.'

'Nothing between us. You and John?'

She shook her head. 'No, nothing.'

'Good. See, we're getting somewhere.' He smiled, but she didn't reciprocate. 'Now, what else are you worrying about?'

*The Irish Midwife*

'At Christmas, after the game . . .'

'Yes?'

'What did you think of my ones?'

'I liked them. Your ma and da seemed lovely, and your brother Gerard seemed sound. Why?'

'What do you know about them? About my family, my background?'

He thought about this, choosing his words carefully. 'I know you live in West, somewhere near St James's and the Whiterock Road. I know your da and your brother work in the mills, and that your brother is a supervisor.' He thought for a moment. 'I know there are six of yous . . . Gerard, then Antoinette, then you? Is that right? And the younger ones . . . there's a young fella who likes hurling.'

'Joe.'

'Joe, yes!' He tried to remember the others. 'The wee girl . . . Aiveen!'

Now she did smile. 'Aye, Aiveen. My wee darlin'.'

'And I'm sorry. I know there's one more, but I can't remember . . .'

'Our Sheila. She's fifteen.'

'Sheila! Sheila. Now what else do I know? Your Gerard is a handy footballer. He got married last summer, I think. Your sister did too. Am I right?' She nodded. 'What else? You went to St Dominic's. Er . . .' He was beginning to run out of facts.

'If you were to guess, what sort of house would you think we live in?'

He shrugged. 'The most likely option is one of the red-brick terrace houses. They're the most common type in that part of Belfast.'

'You'd be right.' She took a breath. 'You've been in one?'

## Seána Tinley

He had to think for a minute. 'Yeah, I think I have.' Vaguely, he had a memory of an older man. Cardiac problems. One time he was out with Da.

'There are two rooms upstairs, two downstairs. An outhouse out the back.'

'Like Mrs Halliday's in Stoneybatter?'

'Similar, yes.'

'How many rooms are there in your house, Dan?'

He froze. *What a question!* Still, he was getting somewhere. Her expression was half-defiant, half-uncertain, and his heart warmed, sensing the emotions that must be churning through her. This was clearly a major issue in her head. His task was to make it all right, without diminishing the very real anxiety she was feeling. He felt as though he was walking on a tightrope – like a circus acrobat. One misstep and she'd withdraw.

'Well?'

Her question was a trap, he knew. If he revealed that he couldn't, off the top of his head, answer it, she'd get even more wound up. The truth was he had no notion how many rooms there were. *A lot.*

'More than four,' he said softly. 'Why?'

'Because we're different. We're from different backgrounds. You have a big house, plenty of money, you went to boarding school, your da's a doctor . . . Whereas I'm a milly from Rockville Street. I started in the mills before I left school at fourteen. I've no exams, and not a ha'penny to spend.'

Knowing he needed to be careful, he let her see some of his genuine puzzlement. 'Why does any of that matter?'

'Because it'll never work long term. This place' – she gestured about vaguely – 'is like some sort of fairyland. It has indoor baths and we eat meat six days a week. Here everybody has a bed of their own and we swan about Dublin together as though there are no differences between us. But back home in Belfast . . .' She closed her eyes briefly. 'Impossible.'

'What are you saying?'

'I – I don't know.'

'Let me ask you a question. Do you like me?'

She nodded, lips clamped together as though it would be wrong to admit it out loud.

'Do you *want* to be my girl? I mean, if it wasn't for all the worries in your head.'

'Yes.' Her voice was small, but his heart was thumping with each victory.

'So why don't we just, like, give it a go? No promises, no expectations. Just be my girl.'

'For now?'

'What do you mean?'

'We can be together in Dublin. But not Belfast.'

He recoiled a little. 'Are you saying that we have to break up once we qualify? That we can't—'

'Yes. Exactly. Together in this' – she gestured vaguely – 'fairyland. But not in real life. Belfast. Our families . . .' She lifted her chin. 'Take it or leave it.'

Well, that was an easy decision! He grinned. 'I'll take it.'

# 29

'I'll take it.'

Peggy could hardly believe what she was hearing. It was going to happen – and in the only way it *could* happen. It was early March, and they wouldn't return to Belfast until the end of August. Nearly six months! Six months of Dan Sheridan being her fella!

Joy blossomed within her, radiating through every part of her. Sitting on soft grass in the Rotunda Gardens, surrounded by beautiful trees and flowers and birdsong, with the sun shining warm on her face and Dan Sheridan smiling at her. Surely this was the most perfect moment anyone had ever experienced?

She smiled back, and held his gaze. They stayed like that for a long, breathless moment, then leaned in for a kiss. Gentle it was, and tender. Their kiss on the train had been swift, desperate, unexpected. This was the opposite. It was known, anticipated, savoured.

Peggy's eyes fluttered closed as his lips brushed hers. Her heart was racing, and her entire world was now reduced to physical sensation. His lips were moving on hers, sending what felt like electricity running through her. Then his tongue briefly touched her lips, and she gasped, opening her mouth. Now the kiss deepened, their tongues meeting in a sensual dance. His hand was on her face, his thumb caressing her cheek.

Afterwards, they opened their eyes again, and smiled once more. He lifted her hand to his lips and kissed it, closing his eyes. Her heart melted at the sight. Dimly, she was aware there was danger there. How would she manage once they broke up? But that was a problem for another day. She would make the most of the months ahead, as it was all they would ever have.

They sat for hours in the sunshine, even skipping the Rotunda dinner. What they had was too new for public inspection, and Peggy knew that Anne would have a hundred questions once she saw her. Keeping it secret was not an option – Peggy felt as though she were a flame of happiness, visible wherever she went.

Dropping their books in their rooms, they walked down to Bewley's hand in hand, and enjoyed a delicious lunch which Peggy could barely remember afterwards. And they talked. About everything. Their studies. Their childhood. Their observations of the world – from the people around them to the worrying news from Europe.

Wandering around Trinity, St Stephen's Green, and Merrion Square – where Oscar Wilde had grown up – they cemented the bond between them on that very first day.

But they had to face reality, and as the warm sunshine gave way to the coolness of evening they turned back to the Rotunda. As they approached Parnell Square they dropped their hands in case someone they knew might see them, both expressing nervousness at the slagging they were about to endure.

## The Irish Midwife

'We'll just have to get it over with,' said Dan. He sent her a glance that held so much warmth that her heart skipped a beat. 'And it's worth it.'

They parted at the corner, Peggy heading to her room. It was well after eight, so Anne was likely to be there . . .

'Howya!' she said brightly – while knowing she had no chance of brazening it out.

'Oh my God!' Anne jumped up, her expression full of excited anticipation. 'Were you out with Dan?'

'I was.' Peggy inclined her head, knowing that she was beaming with barely contained happiness.

'And?'

'We're now a thing,' she began, 'but only—'

That was as far as she got. Anne squealed and leapt towards her, enveloping her in a huge hug. 'I am only delighted for the two of ye!'

Peggy hugged her back, saying, 'Well I'm delighted too.'

'What about all your worries? Do you know now that he doesn't care about your background?'

'Ah, well. You see, I care about his. Maybe I am a back-to-front snob, I dunno. But I basically said I'd only go out with him here. Not in Belfast.'

Anne looked confused. 'But you both could be living in Belfast permanently from September.'

'Or maybe he'll stay here. This can't last, Anne. It's only for Dublin.' Peggy grinned. 'But I fully intend to enjoy it while I can.'

'Enjoy it? What if you . . . you know . . . what if you fall for him even harder?'

'I'm only copying you and Paudie. At this minute I don't care if Dan is a frog or a prince, I just want to kiss him!'

'Fair enough.' Anne looked a little cynical. She paused for a moment, adding, 'Me and Paudie are open to the future though. We don't know yet, that's all. What you're suggesting is very different – going into it with a deadline for when you'll finish. It seems odd to me.'

Peggy shrugged. 'It is odd. But it was the only way I'd go out with him, so . . .' She grinned. 'So now I'm going out with him.'

Anne smiled back, shaking her head at the same time. 'You're mad. Totally feckin' cracked.'

'Probably!'

\* \* \*

Paudie's slagging was fairly muted, thank God. When Dan told him the news, he shook his hand, saying simply, 'Fair play to ya, boy.'

When Dan then told him that Peggy intended to break up with him in August, he raised an eyebrow in disbelief.

'Yeah, right. That girl is already cracked on you, Dan. Can't really see why, myself. It's not as if you're from Cork or anything. But I can't see her going through with that plan – unless you mess it up, which to be fair you're quite capable of doing.'

'Well, I hope you're right about her and wrong about me!' Dan declared. 'I have six months to convince her that we belong together – and I bloody intend to make the most of it!' He frowned. 'I wouldn't want her staying with me against her will, of course. If she genuinely wouldn't be happy with me in Belfast, for whatever reason, I'd actually have to let her go.'

Paudie whistled. 'Because her happiness is more important than what you want? Jesus, Dan. You have got it bad.'

Dan's eyes danced. 'I had it bad yesterday too. The difference today is that I have six months with her. She literally said "Take it or leave it"!'

'So you took it? Good lad. Right! Time to go down for supper. Brace yourself, my friend, for you and Peggy are about to get the greatest roasting of your lives!'

At this, Dan laughed out loud. 'Bring it on! I'm ready!'

★ ★ ★

Their friends were agog, and pleased, and there were lots of I-told-you-sos. Peggy endured it all with only a slight blush, for Dan was opposite, sending her warmth and reassurance, and Oh! She was so, so happy. Afterwards, when the conversation moved on, there was an air of not-quite-real-ness about everything. How could they all sit there calmly discussing irrelevancies like exams and tests when she and Dan were now together? Surely the whole world had changed. A warm glow burned inside her chest, flaring when she looked at him or watched him speaking. My God, he was amazing! *And he is mine!* Impossible. Totally impossible. And yet . . .

After supper, as they were all walking out, he whispered in her ear, 'Meet you outside, by the gate to the gardens. Five minutes!' A shiver went through her, and she nodded.

Paudie and Anne often met for a last chat after supper, she knew. *And now it's my turn.* After going to the bathroom, washing her hands, and making sure her hair looked all right, she slipped out of the side door and round to the gate. Dan was already there, and her heart leapt as she saw him. As she approached he opened his arms, and she went into them as if it was the most natural thing in the world. They kissed hungrily, passionately, breaking apart breathlessly after what seemed like a long time.

'Peggy, Peggy,' he murmured, and the desire within her flared at him saying her name. 'You are wonderful.'

'You're pretty nice yourself,' she responded, unable to match his intense words. *It's too much. I can't . . .*

Stepping back deliberately, she took both his hands, saying, 'Supper wasn't as bad as I thought it would be.'

'True! We got away lightly, I think.' They spoke then of their friends' reactions at the table. Peggy didn't mention her private conversation with Anne.

'Within a week we will be old news,' he said, 'thank God.'

'I do hope so, for I hate to be the focus of everybody's attention. I just cringe.'

'Is that right?' he mused. 'I never would have thought that about you, because you always seem so composed. I'm looking forward to getting to know the real you. The parts you keep hidden.'

Alarm bells were going off in Peggy's mind. *Never, ever tell him about being a handywoman!* She would have to learn how to share her real self while leaving out something that was a major part of her. It was so frustrating, for under other circumstances she'd have loved to get to know him fully, and let him get to know her fully. *Impossible.* For the first time, she began to appreciate how tricky a path she'd chosen. Still, to be with Dan – even for six months, even while holding back . . .Yes, it was worth it.

## The Irish Midwife

Peggy and Dan soon developed a wonderful routine. Like the other courting couples they swapped their off-duty days to maximise their time together, despite eye-rolls and teasing from their classmates. They sat together when they could – in Mass, at dinner, and in any joint lectures. They studied together – sometimes just the two of them, sometimes with more of their friends. They shared their thoughts, hopes, and fears every day with one another – usually the small things, the things of now. Occasionally Dan would talk about his parents, and the pressure he would feel – particularly, it seemed from his mother. Peggy couldn't advise him, but would listen with a sympathetic ear. She was used to strong mothers, but wondered if Mrs Sheridan was perhaps a bit too pushy at times. But then, Dan was an only child, with far too much attention on him.

They held hands when outside the hospital, and kissed any time they could – during their post-supper goodnights, at the cinema, in a dozen dark Dublin doorways when no one was around. Both knew it would be wrong to go further since they weren't married, so they applied restraint – which was at times challenging to say the least. In her heart of hearts Peggy had often daydreamed about being naked with him, about sleeping in the same bed as him, about waking up with him. But such dreams were only dreams, and she had to keep her feet on the ground. And so neither pushed for more than kisses, despite the need inside, for they had both been reared to wait for marriage.

*Marriage!* A pang would go through Peggy at the very thought of it. Paudie and Anne could consider that possibility. Peggy and Dan couldn't. It was impossible from her perspective, and he had happily agreed to a temporary relationship. They would part on leaving Dublin, and she would just have to take the pain.

Unfortunately, having debated whether to go for Belfast or Dublin after qualifying, Dan had decided on Belfast. The reasons weren't fully clear to Peggy, but she assumed the call of home had been too strong. For her part, she was completely torn inside by her own impending qualification. It would be such an achievement for a young woman from the Rock streets to qualify as a proper *thing* with a job-name and a badge. All her life, she'd be able to call herself a midwife. Her interview at the Royal was coming up soon, and while she was nervous about it everyone assured her that she would fly through it.

But finishing her course meant saying goodbye to Dan. It was now July, and they had just over a month left. Worse, it now looked as though they may well end up both working in the Royal. She would have to be strong, and adapt to life without him, while seeing him all the time. It didn't bear thinking about. All she could do for now was to live for every moment, and push away the sense of impending doom that threatened to overcome her. Some days that was easier than others.

Frustratingly, they were only occasionally allocated to support the same woman in labour. While there was no rule that said couples couldn't work together, Peggy suspected that some of the sisters deliberately kept courting couples apart while on duty. She and Anne had discussed it many a time, with Anne also convinced the same was true of her and Paudie. On one day in late July though, with the hospital busy and a couple of the students struck down with the summer cold, Peggy and Dan were both assigned to look after Mrs Costello, who had recently arrived in labour.

Peggy was there first, and went through her usual process of sitting with the woman, getting to know her a little, and building some trust very quickly. This was Mrs Costello's first baby, and she had sensibly stayed at home while in early labour, as her ma and sisters had advised her.

'They told me it was time to go in once the pains were coming every couple of minutes, so here I am!' She was a merry young woman in her mid-twenties, with glorious red hair and a lovely smile.

'How did you come in? Did someone bring you?'

'Aye, my husband drove me. We have a car,' she said, with more than a hint of pride.

'Wow!' Peggy looked suitably impressed. 'You may hang on to him!'

'Aye, I think I'll keep him around, Nurse!'

Another pain came then, so Peggy quietened while Mrs Costello breathed and paced her way through it. 'Well done,' she said softly once it had passed. 'Now, do you mind if I have a feel of your tummy, to see which way the baby is lying?'

'Aye, of course. Do you need me to lie down?'

'Only for a minute. I promise you can get straight back up.'

Mrs Costello held up a hand, and began breathing harshly, her eyes closed and her face contorted with pain. The pains were clearly very close together. Peggy put a hand on her shoulder to comfort her, then frowned. Mrs Costello's skin felt hot.

Her heart sank. Infection was one of the greatest risks to the baby – and the mother. Thankfully, at that moment the

## Seána Tinley

door opened and Dan came in. Relief flooded through her. Whatever the next few hours brought, at least they would be together. She glanced at the clock. It was a little after five in the afternoon – three hours until their shift finished. Hopefully Mrs Costello would give birth by then.

Holding a finger to her lips, she gave him a worried face and shook her head slightly. Closing the door quietly, he waited.

'Here's Dr Sheridan who'll be looking after you as well,' she said softly as Mrs Costello's pain ended.

'Not quite a doctor yet!' He smiled. 'Nice to meet you, Mrs Costello. I'm Dan, and I'll be qualified in about three weeks.'

'So you're basically a full doctor then?'

'Ah, now, we have to wait for the final whistle, don't we?'

'Fair enough.' She smiled back at him, and Peggy's heart warmed at the rapport that was clearly already building between them. *Dan is amazing!*

'How are you feeling in yourself, Mrs Costello? You feel a bit hot to me.'

'Ach, I've been feeling rubbish for about a week,' the woman said. 'You know when you're hot one minute and cold the next? It's this summer cold that's going about. It keeps trying to get me, I think.'

'Have you a sore throat? Runny nose?' Dan was straight in there.

'No, nothing. Only the hot and cold.'

As Dan took the woman's temperature and looked inside her mouth, Peggy tried to maintain a calm appearance. There was no reason to think anything might be wrong. It was probably just a cold.

## The Irish Midwife

After the next pain had passed, Peggy helped Mrs Costello to lie down, at the same time asking her if the baby had been kicking as much as usual.

'Oh no, it's been very quiet. But everybody says they get quieter at the end, when they're near ready to be born. Is that not right?' Suddenly there was fear in her eyes.

'Well, they have less space to move around in, that's for sure,' Peggy said diplomatically. All of her handywoman instincts were screaming at her. At the same time her hands were moving, identifying the baby's presentation and position. 'Baby is head down, which is good. Now, let me have a wee listen.'

Taking her Pinard, she pressed it to exactly the right spot and bent her ear to listen.

*Nothing.*

She tried it a little to the left, to the right, higher, lower. Still nothing. Wordlessly she straightened, handing the Pinard to Dan before moving round to take Mrs Costello's hand.

Dan listened, moving the Pinard around as Peggy had. *Please God, let him find the heartbeat!*

'Can I help you up, Mrs Costello?' he said, and together they helped the woman into a sitting position.

'What's wrong, Doctor? What is it?'

'I wasn't able to find the baby's heartbeat there now, and I don't think Nurse Cassidy found it either.' Peggy bit her lip *This is terrible.*

'What? Are you saying my baby is dead?' She was gripping Peggy's hand tightly, and Peggy's heart was sore at her distress and pain. Then another contraction took her, and her focus went to managing it.

Once it was done, she started talking and crying all at once. She had thought she had the cold. Had felt unwell but thought nothing of it. That everyone had told her not to worry that the baby wasn't moving.

'But I *knew*, Nurse. I knew, in here!' With a stabbing motion she indicated her heart. Putting a hand on her tummy, she added, 'And in here. I felt . . . cold inside. Oh, my baby, my baby!'

Peggy held her while she cried, and held her again and again during the hours that followed. The night team arrived, but neither Peggy nor Dan were willing to leave. He had already gone out to tell the sister and the obstetrician on duty. There was nothing to be done though, beyond preventing any infection from spreading to other women, and caring for Mrs Costello as compassionately as they could. The poor woman had to continue with her labour, knowing that in all likelihood her baby was already gone.

# 30

The bravery of women – their strength, and courage – was something that Peggy knew well. Every woman who endured labour, or bravely underwent a caesarean, or struggled with feeding but persisted – all of them were brave, Peggy knew. But Mrs Costello was something else.

On and on she endured, through the slow progress of a first-time labour, and with her heart broken and her temperature spiking. Peggy gave her what comfort she could, both physically and emotionally. Finally, sometime in the darkest part of the night, she began pushing, and birthed a well-developed full-term baby girl at two thirty in the morning. The baby was, Peggy saw, perfectly formed, but her skin was mottled and discoloured in places, indicating that she had been dead for some time. Swiftly, Dan tied and cut the cord – no reason to wait in this case – and Peggy took the child over to the side table to wrap it up.

Mrs Costello was no longer crying. She was numb, exhausted, empty. Dimly, Peggy recognised what she must be feeling.

'I don't want to see it.' Her voice was flat.

'Are you sure?' Peggy turned, cradling the little one in her arms. As handywomen, she and Aunty Bridget had always left it up to the woman to decide.

Mrs Costello glanced up, her expression uncertain, then slowly she opened her arms.

Peggy walked back across to her – slowly, carefully, giving her every opportunity to change her mind again. But Mrs Costello lifted her chin, and accepted the baby into her arms. Fresh tears came then, which Peggy thought was probably a good thing. With her free hand she traced the baby's features as if committing them to memory.

'Boy or girl?'

'A wee girl.' The lump in Peggy's throat was so painful she could barely speak.

'Muireann.' Her gaze flicked briefly to Peggy. 'That's the name we picked for a girl – me and my husband.'

'It's a beautiful name.'

Mrs Costello moaned as another labour pain took her. 'That'll be the afterbirth coming away,' said Peggy. 'Can I take her – only for a few minutes?'

Mrs Costello nodded, and Peggy took the baby into her arms while Dan received and inspected the afterbirth. Almost immediately afterwards the woman asked for her baby back and Peggy complied, her heart breaking for the bereaved mother. Rummaging in Mrs Costello's bag she found a white, hand-knitted blanket. 'Would you like this?'

'Oh, yes please. Me mam knitted that blanket for her.' Peggy helped her wrap the baby in the blanket – leaving the towel in place so Mrs Costello would not see anything that might distress her more.

'Would you like us to get your husband?' asked Dan softly.

She nodded, the very mention of her husband upsetting her anew. Dan slipped outside, Peggy hoping that their colleagues had managed to contact Mr Costello. Thankfully,

## *The Irish Midwife*

he must already have been in the hospital, for Dan returned only a few moments later with a bewildered-looking young man. As the couple shared a tearful greeting, Dan and Peggy stepped outside to give them some privacy.

The hospital was dark and quiet, the world seeming to still in sympathy for the loss of a wee life, never lived. Dan opened his arms to her and Peggy stepped into his embrace, vaguely sensing a parallel with Mr and Mrs Costello and baby Muireann. The difference was that she and Dan had one another – alive and well and caring. A sob escaped her and his arms tightened about her. She moved to place her cheek next to his, and discovered that he, too, had been overcome with emotion.

Neither spoke. Well, what could anyone say in such a moment? They stood there, Peggy feeling comforted by Dan's presence, his understanding, and the mighty connection between them. He too, was getting comfort from her embrace, she knew.

Gratitude flowed through her now. For menfolk. For Dan and Mr Costello and Mr Halliday and Da and all the men who were so good to their women. Yes, women were strong, and women together were even stronger, but there was also something very special in the bond between man and woman. Right now, just a few feet away behind a closed door, Mrs Costello would be receiving comfort and strength from the man who loved her.

Peggy had seen stillbirths before – as a pupil midwife, and as a handywoman. Sometimes the woman had an obvious infection, other times there was no apparent reason for it. Gradually, her sense of professional duty was returning, buoyed by the strength she was getting from Dan. She straightened, and they looked at one another for a long, long moment. The communion in that look was like nothing Peggy had ever known. She nodded then, and stepped away. Time to return to Mrs Costello.

Soon afterwards, the couple were ready to say their farewells to their wee deceased baby. Having completed writing her notes, Peggy stepped outside again briefly to allow them to say goodbye. Dan had sunk onto a nearby bench, head in hands, but she couldn't go to him now. She needed to stay strong and complete her duty. Returning to the bereaved parents, she spoke softly to them, and Mrs Costello placed one last kiss on her daughter's forehead. Mr Costello stroked her wee face, then they handed the baby to Peggy. As she walked out of the room, Mrs Costello's fresh sobs followed her. Walking carefully, she took the precious bundle to a side room, where Sister Dolan was waiting.

'Well done, Peggy,' she said, placing a kind hand on Peggy's arm, and Peggy almost gave in to the grief within her.

Blinking back tears, she said, 'It's a girl. Her mother called her Muireann.' Frowning, she asked, 'What do we do? There'll be no priest, no funeral.'

'No. We have wee boxes.' Opening a cupboard, Sister Dolan extracted a small wooden box. Not a coffin, just a plain rectangular box. 'Set the baby down here, and I'll examine her.'

Peggy did as she was bid, then stood watching as Sister completed a top-to-toe examination, handling the baby with great care and respect. She described her observations as she did so – including the signs that the baby had been dead for at least four or five days in the womb.

## The Irish Midwife

'Now,' she said, 'let's wrap you up in this beautiful blanket, Muireann.' This she did, discarding the towel into the bin, and then placed Muireann into the box. Together they fitted the lid, then carefully washed their hands. Astonishingly, Sister Dolan then produced a small hammer and some tiny tacks from another cupboard, and together they secured the lid – one tack at each corner. 'That's to prevent any accidents if someone trips or falls while carrying the box,' she said briskly. 'Now, do the family want to take her, or is she to be looked after by us?'

'I'll check,' Peggy said as Sister Dolan began writing up her notes and observations.

'Bring Midwife Logan with you,' she said. 'I'm taking you off the duty roster for tomorrow and Monday. Mr Sheridan too. You've both worked . . .' she thought for a moment, 'twenty-one hours straight.'

It certainly felt like it. 'No way was I leaving her, though,' Peggy said quietly. 'She'd built a relationship with me – with us.'

'Quite right, Peggy. I commend your compassion. Now' – her tone turned brisk again – 'hopefully Mrs Costello can get some sleep. Her husband can come back at visiting time.'

Peggy knew the rules. 'Yes, Sister.'

Dan had gone when she returned. She asked the senior doctor where he was, not caring in that moment whether he knew that they were courting.

'I told him to go. He's off duty now. You both did a sterling job.'

*A sterling job.* They had done the best they could. She glanced towards the bench where she had last seen Dan, feeling his absence. Stepping into the room, she introduced

## Seána Tinley

Midwife Logan, and advised Mr Costello that it was time for him to go. Squeezing Mrs Costello's hand, she promised to come back later. The woman looked exhausted, her eyes closing. Peggy left Midwife Logan to check on her and make her comfortable, then she and Mr Costello left.

'What happens now, Nurse?' he asked.

'Peggy,' she said. 'Call me Peggy. Unfortunately they won't give the baby a proper funeral, because she didn't take a breath.'

'Aye,' said Mr Costello harshly, his face twisting. 'Limbo or purgatory or something.'

'However,' Peggy added, 'if you promise not to open the box, I can pass Muireann to you. Have you a family plot?'

'We have. My ma and her parents are buried there. Glasnevin Cemetery.'

'Bury her there. Say nothing.'

'Thank you so much. That means everything! It'll give us both comfort in the times to come to know she's buried in holy ground alongside her granny.'

'A wee innocent like that is perfectly entitled to be buried with her family, no matter what the Church says,' said Peggy firmly. 'You have the car?'

'I have. Me and me da will do it as soon as the sun comes up.'

'Good. Bring the car round to the Parnell Street side. I'll meet you there.'

Dawn was breaking as Peggy watched Mr Costello's car depart up the deserted street. 'Goodbye, Muireann,' she whispered.

Midwifery was all about new life, but occasionally a wee soul wasn't destined to live. The handywoman knew

## The Irish Midwife

about death as well as life, and so Peggy knew she herself would be all right. She would grieve for the Costellos, and she would not let fear or grief stop her from supporting other women.

Weariness was now beginning to overtake her. Making her way up the stairs to her room felt as though she was climbing Sliabh Dubh at home. After minimal ablutions she fell into bed, and was asleep as soon as her head hit the pillow.

Peggy slept until mid-afternoon, and awoke with a groggy head. It was Sunday, but the hospital chaplain had told them all at the start of the year that it was acceptable to miss Mass if they were on duty or had come off night duty. After bathing and dressing she grabbed some tea and toast then visited Mrs Costello. The woman was pale, her eyes red, but she was calm. She thanked Peggy and hugged her, even making quiet mention of Glasnevin Cemetery, for her husband had been allowed in to see her briefly a little earlier.

Leaving her, Peggy felt the usual inadequacy when trying to comfort someone who was bereaved. There was no way to actually ease their pain, and because a stillbirth was only spoken about in hushed tones, Mrs Costello and her husband would miss out on a wake and all the support that could provide. No priest, no wake, no one even speaking of it . . . It was almost as if there was something shameful in it. *It's so wrong.*

Dan had apparently already been to see Mrs Costello. She found him in the common room and slid into the seat beside him. Others were present, so they limited themselves to a hand-squeeze under the table, then talked in low tones about last night's events. It was comforting to be with him again. Peggy could feel her insides starting to settle as their conversation moved on to more mundane matters – like how great it was to be off two days in a row.

'We should go somewhere. Get out of here,' Dan said suddenly. 'The weather's great, and we're not on again until Tuesday. What do you think?'

'You mean for a couple of hours? It's already three o'clock. Hard to get anywhere and back today.'

'No. I mean' – his voice dropped – 'stay somewhere. Get a hotel. Two rooms, of course,' he added hastily.

Peggy shook her head. 'I couldn't afford—'

'But I can. My treat. I have plenty of money. I need this. *We* need it, after last night.'

He was right. They needed to get away from the pain and heartache of Mrs Costello's loss. In terms of the money, they *were* courting, so he often paid for things. And two rooms, so she needn't worry he might be doing it to pressure her . . . She shook her head. He had never pressured her. In fact, it was just as often he who put a stop to things . . .

The notion was tempting. Definitely tempting. 'But where would we go?'

He took her hand. 'Let's just go to the station and see what's available. It'll be an adventure.'

Energy was now racing through Peggy at the notion. To stay in a hotel. To go impulsively, with no plan. To be with Dan, and nobody watching them. She grinned.

'Aye, go on then. Let's do it!'

# 31

Half an hour later they met under Clerys' clock, thinking it prudent to leave the Rotunda separately. Peggy had left a note for Anne, with strict instructions to tell no one where they had gone or for how long.

When she got there Dan was already waiting, a canvas bag slung on his shoulder and a huge smile on his face. He picked her up and swung her round, then planted a kiss on her lips. 'This is some craic!'

'It so is! I've never been adventurous, but this is such a daring thing to do. Love it!'

The train station was only a short walk away, and they stood looking at the list of upcoming departures, along with some helpful posters aimed at tourists. The Great Southern Railways owned a touring company, and so they opted for a bus trip to Wicklow, rather lyrically described as the Garden of Ireland, with one night in a hotel, dinner, breakfast, and a trip to Powerscourt Waterfall included, returning to Dublin by ten o'clock tomorrow evening. Dan made sure to pay the extra for two hotel rooms, a helpful porter told them where to find the bus, and twenty minutes later they were on their way.

The sense of adventure stayed with Peggy the whole time as the bus ambled through south County Dublin and on to

Wicklow. She exclaimed at glimpses of the sea, at the Wicklow mountains, and was fascinated by the pretty villages they passed through. Finally they arrived in Enniskerry, and the bus pulled up in the village square.

The Powerscourt Arms was a beautiful old building – painted white, with the woodwork on the gables and porch a neat, glossy black. A notice in the lobby informed guests that the hotel had been built in 1715, making it even older than the Rotunda.

The clerk at the desk took their details and gave them each a key. Peggy was in room 9 while Dan had room 5.

'Here's mine!' he said as they walked together along the well-lit corridor. 'Want to see?'

His room was neat and clean, with a large bed and views over the yards and rooftops of the village, and the Wicklow mountains in the distance.

'This is lovely!' said Peggy, trying *not* to think about him sleeping in that bed, right there. 'Right! Let's find room 9.'

Throwing his bag on the bed, he accompanied her back out to the corridor. She opened the door to her own room, and—

'Oh my God!' It was stunning. It was about twice the size of Dan's, with a four-poster bed, a sofa and an armchair. She had genuinely never seen anything like it in her entire life. Setting her bag down, she walked to the window. It looked to the front, with views over the square and the countryside beyond.

Dan whistled through his teeth. 'You've won the sweeps, Peggy! What a room!'

*The Irish Midwife*

Immediately a pang went through her. 'And you've paid for both. I feel bad. Do you want to swap? You should have the better room!'

Smiling, he put his arms around her. 'You're such a good person, you know that, Peggy Cassidy?'

'I'm serious! How can I take this, when you're paying for everything?'

He kissed her lightly. 'Because you deserve the best.' Stepping back, his tone turned brisk. 'I'm heading to the bathroom. Meet you downstairs in ten minutes?'

She agreed, and after he left couldn't help dancing around the room in joy. Never had she stayed anywhere this beautiful. Swiftly she emptied her little bag – nightgown under the pillow, toothbrush and hairbrush on the polished bedside table, her clothes for tomorrow in a drawer. There was a pile of towels on the chest of drawers, and she touched them just because. They were thick and soft and fluffy – a far cry from the thin practical towels she had used all her life – both at home, and in the Rotunda. Slipping her handbag over her arm, she left the room, carefully locking the door. Astonishing to think she would get to sleep there tonight. After a quick visit to one of the bathrooms dotted along the corridor she headed downstairs.

Dan was waiting, and her heart lit up on seeing him. *Remember every moment.* Somewhere in the back of her mind she was aware that July would soon be over. That meant they had only a month left, for in late August their time together would come to an end. Resolutely, she ignored it. *Now* was what mattered.

They wandered around the village, then followed signs for the nearby woodland walks. The place names on the map were wonderful. Carrickgollogan. Barnaslingan. Djouce

Wood. Powerscourt. There was even, a few miles away, a place called Crone Wood. Peggy nodded inwardly. Somewhere near here, maybe a long time ago, had lived a cailleach. *Witch. Hag. Wise-woman. Handywoman.* Women through the ages connected by the wisdom handed down from generation to generation. From knee to knee, as the phrase went in Irish.

The evening was cloudy but still bright, the woods alive with sound and scent. Peggy breathed it all in, committing as much as she could to memory. The path rose, and she was grateful for Dan's steadying hand as she nearly went over on her ankle a couple of times. Her best shoes were not, perhaps, most suitable for the terrain, but she didn't care. She was dressed in her Sunday best from head to toe, for today was special.

They crested the hill, and suddenly a dramatic vista opened up in front of them. The valley spread out for miles ahead, culminating in the sweeping verdant slopes of the Sugarloaf Mountain.

'Wow. So beautiful!' Lost in admiration, Peggy stood exclaiming, then turned to see why Dan wasn't saying anything.

'Yes, you are,' he said, and the sincerity in his voice made it feel like her heart turned over. 'I got you something.'

Only then did she realise he was holding a small wrapped present. 'For me?' she asked stupidly.

He put it into her hand. 'Aye.' He gave a short laugh. 'It's been in my canvas bag for ages – I could never find the right moment to give it to you.'

'Dan! You don't have to buy me presents!'

'Well, open it then. Don't just stand there!'

## The Irish Midwife

Carefully opening the wrapping, Peggy saw that inside was a small wooden box. She lifted the lid, and saw—

'Oh, Dan! Thank you!'

It was a fob watch, silver-coloured, with a white enamel face and numbers etched in black. The twelve was red, with a red medical cross below. She turned it over, loving the smoothness of it under her thumb, and opened the little clasp at the back. She stilled. There were tiny numbers and symbols etched into the metal. 'Wait. Is this – is this *real silver*?'

He shrugged. 'Only the best for the best girl.'

'I can't—'

'Yes, you can,' he said firmly. 'I don't want any nonsense.'

'But—'

'But nothing.' He pretended to huff. 'You could say thank you, like.'

'Thank you, thank you!' Throwing her arms around him, she kissed him fervently, knowing that he had managed to get her to accept his outrageous gift. Knowing too, that she would treasure it until the day she died.

'I love it,' she said quietly when they finally walked on. 'But why was it wrapped in Christmas paper?'

He shrugged. 'It was a Christmas present for you. I brought it to the game that day.'

The day she had been so cool with him. 'Ach, I'm sorry, Dan. I was feelin' so awkward about you meeting my ones, and realising I was – you know, poor. I thought you wouldn't want to be friends with me after that.'

'Is that really what you thought of me? That I wouldn't be friends with you because of your Da's job?'

She shrugged. 'Yes. It seemed impossible for the likes of you and the likes of me to . . . you know?'

'And now?'

She stopped, stunned. 'Now, I . . . don't know.'

He looked cross. 'You don't know? We've been together for nearly six months. Is there any part of you that still wonders if I'm a snob?'

'Well, no. But—'

'But what?'

'I don't know!' she burst out. 'In here.' She jabbed at her chest. 'I'm confused and I don't know *anything*, and the thought of Belfast fills me with . . . with terror. And . . . and hopelessness. And so I avoid it. I can't think about it. I just can't!'

'All right.' He seemed remarkably calm. 'I can see that you're upset about this. I'm going to leave it for now, but we will talk about this again. And to prepare, I want you to try and work out what's going on in your mind. The terror. The hopelessness. Will you do that for me?'

She nodded, unable to speak, almost overwhelmed by the strong emotions within, by the confusion raging through her. With a muffled exclamation he drew her into his arms. 'Ah, Peggy, Peggy. You'll be the death of me. You know that?'

He kissed her cheek, her nose, her cheek again. Turning her head, she found his lips, pouring into the kiss all the things she could not say. Ignoring the tears streaming down her cheeks, she deepened the kiss, passion rising within her. When they eventually parted they were both breathless, and the doubts that usually assailed her had temporarily eased. The smile they shared hit her squarely in the heart.

*Jesus!* For the first time it hit her – how hard it was going to be to break up with him. Nothing had changed. She was still Peggy Cassidy, milly and former handywoman, and he was still Dr Sheridan's son. How could she ever bring him home to Ma – the son of the man who had reported Aunty Bridget? How could she do that to her family? And yes, he wasn't a snob. But she would bet ten pounds his parents were. *No. Impossible.*

Ruthlessly, she pushed away the feeling of dread in the pit of her stomach. She was in the middle of one of the greatest adventures of her life. No way was she going to ruin it by thinking about terrible things.

'You're very quiet.' He was looking at her as they walked back towards the hotel. 'Are you all right?'

'I'm more than all right.' She was never one for gushing, and rarely said things like this out loud. But today was special. 'This whole thing is amazing.'

He exhaled. 'Good. Sometimes I can tell what you're thinking, how you're feeling. Other times . . .' He shrugged. 'I want you to be happy, Peggy.'

'I am happy.' And she was. Truly, deeply happy. As they meandered on, she allowed herself to really feel it. The most beautiful feeling, deep inside. *Happiness.*

★ ★ ★

Dinner was included in the price of their trip, and Dan was determined to make it special. His feelings for Peggy were deepening by the day. Looking back, he had already loved her at Christmas when he had bought her the watch. But now . . . now, *love* was too small a word for how he felt. She was everything. Compassionate, kind, smart, caring . . .

Loving, almost. He could not be certain, but surely the way she looked after him as he did her meant something?

She worried about him, teased him out of bad moods, helped him prepare for exams . . . she *knew* him, better than anyone knew him. As he did her.

As he waited for her in the hotel reception, he reflected on how well matched they were. They shared the same notions, the same values. They had the same ideas about the world. Oh, they disagreed at times – in fact they'd had some great debates. They even annoyed one another from time to time. But they fit. They matched. They belonged. He knew it in his bones. But did she?

He rose as she arrived, smoothing his tie. *Feck, that smile!* It made him light up from within. Not caring who might be looking, he kissed her cheek.

'What was that for?' she asked, her eyes dancing.

'For being too beautiful to resist,' he replied, and was rewarded by a slight blush on her part.

The waiter showed them to their table, seating Peggy in a formal way before giving them each a menu, then handing Dan the wine menu. Peggy had confessed earlier that she'd never eaten in a proper restaurant before, and that she was quite nervous about it, so Dan was determined to ease her worries.

'We'll have a bottle of the Shiraz, please,' he said as Peggy perused the food menu. 'I hope you don't mind me choosing the wine,' he said.

'Not at all, for I only know how to drink it, not choose it!' She gave a mischievous giggle. 'And I'm not even that experienced in drinking it! Or any alcohol, to be fair. But today is a day for adventures, and so I'm going to drink wine.'

Making a mental note not to let her over-indulge, Dan made a comment about the food menu, and they both made

## The Irish Midwife

their choices. The waiter returned with the wine then took their food order. As he was walking away, Peggy leaned forward, asking in a whisper,

'Why did he make you taste it first?'

Dan shrugged. 'They always do that. I think it's' – he dropped his voice, glancing around to make sure no one was listening – 'in case it might be off!'

'No!'

'Yup.'

'But it's so fancy here! Would they really serve something bad?'

'Well the wine has probably been sitting in their cellar for a few years, so of course it could be!'

They sat, and ate, and drank, and talked. They talked about the Costellos without mentioning their name, about Dan's final exams next week, about Peggy's upcoming interview in Belfast.

'Do you feel ready for it?'

She bit her lip. 'Yes and no. I've been more or less told the sorts of things they're likely to ask. What I don't know is whether my brain will work, or whether it'll just freeze up, and I'll be left making an eejit of myself!'

'Would it help to practise your answers?'

'Actually,' she said slowly, 'that's not the worst idea you've ever had. But not now. Not tonight. The interview is on Thursday, so I'm going up home on Wednesday.'

'And when will you be back?' *How long will I have to manage without you?*

'Friday. I'm on duty Friday night.' She sent him a keen glance, taking another sip of wine, then licking her lips delicately. 'What about you?'

'Sorry, what?' His gaze was still on her lips.

'What about your exams next week? Are you ready?'

'Aye. It'll be grand. We're all well on top of it. The harder exams were those February ones. At this stage I think they *want* us to pass, you know?'

She considered this. 'That could be true. Now that we're in our last few weeks of midwifery training, they're putting us under less pressure. They expect us to know things now. And we do. We actually do.'

'Excuse me.' It was their waiter. 'We're closing up for the night, so . . .'

'Oh! Of course! Apologies.' They both stood, Dan realising the other diners were long gone and they were the only ones left. 'Thank you.'

They continued to chat about exams as they mounted the stairs, Dan putting a steadying hand under Peggy's elbow at one stage as she nearly missed a step. *How much wine has she had?* He reflected on this as he waited outside the bathroom for her, not wanting her to fall down or to be accosted in some way. Any low-life could be roaming about the hotel in the hopes of finding such an opportunity. Yes, it was unlikely, but . . .

She emerged, her face pink from being recently washed, and made for her room. He stifled a grin at the notion that, even tipsy, she had carefully had a wash before bed. Again, he hovered as she fumbled with her key. She'd had three glasses. Maybe four. *Hmmm.* Enough, given that she rarely drank.

She was still talking as she entered the room, and clearly expected him to follow. He hesitated, suddenly uncomfortable. 'Well, good night, then.' He stayed in the doorway, not wanting to step inside.

## The Irish Midwife

She kept walking, turning on the bedside light before crossing to close the curtains. There was a definite sway in her step as she turned towards the sofa, and her hands flew out to keep herself steady.

'What? No goodnight kiss?' She was definitely pouting. He had never seen her pout before. It was extremely endearing.

*Lord, don't do this to me!*

'Actually, I need the bathroom myself. I'll come back and kiss you in a minute.'

Closing the door, he made for the same bathroom she had recently vacated, relieving himself before washing his hands and face – desperately hoping that a dash of cold water would quieten his thoughts. *Peggy. Alone. Beautiful. Four-poster bed.*

*Bloody hell!*

Once he'd judged a decent amount of time had passed, he emerged. Hopefully she'd have settled a bit. He knocked on the door.

'Come in.'

*One quick kiss, then get out of there!*

Swiftly he entered, closing the door behind him. He turned, looking towards the sofa where he had last seen her. She wasn't there.

'Peggy?'

*Oh, feck!*

She was sitting on the bed wearing some sort of white nightgown and, he suspected, very little else.

'I had the best day.' She rose, the light behind her clearly outlining her shapely legs through the thin cotton. *She probably has no idea . . .*

'Thank you, Dan,' she continued. 'I'll never forget it.' Sliding her arms around him, she lifted her face for his kiss, as she had done hundreds of times these past few months.

# 32

Dan was lost. Her breasts, unencumbered by whatever undergarment she usually wore, were pressed against his chest. Just two layers of fine cotton between his skin and hers. And they were together in a hotel room. Alone.

'Peggy,' he said hoarsely, taking her mouth in a kiss of passionate desperation.

Unfortunately, she responded. Responded with a passion to match his own. Her hands were on his back, in his hair, now on his bottom – pressing him closer to her.

His hands were busy too – on her bottom, her breasts, and back again. He groaned, then bent his head to find her nipple with his mouth through the thin fabric. She threw her head back, and he gloried in the sight of her, the feel of her. They had occasionally got a little carried away like this before – but always in a situation where they couldn't take it further. And always before, she had been wearing many more clothes. It was wonderful . . . yet his conscience wouldn't rest.

'We have to stop,' he managed.

'I know,' she said, while at the same time her hands were exploring the front of his trousers. Through his clothing she stroked and squeezed, till he thought he might disgrace himself.

'Stop, stop.' He arched his hips away from her, grabbing her hands.

'Dan, please. I want to.'

'So do I. You have no idea how much. But I don't want to get you pregnant, Peggy.'

His words had an instant effect, as though someone had thrown a bucket of cold water over her.

'No, I don't suppose you do.' Her expression changed, became shuttered.

Inwardly, a new idea struck him. He *did* want to get her pregnant. He wanted her and only her to be the mother of his children. But only after they were married. Never could he allow anything bad to be said about her. And it always seemed to be the girl who got blamed when pregnancies happened.

'You're right, of course. We can't risk a pregnancy.' Her expression had cleared: his Peggy had returned. 'But, feck, that was class!'

He feigned shock. 'Peggy Cassidy!'

'I know.' She giggled. 'Sometimes I wish I wasn't a good Catholic girl.'

'Ah, but then you wouldn't be my Peggy.' He exhaled through his teeth. 'And you're right,' he said soberly. 'It was class. You're . . . you're so beautiful. And I want you so much.'

She sent him a saucy look. 'Will you . . . is this frustrating for you? Like, what does it do to a man, to go that far without . . . finishing?'

He sent her a wry smile. 'I have every intention of . . . er . . . finishing, once I get to my room.'

'Oh, really?' she asked archly. 'Because I do too.' Her eyes danced. 'If you teach me, could I help? I mean, just my hands. No risk of pregnancy.'

Shock held him speechless for a minute, then the possibilities flew through his mind. It would be up to him, he knew, to ensure that there was no risk of pregnancy. Hands only . . .

'Only if I get to return the favour.' He allowed a devilish look into his eye, deliberately using words that she'd said to him before. 'Take it or leave it!'

Her eyes widened, then she grinned. 'I'll take it!'

★ ★ ★

Peggy stretched, snuggling closer to Dan, who was sleeping at her back. Half-asleep, she was aware enough to try to notice, and *remember*, how it felt to be sharing a bed next to him. He tightened his arms around her, planting a sleepy kiss on the back of her neck.

Gradually she realised that pale morning light was peeping around the edge of the curtains. He realised it too, for he murmured,

'I have to go before the staff wake up.'

Turning around to face him, she kissed him, smoothing his hair back from his forehead.

'Are you all right?' he asked, the usual worry lines furrowing his brow when he was concerned about her.

'I'm great,' she said, tracing the lines with her finger. 'No regrets.'

'No regrets. Good.'

He got up then, and found his clothes in the half-light. They had both stuck to their deal last night, and it had been the most wonderful experience of Peggy's life. Neither had been touched intimately by another person before, but they had coached one another into a very successful outcome – and with no risk of pregnancy.

'Goodbye, beautiful,' he said, planting a last, sweet kiss on her lips. 'I'll see you downstairs at half eight.'

And then he was gone, and Peggy slid into the warm place in the bed he'd left behind, closing her eyes again as sleep reclaimed her.

\* \* \*

It really had been one of the peak experiences of her life, Peggy reflected as she walked down the Falls Road towards the Royal Maternity Hospital. And really, she had surprised herself by how little she regretted it. All those messages she had heard over the years from nuns and priests, and Ma and aunties – that a girl had to be careful, that men couldn't control their urges, that a girl who 'got herself pregnant' was to be condemned . . . it all seemed foolish now. Dan had been entirely able to control his urges, sticking rigidly (and delightfully) to their agreement. The whole process had been fascinating, and wonderful, and deliciously forbidden. And when he had touched her . . .

She had to stop thinking about it. About him. They had returned from Enniskerry three days ago, and she was about to enter the Royal for a job interview – possibly the only time in her life she would have to endure such an ordeal.

The building was new, clean, and modern, and had apparently been designed in light of the most up-to-date understanding of how a maternity hospital should be laid out. The porticoed entrance looked grand and impressive, and Peggy took a careful breath before pushing open the door. Once inside, she went up three shallow steps to where a sign was posted a little further along. *Interview candidates*, it read, *please wait to be called*. There was an arrow pointing to a door on the left.

Tentatively, Peggy stepped inside. Two other girls were already there, and with a tight smile she made her way to an empty seat. It was an interesting room, with windows either side of the fireplace, and a dresser with a full set of china by the wall. The chairs and settees were upholstered in red, which added a sense of warmth to what might otherwise have been a fairly stark room.

'What time are you in at?' one of the girls asked, sending her an inquisitive look.

'Eleven. You?'

'I'm quarter to eleven.'

'And I'm quarter past.' The second girl made a face. 'I'm far too early, which won't help the nerves.'

They shared their names then, and details of their training. Maisie – who had arrived far too early – had trained in England, while Priscilla had trained in the Union Infirmary in South Belfast.

'So why are you applying to the Royal?'

Priscilla shrugged. 'Some of the people in the Union Infirmary aren't very nice.'

'Oh. I'm sorry to hear that.'

The door opened, admitting a tall midwife wearing what must be the Royal uniform. It was almost identical to that of the Rotunda, though the dress was darker. And of course the badge was different.

'Priscilla Gildea, please.'

Priscilla stood, her demeanour suddenly tense. 'Good luck!' Peggy mouthed as she followed the tall woman out.

Once the door was closed again she and Maisie chatted, Peggy not wanting to give into nerves. Apparently this room, so Maisie informed her, was Matron's sitting room.

'Matron has a sitting room?'

'Yup. There's another room opposite for the use of the lead obstetrician.'

Maisie was nice, and it was reassuring to know there was someone here who might become a friend – assuming they were both offered positions, of course.

All too soon the door opened again. 'Margaret Cassidy.'

Even the use of her formal name gave Peggy butterflies. No one called her Margaret. Even the seniors in the Rotunda had learned to call her Peggy.

'I'm Sister Muriel Hanna. Your interview will be in Matron's office. Have you come far today?'

They went back down the three steps towards the entrance portico, but then turned left along a narrow corridor. There was a window on the left and some doors on the right.

'Oh, no, not far. I walked here from home.'

Straight ahead, at the end, was another door, the word *Matron* painted on the woodwork in gilt letters. Inside was a formidable-looking woman with grey hair and an uncompromising expression. She was seated at a desk but rose as they entered, stepping towards the table in the corner. The room, Peggy saw at a glance, had a fireplace, three windows, and a carpet. *Very fancy.*

'Good morning, Miss Cassidy.' Matron gestured towards an empty chair. 'Please sit down.' Peggy sat, and Sister Hanna sat opposite, alongside Matron.

*The Irish Midwife*

Matron looked through the papers in front of her. 'I see you trained at the Rotunda, Miss Cassidy, yet you're from Belfast. Why go to Dublin?'

Thankfully, Peggy was ready for this question. 'I have relatives in Dublin and felt it was a good opportunity to train there. I'm a Belfast girl though, so always intended to come back.'

Technically she did have relatives in Dublin – both Ma and Da had cousins there. The fact that she hadn't seen them since starting her training was of no matter.

'Why do you want to be a midwife, Miss Cassidy?'

Peggy's confidence rose. So far, so good. She spoke of passion and knowledge, and being with-woman. Both Matron and Sister wrote down her answer, both expressionless.

'Here's a theoretical situation for you. How would you manage this?' Matron went on to describe a fictitious woman who was clearly displaying symptoms of infection. Trying not to think about Mrs Costello and her tragic outcome, Peggy calmly went through the actions she would take as a midwife – both in caring for that woman and baby, and in preventing the infection from spreading to anyone else.

Matron nodded. 'When do you qualify?'

'Next month, so long as I pass the final oral exam.'

'Specifically?'

'Oh, the ceremony is on Friday the twenty-fifth of August.'

'Very well. Assuming you pass your remaining exams, please report to Sister Hanna at half past eight on Monday the twenty-eighth. Make sure you bring your certificate from the Rotunda.' She half smiled. 'Welcome to the Royal, Miss Cassidy.'

# 33

*Friday, 25 August 1939*

'Congratulations, ladies. You are all now qualified midwives. When your name is called, please step forward to receive your certificate and badge.'

Pride soared within Peggy. *I've done it!* She was near the start of the list, and walked forward calmly, her confidence boosted by her gorgeous new dress. She had taken the head staggers and joined some of her friends on a shopping trip a few days ago, as she still had most of the funds assigned for her 'pocket money' during the course. Anne had got her to try on the dress, and Peggy had fallen in love with it as soon as she had put it on.

It was calf-length, bias-cut, and the fabric featured pink flowers on a black background. It was the most glamorous thing she had ever owned, and it was made of silk georgette. Actual silk. The feel of it swishing against her calves as she walked to the front of the lecture room was fabulous.

Returning to her seat beaming with pride, she clapped for all the others, occasionally touching the Rotunda badge now pinned to her chest. The medical students were all at the back of the hall, clapping and occasionally whooping as their friends received recognition after a year of training. Their own ceremonies would be at their universities in the coming weeks, as the Rotunda placement was only one element of their studies.

The new cohort of medical students had arrived a couple of weeks ago, and from today were taking over the student medical rota. That meant the old medical students were all now free.

Free to go. Free to work. Free to have their hearts broken.

The dark cloud that seemed to have followed Peggy around these past few weeks had been steadily growing. It was now enormous, threatening to engulf her as soon as she looked at it. And so she did not look anywhere near it, keeping her mind on the present, living from day to day, moment to moment. She could not, *would* not give in to emotion. It was going to be hard enough to say goodbye to Dan tomorrow, without living it ahead of time.

Tonight, they were all going out on the town. There was a dance on in the Halla Banba, at the top of Parnell Square, and Peggy intended to dance all night. She and Dan had never danced together before, and she was looking forward to being in his arms in public, perfectly legitimately. She still remembered every detail of their night together in Enniskerry, and remained fiercely glad they had done what they had done. No one's virginity had been lost, no sperm had been allowed anywhere near the vicinity of a potential ovum, and she and Dan had experienced one of the best, most extraordinary nights ever.

As they walked to the dance hall, the girls passed men selling the evening newspaper. The headlines screamed out about the new pact agreed today between Britain and Poland, which was a direct response to the German-Russian pact signed on Wednesday. *It's all formalised now*, thought Peggy.

## The Irish Midwife

*Once misstep and there'll be war.* Change was most definitely in the air. Pain, too. And tragedy.

But not tonight.

With Anne, Mary, and Joan, Peggy paid the entrance fee and went inside. The place was already busy, with young men all seated or standing on the right, women on the left. They bought tins of delicious fizzy drinks called Club Orange, and wandered around chatting to some of the other newly qualified midwives.

'You're a midwife!' they kept saying to each other.

'Yes, and you're a midwife, too!' It felt strange, but so, so great. *I'm a midwife.*

The band was ready, and the *fear an tí* – the host – called the first dance, which was *Ballaí Liomnaí* – 'The Walls of Limerick'. This one required two couples per set, so Peggy grabbed Anne and waited for the lads. Over they came, and they all took their places on the dance floor.

They had all been taught the céilí dances in school and the 'Walls of Limerick', being the simplest, was the first one that most people learned. Holding hands with Dan, Peggy advanced and retired, then swapped places, danced briefly with Paudie, then came back to Dan for the swing. Moving round to the next couple, they prepared to do it all again.

With the shadow of war hanging over them, and with the numbers in the dance hall swelled by a large group of young men and women who had just finished their studies, the atmosphere was definitely feverish. True to her word, Peggy danced every dance, Dan by her side. They had to count carefully during the 'Waves of Tory' to make sure they would end up together when the marching lines became couples for the reel part.

'I'm thirteen from the top!' Peggy shouted across the floor to where Dan stood in the line of boys.

'Thirteen! Got it!' He counted too, and when they marched down the lines, meeting under an arch of hands, they claimed one another with a triumphant smile.

Finally, it was all over. Standing by his side as the band played the national anthem, Peggy felt the first sting of tears behind her eyes. The thunderstorm in her heart would soon be upon her. *Not yet.* She had to hold on for a little longer. Bad things were coming, and they were inevitable.

## Saturday, 26 August 1939

Despite the late night, Peggy had set her alarm for six in the morning. Anne grumbled in her sleep, then turned over, while by the light of morning coming through the curtains, Peggy packed up everything of hers from their little room. *My last morning waking up here.*

When she returned from the bathroom Anne was awake.

'God, you're packed and all!'

'Aye. Got to be organised,' Peggy said lightly. 'Now, you will reply when I write to you?'

'Course I will. We're best friends, you and me.' She yawned. 'I better get a move on. Can't miss our last Rotunda breakfast!'

Peggy dressed while she was gone, stuffing her nightgown into the last corner of her bag. It was fuller than it had been when she came a year ago – the main additions being two textbooks, three notebooks filled with all her lecture notes, and her lovely new dress. She also had a new midwife's badge and a silver fob watch, which she had not yet used.

## The Irish Midwife

Sitting the bag on her bed along with her coat, she took a breath. This had been a special time, in a special place, with special people. And now it was over.

The air at breakfast was definitely strained, as everyone braced themselves for the goodbyes to come. Paudie was visiting Anne's family next week, and they intended to do their best to keep their relationship going. Peggy ate very little, the sick feeling inside her growing by the minute.

Afterwards, Dan said, 'Outside?' and she nodded.

He took her hand as they walked through the doors and out into the gardens. *The last time. The last time.*

'It's so strange to think we'll never be back here as students.'

'I know. Doesn't seem real, somehow.'

He led her onto the green where they'd first got together, then stopped, taking both her hands.

'Peggy,' he began, and her heart sank. 'I've tried to talk to you a few times recently about what happens in Belfast, but you'd never talk about it.'

She swallowed. *It's time.* 'I know. I didn't want to spoil our last few weeks together.'

'What do you mean, *spoil*? You're surely not still thinking we should break up?'

She looked at him, afraid to say it out loud.

He looked her directly in the eye. 'Tread softly, Peggy.'

*The Yeats poem!* His voice was low, and a pang went through her. *Tread softly, for you tread on my dreams . . .*

She had to be brave. Had to tell him.

She took a breath. 'Nothing's changed, Dan. We could get away with being together here, but it would never work in Belfast.'

He dropped her hands. 'Why the fuck not?'

She flinched at his curse word, and he visibly tried to get himself under better control.

'You say nothing's changed,' he said, his tone tight. '*Everything's* changed, Peggy. Everything!'

She set her chin, shaking her head.

'So, all this . . . Was it some sort of *game* to you?' The hurt in his eyes was almost her undoing.

'No! It was real, and lovely.' She could hear her voice shaking. 'But that was the deal. You knew from the start.'

'Take it or leave it.' His tone was harsh, his face twisted.

'Yes.' *If I have a fairy godmother,* she thought, rather randomly, *now would be a very good moment for her to show herself.* But magic only happened in fairy tales and pantomimes.

'Jesus, Peggy!' He looked directly at her, his eyes filled with pain. 'I feel like I don't know you suddenly.'

'Maybe you never did.'

'No. You're wrong. I do know you, and this makes no sense.' He took a breath. 'When we were out walking in Enniskerry, you spoke of terror and hopelessness.'

'I remember.'

'Can you explain that to me?'

*Not without betraying my Aunty Bridget.* 'I know you're not a snob, Dan. I *know* that. But our worlds are so different. And Belfast feels like, I dunno. Like those dividing lines are stronger than they are in the south.'

'This is bullshit, Peggy. I cannot believe that you're doing this, after everything that's happened between us.' His voice was raw with anger, fuelled by pain. All she could do was stand there and take it, as best she could. 'I can't do this right now, Peggy. I—'

Holding a hand up – whether as a barrier or a plea, she could not tell – he then turned and stormed off. The only other time he'd done that was when they'd all been teasing him at supper, six months ago.

For a long moment Peggy stood there numbly, unable to move or think or feel. She watched until he turned the corner and disappeared, then just stayed there, frozen by anguish.

Birds were singing, and a slight breeze was making the leaves in the trees nearby rustle. And it was all entirely meaningless. She felt strangely detached, as though watching a play. This could not be real. She could not possibly have deliberately and knowingly hurt him, and herself in the process. Could she?

Movement came back first, and a feeling of urgency. She had come close to breaking down there now, to dropping the whole stupid idea of breaking up with him. She had so wanted to throw her arms around him and tell him it was all a mistake. And that would never do. She had to run, now, and get as far away from him as she could.

Walking quickly, she made for the sanctuary of the nurses' home.

Even if the difference between them in class could be overcome – and that was a massive *if* – that still left the fact that Dr Sheridan had reported Aunty Bridget.

The only reason Peggy was even here in Dublin was because Aunty Bridget was dead, the savings she had gathered for her old age useless to her. It would be the worst of betrayals for Peggy to fall in love with a Sheridan – the family that had contributed to her beloved aunt's death. Unknowingly, perhaps. Unintentionally, certainly. But Dr Sheridan had still done it.

*Seána Tinley*

Her family had been polite to Dan at Christmas, for which she was grateful. But she would never forget the way Da had said, 'The one who—' and the way Ma had cut him off.

*The one who* reported Ma's sister. *The one who* brought the police into it. *The one who* . . .

She *knew* Dan, *knew* he was a good person. His father might have thought he was doing a good thing by reporting a handywoman. It didn't really matter. He was still The One Who.

And that meant it would be unfair of her to lead Dan on by pretending they might have a future. While it was killing her to know how much he was hurting right now – hurting because of her – all she could do was hope that he got over her quickly. It was unfortunate that he was going to be working in the Royal too, but at least the move to Belfast meant a fresh start for both of them. New routines. New friendships.

Swiftly, she walked up the stairs and along to her room. Anne was packing, and Peggy managed a reasonable goodbye before putting on her coat, picking up her bag, and walking out. Within the hour she was on the train, steaming north to Belfast, alone.

★ ★ ★

Dan came back to the hospital about an hour later, as he knew he had to. He hadn't yet packed, and he had no idea which train he and Peggy would take to Belfast. That journey would be his last chance to try to understand her reasoning, to try to get her to change her mind. They would have more than two hours to talk. Surely he could manage to turn this around in two hours?

## The Irish Midwife

Her insistence that they still had to break up had come as a shock. To be fair, he had been worried when she refused to talk about Belfast each time he'd brought it up, but he'd managed to convince himself all would be well. Foolishly, as it turned out.

Did she think Belfast was some sort of alien world, totally different to Dublin? Ireland was Ireland, and people were people, and Belfast was little different to Dublin in the ways that mattered. Heading to his room, he began to pack, his mind on the thorny problem of what he might say to her, what questions he might ask . . .

Paudie arrived then, to begin his own packing. 'You all right, bai?'

Dan shrugged, unwilling to lie.

Paudie made a face as he rolled up a shirt and stuffed it into his bag. 'I heard Peggy left already. Did you two have some sort of falling out?'

There was a roaring in Dan's ears. *Shock*, he thought dimly. Aloud, he managed, 'She left? She's gone?'

'Ah, feck it, man, I thought you knew. She went ages ago, took an early train. Anne was really sad about saying goodbye to her.'

Dan's knees suddenly felt strange. Sinking down onto the bed, he put his head in his hands. *Peggy left already*.

'What the fuck happened?' Paudie looked almost as bewildered as Dan felt.

'We spoke outside after breakfast. She still thinks we have to break up before Belfast.'

'So now, then?'

'Yes.'

*She broke up with me. And I had no say in the matter.* The feeling of powerlessness made the hurt a thousand times worse. As if in a trance, he packed the rest of his stuff, gave Paudie what he hoped was a decent farewell, and walked to Amiens Street to take an afternoon train.

# PART III

# 34

*Belfast, Friday, 1 September 1939*

It was hard, moving home, starting a new job, and dealing with a broken heart all at the same time. Peggy's family had welcomed her back home with clear pride, but things had changed. She had changed.

While it was wonderful to be home and to see them all every day, something inside Peggy chafed when Ma asked what time she'd be home, or told her to go to bed as she had an early start in the morning. Having had some independence, it was hard to go back to being treated as a child again. Ma meant well – she couldn't help it – but at times Peggy found herself really struggling not to be cheeky.

Ma had already committed her to help out with the old people's dinner on Saturday, and of course she was expected to do her fair share of work around the house. Having adapted to the luxury of only having herself to look after in Dublin, something inside her was fighting against the idea of being managed by Ma once again.

In Dublin, off duty meant you were free to do what you wanted, so long as it didn't threaten the reputation of the hospital. Here, off duty meant you had time to do tasks for Ma. And she was happy to help, it was just . . .Oh, *everything* was hard.

There was also no privacy, ever. No bathroom to hide in when a good cry was needed. Peggy's tears were saved for deep in the night, with Aiveen and Sheila fast asleep in the big bed beside her. Even then, she had to cry silently, for fear of waking them.

She thought about Dan constantly. In a way, losing him reminded her of the grief she'd felt on losing Aunty Bridget. Like bereavement, except he was still alive. Still wanting to be with her. Oh, the temptation to give up and go to him was so strong. But she'd been raised to do the right thing, even if it was hard.

Should she have told him the whole truth, rather than only focusing on the class differences between their families? He clearly had no idea that Bridget had been her aunt. It was even possible he didn't know what his da had done.

She'd thought about it a hundred times, and each time, she'd come to the same conclusion. Telling him about Aunty Bridget would only add to his hurt, without solving anything. It simply couldn't be solved, for what was done was done. He couldn't bring Aunty Bridget back, couldn't prevent his father from reporting her. And it would always be there – a fault line between her family and his.

Her first week in the Royal had gone well, she supposed. She and the five other new girls – including Maisie and Priscilla – had been given a tour of the (fabulous) building, and various learning sessions explaining how things worked in the Royal. To Peggy's relief it all was very similar to practice in the Rotunda. Maisie had been just as nice as Peggy remembered, though she wasn't so sure about Priscilla.

Dan and the other new junior doctors were expected to start on Monday. The names had been shared on a

## The Irish Midwife

noticeboard near the entrance corridor, and Peggy had felt a sense of déjà vu as her eyes had instantly sought out his name – this time with the word 'Doctor' in front of it. *Dr Daniel Sheridan.* Dr Sheridan. Peggy would have to brace herself to see him again.

Peggy Cassidy and Priscilla Gildea had both been assigned to A Ward, a bright and airy space for postnatal women and their babies. The sister there, Sister Campbell, was strict but fair. On the first day she told them that she ran a tight ship and that she expected them to comply with all of her requirements and instructions.

'Yes, Sister,' Peggy had replied meekly.

First nuns, now midwives. She had basically been meekly saying 'Yes, Sister' most of her life. Inwardly though, she knew herself to be a rebel. Had she not worked as a handywoman, then trained as a midwife? Had she not courted Dan Sheridan, the son of a doctor, and far above her own station in life? Had she not slept in a bed with him for a whole night, and both of them naked as newborns?

Quickly, she diverted her thoughts away from that night. Now was not the time. Sister was holding her early-morning meeting with all the midwives in the office beside the main bay.

'Next Wednesday afternoon,' she was saying, 'the fundraising committee are holding an event in the baby clinic. Many of our donors will be attending, as well as all senior staff, and I have been asked to nominate a junior member of staff to accompany me to represent our ward. Margaret Cassidy will attend on our behalf.'

Peggy gulped, but managed to nod. A wave of nervousness rushed through her, but she countered it by reminding herself of all the senior people – including donors – she'd met during her time in the Rotunda.

'How come *you* got picked?' asked Priscilla as they began making up two empty beds. Her tone indicated she wasn't a bit happy.

'No idea,' Peggy replied. A thought occurred to her. 'It could be because my surname is so early in the alphabet. At school I always got picked on by teachers to do things because of that. Me and Brona Anderson. I bet you get to go to the next one.'

'Hrmmph.' Priscilla was still miffed. Peggy could tell. Peggy suppressed a sigh. Some people had little to be worrying about. Sister was approaching, so she couldn't say anything more.

'When you've done the beds,' Sister said crisply, 'I want you to go to delivery suite and bring back a new mother and her baby. A Mrs Murray in room four. Put her in the empty space at the bottom there.'

'Yes, Sister.'

★ ★ ★

It was hard, moving home, starting a new job and dealing with a broken heart at the same time. Dan was now a junior houseman rather than a medical student, and the new junior doctors had been asked to start today, even though it was a Friday. Today was September first, and apparently it would make the paperwork easier if they started on the first. They would spend the day in orientation lectures, meeting the medical team, and taking part in ward rounds throughout the hospital. And he would maybe see Peggy.

## The Irish Midwife

It had been almost a week since they broke up. He missed her something terrible. They had been inseparable since that day in March, and had basically seen each other almost every day for the past year. Not seeing her, not talking to her, not kissing her, had left a huge hole in his life. A heart-shaped hole.

As if his heartbreak wasn't enough, the past few days had been a waking nightmare in other ways. Being back under his mother's roof, having to account to her for every minute of every day, was slowly killing him. Already she had had Melissa Moore and her mother over for tea, and he'd had to endure their sly hints and Melissa's blatant flirtation for nearly two hours.

It had been a relief to tell Ma he had to work today. The Royal had also asked for volunteers to staff the Sunday-night medical shift, and he'd put himself forward straight away. Like his da, he anticipated working as much as he could get away with for as long as he was living at home.

The news from Europe was also dreadful. Yesterday, the Westminster government had started evacuating civilians from London, and this morning on the wireless had come the news that, despite everything, Germany had invaded Poland during the night. War was upon them, and everyone was now simply waiting for the announcement.

Despite the weak assurances of James Craig – the man currently leading the Stormont government – conscription might well follow – and just as Dan qualified as a doctor. As a healthy man in his mid-twenties he would be among the first called up, he knew. While he was not afraid – though he probably should be – he felt a sense of frustration. History was repeating itself, only twenty years after the Great

War, and fuelled by the same posturing and arrogance that had caused the first war. While Germany were clearly in the wrong, and could not be ignored, the fact that the six counties of the north-eastern part of Ireland had not won independence with the rest of the country meant that those who did not see themselves as British, those who could not understand Britain's need to be Policeman of the World, well, they would get caught up in matters whether they wanted to or not.

Paudie would not be conscripted, and nor would any of Dan's other friends from the south. The Irish Free State had already signalled that its neutrality would be preserved, and so the lads that Dan had trained with would all be free to pursue their work as medics without being dragged into a war that was none of their doing.

Should he have stayed in Dublin? The Rotunda had a few vacant posts for his level, and apparently the Coombe and Holles Street hospitals in the capital also had junior doctor posts available. He sighed. Too late now.

The truth was he'd chosen Belfast because of Peggy. And Peggy had broken up with him. Would he have been better to follow his own path? Or should he have tried to persuade her to stay in the Rotunda? They could have had a good life in Dublin – marriage, children, satisfying work . . .

But there was no point daydreaming. They were both in Belfast, and Peggy couldn't have made it clearer that she didn't want to be with him. And all out of some sort of inverted snobbery. *Damn it!*

\* \* \*

## The Irish Midwife

Delivery suite was apparently fairly quiet, which was good. They'd been told earlier in the week that over 70 per cent of Belfast mothers gave birth at home, and that this was expected to continue. The bed numbers in the Royal had been planned accordingly, and the midwives spent at least half their time out on the district. Peggy couldn't wait to get out and about among the women of Belfast, and suspected that home births would always be her favourite. For now though, she would learn all she could about what was needed of her in the hospital.

They chatted as they walked to delivery suite, Priscilla asking her where she lived.

'The Rock streets,' Peggy said flatly, knowing what Priscilla was angling for. 'Off the Falls Road.'

'Oh. I'm from Ravenhill.'

*I bet you are.* Working-class Catholic, middle-class Protestant. Worlds apart. Thankfully they had now arrived in delivery suite.

'Yes, Mrs Murray is ready for the postnatal ward. Room 4. Thanks, girls.' The midwife on duty pointed to her left, and Peggy followed Priscilla inside the room.

'Good morning, Mrs Murray,' Priscilla announced brightly to the woman in the bed. 'I'm Midwife Gildea and this is Midwife Cassidy. We've been asked to bring you to the postnatal ward.'

Mrs Murray's eyes widened as she saw Peggy. 'Peggy! Peggy Cassidy! So lovely to see you again!' With dawning horror Peggy just stood there, knowing that Mrs Murray was going to say something incriminating, yet being unable to stop her.

'. . . Especially after the way you looked after me with my first,' Mrs Murray continued. 'You and lovely Mrs Devine. Best handywoman in Belfast!'

Priscilla's head turned towards Peggy, a look of shocked questioning giving way to realisation then slyness, quickly hidden.

*Feck! Jesus, Mary and feckin' Joseph!*

'Congratulations on your new baby,' Peggy replied, her voice shaking slightly. She walked across to the cot and looked inside, though she couldn't really take in what she was seeing. 'How many wee ones have you now?'

'This is my third,' Mrs Murray said proudly. 'I've a boy and a girl at home, and now another wee girl.'

'Ah, that's lovely.'

All the while it felt as though Priscilla was watching their exchange closely, her manner reminding Peggy of some sort of bird circling its prey. All the blood had drained from Peggy's face, she knew, for the world seemed to be spinning slightly, and her knees felt as though the bones were too soft to hold her up.

Mrs Murray looked from one midwife to the other then frowned, biting her lip. 'Er, anyway. I'm looking forward to getting a good rest the week or so in the postnatal ward. It's the main reason I decided to have this one in the hospital.'

'Quite right too,' said Priscilla cheerfully. 'Now, let's get your things together.' Taking Mrs Murray's bag, she began putting the woman's belongings into it. Belatedly, Peggy went to help, passing the baby to her mother, and by the time they were pushing Mrs Murray's bed through the corridor she had managed to regain a semblance of self-control.

## The Irish Midwife

Why had she not been prepared for this? It was bound to happen eventually – encountering a woman whom she'd supported as a handywoman. Murray was a fairly common name in the north, so it had never occurred to her that it could be *this* Mrs Murray. *I'm too used to supporting women I don't know in Dublin.*

Besides, Mrs Murray of all people should have known not to mention their previous connection, for it had been her house that the police had invaded that day. Her husband had come to Aunty Bridget's funeral, and had been full of rage – like everyone else, seeing it as no coincidence that the handywoman had suffered the stroke on the very day she'd been lifted by the RUC for the first and only time in her life.

Peggy sighed inwardly. She had literally been in the Royal less than a week, and her secret was already in danger of being revealed. She had even managed to bite her tongue when she had met Dr Fenton yesterday. The man had seemed to her both cold-hearted and arrogant, quite unlike most of the obstetricians. Maybe she was prejudiced against him – but he deserved it, so she didn't care.

Perhaps, she thought hopefully, Priscilla hadn't fully understood the circumstances under which Peggy had previously met Mrs Murray. *Or perhaps she had understood perfectly.* Remembering the sly look that had flashed into the midwife's eyes, Peggy was pessimistic about the chances of Priscilla keeping the information secret. Which meant she might have to lie. And she hated lying. Her whole life had been a lie, this past year.

Had she lied to Dan? Well, no. But she had omitted part of the truth. *What a mess. What a feckin' mess.*

## Seána Tinley

At the end of the corridor they turned the bed into A Ward, carefully manoeuvring it down the narrow corridor and into the bay. Priscilla went off to get a cot for the baby, and Mrs Murray took the opportunity to speak to Peggy in hushed tones.

'I'm so sorry, Peggy. Have I got you into trouble? My God, they really hate handywomen, don't they?'

'Wheesht!' Peggy glanced around to make sure no one was listening. 'They do. It's really unfair.'

'And your poor aunty. But good on you for playin' them at their own game, Peggy! Look at you, uniform and nurse's watch and all!'

The mention of the silver fob sent a pang through Peggy. It was pinned to her uniform alongside her Rotunda badge. Apart from family and country and religion, these were the two things that defined her. She was a midwife-handywoman, and she loved Dan Sheridan.

'God, are you all right?' Mrs Murray put a hand on her arm. 'You look terrible, love!'

Peggy swallowed. She wasn't a bit all right. The thought that she would never let herself think had popped into her head. *I love him. I love Dan.* And she would never be his girl again. Even though he wanted to be with her. Even though she loved him more than anything.

'I'll be fine, thanks.'

'Jesus, I hope so.' Mrs Murray's eyes flicked to something or someone behind Peggy. 'So the birth was very straightforward, thank God. Very quick.'

'Here we go, Mrs Murray.' Priscilla was all charm. 'Do you want baby to go in here now?'

'Nah, I'll keep her with me, Nurse. Thanks.'

Taking the bag of Mrs Murray's belongings from the bottom of the bed, Peggy made a show of putting everything in the tiny bedside cupboard. Thankfully, Sister then called her away to help with the dinners, which allowed her to let her pulse settle. If someone asked her directly about her past, she could not lie. But in the meantime she would hope to avoid the question via evasiveness. It was all she could do.

★ ★ ★

Dr Fenton was just as charming, and just as cold as Dan had remembered him.

'Ah, young Sheridan,' he said, making Dan feel as though he were ten years old and still in short trousers. 'Good to have you on the team.'

'Thank you.'

Some of the other junior doctors were glancing at him curiously. He stifled a sigh. At the first available opportunity he would tell them that his father knew Fenton, but that there was nothing more to it. The last thing he needed was for his new mates to think he had some sort of privileged position. Fenton hadn't even known he was applying, and had had nothing to do with Dan being offered a position. Dan had earned his place on his own merits, fair and square.

'Right. A Ward next. Sheridan, and you two, come with me. The rest of you can take your break.'

*Sheridan and you two.* So disrespectful to the other two junior doctors. As they walked towards A Ward he stole a glance at them. Both were expressionless, but when Dr Lowe met his gaze he made a face. *Feck*. Dan would have to speak to them as soon as an opportunity presented itself. They'd be having their own break, he guessed, after reviewing the women in A Ward.

Once again, he wondered if Peggy would be here. She hadn't been in delivery suite or theatres this morning. Perhaps she was out on the district, or off duty today. God, he was desperate to see her. And he was a fool still to want her when she had literally left Dublin early to avoid having to even travel with him.

The ward had an inner corridor, with a couple of side rooms and a smaller bay. As they reviewed the women in that part of the ward, Dan surreptitiously clocked the midwives. There was Sister, a formidable-looking woman with a stiff manner, along with a pert junior colleague called Midwife Gildea. When he and the others had arrived in Dr Fenton's wake just now, she had appraised them boldly, as if deciding which of them she'd have for dinner. Dan had averted his eyes, pretending to make a note in his notebook as Dr Fenton spoke.

On they went, into the large bay in the main ward. And there she was. *Peggy!* His heart leapt as he drank in every detail at a glance. Her beautiful face. That fine figure – the uniform hugging curves he knew intimately. On her chest was pinned a Rotunda badge, and a silver fob watch.

'This is Midwife Cassidy,' Sister said, and the other two lads murmured something as Peggy said hello. All Dan could manage was a nod of the head. Sister accompanied them as they made their way down the ward, noting all the care instructions that Dr Fenton was throwing out – some of which did not seem particularly logical.

Finally they reached the last woman. 'This is Mrs Murray,' Sister said. 'She had her third baby six hours ago here. All went well.'

'Ah, you'll not be needing us then, will you, Mrs Murray?' Dr Fenton waved a hand towards Peggy. 'This pretty little thing will see to your needs, I'm sure.' He leaned forward, ignoring Mrs Murray's frown. 'I'd call you lucky, for I'd love to be looked after by a girl like that, but I wouldn't trade places with you if I had to go through childbirth!' Guffawing at his own wit he turned away, completely ignoring the cross expressions on the faces of all three women.

Dan was ragin' on Peggy's behalf. What an eejit Dr Fenton was! As they turned to leave, he looked at her again, but she had busied herself with tidying Mrs Murray's bedcovers. *For feck sake!* Now Peggy would probably associate him with Fenton, and he'd have no chance.

He caught the direction of his thoughts. Did he actually still think he had a chance? *Wise up, man!* he told himself, but the hopeful eejit inside him unhelpfully argued that they'd been so close for so long, she couldn't possibly have turned off her feelings for him completely.

What feelings? Could he even be confident she had feelings for him? They'd never said loving things, and had limited themselves to complimenting each other on a regular basis rather than making any declarations. Dan had played things carefully these past months – too carefully, perhaps. What would have happened if he'd told her he loved her?

For he did love her. Madly, passionately, deeply, with everything that he was or wished to be.

## Seána Tinley

'. . . your dinner, lads,' Dr Fenton was saying, and Dan followed the other two out of the ward and down the stone steps to the canteen on the lower floor. While he couldn't read anything into Peggy's behaviour just now, his own heart was clear. He loved her, and he was not going to give up.

# 35

*Saturday, 2 September 1939*

'Now, Granda. Where do you want to sit?'

Granda Joe, leaning on his stick, surveyed the room. 'Over there, love. I think I see my mates Peter and Barney.' He indicated a table to their right, and Peggy walked slowly alongside him as he made his way to his friends. They were in a parish hall in north Belfast, with Granda looking forward to today's dinner and get-together for the elderly. The event was part of the work of the St Vincent de Paul Society, who did a great job supporting the poor and the old. Often the two – poverty and old age – went hand in hand, but even those who weren't living in poverty needed the company of their own generation from time to time.

She joined the three gentlemen for a while, joining in their conversation about the news from Europe, and the understanding that war was now inevitable. The Irish Parliament, Dáil Éireann, was sitting today, with De Valera expected to confirm officially that Ireland would remain neutral, along with most European countries. Meanwhile in London they were evacuating children and mobilising the armed forces.

To Peggy it was all shocking and frightening, but the elderly gentlemen had seen it all before, and simply seemed sad. Once Granda Joe and his friends moved on to reminiscing about the old days, before Belfast had got so big, she sat quietly, enjoying the memories they were sharing. She knew both Granda's friends well, and had met them many times over the years. Today they complimented her on being all grown up, and so pretty with it. Laughing this off, she told them to behave themselves, and got up from their table.

'I'd better go and help. I'm not actually here to sit and chat with you gentlemen all day, you know!'

As she walked towards the kitchens she reflected on their compliments, noting that very similar words had been said about her yesterday by the odious Dr Fenton, yet they had affected her very differently. The elderly gentlemen today had been charming and respectful, whereas Dr Fenton had made her feel a sense of disgust inside.

*Odious* was a word she had learned only recently, but it fitted the man perfectly. Of course he'd been the one to report poor Aunty Bridget. Oh, how she would love to say it to his face. *You are odious*, she rehearsed in her mind, then, realising how foolish she was being, shook off the thought.

Seeing Dan had been a shock yesterday, and coming so quickly after the shock of Mrs Murray's unguarded words, it had left her reeling for the rest of the day. But nothing more had happened, so presumably Priscilla – who she was starting to suspect was not a very nice person – hadn't told Sister on her.

God, Dan had looked gorgeous, and she was so proud of the fact he was now a qualified doctor. Of course, she couldn't speak to him, and her thoughts would have to remain unspoken.

At least the first meeting was out of the way. Now she would begin to get used to seeing him casually at work,

## The Irish Midwife

and eventually, she would get used to not being his girl any more.

The kitchen was a hive of activity, with nearly a dozen women bustling about, preparing food. Grabbing a pinny from the rack, Peggy put it on over her comfortable old dress, tied the strings around her back, then presented herself to Mary Corvin, Peter's daughter, who was coordinating. 'Well, Mary. How are you? I'm here to help.'

'Ah, thanks, Peggy. You're an angel. It's lovely to see you! I saw your Antoinette last week, and she told me she's expecting. Lovely news!'

Peggy beamed. 'Aye, we're all delighted.' *And I'll be there for the birth, thank God.* 'Now, where do you need me?'

'We're nearly ready to start serving the soup. Can you help Miss Moore and her mother with that?' She indicated two women to her left, who were currently ladling traditional Irish broth from a massive pot into small white bowls.

'Will do.'

Making her way across to the mother-daughter duo, Peggy introduced herself and explained she'd been sent to assist.

'Oh, good,' said the older lady, 'for I'm sure the steam from this awful soup will ruin my hair.'

'You look fine, Mother,' said the younger woman. Her gaze swept over Peggy, taking in the faded dress and old shoes. 'Yes, Peggy here can ladle it out, and then you and I can bring it to the dear old people.'

Peggy bristled at her tone, then chastised herself inwardly. Miss Moore and her mother were good enough to volunteer here today. So, suppressing the urge to give the woman a military salute, instead she replied that she was happy to ladle the soup into the bowls, and proceeded to do exactly that, working at approximately twice the speed of Mrs Moore. When they both disappeared, each with a tray full of filled bowls, Mary sent her a couple more volunteers, and before long the pot was empty.

The rest of the meal went smoothly, and Peggy was relieved not to have to work alongside the Moores again. She knew the type – middle-class Catholics who volunteered occasionally to assuage their consciences. She shouldn't condemn them, but given the week she was having, she absolutely didn't care.

Afterwards, up to her elbows in soapy water washing dinner plates and dessert bowls, Peggy listened to the singing and tunes from the hall – old laments and airs, then a few rousing rebel songs. She could tell how much Granda and his friends were enjoying themselves. *This is what it's all about.* Family, and community, and a sense of being in the right place. This was where her broken heart needed to be. For the first time since returning to Belfast, she felt a fleeting sense of contentment.

It was beginning to dawn on her that she might never get over Dan Sheridan. In school, on the dreaded vocation days, she used to pray not to get a calling to be a nun. But she had had a different calling, and one that was, to her mind, equally valid. She had been called to be a midwife-handywoman. Some midwives married, others didn't. Aunty Bridget had got over her childless state, always saying it gave her more time and energy for the women. Mary Corvin, unmarried, was a stalwart of her local community.

There were many paths in life, of which wife and mother was just one. So maybe she was destined to remain single, and to devote her life to others. It wasn't a bad fate, and she had the benefit of knowing what it felt like to be in love. She had even shared a bed with the man she loved for one long, glorious night.

Yes, right now Peggy was in the throes of heartbreak. But she would be all right. She simply had to see it through.

## Sunday, 3 September 1939

*So it is war.* After Mass this morning, Dan had sat by the wireless with his parents and Mrs Kinahan to listen to Chamberlain's announcement. When it came, at around a quarter past eleven, it had sent chills through him.

'I have to tell you now that no such undertaking has been received,' Chamberlain had said, his sorrow clearly evident, 'and that consequently this country is at war with Germany.'

To be fair, Chamberlain had tried for peace – and had also been smart enough to start preparing for war these past months. The British prime minister was certainly no warmonger. And yet, war was here, regardless.

France had also declared war on Germany, who seemed determined to continue their invasion of Poland. In the afternoon the National Service Act was agreed in Westminster, introducing conscription on all male British subjects between eighteen and forty-one who were present in Great Britain. The terminology was interesting. Great Britain, not the United Kingdom.

Since partition the British generally used the term 'United Kingdom' when including the northern six counties of Ireland still under British rule, and 'Great Britain' to refer to the island containing England, Scotland and Wales. From the language it seemed that they had in fact exempted the Northern Irish entirely from conscription, thank God.

'The Unionists won't be happy to be treated differently,' Dan had said, but Da had only shrugged.

'They can still sign up if they want to. Many will. Quite a few Catholics might too, for that Hitler is one bad, bad boy. But,' he mused, 'the British government are smart not to introduce conscription here. The last thing they want is riots and rebellions in their own back yard while they're trying to fight the Germans.'

Dan snorted. 'Our local politicians have all talked many times of refusing to employ Catholics, and of making sure they are a Protestant government for a Protestant people. I bet they'll not turn down anybody who signs up for their war, though.'

'Damn sure. I'm only glad that you won't have to go and fight, son. You're gonna be needed here.' He glanced over at Ma. 'All those poor mothers over in Britain.'

Ma looked genuinely upset, so Dan gave her a hug. 'Ah, you can't get rid of me that easy, Ma— Mother.' He sat down again. 'Besides, we could well be affected here in the north. According to the papers, they're going to bring in a blackout during the hours of darkness in the next few weeks – in case the Germans send bomber planes.'

Ma shuddered. 'Terrible. That Hitler! If I had him here I'd give him a bloody piece of my mind!'

'Now, Ma. You sounded very North Belfast there for a minute,' he teased.

'Daniel Sheridan – you wash your mouth out with soap!' But she was smiling, so at least he'd diverted her mind, even temporarily. She'd even let him call her Ma.

He was still thinking about it a few hours later as he and the rest of the night team met the day crew for handover in the consultants' sitting room, which was directly opposite Matron's red sitting room. The mood was sombre, and no one was crowing about not being conscripted.

'You are needed here,' said Dr Russell, addressing the younger men, and echoing Da's words from earlier. 'If the Germans do decide to bomb Belfast, every doctor will be needed.' He sighed. 'All I can see ahead is a massive loss of life in Europe, and maybe here too. Right now in Poland there are people dying.' He shook his head, his expression one of dejection. 'It is a terrible, terrible thing.' Straightening, his tone became brisk. 'Right. The tutor will base himself in delivery suite overnight. Junior housemen, you are assigned as follows.' He consulted his list. 'Sheridan and Lowe, the wards . . .'

Dan nodded, his heart jumping at the news. Having furtively checked the A Ward roster in the office on Friday evening, he knew that Peggy was on duty tonight. While he had no idea what he would say to her, he intended to make the most of every opportunity he got.

The outbreak of war had reminded him how short life was, and how precious. He loved Peggy, and he was still determined to do all he could to win her back.

★ ★ ★

'Peggy!' Mrs Murray greeted her with a mix of delight and relief. 'I'm so glad you're here. There's something wrong.'

'Hello, Mrs Murray. What is it?' She eyed the woman with concern. This was the third day since the birth of her baby, and all sorts of things could go wrong on day three. The baby was crying, and as Peggy watched, Mrs Murray tried to attach her.

'She won't go on properly. See?' The baby was still fussing, and as Peggy watched she came off the breast.

'Your milk is probably coming in. Could be that?'

Mrs Murray shook her head. 'Aye, I remember the milk coming in from the other two. But that's not it. She's been fussy at the breast from the start.' Her tone changed. 'Ah, that's it. Good girl.'

Peggy observed closely. The baby was in a good position, tummy to tummy with her mother, head up, and with her little chin angled correctly. Listening carefully, Peggy heard a familiar clicking sound, indicating the baby's attachment was not correct, despite Mrs Murray's expertise in positioning her. Sure enough, a moment later the baby lost her grip on the breast, coming off with a wail of frustration.

Mrs Murray looked close to tears herself. 'See? This is happening all the time. Maybe I'm imagining it, but I can't remember my other two being like this.'

'All right. I think I might know what this is. Can I hold her for a second?' Mrs Murray passed over the baby, who was now crying lustily, and Peggy held her so that the light beside Mrs Murray's bed shone directly into the baby's mouth. Sure enough, the front of the baby's tongue was slightly pulled back in the middle, the tongue heart-shaped at the front, and the short frenelum clearly visible underneath, tethering the baby's tongue and restricting its movement.

'It's a tongue tie, Mrs Murray. You weren't imagining it.' Turning the baby so her mother could see, Peggy pointed it out to Mrs Murray. She then moved the baby up to her shoulder, swaying from side to side to try to settle her. Mrs Murray was probably too distressed to try attaching her again

## The Irish Midwife

for another few minutes, and the baby was too distressed to even try. Everyone needed to calm down before trying again.

'I've heard of that,' said Mrs Murray, blowing her nose. 'Doesn't it cause speech problems?'

'It can do, I think,' said Peggy, 'but only if it's not snipped.'

'Snipped? You need to cut it?'

'Aye, I'm sorry. The sooner it's cut, the better. She'll not be able to attach properly with her tongue so restricted.'

Mrs Murray nodded tearfully. 'Poor wee mite. Not a great start in life, is it? And now there's war as well, and my man might have to go and fight in the bloody British Army! It's all terrible.'

'Ach, Mrs Murray. God love ya.' Recognising the other woman was feeling really upset, Peggy held the baby securely with one arm, and took Mrs Murray's hand with the other. 'You've just had a baby, you're on day three. Your milk is coming in and you have the sadness that a lot of women feel around now. And it's not helped by the terrible news from Europe. But did you not hear? No conscription for us!'

'What?'

'Aye. Great Britain only.' Peggy grinned. 'They might have had another Rising on their hands if they'd tried it here!'

'Too right! Well, thank God for that.' She blessed herself, then eyed Peggy sheepishly. 'Sorry about that. I'm not normally so weepy.'

'Ah, you're grand. I'm telling you, it's really common after having a baby. Now, the doctor will be coming soon to do the night ward round. I'll ask him to snip it for you. Is that all right?'

'Aye, thanks, Peggy.' She glanced up the ward. 'And I'm so sorry again for mentioning . . . you know . . . on Friday.'

'Ah, you're all right.' The baby had settled, so Peggy set her down in the cot. She was still awake, moving her little hands and feet about, so no doubt she'd be crying again before long. 'Nothing came of it, thank God.'

'Well, that's a relief!' She glanced behind Peggy. 'Looks like the doctors are here.'

Peggy looked towards the top of the ward, met Dan's gaze, then turned back again, feeling warmth flush up her neck and face. Mrs Murray was giving her a knowing look. 'Aye, he's a looker, that one, and that's for sure.'

'Is he?' Peggy sniffed. 'I hadn't noticed.'

'Ah, you're a terrible liar, Peggy Cassidy. I've known you most of your life, remember. You can't fool me!'

'Good evening. I'm Dr Sheridan. Mrs Murray, is that right?'

The sound of Dan's rich, deep voice was sending a delicious shiver through Peggy. *The body remembers what the mind refuses.*

'Sheridan?' Mrs Murray's tone was sharp, and she sent Peggy a confused look.

'Dr Sheridan's father is also a doctor,' said Peggy in an even tone, sending Mrs Murray a warning look.

'Oh, I see,' said Mrs Murray, though she still looked confused.

Peggy waited while Dan asked the usual questions about Mrs Murray's postpartum recovery, noting her answers in her file. Afterwards he felt her tummy to make sure her womb was shrinking down as it was supposed to, declaring himself content. Peggy avoided looking at his hands and instead kept her eyes on Mrs Murray's face. Once he was done she helped the new mother to sit up again, while Dan asked if the baby was feeding well.

## *The Irish Midwife*

'No. Peggy thinks the baby has a tongue tie.'

'Well, Peggy is one of the best midwives I've ever worked with, so I suspect she's probably right. Do you mind if I check?'

After washing his hands he returned and gently checked in the sleeping baby's mouth. 'Definite tongue tie,' he declared. 'Peggy was, of course, correct. Right. We'll need to snip it, if that's all right with you?'

Mrs Murray agreed, and while Dan was explaining the process to her, Peggy went to fetch what was needed. After she had carefully washed her own hands, the night sister helped her gather together in a sterile kidney dish, some gauze, and a pair of sterile scissors from the autoclave. Dan was still answering Mrs Murray's questions as she returned, and it struck her forcefully that this was the moment when the two parts of her life had finally collided. Mrs Murray, whom she'd supported as a handywoman, and was now supporting as a midwife. Dan, who knew her only as a midwife, but whose surname was clearly familiar to Mrs Murray.

Dan, who was so dear to her.

Clamping her lips together, she pushed the feelings inside her down, away. Those feelings – longing, and loss, and enduring love – were part of what had to be sacrificed. They would fade eventually – or so she hoped.

'Peggy, would you hold the baby for me, please?'

She nodded, picking the baby up, then angling around so that Dan had the advantage of the light. He stepped closer – so close that she could sense his warmth, feel his breath on her cheek. It was agonisingly lovely.

Gently, he opened the baby's mouth, holding her tongue up with the gauze while deftly snipping the thin band of tissue anchoring the baby's tongue to the floor of her mouth. The frenectomy took only a few seconds, and the baby barely protested.

'Nicely done.' She couldn't help complimenting Dan. It was, after all, what she had always done.

'Thank you.' His eyes held hers, their faces inches away from each other, and for a moment Peggy was lost in the wonder of connecting with him again. Then she blinked, recovering her senses, and stepped back.

# 36

'All done!' Peggy said in a voice that by some miracle did not shake. 'Now, we should try and attach her again before she wakes fully and remembers how hungry she is!'

Mrs Murray's eyebrows were raised in a wry acknowledgement of the moment she had just witnessed between midwife and doctor. 'Aye, let's give it a go.'

'I'll leave you to it,' said Dan.

'Thanks, Dr *Sheridan*.'

Was it Peggy's imagination, or was Mrs Murray emphasising Dan's surname? God, this mess was becoming messier by the moment.

Baby Murray, uncaring of all the drama, promptly attached beautifully and fed for over half an hour. Peggy stayed for a while, keeping the conversation light – including telling Mrs Murray that in years gone by, handywomen would have always kept one fingernail long for releasing tongue ties. Nowadays though, it had changed from a fingernail to scissors from an autoclave in hospital, or scissors sterilised in boiling water at home. Either way, the process rarely bothered the babies, and it usually transformed the feeding.

'Well that's for sure. Just look at her, the wee guzzler! Thanks, Peggy. I appreciate it.'

'Ah, it's no bother.'

When Peggy returned to the office, Dan was there chatting to Sister about the news. The other junior houseman had apparently gone to check on the women in the other ward, while Dan had agreed to stay here. Of course he had.

A little self-consciously, Peggy joined in with the conversation, but as there was so much to say about the weekend's events, eventually she felt herself react more normally. The ward was quiet, with only a few women in, and most of them were sleeping. Occasionally a baby would cry, and Peggy or Sister would go to see if any assistance was needed. They brought bedpans to the women too, and changed the sheets for women who bled through their pads. In between though, they returned to the office, to say something new about the war, or conscription, or blackouts.

'Right, Peggy, go you and have your break, and I'll take mine when you come back.'

Peggy stood. 'The canteen will be closed. Where do we go on night duty?'

'Go to Matron's sitting room, but make sure and clean up after you. She really doesn't like finding crumbs or teacups in there – or in fact any sign it's been used!'

Peggy grinned. 'Noted.' Everyone was scared of Matron, and the last thing Peggy wanted was to come to her notice. 'See you in twenty minutes.'

Taking her packed lunch of bread-and-dripping wrapped in paper she left, knowing Dan was probably watching her. He couldn't take his break at the same time, as it was safer for two people to be in the ward at once, in case something happened and one person had to go for help. Yet despite knowing this, she still felt an illogical pang of disappointment that he hadn't followed her. *I'm an eejit. A complete feckin' eejit.*

\* \* \*

Dan chatted away to the night sister, who was very personable, all the while waiting for Peggy's return. The woman was married, which he found interesting, since most of those who'd earned promotion were single. He asked her about it, and she was happy to explain. Her children were well up now, and she had started taking on extra work, like helping with the rosters and ordering stock for the ward. The A Ward sister had asked her if she'd like to take on the role, and she had agreed.

'And, you know what? It's been fine. I only work three nights a week, but it suits me and my family.' She grimaced. 'And I have the next set of rosters to finish by morning, so I better do some work on them.'

*Interesting.* His Peggy had tremendous potential, he knew. He wouldn't want her future to be constrained if she married him. Inwardly, he arched an eyebrow at the multiple assumptions behind his thought, then shrugged. His body was thrumming with hope. Tonight he had made good progress. The way they had all conversed before Peggy went on her break. The way it had felt to work with her again – this time dealing with a tongue tie. The way she'd looked at him afterwards.

*She still feels it.* Whatever 'it' was. Dammit, he had been right!

The mystery of her reluctance still had to be solved though. A thought came to him. As he had approached her and Mrs

## Seána Tinley

Murray at the start, hadn't Mrs Murray been saying that she knew Peggy well? Leaving the night sister to her work, he walked quietly through the ward. Mrs Murray was awake, her soft bedside light on, her baby feeding.

'Well?' he asked in a half-whisper. 'How's the feeding going now?'

'A hundred times better, Doctor. And she's making up for lost time, I think.'

'Good on her!' He smiled. 'I hope she doesn't tire you out too much though.'

'Believe me, I'm better in here than with two wee ones round me at home. I've a wee fella of four and a wee girl of two, and most nights one or other of them needs their mammy.'

'So who's looking after them this week?'

'My ma and my husband's sister between them. People are very good.'

'They are.'

'Did I hear you saying you know Peggy?'

Now there was a definite wariness in her eye, and Dan's attention was suddenly on full alert. 'Aye. She's from West, I'm from West, most people know each other.'

'True. They call Belfast a city, but it's really just a collection of villages all beside each other.'

She nodded. 'That's a good way of describing it.' She sent him a piercing look. 'So your father is a doctor? He's Dr Sheridan?'

The way she said his father's name was odd. Deliberate. The hairs on the back of his neck were standing to attention now. *Is there something to do with Da? But what?* 'He is. Why?'

Her lips clamped together, her jaw set. 'No reason.'

*The Irish Midwife*

No reason? Mrs Murray was angry, and her anger clearly had something to do with his da. But what? None of it made sense.

'Anyway. If you don't mind, Doctor, I'd like to get some sleep now.'

'Of course, of course.'

As he walked slowly back to the office, his mind was working furiously. Mrs Murray's demeanour had entirely changed when speaking of his father. And why had she been so wary when he'd asked what was surely an innocent question about Peggy? Movement ahead caught his eye – Sister was leaving the ward, presumably on her break. Which meant . . .

Yes. There she was. 'Hiya, Peggy.'

She jumped up, clearly intent on leaving the office. Pain lanced through him, enveloped in confusion. *God, what the hell happened between us?*

'No, don't leave on account of me. Sit you there.' His voice cracked. 'I'll go if you really can't bear to even be in the same room as me.'

Seemingly frozen, she just stood there looking at him, and as he watched, the panic in her eyes gave way to – was that *longing*?

'Peggy!'

'No!' She brushed past him, and he caught her scent. Hospital starch, soap, and the essence of Peggy. His eyes half-closed briefly, but this was yet more evidence that she was not cold towards him. So why the hell was she running away? He knew he would have to tread carefully, but by God, he was going to get to the bottom of this!

## Monday, 4 September 1939

After a long sleep on Monday morning, Dan emerged mid-afternoon to find his home had once again been invaded by the Moore ladies. Stifling a groan, he sat silently as they and Ma updated him on the latest news.

Everyone was searching out the gas masks issued by the government last year, as gas attacks were considered likely. He listened, astounded, as the ladies complained at length about how ugly and uncomfortable they were. Was there no practicality at all in these women? Why were they encouraging each other in displaying the worst aspects of their characters?

Air-raid shelters were their next cause for complaint. Householders were now being urged to build shelters as soon as possible. Apparently, Mr Moore had already hired someone to build a shelter in the family garden, with work to begin on Thursday, but Mrs Moore was outraged at the thought of sacrificing her hollyhocks to Hitler.

'I totally agree with you!' declared Ma, with a glance out to her own well-tended garden. 'The thought of destroying our own little piece of Nature . . . and why? Because of Hitler! That awful, awful man.'

'If there are air raids though, having a shelter could mean the difference between life and death,' Dan pointed out bluntly, in his mind thinking of all the Belfast households that didn't have gardens in which to build a shelter. Those tiny yards in the Rock streets, for example . . . Making a mental note to discuss their own shelter with Da, he wondered if Gerard Cassidy and his father were making plans for something, *anything* that might keep them and their family safe.

## The Irish Midwife

'We'll have to sort out Granda's house too.' His Granda and aunt wouldn't be able to build an air-raid shelter.

'They're coming here on Saturday for your granda's birthday, so make sure you have the day off,' Ma reminded him. Since his arrival back in Belfast, he'd insisted they invite their only relatives round more frequently.

'Aye, I've already arranged to be off on Saturday. I'll talk to Granda about it then.'

Melissa, who had been giving Dan doe-eyes since he came in, shuddered dramatically. 'Please stop talking about all these horrible things. Let's talk about something nicer. I'm looking forward to the fundraising committee reception in the maternity hospital on Wednesday, Daniel. Will you be there?'

Since they'd already been told by Dr Fenton in no uncertain terms that they had to attend, he nodded curtly. Mingling with donors and socialites was not his idea of a day's work in the hospital. Yet the committee had been the source of funding for the hospital building, and for the new nurses' home, Musson House, which had opened less than two years ago. They were now raising money for a second nurses' home.

'Aye. How long will it last for?'

Melissa leaned forward to slap his hand in what she probably thought was a playful manner. 'Now, Daniel, don't you be teasing me. It's only to last an hour and a half, maybe two hours, and Dr Fenton is going to make a speech. Your mother and mine will be there, too. Your father as well, I think.'

'How exciting.'

'You, my friend, are a wretch!' Melissa declared, now leaning dangerously close to him and leaving her face near to his. It was all Dan could do not to recoil. Strange how he craved being close to Peggy, yet Melissa – and every other woman on the planet, to be fair – left him cold.

He broke her gaze, only to see identical indulgent looks on the faces of both mothers.

*Jaysus!* He rose. 'Right! I'm off to get some breakfast.'

'But we have tea here!' said Ma, pointing to the tray. 'And cakes!'

He made a face. 'Not for breakfast, Ma!'

Ignoring her call-me-Mother face, he made for the door. Mrs Kinahan's kitchen was calling.

# 37

*Wednesday, 6 September 1939*

Peggy worked Tuesday, but didn't see Dan once. Apparently he was in delivery suite all day – according to Priscilla, who declared him to be a 'dreamboat' and the best-looking of all the new junior doctors, along with Dr Lowe. It was all Peggy could do to keep her face expressionless. Priscilla volunteered to go to delivery suite every time something was required, while Peggy concentrated on looking after the women in A Ward. She and Maisie, the other midwife she'd met ahead of her interview, were forging something of a friendship, and often arranged to meet at dinner break, chatting easily about their new jobs and all the people. Maisie was also wary of Priscilla, which was reassuring.

Wednesday morning was better, because Priscilla was off. Strangely though, she arrived at around noon, in uniform, and was sitting drinking tea in the ward office when Peggy returned from her break, which she had again taken with Maisie.

'I thought you were off today, Priscilla?'

'I am, yeah. But I fancied going to the donors' event.'

'Oh.' *God, she's keen.* 'Does that mean I don't have to go? I really would rather not.'

'Aye, you might be better staying here – if you don't like that sort of thing, I mean.'

There was a condescending edge to her voice. *Would she have said that if I'd been from Ravenhill too?* 'Oh, I don't mind receptions, but our job is to be with the women.'

'Good thing I'm not rostered then, isn't it?'

As she made her way through the ward, tending to the women and babies, Peggy was fuming. Priscilla's tone, the way she had looked down her nose at her – it was exactly the sort of thing Peggy had anticipated as someone from a working-class background who had managed to get a professional qualification. The sooner she was out on the district in West, the better.

A little later Sister Hanna and Maisie came from the antenatal clinic to provide cover while she and Sister Campbell attended the reception, and Peggy accepted the inevitable. *I bet Dan will be here.*

She and Maisie chatted companionably until Sister Campbell signalled that it was time to go. As they made their way down the stone stairs and along the bottom floor corridor, turning right for the baby clinic, Peggy thought what a pity it was that Maisie hadn't been assigned to A Ward.

Sure enough, Dan was present, teacup in hand, chatting to a middle-aged lady who was wearing an actual string of pearls. Something about the woman was vaguely familiar, but Peggy couldn't quite place her. Priscilla was there too, near the door. And there was Dr Sheridan, chatting to Dr Fenton near the line of long windows. The two men who had reported Aunty Bridget, together. Clenching her teeth, Peggy looked away.

As Peggy made her way further into the room by Sister's side, Dan lifted his head and his eyes met Peggy's. She could

## The Irish Midwife

not help it – she was too raw to hide the confusion and longing and anger and despair within her, and he seemed to register it, for his eyes widened. To her right, Peggy half-saw Priscilla's jaw drop in reaction, so she instantly broke Dan's gaze, swallowing hard and looking around as if interested in the event. *God, I need to get a handle on this!*

The baby clinic was a large sunlit space bookended by smaller consulting rooms and offices. Today it was full of people – a mix of white coats, midwifery uniforms, and the great and the good. Matron was there too, and Peggy's stomach clenched at the very sight of her. The woman was, quite simply, terrifying.

'Good afternoon. You're midwives, aren't you?' It was an older gentleman with upper-class whiskers, and Peggy politely joined in the small talk that followed, allowing Sister Campbell to dominate. After a few moments someone else came to talk to the man, who was apparently some sort of 'Sir'. Mumbling a polite goodbye, Peggy moved on, Priscilla joining her instantly.

'This is some craic!' Priscilla declared, adding, 'Already I've seen an actual lord, three ladies, and quite a few sirs.'

'Oh.' Peggy, unimpressed by British ascendancy titles, had nothing to say to this. Walking to the tea table she accepted a cup, with a thank you to the woman serving. Priscilla was still shadowing her. *Well, she probably doesn't know anyone here except me. I'm sure I'd be dumped in a second if she got a better offer.*

Together they made their way towards the centre of the room – although Peggy would have much preferred sticking to the edges, where it was easier to hide. Priscilla's gaze was restlessly moving, searching.

'Dr Sheridan!' Priscilla hailed him from a few feet away. 'So they let you out of delivery suite for this then?'

With a brief glance to Peggy, Dan smiled warmly. 'Aye. Things are grand up there at the minute, so a few of us are here. Er . . .' He glanced towards the middle-aged woman by his side. 'Can I introduce you to Midwife Gildea?'

*Damn it!* Peggy, who had been hovering mutely, now saw that she too would have to come forward and be introduced. To do anything else would be seen as rude. Accepting the inevitable, she took the three or four steps forward to join them.

'This is my mother,' Dan was saying to Priscilla, and Peggy stiffened in shock. Of course! The last time – indeed the *only* time – she had seen Mrs Sheridan had been at the train station at Christmas. Just after she and Dan had kissed for the first time.

'And this is Midwife Cassidy.'

Peggy shook the woman's hand, murmuring something polite. There was an instant's silence, which Priscilla filled by complimenting Mrs Sheridan's dress. Dan's mother looked pleased, smoothing a hand over her skirt, and telling them about the boutique where she had found it. *Boutique.* Even the word was alien. Peggy had seen it in newspapers, but had never before heard it spoken, much less met anyone who shopped in such places. And how would a boutique mother react if her son – her only child – turned up with a milly for a girlfriend?

*See? I'm not suited for this.* Even the conversations were making Peggy feel uncomfortable. In the West Belfast community, there were no false compliments – only real ones, and even they were usually delivered with an ironic twist.

Mrs Sheridan and Priscilla chatted away then, discovering mutual acquaintances from Ormeau. Peggy glanced around. People were still arriving – including, she saw,

## The Irish Midwife

Mrs Moore and her daughter from the old people's dinner. Cynically, she wondered if this was how they spent their days – attending receptions where they could feel good about themselves.

*Stop it, Peggy.* God, she was becoming so judgemental! The Moores were probably doing what they could to help the Royal, and they had genuinely worked at the old people's dinner. She needed to be more open-minded.

The problem was, she realised, that she herself was so worried and anxious inside – like an over-wound clock. The Moore ladies looked around, then made straight for the Sheridans. *Of course they know one another.*

'How lovely to see you! And Daniel!' Both kissed Dan's cheek, and as the younger Miss Moore stood on tiptoes to do so, Dan flushed slightly.

*Feck!*

What did that mean? Was there something between them? Peggy looked at Miss Moore again, this time with an assessing eye. She was pretty, to be fair, and extremely well groomed. But there was a – a *languidness* about her which Peggy didn't think would suit Dan at all. Languid. Another fancy word she had no right knowing. *Our ones will think I've swallowed a dictionary if I start talking like them ones!*

Dan was again performing introductions, and this time he lit on Peggy first. 'This is Midwife Cassidy. This is Miss Melissa Moore.'

Miss Melissa Moore was frowning in half-recognition as she stuck out a limp hand. The name perfectly suited her, Peggy realised. Frilly, feminine and lah-di-dah. And, to be honest, slightly comical. Like something out of a music hall. *Miss Melissa Moore.* West Belfast names were sturdy. Peggy.

Sheila. Aiveen. Even Antoinette – Ma's only vanity selection – had been named after Da.

'We've met,' Peggy said neutrally. 'At the old people's dinner last Saturday.'

'Oh!' she exclaimed. 'It's the soup-kitchen girl!'

Priscilla giggled at this, but Miss Moore's mother, seizing the opportunity, proceeded to talk at length about all of the volunteering her daughter did. Mrs Moore didn't even speak to Peggy. Or to Priscilla, to be fair. It was as though their uniform made them invisible.

Mrs Sheridan said little, which was interesting. The Moores were obviously friends of hers, but maybe Mrs Moore's rudeness was blatant enough even to make someone of the same ilk slightly uncomfortable. Or maybe not.

Dan eventually intervened, asking his mother if the man had arrived that morning to start working on their air-raid shelter. Well of course the Sheridans would get a man in to do it. Buy the materials, pay a labourer, sacrifice one corner of what was probably a massive yard or garden. His mother frowned.

'Yes, and he's already started digging up a corner of the lawn!'

The Moores commiserated, loudly and dramatically, while Peggy suppressed the urge to raise an astonished eyebrow. They were lucky to have a bloody lawn in which to build their shelter; Da and Gerard were currently trying to figure out what sort of makeshift shelter they could construct in the Cassidys' tiny back yard.

Peggy couldn't help it: she had to look at Dan. This was exactly the sort of situation that always had them eye-rolling, and they'd usually talk about it afterwards. Their eyes met,

## The Irish Midwife

and shared understanding passed between them. He was laughing inside, as she was. She knew it, as well as she knew her own name.

Time stood still as other emotions flashed through her. *This is Dan, and we're looking at one another.* Joy, love, loss, a sense of rightness . . . Peggy tore away her gaze, to find that the conversation had stopped, all four women staring at them with expressions ranging from horror (Dan's mother) to anger (both Melissa and Priscilla) and confusion (Mrs Moore, who was clearly not the most perceptive of women).

*Ah, feck!*

'Ladies and gentlemen! Honoured guests!' Dr Fenton was beginning his speech, Dr Sheridan senior standing nearby. Thankfully, everyone had to turn to listen.

As he rabbited on, Peggy wondered how quickly she could escape. Setting down her cup on a nearby table, she glanced towards the door to her right, realising she was literally only a few steps from it. Soon she could return to the relative safety of A Ward, away from the Moores and the Sheridans and Dr Fenton and Dr Sheridan senior – the two signatories to the complaint against Aunty Bridget. She wouldn't even have to cope with Priscilla, for she wasn't on duty today.

The speech ended, those without teacups in their hands clapping, and Peggy joined in politely, looking away from the group that she was standing with. To her relief, Sister Campbell was beckoning her.

Murmuring an 'Excuse me,' she made her way across to where Sister was standing with Matron.

'Midwife Cassidy,' Matron began, and Peggy's eyes widened, her heart thumping wildly. *Why is she speaking to me? Have I done something wrong?*

'Sister Campbell has just been telling me about your prompt actions in diagnosing a tongue tie.'

'Yes, Matron. It was very obvious, to be fair.'

'Ah, but no one else had spotted it, and this was a day three baby. Well done.'

What could she say to this? 'Thank you. Thank you both.'

There was a pause. 'How are you settling in?'

Matron couldn't really be interested, but Peggy knew what to say. 'Very well. I'm enjoying it, and everybody has been kind and welcoming.'

*Except perhaps Priscilla Gildea.* She glanced back. Dan had left the ladies to it, and was currently chatting to Dr Lowe. Priscilla though was still with Melissa, and seemed to be telling her something. Melissa was listening intently, a shocked expression on her face, then she glanced at Peggy. In dawning horror, Peggy suddenly realised *exactly* what Priscilla must be telling Melissa Moore.

*No!* This was it. She was about to be exposed.

# 38

*Oh, fuck. Oh, sweet Jesus, Mary and Joseph. Oh, Holy God and all the saints and angels.*

Priscilla had said nothing all week, and despite knowing her to be small-minded and vindictive, Peggy had actually begun to hope she wouldn't do anything about what Mrs Murray had revealed. She should have known better. Priscilla had simply been biding her time, choosing her moment so as to inflict maximum damage.

As Peggy watched in horror, Melissa walked briskly across the room to her mother, leaning in and speaking to her in an animated manner. She was clearly relaying whatever it was Priscilla had told her. Priscilla had followed Melissa, and was looking smug as you like. The two young women were well-met. *Two absolute cows!*

Turning back, Peggy saw that both Sister and Matron were looking from her to the ladies and back again. *Feck!* Midwives were smart, and her bosses had clearly realised that something was going on.

'Are you all right, Midwife Cassidy? You look very pale.'

'No, I – is it me, or is it very warm in here?'

Sister took charge, as sisters did. 'Sit down a second. Here.' She indicated a couple of nearby chairs, taking Peggy by the arm but thankfully sitting with her. 'Are you feeling faint?'

'A bit.'

The truth was that Peggy's head was spinning, her knees were like jelly, and her stomach was sick. Everything was about to unravel. Aunty Bridget's life's work. Her entire savings. All Peggy's hard work and studies. Dan. She had been here for less than a fortnight, and was about to get booted out. They might even report her to the police.

Sister brought her sweetened tea and Peggy drank, lifting her cup with a trembling hand. She was frozen, unable to think or feel or plan. All sense of control over her life had abruptly evaporated. She was at the mercy of other people, at the mercy of events.

Matron had moved on, thank goodness, and was now talking with Dr Fenton. Peggy breathed in and out, her knees trembling. Longingly, she glanced at Dan's back. Once the Royal got rid of her, she would never see him again.

As on the morning she had finished with Dan, Peggy felt as though she was watching a play. But this time she was the victim, helpless to resist as multiple conspirators prepared to attack. This was her Ides of March.

She went over it again – that mistaken sense of security. Foolishly, she had thought that because Priscilla hadn't mentioned anything, she had got away with it. No, Priscilla had simply been looking for the perfect moment to strike. And now, she had clearly found it.

*Not a cow, then. A snake.*

Helplessly she watched as Mrs Moore, an angry, determined expression on her face, crossed the room to accost Matron and Dr Fenton. Watching their reaction, and the back of Mrs Moore's head, Peggy could tell the moment

*The Irish Midwife*

Matron and Dr Fenton realised what Mrs Moore had to say. All expression disappeared from Matron's face, while Dr Fenton looked cross, his colour rising.

He then spoke at length, his manner first angry, then determined. Straining to hear, Peggy managed to catch a few words during a slight lull in the hubbub. Mrs Moore was saying something about donors not being happy.

'I trust this will be dealt with appropriately?'

Matron nodded, her mouth a straight tight line. 'You may depend upon it.'

Peggy was gripping the handle of the teacup so tightly she was afraid it might break. Setting it down beside her, she rose as Matron approached.

'Come with me, please, Midwife Cassidy. You too, Sister.'

Peggy followed, now trembling from head to toe. At the last, just as she was following Matron and Sister Campbell through the door and out of the baby clinic, she glanced at Dan, seeing his jaw drop in shock at the state of her. Then she was gone, in her head saying a farewell to the clinic, to the Royal, to midwifery, and to her beloved Dan.

★ ★ ★

Dan felt shock rippling through him. Where was Peggy going? And why did she look as though she had just seen a ghost?

'I have to go,' he said to Dr Lowe, uncaring what he was revealing.

'Why?'

Belatedly, Dan realised that no one else seemed to have noticed.

'Something's wrong with Peggy – with Midwife Cassidy.'

He had already started to move when he felt a small but determined hand on his arm. 'I wouldn't, if I were you.'

It was Melissa. Confusion swirled within him. 'Wouldn't what?'

'I know you probably fancy her, but that midwife you were eyeing up earlier . . . well, she's about to get fired, if I'm not mistaken.'

His jaw dropped. 'Fired? For what?'

She giggled mischievously. 'She has a terrible secret, which was accidentally revealed by some new mother in the ward.'

'A secret? What secret?'

Melissa's expression changed. 'Don't be getting so worked up, Daniel. You hardly know the girl.'

'What. Secret.' He spoke through gritted teeth.

She sniffed, lifting her chin. 'Well, I don't like your attitude, so I'm not going to tell you. And if you think you can go on like that after we're married, Daniel—'

'I wouldn't marry you if you were the only girl left in Ireland, Melissa!' he retorted, having had quite enough of her games. 'And my name is Dan, not Daniel!'

Ignoring Dr Lowe's sudden grin, he turned on his heel and marched out, hurrying along the baby clinic corridor, then up the narrow stairs, half-running towards Matron's office. *Damn!* He was just in time to see the door closing behind them.

Knowing he could get fired too if he barged in, he paced up and down the entrance corridor for what seemed like an hour, but was probably only ten minutes. What in God's name was going on?

\* \* \*

## The Irish Midwife

'Please, sit.'

Peggy sat, noting randomly that this was the same chair she'd sat in for her interview. There was a nice symmetry in that, she thought, a little hysterically. Sister Campbell sat too, taking out a notebook and pen, her face tight and closed.

'One of the members of the fundraising committee has highlighted an issue to me,' Matron began, her face expressionless and her tone even. 'An issue involving you, Midwife Cassidy. Now, do you have something to say to me?'

*Is this the part where I grovel, and apologise, and beg to keep my job?* For an instant, Peggy saw two paths opening up before her. Both had the same destination, and so, defiantly, she chose the one that would respect Aunty Bridget and every other handywoman who'd ever supported another woman giving birth.

'Yes, Matron.' She squared her shoulders. 'I worked as a handywoman before training as a midwife.' As she said the words, an overwhelming sense of relief overtook her. It was done. No more secrets.

Matron remained impassive. 'Tell me more. How did this come about?'

And so Peggy spoke for a good ten minutes. How she had been a half-timer in the mill until finishing school at fourteen, but had already been helping her aunt occasionally – her aunt being a well-established handywoman. How she had asked to remain a half-timer because her aunt thought she had a talent for supporting women.

Then the questions began. How many births had she attended? Was her aunt aware of germs and hygiene? What did she do if she suspected infection? What if a woman suffered a post-birth bleed? At what point and for what reasons did they call for a doctor?

Peggy answered them all, steadily, calmly. It felt good to be able to talk about Aunty Bridget's wisdom and skill.

'Midwife Cassidy, what is your aunt's name?'

Peggy gave a sad smile. 'Bridget Devine. She died.' Tears pricked her eyes. Strange that she had not cried for herself. Not once. But the uncovering of her secret now meant that Aunty Bridget's legacy had been wasted, her death somehow made meaningless. 'She left me her life savings so I could train as a midwife. Twenty-two pounds it cost for me to train in the Rotunda.'

'And that's why you went to Dublin? To try and keep this secret?' Reaching behind her, Matron offered Peggy a paper tissue.

'I do have relatives down there, but yes, that was the main reason. I'm sorry I couldn't be open with you during my interview.'

'Sister Campbell, could you bring us some tea, please?'

'Yes, Matron.'

Peggy frowned. Why was Matron getting Sister to leave the room? With a sense of trepidation, she waited.

★ ★ ★

Dan was leaning against the wall in the corridor outside Matron's office. He hadn't dared to move closer to eavesdrop, but was determined to wait until he found out what the hell was happening. Finally the door opened, making him straighten, but it was only Sister Campbell. Walking past without a word, she made for Matron's red sitting room,

## The Irish Midwife

and he followed. Once inside, she checked and turned on the plug-in kettle. *She's making tea? Why?*

It made no sense. If Peggy was to be fired, why would they be kind to her? He nodded slowly. *Because, at heart, they are kind women.* Strict, perhaps, and unbending, but they wouldn't be midwives if they didn't have compassion. They could be kind, but still fire her.

'Er, Sister?'

'Yes, Dr Sheridan?' Her face gave nothing away.

'Is – is Peggy all right? Midwife Cassidy, I mean?'

'Well, no. But I can't say very much, you understand.'

'Why? What's going on?'

'Someone has reported her.'

'For what?'

She looked distinctly uncomfortable. 'Matron was clear that there is to be no gossip, and so I am saying nothing more. I suggest you return to your duties, Doctor.'

Frustrated, Dan marched out, pausing at the bas-relief which symbolised the Royal Maternity Hospital. It was just past the red sitting room, at the junction between the entrance wing and the main corridor. Helplessly, he stood there staring at it unseeingly, his mind racked with speculation and distress on her behalf. *Someone reported her . . . Fired . . . Terrible secret.* What in God's name was she supposed to have done?

The bas-relief came into focus. It was nicely sculpted – the figure of a mother holding a baby, another child standing by her. Suddenly his mind was clear.

*Mrs Murray!*

Suddenly he *knew*, was absolutely certain that she held the key to all this. Making straight for A Ward, he hesitated.

*Damnation!* It was visiting time, and every mother had someone by their bedside. Should he come back later? *No.* This couldn't wait. Down the ward he went, pausing at the last bed on the left.

'Oh, hello, Doctor. This is my husband, John.'

With a token nod to the husband, he walked up the side of the bed. Mrs Murray was frowning now. 'What's wrong? Something's wrong, isn't it?'

He nodded grimly. 'It's Peggy.'

'Oh, sweet Jesus!' She blessed herself.

Her husband was looking from one to the other. 'What is it? What's happening?'

'I'm told,' said Dan grimly, 'that she is currently getting fired from her job, because of a secret revealed by a woman.'

'Ah no, no!' Mrs Murray's hand flew to her mouth. 'I didn't mean anything by it. I didn't know, I swear!'

'What the hell happened?' the husband demanded. 'Somebody better explain damn quick!'

Mrs Murray turned to him, her expression distraught. 'I let it slip about Mrs Devine and Peggy. I didn't know it would be trouble for her.'

'Peggy? Peggy Cassidy?'

So Mr Murray knew Peggy, too. But who was this Mrs Devine?

She nodded. 'She's a midwife here. I said about her and her auntie being handywomen.'

In an instant, everything became clear. Peggy had been a handywoman before training in the Rotunda!

Dan's mind flew around the new information, making linkages, working things out . . . He had even suspected it once, he realised.

*The Irish Midwife*

'Well, don't look so cross with me, Doctor! It was an accident!'

He must have been standing there frowning as he thought it all through. Before he could say anything more though, Mrs Murray added, 'And besides, you're one to talk!'

His jaw dropped. 'What? Me?'

'You know who he is, don't you?' she said to her husband, indicating Dan via a toss of the head. 'He's the son of Dr Sheridan!'

Mr Murray rose, his brow furrowed and his face flushed. 'Your father killed a good, good woman. Bridget Devine was well loved in West Belfast, and her whole family well respected.'

Dan felt the blood draining from his face. 'Killed? My father has never killed anyone! How dare you!'

Mr Murray was unmoved. He shrugged. 'Maybe you genuinely didn't know. Then I suggest you ask him about it. It was him and – what was the name of the other fella?' he asked his wife.

'Fenton.' She almost spat the word.

'Dr Sheridan, could I have a word with you please?' It was Sister Hanna, and – *Fuck!* He was in trouble himself now. But he didn't care. It was all too much. Peggy, Melissa, his da . . .

Wordlessly he left the Murrays, following Sister to her office.

'What happened just now, Dr Sheridan?'

'There's a . . . situation underway which Matron is involved with,' he said, choosing his words carefully. 'She's in her office, along with Sister Campbell and – and another person.'

Now Sister Hanna looked puzzled. 'Right?'

'Matron wants no gossip, so I better say no more.' He rose. 'I need to go. Er – if Mrs Murray wants to discharge herself today or tomorrow, she can. She's fit and well, and the baby is thriving now.'

Sister Hanna nodded. 'Understood.'

'Thanks. Er, sorry I got a bit heated there. It relates to . . . to the other situation.'

She held up a hand. 'I am quite sure I don't need to know, Dr Sheridan.'

'Thanks. And you're right. You really, really don't.'

# 39

*Now what?* The door closed behind Sister Campbell, and Matron's demeanour changed. Suddenly her face was relaxed, her shoulders too. 'Peggy.'

*She's using my first name?* Peggy was totally confused.

'Yes?'

'I knew your Aunt Bridget.' Her words dropped into the silence like a stone into a millpond.

'You did?'

'Aye. She trained me. Years ago.'

'Trained you? But—' Impossible thoughts were flying around Peggy's mind.

A mischievous look appeared in Matron's eye. 'Can't you work it out?'

Peggy gasped. 'You—' She was almost afraid to say it out loud. 'You were a handywoman too?'

'I was, and a damn good one! It's why I went into midwifery. Many of us older midwives were handywomen first – a fact that I shall have to remind Dr Fenton about, I think.'

'But—' Peggy put a hand to her head. '*You* were a handywoman?' It just seemed impossible. She knew she was repeating herself, and probably seemed really stupid, but her mind couldn't cope.

'Have you not realised yet? Midwives *are* handywomen, and handywomen are midwives.'

'Yes! That's what I think too! It's the same, except midwives know more of the theory and science.'

'Ah, Peggy. I love your optimism. There's more to it than that.'

'What do you mean?'

'Many men don't trust or value women as they should. And many in the middle classes don't trust or value working-class people. Handywomen are generally working-class women, remember. I certainly was. The Midwives Act was an attempt to create a new profession of so-called "respectable" girls – by which they meant middle-class girls.'

'As if girls like me aren't respectable!' Peggy felt outrage burn within her.

Matron nodded sympathetically. 'Plus there's the fact that male doctors want to control and manage birth, and that means getting rid of handywomen – who are totally independent – and replacing them with midwives, who work within the systems set up by those very doctors.' She shrugged. 'It's all about control – for some of them, at least. If it was actually about preventing infection and making use of medical science, they'd have *trained* the handywomen, not outlawed and prosecuted them.'

Peggy's eyes widened. 'I've never thought about it that way before.'

Matron smiled. 'Give it a few more years, and you'll be as cynical as me, Peggy. But you'll still be a damn fine midwife.'

Someone was calling at the door. Peggy jumped up to open it, and there was Sister Campbell, holding a tray with

## The Irish Midwife

a pot of tea, and three china cups and saucers, along with a beautiful matching milk jug.

They all gathered round the small table and Matron poured. The whole thing seemed surreal. Like a dream. Matron had known Aunty Bridget! Matron was a handywoman!

Did that mean Peggy wasn't getting fired after all? Unfortunately, Peggy didn't understand hospital politics. Donors would have a lot of sway, surely? Doctors, too? But Matron was . . . *formidable*. Yet another fancy word – far too fancy for a milly.

*But I'm not a milly any more.* Fierceness ran through her. *I'm a handywoman-midwife.*

Once they had all had a few sips of tea, and Matron and Sister Campbell had had a brief conversation about the reception, Matron turned to Peggy again.

'Midwife Cassidy,' she said formally, and Peggy's heart couldn't help clenching in fear – even though she now knew things about Matron that she suspected no one else in the Royal knew.

'Yes?'

'I'm curious about something. How did this information come to light today? How did Mrs Moore discover that you used to be a handywoman?'

'I don't know for certain, but . . .' She went on to tell them of Mrs Murray's spontaneous words in front of Midwife Gildea.

Matron looked thoughtful. 'I thought that might be it. I saw her speaking with Mrs Moore's daughter downstairs.'

'Er, Matron – Midwife Gildea isn't rostered to be on today,' Sister Campbell offered. 'She only came for the reception.'

## Seána Tinley

'Why would she do that? Seems a little unusual.'

'I had thought it was to support the hospital.'

'And what do you think now, Sister Campbell?'

'It's possible she came in order to tell people about Midwife Cassidy.'

Matron checked her fob. 'The reception will continue for another half-hour. I think it's time we all return to it, don't you think?'

'R-return to it?'

*Back to the Moores, and Dr Fenton, and Dr Sheridan, and Priscilla?*

*And Dan?*

Matron rose. 'Follow me, ladies!'

Matron led the way, impassive as ever. But Peggy had seen another side to her. *My God, what is she planning?*

Downstairs they went, Sister Campbell and Peggy flanking Matron like army lieutenants. Peggy felt what must surely be a hysterical giggle try to bubble up inside. As they walked along the lower corridor people gave way left and right – midwives, husbands, Dr Lowe. He met Peggy's eye, and there was something intent about his expression. But there was no time to think about it, for they had arrived at the baby clinic.

\* \* \*

Dan met Dr Lowe as he left A Ward. 'Dan! You've just missed her!'

'Who?' His heart, still thumping from his encounter with the Murrays, now skipped another beat.

'Midwife Cassidy. She's with Matron.'

## The Irish Midwife

He was already starting to run. 'Where?'

'Heading towards the baby clinic.'

'Thanks.' The reception? Why was Matron taking Peggy back there – to humiliate her in some way? *For fuck sake!* With no clear idea what he was going to do, Dan knew only that he had to get there as soon as possible. As for the strange accusation that his father had somehow been involved in the death of a Mrs Devine, who was a handywoman and had possibly been Peggy's aunt . . . It would have to wait until later. Right now his priority was to get to Peggy.

\* \* \*

The crowd at the reception had thinned a little, but the key players were all still there. All but Dan.

Peggy didn't know how to feel about this. While she was always – *always* disappointed not to see Dan, things had changed in the last half-hour. She could tell him now – at least, tell him that she had been a handywoman. As for the rest, her head was in a whirl. Might she still be able to prevent him from finding out about his father's part in Aunty Bridget's death? It would hurt him terribly once he knew, and she didn't want him to be hurt. God, she needed time to think.

But here she was, and everyone was looking at them, and *Oh, Lord!* How she wished she could hide in the corner.

'Stay with me, ladies,' Matron murmured as she led them towards the tea table. *More tea*, Peggy thought a little hysterically, *and I haven't been to the bathroom for hours*. But midwives and nurses were known to have bladders of iron, and Peggy was no different. Once they had each received a cup they stood near the tea station, Matron calmly asking Sister Campbell whether the new rosters had been drawn up for A Ward.

'Oh, yes,' Sister Campbell replied. 'The night sister did them on Sunday night.'

'Matron?' They turned. It was Dr Fenton, accompanied by both Mrs Moore and her daughter. Miss Melissa Moore's eyes were shooting shrapnel in Peggy's general direction, while her mother looked serenely confident. At the far side of the room, Dr Sheridan senior was watching keenly – though he was too far away to be able to hear what was being said.

'Yes?' Matron's steely look was the terror of the junior midwives. It was nice to see it being directed towards someone as deserving as Dr Fenton.

'Might I speak with you in private?' he asked, his gaze flicking briefly to Peggy.

'If it's about what we discussed earlier, I can inform you that the matter has been resolved to my satisfaction.'

'But . . .' he began to bluster, his mouth opening and closing. 'But it hasn't been resolved to *my* satisfaction.'

Mrs Moore intervened, her tone smooth as silk. 'Matron, I'm sure the committee and donors will wish to know if there are any – ahem – *illegal* activities being perpetrated by anyone associated with the Royal Maternity Hospital.'

Matron was unmoved. 'You may inform the donors and the committee that nothing of that nature is taking place.'

'But there may be individuals who have done such things in the past!' Melissa's face was twisted with anger. 'People like that should not be working here!'

'Melissa.' Shockingly, it was Dan. He stepped closer. 'Stop.'

## The Irish Midwife

She glared at him, her jaw dropping.

'Miss Moore is correct.' Matron remained serene, but her words sent shock rippling through Peggy.

'By that I mean,' she continued, 'that there *are* individuals in this hospital who have, for example, worked as handywomen in advance of their midwifery training. I am one of them, as you may recall, Dr Fenton. Now, does the fundraising committee wish for me to tender my resignation?'

'Lord, no!' Dr Fenton looked horrified. 'We can't have that, Matron. Would be more than my life's worth if I was the cause of you leaving.'

Matron inclined her head in a regal manner. 'Then I trust this matter is at an end.'

'Oh, absolutely, absolutely.' He coughed. 'Well, I'm glad we cleared that up. Now I really must go.'

And with that, he scurried off – as well he might, for both Moore ladies looked seriously displeased. *Bullies are always cowards.*

\* \* \*

'Daniel.'

Stifling a sigh, Dan turned towards his mother, who was standing a little distance away with Midwife Gildea, wringing her hands.

'Yes, Mother?' With a nod to Peggy and the other ladies, he approached them, noticing as he did so that Da had moved towards Matron, who was even now stepping aside to speak to him privately.

'What is going on?' Ma hissed.

'Melissa Moore just tried to get a midwife sacked.' He glanced sternly at Midwife Gildea, who dropped her gaze, murmured an excuse, and walked off.

'What? Why?'

'I *think* it was because I looked at her in an unapproved way earlier, but I can't be certain.'

'Daniel! This is not the time for your humorous comments! Apparently you really upset Melissa earlier. Mrs Moore wouldn't tell me exactly what happened, but Melissa looked as though she was crying when you were gone.'

Dan rolled his eyes. 'She'll survive, believe me.'

'That's no way to talk about . . .' Her voice tailed off.

'About who, Mother? Your friend's daughter?'

'No. *Your* friend. You two like each other, do you not?'

'Absolutely not! She may think she likes me, but we barely know each other.'

'But you can get to know one another. Melissa is exactly the sort of girl—'

He wasn't taking this any longer. 'No, Mother. I can promise you right now that I will never marry Melissa Moore. The very thought gives me the horrors.' Ma's shocked expression was now giving way to confusion. 'She is vain, empty-headed, and self-absorbed, and what she tried to do today is unforgivable. I heartily dislike her.'

She gasped. 'You – you dislike her? I had no idea!'

'No, because I was raised to always be polite. And because what you wanted got in the way of seeing the truth. But you know what? I'm done with being polite.' He glanced across to where Melissa stood, her expression sulky, her mother clearly trying to placate her. 'That

*The Irish Midwife*

absolute *turnip* nearly ended the career of one of the best midwives I know.'

'Daniel Sheridan!' Ma was trying desperately not to laugh. 'A turnip? Really? Is that the best you can come up with?'

He grinned. Ma might be a pain at times, but she was no Mrs Moore.

'Anyone can be a turnip occasionally. Melissa has decided to make a career of it.'

Ma looked at him assessingly. 'So, the other girl – the one you were exchanging glances with earlier . . .'

He tensed. 'What about her?'

'Is she . . . are you . . . ?'

'What, Mother? Are you asking if she's my girl?' He gave a twisted smile. 'No. She used to be, in Dublin, but she broke up with me.' He swallowed, realising that Ma could see the pain in his eyes.

Her hand flew to her mouth. 'Oh, Daniel!'

He grimaced. 'I don't know how to persuade her to get back with me, but I intend to try.'

'Well, how dare she break up with you in the first place!' Ma looked fierce. 'And who is she? Where is she from?'

'She's called Peggy Cassidy. You saw her once before – at the train station last Christmas.' He might as well tell Ma everything. 'The Cassidys live in a two-up two-down in the Rock streets, and she worked in the mills and as a handywoman before training as a midwife. Her family are all millworkers,' he added bluntly. 'And she's the best girl I've ever known.'

'I see,' said Ma. 'I see.' Her expression was a mix of disappointment and thoughtfulness.

'I'm sorry I didn't choose someone you approve of, but she's my choice. *If* I can win her back.'

'Well,' said Ma, 'if she's your choice she must be special. But I can't pretend to be happy about it, Dan. You and a milly! You know how hard I worked to escape all that.'

'Not you.'

'What?'

'Your *da* worked hard to ensure you escaped. He saved all his money to send you to that fancy school. Your sister didn't want to go, but you did. You never worked in the mills.'

'Well, that's true, but—'

'It was Granda who worked hard, wasn't it?'

'Yes, but I had to survive in boarding school among all the rich girls, knowing I was a coalman's daughter from North Belfast.'

Now this was an open goal. 'And Peggy's family somehow managed to find the money to send her to midwife training, where she had to blend in with all the girls from well-to-do families.' He pressed his advantage. 'She's *you*, Ma. She's you.'

Ma's jaw dropped, and her gaze sought Peggy, who was still standing with Matron and Sister. 'Maybe. I only hoped you'd find someone who was a good match for you.'

He nodded firmly. 'Oh, I have, Ma. She's the perfect match. Now somehow I have to make her see that.'

# 40

'Well, I'm glad that's all sorted,' Matron declared, taking another sip of tea. She had been speaking to Dr Sheridan senior, but was giving no clues as to the content of their conversation. *Was he trying to get me fired too?* Well, if he had been, Matron had clearly been unmoved. *Formidable.*

'How are you doing, Midwife Cassidy?'

'Fine, I think. Relieved. It's all been hanging over me for a long time.'

'I'm sure. I need midwives here who have a bit of steel in them. I think you will do very well in the Royal.'

Peggy gulped. 'Thank you.'

Sister Campbell, who was smiling broadly at Matron's words, suddenly frowned. 'I think Midwife Gildea may be leaving. Did you want to speak to her today, Matron?'

Sure enough, Priscilla had set her cup down and was currently sidling towards the door.

'Yes, bring her here, please.'

Handing her own teacup to Peggy, Sister Campbell hurried to intercept Priscilla. As they approached, Peggy saw that Priscilla looked worried and guilty and yet, part-defiant.

'Midwife Gildea, may I ask if you are on duty today?'

'No, Matron.'

'Then why are you here, and in uniform?'

'I . . .' She shrugged. 'I thought it might be fun.'

'You think attending a formal reception to which you are not invited is *fun*?'

'No, Matron.'

'And is telling tales on your colleagues also *fun*?'

'No, Matron. I'm sorry.'

'It is not only me you need to apologise to.'

'I'm sorry, Peggy.'

Peggy nodded.

'When are you next on duty, Midwife Gildea?'

'Tomorrow. Eight a.m.'

'Come and see me at nine, after the handover meeting. But you should be aware, I am not impressed at all with your actions today.'

'Yes, Matron.'

'You may go.'

She went, her head down and shoulders drooping.

'Right!' Matron's tone was brisk. 'I think I have achieved what I needed to. Midwife Cassidy, you may return to A Ward.'

Peggy caught the slightest hint of humour in Matron's eye. *I actually love this woman!*

'Yes, Matron.'

Her heart was swelling in relief as she walked calmly towards the corridor. To get there, she had to pass Dan and his mother, and she hadn't had a second to think about what she might say to him. Or what it all meant.

'Peggy!' His voice, her name. Predictably, her insides melted and her heart rate – which had only just begun to settle – was off like a steam train again.

He was beckoning for her to approach. As she took the few steps towards him and his mother, her heart was filled

## The Irish Midwife

with a maelstrom of conflicting emotions – love, fear, trepidation, hope, pessimism.

'How are you?' The sincere concern in his eyes was almost her undoing. Fighting the urge to throw herself into his arms and tell him every detail of today's drama, she contented herself by saying that she was fine, thank you.

'I bet you're not a bit fine. I bet you're shook, as our friends would say!'

She couldn't help smiling. The word brought her instantly back to the staff dining room in the Rotunda, with Anne and Paudie and Mary and . . . oh, all of them.

'I am a bit shook, to be fair,' she admitted. 'But by some miracle it's all worked out better than I could have hoped.'

'So let me see if I've got the story straight. Mrs M—Or rather, the mother whose baby had a tongue tie, told people that you used to be a handywoman. Is that right?'

'Not *people*. Just one person.'

'Midwife Gildea?'

'Correct.'

He rolled his eyes. 'I did wonder. I hope that was Matron telling her off just now.'

'It was.'

'Good.' They shared another smile, and her heart warmed.

'And . . . your aunt was a handywoman?'

Peggy tensed. He was getting too damn close to the other part of the truth. 'She was, but she died.'

'I'm sorry.'

*He has no idea about what caused her death, clearly.*

'And she was your mother's sister?'

'Aye. They were both Doyle to their own name. Aunty Bridget was the eldest, and Ma the youngest. There was a fair age gap between them.'

'Were you close to her?'

She nodded. 'Very close. I worked with her when I was younger. But,' she hastened to add, 'I haven't been a handywoman since going to the Rotunda.'

'No, because you're a midwife now.'

She lifted her chin. 'They're basically the same thing.'

He was about to ask something else, she saw, and so hurriedly added, 'I actually need to go. Matron has directed me to return to my duties, and she is not someone you want to cross.'

'Definitely not!'

All the while, Dan's mother had been watching them closely. 'Miss Cassidy.'

'Yes?' Peggy looked at her, feeling decidedly wary.

'We are having a small tea party for my father's birthday this Saturday at our home. I would be delighted if you could attend.'

Dumbstruck, Peggy could only stare at her for a moment. *She's inviting me to her house? But – does she know about my background?* Her eyes flew to Dan. He was half smiling, his expression urging her to say yes.

'Yes,' she said. 'I mean, I'd be delighted. I'm off duty. Thank you for inviting me.'

'Excellent. Four p.m., 25 Derryvolgie Avenue.'

'Four p.m., 25 Derryvolgie,' Peggy repeated dutifully, her mind now awhirl with an entirely new set of problems. 'I'll see you both then!'

With a last smile towards them she left, head held high.

## The Irish Midwife

\* \* \*

Dan was called to an emergency in theatre soon afterwards, and didn't get the chance to go to A Ward before the end of his shift. He actually ended up staying late, as the case was complex, and he wanted to be sure the woman was all right when she came round from the anaesthetic. Finally, though, it was time to leave, and as he cycled through the darkening streets of Belfast towards home, he was able to think for the first time about everything that had happened.

Peggy had clearly been worrying about what would happen to her if her past work as a handywoman came to light. Today, that problem had gone away. Matron had been decisive, Melissa both vacuous and vindictive. *And vanquished!* he added, laughing inwardly at his own word games. He suspected he'd see a lot less of her in future – although the Moores had already been invited to Granda's tea party on Saturday.

The other barrier remained – the difference in their family backgrounds. But Ma was definitely softening – helped, no doubt, by the respect Matron had shown towards Peggy today. His own insight – that Ma and Peggy had had similar paths in terms of rising in the unspoken ranks of society – would make her think, he knew. And she had invited Peggy to their house on Saturday. *Fair play to ya, Ma!*

Peggy would be nervous, he knew, recalling how out of place she'd felt when they sat down to dinner at the hotel that night. And yet, she had soon relaxed, their conversation and easy connection leading to what had been beyond doubt the best night of his life. But he would be there with her on

Saturday, and hopefully she would feel at ease, eventually. So long as there were no disasters.

There was one more strand to the mystery of Peggy's withdrawal. Mrs Devine. Why on earth had the Murrays accused his father of having killed her? Yes, and they had accused Dr Fenton too.

Da was a GP, Dr Fenton an obstetrician, and Peggy's aunt was likely to have been past childbearing age when she died. The only manner in which his father and Dr Fenton had any influence over life and death was in the provision of medical care, but Dan couldn't for the life of him figure out how an obstetrician and a GP could *both* be accused of killing her.

Once home he had some supper, then waited until Ma had left the room to have her bath before broaching the subject.

'Did you ever have a patient by the name of Devine, Da? A Mrs Bridget Devine.'

His father frowned. 'I don't think so, yet the name seems familiar.'

He thought for a few minutes, while Dan picked up the paper and tried to pretend he wasn't desperate to hear Da's answer. The news was worrying. The United States had, as widely predicted, declared neutrality, while the German army were thought to be currently moving towards Krakow. Westminster had passed the National Registration Act, requiring every man, woman, and child to carry an identity card. There were also predictions of food shortages. He sighed.

'I've got it! She was a handywoman in West Belfast. A good one, too.' Da eyed him curiously. 'Everything is about handywomen today, it seems.'

## The Irish Midwife

'Oh, so you know a midwife nearly got fired this afternoon?'

'Aye. I spoke to Matron about it. Fenton was all worked up and told me he wanted the poor girl sacked. I told Matron I had no issue with handywomen, and neither did most GPs.' He grinned. 'She had it all under control though. A redoubtable woman. Fenton scurried away with his tail between his legs!' He sent Dan a keen glance. 'Now, why did you ask me about Mrs Devine?'

*This is it. Now how do I do this without annoying him?* 'Did you know that she died?'

Da shrugged. 'No – although I haven't heard of her practising for a few years, so I suppose she must have retired or died. Why the focus on her?'

'Had you ever any connection with her? Ever treated her for anything?'

'She was never a patient of mine, that's for certain.'

*This is so odd.* 'What about Dr Fenton?'

'From the Royal? The obstetrician?'

'Aye. Had he any connection with her?'

Da's eyes widened. 'He did! I remember now. Do you mind the day we were in Queen's, and he was so pompous it damn near put you off studying medicine?'

Dan strained to remember. 'Vaguely.'

'Fenton told me that day that he'd put in an official complaint about Mrs Devine for being a handywoman.' He scowled. 'The cheeky get put my name on the complaint too, without my permission. He's always been an arrogant so-and-so.'

Shock rippled through Dan as he recalled the incident. 'Dr Fenton wasn't happy that the handywomen were undercutting the medicine men by charging a smaller fee.'

'I hadn't remembered that part, but you're probably right. He used to rant all the time about handywomen being dangerous. Still does, occasionally.'

'Did you ever challenge him for using your name without your permission?'

'No point.' Da shrugged. 'It was already done. That poor woman would have been fined though, if the police followed up on it – though as I recall, Fenton said they hadn't seemed that interested.' His face twisted. 'Bloody Fenton. This is why I'm glad I never went into hospital medicine. I'd have eventually decked him – or somebody like him.'

'Most of them are actually very nice, you know.'

Da wasn't really listening. 'Why all the questions about Mrs Devine?'

Dan took a breath. 'A new mother and her husband today accused you and Dr Fenton of . . . Now this is going to sound awful, and far-fetched . . .'

'Accused me of what?'

'Of killing her.'

His jaw dropped. 'You *what*? Are you actually serious?'

'Yup. Sorry to break it to you, but—'

'No, no, you've done the right thing by telling me.' He frowned. 'Sometimes stories go about – especially in tight-knit communities like West – and they get changed, or confused . . . I wonder what happened there.' He tapped a finger on the arm of his chair. 'So many possibilities, but it has to be connected with Fenton reporting her. Might she have stopped working and suffered poverty? There are many ways to die, and people know. They *know*.'

'I'm so sorry, Da.'

## The Irish Midwife

'You have to be thick-skinned in this game, son. There are times when your patients do die, and you always wonder, what more could I have done? What could I have done differently? It is, sadly, part of being a doctor.' He sighed. 'I do wish I'd formally challenged that complaint at the time though. I have no real issue with handywomen – though of course it's great now there's proper midwifery training.'

'We need them to know the truth.' Whatever way Mrs Devine had died, Peggy and her family must surely believe it was connected to that report. And how could she be Dan's girl under those circumstances?

'Honestly, son, it's best to let it go. You have to choose your battles in life, Daniel. People are going to say whatever they want about me anyway. My judge is in here' – he pointed to his chest – 'and up there . . .' – he pointed in the general direction of the heavens.

'Normally, I'd agree with you but, as you said yourself, you have to pick your battles. And this is one that I think we have to fight.'

'Why's that?'

'Because . . . there's a girl.'

'Ah.'

'Mrs Devine's niece. Peggy Cassidy. It was her who nearly got fired today. We were courting in Dublin, but she insisted on breaking up with me once we went back to Belfast. I didn't understand why. But now I'm beginning to.'

'Fair enough.' He eyed Dan keenly. 'She matters to you, this girl.'

Dan's throat tightened. 'Yes.' It was little more than a croak.

Da stood, checking his watch. 'It's maybe a bit late, but this can't wait. Let's go.'

Confusion raced through Dan. 'Where are we going?'

'To your girl's house. I assume you know where she lives?'

'Not exactly. I know it's the Rock streets.'

'That's good enough. Now, let me get my coat. You can tell me more in the car.'

# 41

It was nearly supper time in the Cassidy house. The wireless was on low, some sort of soft orchestral music filling the house with resonant beauty. The tea was brewing, some of today's soda bread and a pat of yellow butter ready on the table. There was dripping too, for both Da and Granda preferred bread-and-dripping to butter.

Wee Aiveen was in bed, Joe was sitting on the floor in the living room finishing his homework, while Da and Granda sat in chairs by the fire. Peggy, Ma, and Sheila were bustling about the kitchen at their tasks, with hardly a word needed. They all knew what to do.

Peggy's brain was still trying to work out and understand everything that had happened today. She was getting used to the fact that Matron herself had been a handywoman, and had stuck up for her against both Dr Fenton and the Moore ladies.

In fact, reliving key moments was giving her the same buzz as when they happened. Matron revealing her past work . . . Telling Peggy she would be a damn fine midwife . . . Threatening Dr Fenton with her own resignation . . .

*What a woman!*

She had also dealt with Priscilla very well, Peggy thought. She could easily have taken Priscilla to her office right then

– as she had done Peggy. By making it nine tomorrow it ensured Priscilla would be worried all night.

And Priscilla couldn't exactly leave and get a job at the Union Infirmary. *They're not very nice there*, she had said. Cynically, Peggy wondered what part Priscilla had played in her own downfall. Some people seemed to suffer conflict everywhere they went, almost as if . . .

Then there was Dan. And his mother. He knew almost everything now – apart from his father's role in reporting Aunty Bridget. Maybe he would discover that as well, but one thing was for certain – she couldn't be the one to tell him.

Why had she agreed to go to their family party? The head staggers must have overtaken her, for really on reflection it was a very bad idea. His mother was probably just being nice, inviting one of Dan's friends. She may well have invited others – the Moores, Priscilla, Dr Lowe even. He and Dan seemed to be getting on well.

But she, Peggy, was likely to be a fish out of water in their house. *I am such an eejit for saying yes.*

There was a knock at the door. Sometimes Gerard or Antoinette popped in at supper time, but they never knocked – they just walked on in. Maybe it was a neighbour looking to borrow some tea.

'Answer the door, Joe,' Ma said and Joe, protesting under his breath, got to his feet. A moment later he appeared at the kitchen door.

'Well?' Ma sounded impatient. 'Who is it?'

'It's a doctor. Two doctors.'

Peggy caught her breath. *Is someone unwell? Do they need my help?* One of the neighbours, maybe. Drying her hands

## *The Irish Midwife*

on a tea towel she followed Ma out to the living room, then froze. Dan and his father were standing in the doorway.

Da was already on his way to the door. 'Come in.'

They stepped over the threshold, Dan's eyes meeting Peggy's. His brow was furrowed, his jaw tight. Peggy couldn't quite believe what she was seeing. Dan, here, in her own front room? What the hell was going on?

'I'm Dr Sheridan, and this is my son, Daniel – who also happens to be a doctor.'

'Yes, we've met Dan. Hello again.' Da's tone was neutral, Peggy noted. Not hostile, but certainly not relaxed. He was clearly curious to hear what they had to say.

'Hello, Mr Cassidy, Mrs Cassidy.' Dan looked at her again. 'Hello, Peggy.'

'Hello.'

There was a silence. 'Is nobody going to introduce me, then?' Granda Joe piped up. This seemed to break the tension a little. Granda Joe found it hard to get up, so both Dan and his father had to cross the room to shake his outstretched hand.

'And this is Peggy,' said Dan to his father.

Dr Sheridan looked at her keenly as he shook her hand. 'A pleasure to meet you, Peggy.'

'Will you take a cuppa tae, Doctor?' Ma's hostess instincts had kicked in.

'I will, and thank you.'

'Sit yourselves down then. Peggy, love!'

Nodding, Peggy made for the living room cabinet and took out the good china. They only ever used it for Christmas and wakes and visitors. Once she had washed it of any dust and carefully dried it, she passed the plates, cups, and saucers to Sheila, who set them on the table.

Da had brought Granda Joe to his usual seat at the table, and Granda was currently questioning Dan and his father about what they thought about the Germans, and Poland, and the Yanks keeping out of it. Da joined in – seemingly despite wishing to be standoffish. Ma and Peggy took the last two seats at the table, while Joe and Sheila went to the kitchen to have their own supper standing up – and earwig as much as they could.

Ma poured, and they all helped themselves to some delicious home-baked bread. With only two children at school, Ma could now afford better ingredients, so there was no risk of grit in the flour, thank God. Dan's father, Peggy noticed, helped himself to bread-and-dripping, declaring it was a treat he hadn't had in a long time.

'So,' said Da, after a few minutes. 'What brings you to us tonight, Dr Sheridan?'

*Here we go.*

Dan's father set down his cup. 'It's about Mrs Devine, Mrs Bridget Devine, who I believe' – he looked at Ma – 'was your sister.'

Ma nodded, her face tight.

'I found out today that some misinformation has been circulated. But first, may I ask how she died? If you feel up to speaking about it?' His tone was gentle, his expression open and filled with compassion.

Ma looked at him for a long moment, while Peggy held her breath.

'All right.' Ma looked him directly in the eye. 'She died of a stroke in her house, after being held by the RUC for the best part of a day.'

He gasped. 'The RUC?' He shook his head slowly. 'Because of the complaint that she was a handywoman.'

*The Irish Midwife*

Ma nodded. 'Correct.'

Dr Sheridan took a long breath. 'I want you to know, Mrs Cassidy, that I did not make that complaint. My name was added to it without my knowledge or permission. I regret that I didn't challenge it at the time.'

'Is that a fact?'

'It is. And I am so, so sorry. That complaint should never have been made. I didn't agree with it then, and I certainly don't agree with it now. Mrs Devine was an excellent handywoman.'

Ma nodded, exhaling. 'Well it's good to hear that. And I'm glad to hear that you didn't report her. Thank you for coming to tell me.' She took another deep breath, the tension in her shoulders easing. 'That – that means something.'

'What I still don't understand,' said Granda Joe, 'is why the RUC took her to the station in the first place. They could have done it through letters and papers and fined her.'

Da shrugged. 'That part is obvious. Name of Devine, West Belfast. Do you seriously think they'd have lifted a Protestant?'

'Aye, you have the right of it.' Granda Joe tutted sadly. 'This place will never change, and we will always be the lowest of the low.'

'Still,' said Dan's father, 'at least they didn't force conscription on us.'

'Bloody sures!' Da said fiercely. 'They'd have had rioting on the streets if they'd tried to force Irishmen into the British Army. Enough of us have died for them over the centuries.'

'Aye, the same British Army that guarded the food leaving Ireland when we were all starving!' added Granda Joe.

'Do you remember the Hunger?' asked Dan curiously.

'I do, son. I do.' Granda Joe – seemingly delighted to have a new audience – began to share his memories, and Dan told him that his own granda had been born shortly afterwards.

*Strange to think I might meet Dan's granda on Saturday.* Briefly, Peggy took herself out of the moment, noticing that Dan and his father were in her house, that the final secrets were out, and that, somehow, the sky hadn't fallen in. *How is this even happening?*

Dan met her gaze, and his small smile was filled with everything she might have hoped for. Tremulously, she smiled back. Maybe, just maybe, things would work out.

## Friday, 8 September 1939

'When's your break?'

Dan had poked his head into the A Ward office, and her heart lifted at the sight of him.

'Twelve.'

'Right. I'll try to take mine then. See you in the canteen?'

She nodded. It was exactly like the old days in the Rotunda – snatching brief moments together when they could. *I have so much to say to him!*

Yesterday Peggy had been out on the district all afternoon, shadowing an experienced midwife. Apparently Matron had personally discussed her future with her team of sisters, and this had been the outcome – in effect, an accelerated promotion. She was to do two days and two nights on the district next week, and in the longer term she would be part of the district team. She would still have to do some hospital work, which she welcomed, for it would be good to straddle both worlds.

Twelve was quite early, and as she slid into a seat opposite Dan, she was relieved to note there was no one sitting near them.

'Well, how are you, Peggy?' His eyes were on hers, blue and gorgeous and warm, setting butterflies off inside her.

'I'm good. Better than I have been for a long, long time.'

'I'm sure. You've been carrying so much inside you. You could have told me, you know. All of it.'

'I didn't want you to know that your da's name was on that complaint.'

He nodded slowly. 'You're very good. But being without you has been far, far worse than any worry I might have had over it.'

She chewed her lip. 'Dan, I—'

'Now don't you start worrying again. The whole thing is sorted, and there'll be no strife between our families over it. I have to say, your ma is very forgiving. A good person.'

'She's class, my ma. But how can you be so sure everything will be all right between them all in the longer term?'

'Your ones don't strike me as the sort of people to be holding a grudge over something that wasn't even true. Although,' he grimaced, 'my da is ragin' at himself for not calling Fenton out at the time, and not sticking up for your aunt against him. He could have done something, and he didn't. He spoke about it in the car on the way home.'

'Ah, God love him, he doesn't need to feel guilty. How many times have we been told about unhelpful guilty feelings in our training? If there's learning after something bad happens, we'll take it. But we're all only human.'

'That's kinda what I said to him. But genuinely I think it will be all right. My da and your family got on great the other night!'

She had to smile. 'They did, didn't they?'

'Aye, once your Granda Joe started on about the famine, I knew my da would be hooked.'

'And then all of them talking away about the political stuff!'

'I know. It was class.'

'We're a good fit, you and me, Peggy.'

'Are we though? It's not only about my aunt and what happened to her. We're also from very different backgrounds.'

'That's only money. Our backgrounds are the same – as those political conversations showed the other night.'

'Aye, only a rich boy could say "it's only money"! Your mother—'

'Ach, she'll be fine. She's already started coming round. She even invited you tomorrow.'

'Yeah, that's what I'm worrying about. What if I make some mistake – use the wrong spoon or something? I assume the Moores will be there?'

He laughed. 'There are no wrong spoons! You'll be grand.' Daringly, he touched her hand. 'Ma is friends with Mrs Moore, so they do tend to get invited. But their little scheme backfired, remember?'

She took a breath. 'Tell me honestly, Dan. Does your mother want you to marry Melissa Moore?'

He opened his mouth to deny it, then nodded, grimacing. 'She did, aye. But I think she went off her a bit at the reception.'

Peggy put a hand to her head. 'You see? How can I get back with you, knowing that your ma won't want me?'

'So you are planning to get back with me, then?' His voice was soft.

## The Irish Midwife

'No – yes – I don't know!' She put her head in her hands. 'I'm still coming to terms with the stuff about Aunty Bridget being all right now. I've believed for so long, in here' – she put a closed fist to her chest – 'that us being together is impossible. It's hard to adapt to things changing, you know?'

'Not really, to be honest. I adapt to things quicker than you, I think. But I *know* you, Peggy Cassidy. And I'm pretty sure you want to get back with me.'

'I do, Dan.' There! She had said it out loud. 'I really do. But I feel . . . I dunno. There's a hopelessness inside me – like it could never work out.'

'You've used that word before.'

She sent him a quizzical look.

'In Enniskerry, on the walk, you said you felt hopelessness and terror. I told you I was going to come back to that later, to ask you to explain.'

She nodded slowly. 'The terror was about being found out as a handywoman, and about my family hating your father.' Her eyes widened. 'That's gone now. It's like – vanished!'

'Good. We're getting somewhere. Now, is that hopelessness all to do with the difference in our fathers' jobs, and what that looks like?'

'Yeah. Like, you've seen our house. We have very little. My family is class, and I'm proud to be part of the Cassidys, but your ma might not be too impressed.'

'What about my da?'

'What do you mean?'

'Forget my mother for a minute. Are you still worried about my da, and what he might think?'

'No. Not any more.' She grinned. 'He got stuck into that bread-and-dripping like he was a starving man!'

'He certainly did!'

'But he probably doesn't know about us – that we were courting, or that you want to get back with me.'

'Oh, he certainly does!' Dan declared cheerfully. 'I told him last night, before we went to your house. In fact, that was why he insisted on going immediately, even though it was getting late.'

Peggy's eyes widened, recalling the intense way Dan's father had said 'A pleasure to meet you'.

'Really? Wow.'

'My ma knows too. I told her at the reception.'

'You what?' She caught her breath in amazement.

'Aye. And *then* she invited you to our house tomorrow.'

'You're joking me!' Her eyes narrowed. 'Are you letting on, Dan Sheridan? To try and bring me round?'

He held up both hands, laughing. 'No! Swear to God.' He sobered. 'It's the truth.'

'But – Melissa!'

He face twisted. 'Aye. To be fair, Ma will still need to come round a bit. But by inviting you, she's shown she wants to try.'

'Aye – or she's gonna put me to the test, and if I fail, she'll tell you exactly why I'm so unsuitable!' She glanced at her fob. 'I have to go.'

He grabbed her hand as she rose. 'But you are still coming tomorrow?'

She lifted her chin. 'Bloody sure I am!' Sending him a mischievous wink, she headed off, feeling his eyes on her as she did so. Dan was right. Most of the hurdles had already been overcome.

There was now only one remaining: Mrs Sheridan.

# 42

'So what is it exactly that you're going to?' Ma watched as Peggy buttoned her good coat and pulled on dainty white gloves. She was wearing her graduation dress, and the swish of silk against her calves gave her a hint of the confidence she'd felt in the Rotunda that day. *I'm a qualified midwife – a professional young woman.*

She picked up her handbag, checking that she had some money and a clean handkerchief inside. 'It's a tea party for Dan's granda's birthday.' Hooking the handbag on her arm, she then picked up the small birthday present – some homemade fudge for Dan's grandfather – tucking it into the bag. If he was anything like Granda Joe and his friends, he would enjoy it.

'And how many's going to it?'

Peggy shrugged. 'Mrs Sheridan described it as a "small party", but sure who knows what that means?'

'Aye – could be thirty people at it! Even for an oul' man's birthday!' She tilted her head. 'Would that be his ma's da or his da's da?'

Peggy smiled at the rhyme, saying, 'His ma's da. I know Dan only has the one grandparent left. He only has one aunt too – his ma's sister, so I assume she'll be there too.' She straightened. 'I just hope they like me.'

'And sure why wouldn't they?' Ma wagged a finger, only half-scolding. 'You be proud of yourself, and what you're achieving in your life.'

'I am. Thank you. And Ma . . . ?'

'Yes?'

'I'm proud of you, too. Of being a Cassidy. Of living in this lovely wee house and being part of a loving family where we all look after each other.'

Ma enveloped her in a hug. 'Ah, get on with you now. And enjoy the party!'

'I will!' Peggy replied automatically, crossing her fingers nervously.

It took a good half-hour to walk to Derryvolgie Avenue. On turning into it from the Lisburn Road, the first thing Peggy noticed was the greenery. Every home had lush hedges and lawns in front – yes, and there were trees, too. In a terraced street, reaching number 25 would take only a minute or two, but here . . . Each house stood alone, the plots wide enough to easily accommodate six or seven houses like those in the Rock streets.

As she passed mansion after mansion, Peggy could feel the confidence ebbing out of her. Who was she anyway? Only a milly in a shockingly expensive dress. She didn't belong here. She never would.

The Sheridan residence was stunning – a two-storey house with a round bay on the left and a recessed arched doorway. Without thinking about it, Peggy counted the chimney caps on top of the roof. There were two stacks, one on each side, and each stack had five chimney caps. Five! Did this house really have ten fireplaces? For three people?

Almost, she turned back. But Ma would be disappointed in her if she did. And to be honest, Peggy would be disappointed in herself. So with a deep breath, she walked up the gravel drive and rang the doorbell.

The door opened, and Peggy saw a middle-aged woman she'd never met before in her life.

'Oh! Sorry, I must have the wrong house.' *I was sure this was number 25.* 'Can you tell me where the Sheridans live, please?'

'Ach, sure you've the right house, love. Come on in!'

Confused, Peggy stepped inside. Might this be Dan's aunt? She was *very* friendly – reassuringly so.

'I'm Mrs Kinahan,' the woman said. 'You must be Daniel's friend from the Royal. Now, let me have that coat of yours and I'll put it away for you. Sit that down here.'

Peggy did as she was bid, setting down her handbag briefly while she took off her coat and gloves, stuffing the gloves into the pockets. 'Thank you.'

'Peggy!'

Suddenly Dan was walking towards her, and his smile instantly settled her nerves a bit. 'So glad you came! You look gorgeous!' He kissed her cheek, taking her hand at the same time, and Peggy was conscious of Mrs Kinahan's blatant curiosity.

Blushing a little, she murmured that she really hadn't been sure if she would come.

'But you did.' He still had her hand. 'You did.'

Mrs Kinahan had bustled off somewhere with Peggy's coat, so she asked, 'Is Mrs Kinahan your aunt?'

'No, she er . . .' He gave a sheepish half-smile. 'She works in our house.'

Peggy sent him a look, shaking her head. 'And here's me, so green that the possibility you have a servant never occurred to me.'

'She's not a servant.' He was frowning now. 'She's a highly efficient cook and housekeeper, and one of my favourite people in the world.'

Noting this with interest, Peggy replied firmly, 'I don't mean to be disrespectful of Mrs Kinahan.' Glancing about at the spacious hallway, wide staircase, and numerous framed pictures on the walls, she added, 'I'm sure she works hard.' Keeping this place clean would be a quare task.

'But you're wondering what my ma does all day, right?' He gave a crooked smile. 'I can read you like a book, Peggy Cassidy. And I'll say this: if this is going to work, you and ma *both* need to not judge each other.'

His words rattled through Peggy forcefully. 'That's a fair point. Reverse snobbery is just as real as snobbery.' Her eyes dancing, she added, 'It's the same thing, only with poverty and injustice on one side.'

He laughed at that, and Peggy's heart warmed. He understood her, this man. But she did need to avoid getting overwhelmed by the evidence of riches all around her, and simply treat them as people. An image of Dan's da enjoying bread-and-dripping at the Cassidy table flashed through her mind.

'Right, let's go in. Da's away to get my granda and my aunt, and they're not back yet.'

'Oh.' Dan's da had been nothing but friendly towards her, and she had hoped he would be there the whole time. Not that she needed a shield, she reminded herself – although Dan would probably see himself in that sort of role today.

## The Irish Midwife

She was proud to be Peggy Cassidy, and she was going to be polite and respectful to everyone.

The door to the left was ajar, and the hum of conversation increased as Dan pushed it open. Peggy had dropped his hand before any of them could see, and he sent her a tolerant look. *In your own time,* he seemed to be saying, for which she was grateful.

As Peggy swiftly scanned the room, the first people she saw were Mrs Moore and her daughter. Melissa was wearing a very chic green dress, and Peggy was glad she had her graduation dress on. At least she didn't *look* out of place. Melissa was standing talking to a young man with an expensive suit and a rather florid appearance, while her mother was sitting with Mrs Sheridan and another middle-aged lady. In chairs by the bay window two gentleman sat, one puffing on a pipe.

'The Moores and the Harbinsons are the only other people invited,' Dan explained in a low tone. 'My ma is very great with Mrs Moore, as you know, but also with Mrs Harbinson.'

'And the younger fella?'

'Richard Harbinson. Solicitor. I was made to play with him all through the years, but we're very different.'

'Enough said.' Peggy sent him a sidelong glance, and he caught his breath.

'If you keep looking at me like that, I'm going to kiss you in front of all of them!'

'Stop it!' she hissed, while inwardly her heart leapt at the thought of his kisses. *It's been far too long since we kissed!*

'Peggy!' Mrs Sheridan was approaching. 'Thank you for coming!'

## Seána Tinley

Shaking her hand, Peggy gave a warm smile. If Mrs Sheridan disapproved of her, it was hard to tell. 'Thank you for the invitation, Mrs Sheridan. I'm glad to be here.'

'Let me introduce you to our other guests.' Mrs Sheridan took her across the room, but Peggy knew Dan was watching. 'You've met Mrs Moore, of course. This is Mrs Harbinson.'

'Yes. Hello. Nice to meet you.'

Mrs Moore replied politely, while Mrs Harbinson gave what looked to be a genuine smile. 'You're a midwife at the Royal, I understand?'

'I am. Just recently qualified. I trained in Dublin with Dan.'

'Ah, so that's how you know each other. You midwives and doctors do splendid work, you know. Splendid!'

Unsure how to respond to this, Peggy offered a 'Thank you.'

Mrs Sheridan took her on to where Melisa was standing with young Mr Harbinson. 'Melissa you know. This is Mr Richard Harbinson.'

Melissa murmured something unintelligible, while Mr Richard Harbinson's gaze swept over her from head to toe. He stuck out a hand.

'*Enchanté*!'

*I presume that's 'enchanted' in French. What an eejit!*

She shook his hand and gave a polite smile, but didn't speak. He was the sort of man, she reckoned, who needed no encouragement whatsoever.

'And finally this is Mr Moore, and Mr Harbinson.' The two older men rose, shook her hand politely, then returned to their conversation.

## The Irish Midwife

*Whew!* The first part of the ordeal was over. Although she should really try not to think of it as an ordeal. She could almost hear Dan's voice in her head, being sensible, and holding up a mirror to her imagined disasters.

'Now, would you like some tea? Or a sherry, perhaps?'

Tea, please.' One did not drink alcohol when properly meeting the parents of the man you loved.

Crossing to the side table, Mrs Sheridan poured some tea into a beautiful china cup, adding a dash of milk at Peggy's request. 'So, Peggy, tell me a bit about yourself.'

*Here we go.*

Trying not to appear tense, Peggy gave a short history – where she was from, how many brothers and sisters she had, and what her parents did.

'We all work in the mills, and are glad of the work,' she said evenly. 'This Great Depression doesn't seem to be easing at all.'

'It's really terrible,' Mrs Sheridan agreed. 'No wonder they call this the devil's decade. And now we have war as well.' She eyed Peggy keenly. 'But how come you managed to get your midwifery training?'

Peggy knew exactly what she was asking. 'My Aunty Bridget was a handywoman, and she trained me to be one. She was widowed young and had no children, and she left me her life savings when she died – with strict instructions that I was to use it for midwifery training.'

'Ah, the handywomen were great – not that we're allowed to say that in some company.' She leaned closer, adding confidentially, 'I had a doctor at Daniel's birth, but I'd have been better with a handywoman or midwife.'

Something in her expression had put Peggy's midwifery antennae on full alert. 'What happened?'

'He made me lie on my back, for a start. Poked and prodded at me constantly. I couldn't get peace to concentrate on my labour, if you know what I mean. The whole thing ended up stalling.'

Peggy grimaced. She'd seen that happen too many times. Interference with nature. Making themselves the centre of attention instead of being invisible and supportive. Sister Guinan. Dr Fenton. It was the opposite of what women needed.

Mrs Sheridan shrugged. 'I ended up having a caesarean section, and apparently bled dreadfully while being operated on. The surgeon had to remove my womb, so no more babies.' Her eyes glistened with unshed tears.

'Ah, Mrs Sheridan, I'm so, so sorry.' Instinctively, she reached out, and Mrs Sheridan took her hand gratefully.

*Woman to woman.* Some things were universal.

'Caesareans can be needed to save the life of the woman and baby,' she said softly, 'and major surgery carries risks. But it's also true that things generally go better when women aren't interfered with.'

'I know. I truly think it could have gone differently. And I wish it hadn't happened to me. But,' she added fiercely, 'I will defend midwives to my dying day!'

'I love that passion. Is that why you joined the fundraising committee?'

She nodded. 'A proper maternity hospital was well overdue, with midwives for any woman that wants one, and doctors when they're needed. Some of the others are on the committee simply because it's a good thing to do. For me,

## The Irish Midwife

though, it's driven by a fire inside me. And part of that fire is the need to stand up for midwives.'

Peggy nodded. 'And in standing up for midwives you stand up for women.'

Another moment of shared understanding passed between them, interrupted by the door opening.

'Ah, here they are!' said Mrs Sheridan, her demeanour returning in an instant to poised South Belfast lady.

Peggy turned to see Dan's father enter, accompanied by an elderly man and a middle-aged woman, both of whom she knew very, very well.

Shock gave way to delight and she broke into a smile, awaiting her moment. Sure enough, the woman scanned the room, her face lighting up when she saw Peggy.

'Peggy!' She touched her father's arm. 'Look who it is, Da! Peggy Cassidy!'

Peggy had already crossed the room. 'Mary!' They hugged, then Peggy took Peter Corvin's hand.

'How are you, Peter? Happy birthday to ya!'

'Ach, thanks, Peggy. I'm ninety today, you know!'

'I do know! I'm here to tell you Happy Birthday – though to be fair I didn't know Dan's granda was Peter Corvin, my own granda's best friend.'

'Dan?' Mary asked sharply. 'You know our Daniel?'

'She does.' Dan was there, shaking his head at the turn of events. 'And I didn't know you knew the Cassidys.'

'Oh, we know them very well,' said Mary. 'Lovely family. But how do you two . . .' She looked from Dan to Peggy and back again, then slapped a hand to her head. 'Of course! Peggy, you're a midwife now, so yous must have met at the

Royal. Or – wait, where did you train? You've been away, haven't you?'

Peggy met Dan's eyes, and there was a clear question in them. With the slightest of head movements, she gave him a 'yes' and he breathed in sharply.

'Actually,' he said, taking Peggy's hand in full view of everyone, 'Actually, Peggy trained in Dublin. And we've been courting since March.'

As everyone in the room (except Melissa and her mother) exclaimed with delight and pleasure, Peggy blushed a little, but left her hand in Dan's, where it belonged. Finally, everything was working out perfectly.

# 43

Mr Sheridan had offered Peggy a lift, but she had instead accepted Dan's offer to walk her home. What she needed right now more than anything in the world, was time alone with him.

They had so much to talk about – the fact that their grandfathers were best friends, Mrs Sheridan's unexpected warmth towards Peggy, the way Peggy had been made so welcome in the Sheridan home.

'It was totally different to what I expected,' she admitted, enjoying the sensation of his warm hand enveloping hers. Despite the chill in the air, she had decided to leave her gloves in her coat pockets.

'What, so all those pictures in your head of the various ways in which it could be a disaster turned out not to happen?'

'Something like that.'

The night was cool, and the clouds looked ominous. As the first drops of rain began to fall they stopped walking, Dan opening up the large umbrella he'd taken with him. Putting his free arm around her, he held it over them both, yet they didn't walk on straight away. They simply stood there, looking into one another's eyes by the flickering light of a nearby streetlight.

Blackout rules were soon to be brought in, but for now the streetlight gave enough light for Peggy to see the handsome face of the man she adored. The rain quickly became a downpour but they were safe together, enveloped in their own private world, shielded by the umbrella and the moment and the music of the rain.

She had to say his name. 'Dan.'

Exhaling forcefully, he gathered her into his arms. Willingly she went, not thinking, not aware of anything but the need to be there again. Bodies close, her eyes closed, savouring every sensation. Her pulse racing and her breathing quickened. His cheek on hers, moving a little, exploring a strange familiarity. Now they moved together, slanting for their first kiss in a fortnight. His free hand on her back, his tongue dancing with hers, the warmth of his chest permeating through.

Eventually they surfaced, sharing a beautiful smile. Peggy's heart felt as though it might burst from her chest, so full of love it was. *This man!*

Dan had remained steady and true through all of her secrets and anxieties, all of her rejections of him, all of the hurt she had caused him. The whole time, he had been steadfast, reliable, loving. It was she who had held back, paralysed by doubts and fears and secrets.

They had never before spoken directly of their feelings, but Peggy felt she should be the one to break through that barrier, since it was probably one of her making.

'Dan,' she began, 'back there you told your family that we're courting.' Her hands were on his shoulders, his free hand at her back holding her close to him, the umbrella angled above them, keeping them dry.

## The Irish Midwife

'I did. I hope you didn't mind, but I thought it would be all right.'

'You were right to do it. My worries have delayed it for a long time, but I'm actually delighted we don't have to be secretive any more.'

'Or apart. That was a bloody nightmare, Peggy.'

'I know, and I'm sorry. It was a nightmare for me too, if that makes it any better.'

'Actually, it does. My biggest worry was that you didn't feel for me what I feel for you.'

She nodded, taking a deep breath. 'The obvious question here is for me to ask you what it is you feel for me, but I'm not going to do it.'

Wariness appeared in his eyes. 'Why? Because you don't want to hear my answer?'

'No. Because I want to say it first. It's the least I can do.' She took a breath. 'I love you, Dan Sheridan.'

'Peggy!' He kissed her again, the kiss of a dying man offered a reprieve.

'I love you,' she said again as his lips moved to her cheek, her nose, her cheek again. 'I love you.'

'And I love you, Peggy Cassidy.' He leaned back, suddenly serious. 'I've known that you're the girl for me for a very long time.'

'You have?'

He nodded. 'I bought that fob watch for the girl I love.'

'But we weren't even courting then!' she gasped.

'Aye, but I knew anyway, and I've never wavered from it.' He paused, taking a deep breath. 'Peggy Cassidy,' he said, in a tone that made her heart pound, 'will you marry me?'

*Yes!* Her heart cried, but she had to be certain. 'Are you sure, Dan? You know everything about me now. I'll never say words like "splendid" and I don't know how to arrange flowers or be on a committee. Are you really sure?'

'I've never been more certain of anything,' he said, his expression serious. 'I want the sort of home where everyone is called "love", not "dear". I want my family to be a cast of thousands, not just a handful of people. I want the sort of family only you and I can make – the best of the Cassidys combined with the best of the Sheridans. That's what we can do. Together.'

She smiled. 'Then yes! Yes, I will marry you! I—'

He was kissing her again, and she was lost in the storm. The rain danced about them in celebration, and the happiness within them and between them shone like a beacon of hope in the darkness of 1939.

# Author's Note

For thirty years – since I was pregnant with my first baby – I've been fascinated by pregnancy, birth, and the early days of motherhood. I've volunteered with childbirth charities, led workshops with women and their partners, guest lectured student midwives, and acted as a women's representative in various change initiatives in Ireland and in Britain. I also had the enormous privilege to work as a senior manager in the health service, and recently managed the wonderful Belfast maternity service for four years. It was after leaving that job that this book poured out of me, inspired by the amazing women and midwives and doctors I worked with.

I was also fascinated to learn about handywomen – nothing to do with DIY! A handywoman in Ireland was a traditional midwife – never formally trained, but holding the wisdom of generations before her. Some of these *mná cabhartha* were undoubtedly more skilled than others, and in the days before germ theory came to be understood, women could die from infections. As well as supporting women through childbirth, the handywoman would also lay out the dead and sometimes sit with the dying. During the early decades of the twentieth century, handywomen in Ireland were replaced by trained midwives. However, there is evidence of Air Raid Wardens calling on the aid of local handywomen during the Belfast

## Author's Note

Blitz in 1941, so we know some were still practising right through the 1930s.

This story takes place during that time – the overlap period when a few handywomen were still working, and many midwives were being trained. In that sense Peggy's journey represents the wider journey of the professionalisation of midwifery in Ireland. I do hope you enjoyed it.

# Acknowledgements

This book has been something of a passion project, so bear with me while I thank a wide range of people who influenced its gestation and birth.

I'd like to begin by thanking my editor at Hodder & Stoughton, Lucy Stewart. Lucy 'got' this book from the start, and has championed it all the way to publication. From the day we met at the RNA one-to-one sessions, we hit it off. I love her enthusiasm and positivity, as well as her immense knowledge and skill. Thank you, Lucy.

I'd also like to thank my agent, Elizabeth Winick Rubenstein at McIntosh & Otis, and her co-agent Anna Carmichael at Abner Stein. Both women have worked so hard to support me on this road to publication, and I am immensely grateful.

To my writer friends, particularly Saoirse Morrigan, Colette Cooper, Jean Fullerton, Katie Ginger, Ali Henderson, Suzie Hull, Leona Larkin, Lara Lawson, Karen Maxwell, Linda McEvoy, and Lucy Morris. You have encouraged me at every turn. Thank you.

This book would probably not have been published without the support of the Romantic Novelists' Association. The RNA has been my tribe and my support in the past few years of writing, and along with my Facebook clan – Tinley's

## Acknowledgements

Tattlers – has been vital in my development as a writer. I am honoured to be the current chair of the RNA.

At a crucial point in developing this story I was selected for a writing residency at Cill Rialaig, co-ordinated by the Irish Writers' Centre and funded by the Arts Council of Northern Ireland. I am grateful for this support and would strongly encourage other professional Irish writers to experience a Cill Rialaig residency.

Supporting women with pregnancy, birth and breastfeeding was my first true passion – before I discovered the joys of writing – and it is in my bones at this point. This book has been based on decades of knowledge and experience as a birth worker and a health and social care manager, and built on the wisdom of generations of women before me.

I'd like to thank all of the women and their partners/birth partners who allowed me into their homes and into their lives for antenatal and postnatal information and support.

I'd also like to thank all of those who shaped my journey in supporting women – the birth workers, practitioners, tutors, campaigners, and volunteers in NCT, BirthWise NI, Breastival, the NI Maternal Mental Health Committee, the RCM, AIMS Ireland and Ciudiú, as well as the health and social care leaders who involved me as a service user representative to help shape services – Maternity Services Liaison Committees, the wonderful GAIN guidelines, the audit work for home birth in the south of Ireland, the Midwifery Unit Network, the NI Maternity Strategy and NI Breastfeeding Strategy, the NMC *My Future, My Midwife* work, involvement in amazing research including the systematic review on NI Breastfeeding, the MuM-PreDiCT study, the

## *Acknowledgements*

ASPIRE-COVID research, those who supported me to guest lecture to student midwives and on PoSoM, and others.

The team at the Royal Jubilee Maternity Service are an outstanding group of professionals, providing a wonderful service to the women and babies of Belfast. It was a privilege to be your service manager for four years, and I think you will recognise some of the locations in the book!

Special thanks to all of the midwives, obstetricians, neonatologists and neonatal nurses who have shaped my journey – there are too many of you to name, but know that you are in every line of the positive stories in this book.

A special thank you to Dr Patricia Gillen, midwife, who read the manuscript and suggested important edits.

I wrote this for women, and for midwives like Philomena Canning RIP (who once spent two days in my home). She will remain the Aunty Bridget for many wise Irish midwives.

My new colleagues at Parkinson's UK have been cheering me on for over a year now – thank you for your support!

Finally, I'd like to thank my family; my husband Andrew, our children Danny, Aoife, and Maeve, along with Becca, Sam, my parents Tommy and Sheila, and the wider McCoy, Tinnelly, and Talbot families – with a special mention for our darling Clodagh!

Your love, encouragement, and support has been incredible. Thank you all.

# Reading group questions

1. Were you familiar with the term 'handywoman' before you started reading? What did you learn about attitudes to birth in the time period from the book?
2. Did anything happen that you were particularly surprised or shocked by? Or was the depiction of life in Ireland in the 1930s just as you were expecting it to be?
3. Peggy has to make many difficult decisions throughout the book. Did you agree with all of her choices? Would you have done anything differently? Should she have told Dan about her past earlier, for example?
4. Peggy has to remain calm under a lot of pressure when delivering babies, even though she's so young and has no experience of it herself. How do you think you would be in her position? Were you impressed by her?
5. At times, the living conditions described sound incredibly tough. How do you think you would have coped living in similar conditions?
6. In Peggy's era, women gave birth at home far more often than in hospitals, which is different to our attitudes to birth now. Did the book change your attitude to birth at all?

*Reading group questions*

7. The book draws attention to stories of women who have never been widely discussed or celebrated, and yet who helped their communities in every way possible. Do you think this is an important part of history to learn about and discuss?
8. What do you think is your overall takeaway from the book? What feeling are you left with after reading it?

Loved *The Irish Midwife*? Look out for the next book in the Irish Midwives series . . .

# *The* Irish Midwife *at* War

As 1941 hits, so does the Belfast Blitz, and in addition to delivering babies, the Irish Midwives are forced to put all their medical training to the test to save as many people as they can. . .

## Spring 2026